UNDER THE
MIDNIGHT SUN

Also by Tracie Peterson and Kimberley Woodhouse

All Things Hidden
Beyond the Silence

THE HEART OF ALASKA

In the Shadow of Denali
Out of the Ashes
Under the Midnight Sun

www.traciepeterson.com   www.kimberleywoodhouse.com

Books by Tracie Peterson

GOLDEN GATE SECRETS

In Places Hidden
In Dreams Forgotten
In Times Gone By

HEART OF THE FRONTIER

Treasured Grace
Beloved Hope
Cherished Mercy

SAPPHIRE BRIDES

A Treasure Concealed
A Beauty Refined
A Love Transformed

BRIDES OF SEATTLE

Steadfast Heart
Refining Fire
Love Everlasting

LONE STAR BRIDES

A Sensible Arrangement
A Moment in Time
A Matter of Heart

LAND OF SHINING WATER

The Icecutter's Daughter
The Quarryman's Bride
The Miner's Lady

LAND OF THE LONE STAR

Chasing the Sun
Touching the Sky
Taming the Wind

STRIKING A MATCH

Embers of Love
Hearts Aglow
Hope Rekindled

SONG OF ALASKA

Dawn's Prelude
Morning's Refrain
Twilight's Serenade

ALASKAN QUEST

Summer of the Midnight Sun
Under the Northern Lights
Whispers of Winter
Alaskan Quest (3 in 1)

BRIDES OF GALLATIN COUNTY

A Promise to Believe In
A Love to Last Forever
A Dream to Call My Own

DESERT ROSES

Shadows of the Canyon
Across the Years
Beneath a Harvest Sky

HEIRS OF MONTANA

Land of My Heart
The Coming Storm
To Dream Anew
The Hope Within

LADIES OF LIBERTY

A Lady of High Regard
A Lady of Hidden Intent
A Lady of Secret Devotion

WESTWARD CHRONICLES

A Shelter of Hope
Hidden in a Whisper
A Veiled Reflection

YUKON QUEST

Treasures of the North
Ashes and Ice
Rivers of Gold

• • • • •

House of Secrets
A Slender Thread
What She Left for Me
Where My Heart Belongs

THE HEART
of ALASKA
BOOK Three

UNDER THE MIDNIGHT SUN

TRACIE PETERSON
AND KIMBERLEY WOODHOUSE

BETHANYHOUSE
a division of Baker Publishing Group
Minneapolis, Minnesota

Published by Bethany House Publishers
11400 Hampshire Avenue South
Bloomington, Minnesota 55438
www.bethanyhouse.com

Bethany House Publishers is a division of
Baker Publishing Group, Grand Rapids, Michigan

Printed in the United States of America

Library of Congress Cataloging-in-Publication Data
Names: Peterson, Tracie, author. | Woodhouse, Kimberley, author.
Title: Under the midnight sun / Tracie Peterson and Kimberley Woodhouse.
Description: Minneapolis, Minnesota : Bethany House Publishers, a division of
    Baker Publishing Group, [2019] | Series: Heart of Alaska ; #3
Identifiers: LCCN 2018033955| ISBN 9780764219252 (trade paper) | ISBN
    9780764219498 (cloth) | ISBN 9781493417308 (e-book)
Subjects: | GSAFD: Christian fiction. | Love stories.
Classification: LCC PS3566.E7717 U52 2019 | DDC 813/.54—dc23
LC record available at https://lccn.loc.gov/2018033955

Scripture quotations are from the King James Version of the Bible.

This is a work of historical reconstruction; the appearance of certain historical figures are therefore inevitable. All other characters, however, are products of the authors' imagination, and any resemblance to actual persons, living or dead, is coincidental.

Cover design by Dan Thornberg, Design Source Creative Services
Front cover photo of Curry, Alaska, courtesy of Kenneth L. Marsh, author of *Lavish Silence*

Kimberley Woodhouse is represented by The Steve Laube Agency.

18 19 20 21 22 23 24   7 6 5 4 3 2 1

This book is lovingly dedicated to my
beautiful friend Jackie Hale.

God blessed me immeasurably when He brought you to me.
You are one of a kind.
Your honesty, encouragement, love, and—let's be
honest—amazing wit and sarcasm have been a joy to
me. I love how you call me your twin (even though you're
younger, cuter, taller, and—ahem—thinner) and how it
doesn't take anything for us to laugh or cry together.
You are a gift.

Every once in a while, God brings someone special into our lives . . .
and it's hard to say good-bye. Wow. Is it ever.
Even though the physical distance between us may be much
greater, our hearts will always be connected. Thank God
for technology that helps make the world so much smaller.

You are amazing and loved.
Don't forget that. Our journey has just begun.
I love you dearly.

And to Tayler . . . the *real* Tayler Hale.
I love you more than words can say. Keep your focus on
the Lord, and let your beautiful light shine for *Him*.
Your adopted mom loves you to the moon and back.

—Kimberley

Jackie and Tayler, I have been so honored to become friends
with you beautiful ladies. I pray God's blessings on you
and your family. Thank you for letting me call you *friend*.

—Tracie

A Note from the Authors

We are so excited to have you journey with us once again for the conclusion to THE HEART OF ALASKA series.

The Curry Hotel has become very special to us, and it has been such a joy to hear how much you love it as well. The characters will live on in our hearts for decades to come, even though the series has come to an end. We appreciate the letters you've sent mentioning your trips on the Alaskan Railroad and your brief sightings of where Curry once stood. It is always such a delight to know that the stories interested you enough to further explore one of our finest states. We hope you'll continue to enjoy the richness that Alaska offers.

We hope too that the stories will continue to encourage you spiritually. The stories we've heard from you—our readers— have been so uplifting. We love that the gift of story has been used in your hearts and minds for God's glory: how something one of the characters went through touched your life, or how a particular Scripture drew you closer to God. Writing, for both of us, is a ministry to share the Gospel of Jesus and biblical application. When you send us your letters and emails, they bless us. Thank you.

While we hate to say good-bye to Curry, there's one last story to tell.

Thomas.

Out of all the fun characters, we've heard you cheering him on the most. And we love it.

So it's a privilege to give you *Under the Midnight Sun.*

Kimberley and Tracie

Prologue

White velvet and blue satin.

That's what the snow on the mountains and the brilliant blue of the cloudless sky made thirteen-year-old Tayler Hale think of as she lay on her back on the ridge above their campsite.

Squinting her eyes at the sky, she imagined she was floating in a giant satiny blue bubble . . . high above the rocky peaks that seemed blanketed in white velvet. The thought made her smile. What she wouldn't give to be able to fly above it all. Watch all the activity in the wild from her bubble, write in her journals about it, and draw the pictures she captured in her mind. Just like the woman she so admired, Lady Isabella Bird.

Lady Bird had come to America and traveled all over these very mountains—alone. She wrote in great detail about her adventures in one of Tayler's favorite books, *A Lady's Life in the Rocky Mountains*. Tayler loved every page of it. Her copy was worn from the many times she'd read the account and dreamt of her own future. Isabella Bird's descriptions of the

Estes Park area had given flight to Tayler's desires to become an explorer just like the refined Englishwoman.

Oh, to be as free as Lady Bird. And to be admired for her spirit and knowledge when she'd become the first woman to be allowed in the Royal Geographic Society. She had traveled the world, lending a hand wherever she went, even helping to found a hospital in India. Tayler couldn't have admired her more. Lady Isabella Bird had made a difference, and Tayler wanted to do the same.

As she looked at the sky and mountain peaks surrounding her, she could almost imagine herself an adult, riding on horse-back over the snow-covered elevation on her way to rescue some campers who'd lost their way. It sent a little thrill through her. They'd talk about her as a great woman explorer, an expert on the plants and wildlife. People would flock to hear her lectures on survival in the wilderness.

Her smile grew into a giggle. Tayler's imagination could take her to far-off places with amazing adventures, and surely her mother would scold her for such thoughts. But she couldn't help it. One day, Mother would understand.

Squinting at the height of the sun in the sky, she realized the time. Her dreams of adventure were inspiring, but none of them beat the real-life adventures she had with her brother, Joshua, and his best friend, Emerson.

They'd had camping and mountaineering trips together with her father for as long as she could remember. It was a mystery why Mother allowed her to go for so long—despite all her push-ing for Tayler to "be a lady"—but Dad had a way of convincing Henrietta Hale.

Yet it was all coming to an end.

Reality set back in, and Tayler felt her face scrunch into a frown.

Joshua and Emerson would soon be heading back east to their prep school. The last year of their college preparatory academy was intense and year-round. After that, they'd be headed to Harvard. Would this be their last adventure together? Ever?

She swallowed the question and tried to blink away the tears that threatened every time the thought invaded. A gust of wind blew over her like a whispered answer. Too bad she didn't understand it. If only God would send her *real* answers on the wind.

A rustle sounded behind her and then something dark and scratchy landed on her face.

"Boo!" Joshua's voice. The scoundrel. Always such a prankster.

Tayler swiped at the wool blanket he'd thrown over her but stayed calm and still in her position. "Just remember *who* squeals like a girl when they see a spider and which one of us has *no* trouble catching aforementioned eight-legged critters *and* has access to your bedroll."

"You wouldn't." His upside-down face held a lopsided grin as he bent over her.

She raised her eyebrows. "Oh, wouldn't I?"

He shook his head and plopped himself onto the grass beside her. "You're not playing fair."

"I know." Allowing a smug smile to lift her lips, she sat up. "But you're older, remember? You *taught* me to not play fair. So it's your fault." She tossed the blanket in his direction.

His laugh filled the air, and he threw the blanket back at her. "Yes, let's remember who *is* older, young lady."

She made a face at him and rolled her eyes. "But that doesn't mean wiser . . . *or* more mature. You know, one of these days, you're going to have to grow up and take on responsibility instead of joking around." Lowering her brows, she attempted to look serious. She adored Joshua—he was the best brother in the whole world—and the thought of him truly *growing up* made her sad. But she couldn't allow her feelings to show.

"I'm hurt. I thought you loved my jokes." He put a hand to his chest and played the dramatic sad fellow.

With her right hand, she shoved at his shoulder and laughed. If only these days could go on forever. She often heard other girls her age tell of how much they despised their brothers, but from her earliest memories she'd adored Joshua. He was clever and witty and so wonderfully observant. He had taught her to see the world with different eyes.

"Hey, Emerson and I are going down to the creek to get cleaned up." And just like that he slammed the door on her reverie. "Just wanted to give you some warning. Dad is working on the fish we caught, so he sent me to tell you that he wants your help."

"All right. Thanks." Why didn't he seem fazed by all the change like she was?

"We'll be back soon." He tapped her nose with his finger and jumped back to his feet. "Don't burn any of *my* fish. But you can burn Emerson's."

She stuck out her tongue and then smiled. Leaning back to gaze at the sky again, she sighed. It wasn't fair. Rolling over onto her stomach, she huffed and then propped herself up on her elbows and peeked over the edge of the ridge to the crystal lake below her in the valley. They were all growing up whether they liked it or not. The boys were sixteen now, and their lives were practically mapped out for them—including the much-expected Harvard educations. If only she were sixteen too . . .

Tayler plopped her chin down on her hands and kicked her feet in the air. Mother would definitely disapprove of such unladylike behavior, but *she* wasn't here on this trip. In fact, she never came, because camping was a bit too primitive for her.

And Tayler had heard the hushed conversations between her parents. Mother thought Tayler was getting entirely too old to be traipsing off into the woods and hiking up mountains. In fact, Mother thought her daughter should focus on etiquette and manners, dinner parties and the arts.

But Tayler wanted to go to college. She wanted to study plants and animals and mountains and . . . well . . . everything outdoors. She wanted to travel and see the world for herself, and maybe . . . just maybe even write about it like Lady Bird.

If Mother knew Tayler's real plan, she'd probably lock her daughter up for a good long while.

Tayler giggled and stood, brushing at her skirt. Her mother wasn't *that* bad. But it was scary enough to think of telling her the truth. Dad had an inkling of Tayler's desires, but he would never go against his wife. Never. Men might run the rest of the world, but Tayler's mother ran the Hale family corner of it.

Might as well face it. She was stuck. At least for now. She headed over to the camp to help her dad cook the fish. There would be plenty of time later to talk with her parents about her future. No need to worry them. Once Joshua was away at Harvard, maybe she would venture the subject with Dad.

But that would mean Joshua would be gone. Permanently. Emerson too. And that thought was almost as horrific as telling Mother. A shiver raced up her spine. If only she could go with them. But she wasn't a boy. A fact that had felt like a thorn in her side most of her life. Now that she was getting older, it seemed even more divisive. The fairer sex were rarely allowed into the same circles as men, even though things were changing. Tayler had pointed out the exploits and world travels of women like Lady Bird and the famous journalist Nellie Bly, only to have her mother threaten to limit her access to reading materials.

With a glance over her shoulder to the white-covered peaks,

she vowed to capture this scene with her watercolors later. Perhaps when the sun streaked its last rays across the sky in brilliant color.

The thought made her smile. There was at least one thing she liked to do that Mother approved of—paint.

"What's brought that lovely smile to your face, Tayler?" Dad looked back down as he dredged fish fillets in his special concoction of flour, cornmeal, and spices.

"Just thinking about painting the sunset later." Tying her hair back with a ribbon, Tayler walked over to the bowl they used as a washbasin. "After dinner, I think I'll attempt to capture it for Mother."

Dad gave her a wide grin, his hands covered in white, sticky-looking globs of breading as he worked with the last few fillets. "She'll love that. There's nothing quite like a Colorado sunset over the mountains." He held up his hands and frowned. "And nothing quite like the mess I've made here."

Tayler shook her head and brought him a towel. She couldn't help the laugh that bubbled up. "You say that every time, Dad, and every time you manage to make an even bigger mess."

"But it will taste good." He leaned in with his hands raised high and kissed her on the cheek. "You start frying them, and I'll get this cleaned up."

Tying an apron around her waist, Tayler noticed that he already had the cast-iron skillet heating over the fire. She plopped a heaping spoonful of lard into the skillet and watched it melt, then added another. As it began to bubble and sizzle around the edges, she brought the plate of fish over. Whistling a tune she'd heard from the radio, she began to fry the fish, a few fillets at a time, and then watched them turn a beautiful golden brown.

Emerson Pruitt strode up the hill toward her, his dark, curly hair wet from the stream. Seeing the towel hung over his shoulder and his charming smile aimed at her, Tayler felt her stomach do a little flip.

She'd hung around Emerson and Joshua since she could walk. The boys had been best friends their whole lives. But it had been only recently that Emerson paid Tayler just a touch more attention than he used to. With compliments and special smiles just for her—smiles that were different from the ones he used to give—she thought their parents' wish to see the two families joined might come to fruition one day.

While boys had never before held much interest to her romantically, in the last few months Tayler had begun to think that maybe marrying one day wouldn't be so bad. Emerson liked a good adventure, and it was possible he wouldn't mind the fact that his wife did as well.

"Hey, Tayler, that sure smells good." Emerson gave her a wink as he passed by.

"Well, I hope you're hungry. I burned a few of them just for you."

Dad laughed in the background as splashes of water sounded behind her. "Actually, I don't think the boys should be allowed to eat any of the fish until they help me clean up the mess."

Tayler joined in on the laughter. "I agree. I think they should have to wash *all* the dishes. Even after supper."

Joshua ran up at that moment, his hair dripping into his eyes. "Come on, Pop, you wouldn't do that to two starving young men headed to Harvard, would ya?"

"You bet I would." Dad wiggled his eyebrows at Tayler and then looked back to the boys with a mischievous grin. "Now get over there and scrub while Emerson dries. I'll help Tayler with the rest of supper."

With moans and dramatics from the boys spurring on the

laughter, Tayler finished cooking the fish while Dad pan-fried potatoes he'd cut up into chunks.

Dinner around the fire was another jovial affair, just like everything seemed to be up in the mountains on their camping expeditions. Nothing could be better—at least in Tayler's mind. But as the boys talked about their dreams and how Harvard was a year away for them both, her heart sank. Melancholy washed over her, and the urge to cry hit her like a ton of bricks.

Not one to normally give in to girlish emotions, she stood abruptly. "If you'll excuse me, I'm off to paint the sunset."

The boys seemed to ignore her—they were so caught up in telling a story from prep school—but Dad at least nodded at her as he listened to the boys' story. A second later, he held up a hand to them and turned to Tayler. "Don't forget a rifle, just in case."

"Yes, sir." Tayler felt wounded. The boys didn't even seem to care that she was leaving. They just kept on with their stories. Their banter continued as she grabbed her easel and supplies. Tears pricked her eyes. She wasn't one of them. When they thought of their futures, they probably didn't think of continuing these types of adventures with *her*. Not like she did. The truth hurt more than she wanted to admit. Childish dreams couldn't guide her any longer. What did she want?

Exasperation filled her entire being. Stupid girl tears. She didn't have time for this.

But the entire trek back up the ridge her thoughts pressed on her all the more. Tears escaped and spilled down her cheeks. The boys were fine without her. But in contrast, she wasn't fine without them. They would leave again, and eventually, they'd go far away to college and maybe not even come back to Denver at all. The thought depressed her as she went to the stream to fill her jar with water and then set up the easel.

Joshua and Emerson had each other as friends. Always together. Always backing the other up with support and slaps on the back.

Whom did *she* have?

Wiping her tears, she finished getting her supplies ready and waited for the sun's show to begin. She had plenty of time to wallow in the boys' leaving. She needed to enjoy the little time she had left with them on this trip. And she couldn't allow them to see her crying. Not ever. She'd never hear the end of it. Then they wouldn't want to bring a girl along anymore. And she desperately wanted to be included . . . as long as possible.

And once they were gone? She'd just have to follow in Lady Bird's footsteps and do it all on her own.

Only, the thought of having adventures alone wasn't nearly as appealing.

Dipping her brush in the water, she looked to the sky above and shook off the dreary thoughts.

Capture the picture. That's what she needed to focus on. The deep pinks and oranges that changed the thin, wispy clouds from plain white to glowing masterpieces. The mountain carving a shadow below it as it blocked the light. This would be a beautiful painting, if she could simply get it on the canvas.

Tayler pushed all depressing thoughts aside and poured herself into the work before her. Sometimes growing up was painful. While she couldn't wait to be an adult, she missed the carefree life of her childhood. Besides, adulthood seemed to bring too many . . . responsibilities. Too many emotions and good-byes. And a great many rules and restrictions.

With a sigh, she did her best to remove the clutter of her mind and focus on the colors. A dark lavender added just the right touch to capture the color of the mountains in the setting sun's light.

Laughter floated up to her from their camp below. Well, at least the guys were having fun. Did they miss her yet?

Words escaped her lips, even though there wasn't anyone to answer but the sky and herself. "Tayler, you know full well it's best to get your mind off that." With a huff, she blew a stray hair off her forehead. Even with the stern talking-to, her mind still went back to Joshua and Emerson. What would she do without them?

A rustling in the grass to her left made her pause with her brush in midair.

Whatever it was, it had to be small. The sound quieted and Tayler counted slowly to twenty. Nothing. Probably just a squirrel. Best to finish the painting while she still had light.

Fully immersed in her work, she furiously set about getting the last of it done. Mother would love to have a new piece of art to hang. At least her daughter could do *something* feminine.

Satisfied with the last streaks of pink, Tayler tapped her chin with the handle of the brush and stepped back a foot. The sun would completely set soon, and she'd do well to get back down the ridge before it was dark.

She rinsed her brush and wiped it on the small towel she kept hung on the portable easel. As she stepped toward her bag, a small ball of black fur rambled over to it.

She gasped.

A bear cub.

Intent on her canvas bag.

With another intake of breath, she realized her mistake. Like an idiot, she'd left it on the ground a good ten feet away. And if that weren't enough . . . she'd left cookies in there.

No wonder the bear cub was after it.

Tayler knew better. She really did. But this time, she'd been engrossed in her melancholy thoughts, and she'd made a mistake that might well cost her more than simple embarrassment. Not only had she *not* hung her bag—as she normally did—but she forgot the rifle. She'd never want to kill a baby animal, but she could have used something to scare it off. Because most certainly, there was a mama bear around here somewhere.

Maybe the cub didn't see her. Tayler moved and made some noise so the baby might get scared and leave.

But no. The stubborn little thing glanced at her and stuck its nose back into her bag.

"Shoo. Go on, now. We do *not* want a visit from your mother, do we?" Tayler waved her hands at it and inched toward her bag. The bear made a cute little growling noise and then began munching.

"Great. You found my cookies. Just what I needed. Bear slobber inside my bag." She stepped closer and raised her voice a bit. "Shoo. Go on."

But the bear had its head buried all the way inside the bag now. Maybe it was best to just go. Leave now before Mama showed up. Tayler backed away and then grabbed the painting and her easel in one swift move.

As she turned to head back down the ridge, an all-too-familiar sound made her stop in her tracks. Deep huffs, followed by clacking of teeth.

The mama had found her cub. And she wasn't happy.

Tayler turned her head to see but kept as still as possible. She knew she couldn't outrun it—and shouldn't try—but she also couldn't appear as a threat. Oh, bother, why had she stopped for the painting and easel? As she turned around to see what the bear would do, she held her breath.

The mama bear ambled over to her cub and gave it a sound thump on its backside. The little guy pulled his head out of the bag and made some cute—almost purring-like—noises.

Another few large breaths and snorts from the mama as she stared Tayler down.

Then she moved in front of the baby bear and closer to Tayler—making it clear she was protecting her cub. She clacked her teeth again.

Tayler slowly set down the easel and painting, hoping she would look less threatening to the animal. She backed up two steps with her hands out.

Three more steps. *Oh, Lord, please forgive my stupidity.*

Two more steps. But something rustled behind her.

At the sound, mama bear charged toward Tayler. Before she could even think of what to do, Tayler screamed.

A shot rang out and Tayler covered her mouth. The mama bear snorted in her direction and then swatted her little cub, and they took off at a fast pace away from where Tayler stood.

"Are you all right?" Emerson's voice was beside her.

Tayler watched the bear with her hand over her mouth. Shaking her head, she felt the tears again. How could she have been so reckless?

"Emerson!" Tayler heard her father yell.

"Everything's fine," Emerson called down to camp. "I just encouraged a mother bear to seek another location." Tayler heard her father's laugh, and it only served to make her cry all the more.

Emerson moved closer, set the rifle down, and looked her over. "Are you hurt?"

Without a second thought, she threw herself into Emerson's arms and sobbed up against him. "No. Yes. . . . I don't know."

His chuckle reverberated through his chest.

Tayler pulled back and swiped at her cheeks with the backs of her hands. "It's not funny, Emerson, and you know it."

"Oh, Tayler. I'm not laughing at you. I promise." He reached for her and put his hands on her elbows. "I guess I'm just surprised to see you crying. You've always been so . . . fearless. We've seen plenty of bears before." He pulled her close and ducked his head as if daring her to meet his gaze, which made her insides do a little flip.

She'd never been held by a boy before . . . well, other than her father or her brother. "It's not about the bear. Well, okay, maybe it was a little about the bear . . . but now I know it was you and your scent coming that made her charge. I should be upset with *you*!" She smacked him in the chest and pulled away, the tears streaming down her cheeks in great big drops as her heart beat inside her rib cage. What a great explorer she was . . . screaming at the first sign of trouble. Embarrassment, anger, and grief all battled for center stage in her mind.

"Hey, I was just bringing you the rifle because your dad was worried." Emerson held his hands out as though surrendering. "Come on, what's wrong? You can talk to me. We've been friends forever."

Before she could contain it, her words tumbled out. "Don't you get it? The years of our camping and mountaineering trips like this are over! You and Josh have all your plans and success waiting for you, and I'm going to be left behind. For more etiquette lessons and finishing school and social gatherings. And that's not who I want to be!" She lifted her hands in disgust. "I hate it. I hate that you both are going away. And the future will be different. You have no idea how tough it is being a girl." Tears dripped from her chin, and she gave a huff of exasperation.

"Ah, Tayler Grace . . . you know it's not going to be forever."

"But what if you never come back?"

"Why wouldn't I come back? My home and my family are in Denver. And so are you. . . ."

"Me?" Her voice squeaked on the word.

Emerson raked a hand through his curly hair. "I thought you knew that I was sweet on you." He licked his lips. "I was kinda hoping you would promise to wait for me."

Blinking rapidly, Tayler wasn't sure what to think. Wait for him? As in—being in love and waiting for him to finish school so they could get married—*wait* for him? "I'm not sure I know what you . . . mean?" Her voice squeaked again, making her feel like a small child.

"Come on, Tayler. I know you're quite grown up now. Don't you know that I think you're the one for me? I mean, even our parents know it. They've been planning this for years."

She raised her eyebrows. "But what about all the girls you were talking about with Josh? The ones who go to the girls' school across the way?"

He blushed. "Aw, you know how guys talk. It's all just talk. You must know that I'm your prince. . . ." He moved closer and closer.

A light laugh escaped. "Well, you did scare the bear off, *after* you made it charge at me."

"Whadaya say, then? Will you wait for me and be my princess forever and ever?" He bowed before her in a sweeping and dramatic gesture. Then his look turned serious, and he stepped even closer. His shoes touched hers, and a tiny thrill shot through Tayler.

"Yes." She felt the heat creep up her neck. Emerson's attention *had* been real. He wanted to marry her!

"Promise?" Emerson reached for her hands.

"I promise." Tayler shivered as his nearness took her breath away.

He leaned in and kissed her on the lips, shocking her into silence. It was only a peck, but still . . . Tayler had never been kissed before. Her eyebrows shot up and gone were any thoughts of tears.

Emerson released her and winked, his fun-loving, boyish expression back in place. "That's my girl. Now, come on. I'll get your bag and you collect your painting." He left her side and moved to where the bears had been only moments earlier.

She put a few fingers to her lips and shivered. Was this what it felt like to be in love?

• • • • •

SUNDAY, JUNE 1, 1919—
TURNAGAIN ARM, ALASKA TERRITORY

Kicking a rock along the railroad tracks with his hole-riddled boot, thirteen-year-old Thomas Smith slung his pack over his shoulder. Everything he owned was wrapped up in the tattered blanket he'd tied in a knot. But that was all right. He didn't need a lot.

When winter came back with a vengeance—as it was prone to do in Alaska—he'd have to find a coat and a better blanket.

But he couldn't think about that now.

Food and work were bigger needs. He was on his own. Not by choice, but it had only been a matter of time before the missionaries kicked him out of their makeshift orphanage. Just like all the boys who were old enough to work and too big to feed and clothe anymore.

The tracks stretched in front of him like a blank slate. What would his future hold? While he'd like to be confident and say he was a man and could take care of himself, there was a small part of him that still longed for a family. He'd never had one—at least not that he could remember.

The ground vibrated and Thomas looked behind him.

A short train with a cloud of smoke above its stack headed toward him.

Thomas backed away from the tracks and adjusted his pack. Maybe they would throw some food leftovers at him like the train yesterday. It hadn't been good, but at least it had been food, and his stomach was raw again today. Life as an orphan had taught him not to be choosy.

As he waited for the train to pass, he forced himself not to think about food. Wouldn't be a good idea to get his hopes up. He turned his head to watch, though. Just in case they threw something out for him.

But instead of passing him up, the train began to slow. Thomas's stomach twisted. He couldn't be in trouble . . . could he? Taking a deep breath, he faced forward and kept walking.

"Hey!" a deep voice shouted over the brakes of the train.

Thomas turned. Lifted a weak smile and waved.

A wiry man waved him forward from the railing. "Where're you headed, kid?"

Thomas shrugged.

The man smiled, which made him seem kind, but that impression could be wrong. "You all by yourself?"

This made Thomas a bit nervous. What would they do to him if he was? But then again, maybe the man could help him find a job. Honesty seemed to be the way to go. "Yes, sir."

With a nod, the man hopped down from the train. "Were you the one we saw yesterday on these same tracks?"

The question made him swallow. "Yes, sir. Should I not be walking here? I don't want to cause any trouble. I'm looking for work."

Sighing, the man looked off toward the mountains and then back to Thomas. With his hands on his hips, the man looked down at Thomas's shoes. "I might be able to help with that, but you have to let me know the truth first."

"The truth about what, sir?"

"Where you came from. Did you run away from home?"

"No, sir."

"Where's your family?"

"I ain't got none, sir." Heat filled Thomas's cheeks.

"Not anyone?"

"No, sir. I'm an orphan."

The man's brow furrowed—his smile gone. "Did you run off from an orphanage?"

"No, sir. I got too big to clothe and feed, sir. So I'm on my own now." Hoping his words sounded intelligent enough, he lifted his shoulders. He didn't have a great education, but at least the missionaries had drilled into him that he had to have manners. Respect should go a long ways, shouldn't it? Tears threatened at the corners of his eyes as exhaustion and hunger warred for his attention and his hope drained. "I'd best be on my way. Like I said, I'm just looking for work."

"Hold on." The man held up a hand. "What's your name?"

"Thomas Smith, sir."

"That's a fine name." He rubbed his chin. "Ya know, I've been looking for someone to help me out. It's a hard job, working on the railroad. Probably just have to run back and forth and fetch stuff at first until we put some meat on those bones of yours, but then you could work your way in other jobs."

The flame of hope in Thomas's heart grew into a blaze. A job. An actual job! All he could manage was a nod as the man kept talking.

Holding out his hand, the man gave him another broad smile. "Name's Joseph Carter."

"Nice to meet you." Thomas shook his hand.

Joseph put his hands back on his hips. "First thing, we probably ought to get you some food. Then some decent shoes." He tilted his head toward the train. "Better get moving. There's lots of daylight left in the day to get things done."

Thomas's heart picked up in rhythm. "Yes, sir." He climbed up behind Joseph and grinned. As the train began to move again, he watched the terrain as it floated by. Maybe he'd be okay after all.

A bell clanging in the distance brought Thomas awake. Last night was the first night in years he'd slept through without being woken up by a growling stomach. Jumping up from his bedroll, he ran his hands through his shaggy hair and then put his cap back on. He straightened his bedroll and headed to the privy. No matter what, he wanted to make a really good impression on Joseph's boss. No way he wanted to give the hardened man an excuse to dismiss him—especially not after everything Joseph had done for him. Looking down at the new boots on his feet, Thomas smiled. It was the first time he'd had a new pair of shoes. Ever.

Breakfast passed in a flurry, but Thomas didn't have any problem eating fast. Growing up in the orphanage, he learned he'd better eat as quick as he could, or he might not eat at all.

Joseph took him to his designated job site and went over all the rules of the camp. After he'd explained his expectations, he clapped Thomas on the back and sent him running for water for the workers.

It was an easy trek to the stream, but once he loaded the filled buckets up on the yoke, Thomas realized that they weighed almost as much as he did. The path back to the railroad camp was uphill, and the struggle to carry the load without spilling water was an intense challenge.

Thomas bit his lip and kept trudging ahead. He could do this. Just needed to build up his strength. For the first time in his young life, he had a place to sleep, a job, and a full belly. There was no way he'd give that up.

As he reached the edge of the camp, he stopped to catch his breath. The mountains before him were still covered in snow, the air clean and crisp. Alaska was home to him. He'd never been anywhere else and had no desire to be. Maybe he'd be able to work for the railroad for a long time. Wouldn't that be grand? Especially if he drove one of the trains one day. He'd have a family with the railroad.

A smile cracked his lips as he moved forward again. The men wouldn't take to waiting too long for water.

The clanging of sledges against the rails rang out in steady rhythm. The men slinging them had shoulders and arms that looked like they were carved out of steel themselves. Thomas glanced down at his skinny arms. Definitely needed some more meat on his bones. Just like Joseph said.

He neared the break area and tripped over a rock. Before he could do anything about it, the momentum flung the buckets and the yoke smacked him in the back of the head. Tumbling to the rocky ground, Thomas put his hands out in front of him to brace his fall.

All around him, several men laughed.

Heat crept up his neck and face as pain seared through his palms and knees.

One loud voice rose above the noise around Thomas. "Is that the orphan kid you picked up yesterday, Joe? Doesn't look like he's good for much. . . ."

More laughter.

Other voices competed for attention in Thomas's hearing. Joseph was saying something back to the man, but Thomas couldn't understand it. Picking himself up from the ground, he tried to brush himself off as the men continued to joke and talk around him. He picked up the buckets and the yoke and took off down the hill to the stream as embarrassment filled his entire frame.

So much for finding a family here. He would always be known as an *orphan*.

When he reached the stream, he slammed the buckets into the water. That word had never really bothered him before because all the kids he knew were orphans. But now, things were different. He wanted to be something else. Someone else.

Determination built in his gut. He was gonna be somebody someday. He would. Orphan or not. He'd prove that he was worth something.

1

TEN YEARS LATER
THURSDAY, APRIL 4, 1929—DENVER, COLORADO

As twenty-three-year-old Tayler threw another brown split skirt into her suitcase, a light knock sounded on her bedroom door. "Come in," she called out, and went to look for the matching neck scarves in her closet.

"Miss, you've been called to the study." Millie, her maid since she was twelve, stood in the doorway.

A groan left Tayler's lips as she peeked at her maid. Summoned to the study again? "Is it urgent, do you think? Or has Mother just found another way to word her displeasure? I'm really quite busy packing." She turned back to the closet and found the brown scarves along with the olive-green ones. Just what she needed.

"Miss, it's your mother *and* Mr. Dunham this time. They said you need to come right away."

Tayler peeked around the doorjamb at her maid and then looked to the ceiling. Mother probably convinced the family's lawyer to come by because she thought Tayler needed a stern talking-to. About why she shouldn't go traipsing off to her job.

As if she hadn't heard the first *four* lectures by Mother already this morning. With a sigh, she resigned herself to yet another. Nothing had been the same since Dad died last September. She'd come home like a dutiful daughter to lend her mother support—not that she needed it after all. Thankfully Tayler's job at Yellowstone National Park had been about to end for the winter. Even though her absence hadn't put her boss in a tough situation, how she wished she were there now.

The thought sounded horrible, but Tayler couldn't help it. The past few months had been worse than she'd ever imagined. Mother had always been strong, but when Father died, she'd hardened herself in a way Tayler hadn't expected. If ever Tayler doubted that her mother ran the household, she didn't anymore. Mother had always been a part of the business ventures and decisions. When Father was alive she'd had the decency to downplay her role, but in the last seven months since his death she didn't even attempt to pretend. Rather than spend time grieving, Mother simply got to work. She'd called in Mr. Dunham, demanded a full audit of the family holdings, and made everyone aware of her demands. Henrietta Hale was insistent that the Hale empire be known just like J.P. Morgan and Andrew Carnegie: as business magnates, investors in numerous companies and real estate, philanthropists—and most importantly—well-established in their social standing.

Poor Joshua had been blindsided. He'd expected to take over for their father, but instead he found himself more of a pawn. Tayler could still see his stunned expression when Mother announced she had everything under control and he could return to New York City to manage his own businesses. Maybe when she was older and tired of running everything she would ask him to come take over.

Joshua hadn't been home since the funeral. He buried himself in his work, and even Tayler's repeated pleas that he come home and help her reason with their mother went unanswered for the most part. He'd sent one letter after Tayler had sent him four lengthy diatribes as to their mother's actions and attitude. Especially her insistence that Tayler give up working and remain at home. Joshua's response had been given in one line:

I am sorry, but I can't change the way things are. Mother has made her decision.

Tayler was still at a loss to understand. They'd always been so close, but whether it was the sadness of mourning their father or the harshness of their mother, Joshua had changed and left Tayler alone to deal with the aftermath.

"Miss?" Millie interrupted her thoughts.

Tayler shook her head. "I'm sorry." With a sigh, she resigned herself to the fate before her. The sooner she left, the sooner she could get out of Mother's grasp. "I'd better go down. Can you find the green split skirts for my uniforms as well? There should be three. Just place them on the bed, and I will get them packed when I return." She ran to the mirror and checked her appearance before she went downstairs. No need to alarm her mother by looking disheveled. If Tayler planned to go into battle, she had to have the upper hand.

"Yes, miss. I'll wait for you here."

"Thanks, Millie. You're a dear." She headed out of her room at a brisk pace. Mother hated waiting. But Tayler wondered how many more times she would have to express her feelings and wishes. Goodness, it was almost 1930, for pity's sake. Mother acted as if they still lived in the previous century.

But as Tayler rounded the corner into the study, an unmistakable voice made her stiffen. She'd been ambushed.

Standing in the middle of the study with Mother fawning all over him was none other than that lying, cheating, no-good

Emerson Pruitt. Tayler crossed her arms over her chest and took a deep breath. This would not be pretty. Her temper started to boil, and she attempted to keep a lid on it. "I hear you needed to speak with me?" Lips tight, she glared at her mother. She knew her expression had turned into a scowl, but she couldn't help it.

"Darling, I'm so glad you joined us. Isn't it lovely that Emerson has come to call?" Mother's voice dripped with adoration.

"Lovely." The sarcastic word left her lips unchecked.

Emerson—hands outstretched like she was a beloved family member—strode toward her with that charming smile she knew to be all too fake. "Tayler Grace, it is *so* enchanting to see you." He came in for a kiss, but she turned away at the last second, and he missed.

Walking over to Mr. Dunham, Tayler reached out to shake his hand. "Good morning, Mr. Dunham. How are you?"

His slight groan under his breath told her more than she needed. "Fine. Just fine." In Tayler's opinion, the lawyer had spent entirely too much time at the Hale home since Mother went into a frenzy over managing everything. It wasn't that Tayler disliked the man, but he was just . . . odd. And secretive. He was short and round, and nothing like her father, Martin Hale, who'd been a tall, strong man.

The thought of Daddy brought a prick of tears to her eyes. If he were here, he wouldn't allow for Mother's nonsense. Goodness, he'd encouraged Tayler to go to college when she told them of her dreams and had cheered her on when she gained a prestigious position at Yellowstone National Park. And he'd been especially supportive when she'd learned the truth about Emerson and ended their engagement.

Mr. Dunham cleared his throat and brought her thoughts back to the moment. In the study. Being ambushed. "How are you doing, Miss Hale?"

"Well . . . considering this is the fifth time this morning that I've been called to the study—"

"That's quite enough, Tayler Grace." Mother frowned. Everyone knew Tayler preferred going by just her first name, but Mother—and apparently Emerson—refused to acquiesce.

She sighed.

"Goodness, Tayler Grace, that is no way to greet your guest." Mother scolded and pursed her lips, then motioned to Emerson. "Especially since he's come that we might set the wedding date."

What?

Tayler shook her head and blinked. Taking a deep breath, she stepped forward. "Emerson? He is not my guest, Mother. Nor will he ever be. And there's not going to be a wedding. If you will remind yourself, I broke off our charade of an engagement three years ago."

Emerson looked wounded, and Mother put a hand on his arm. Which he accepted and patted and then appeared ready to cry. The big actor.

Mother pursed her lips. "You were distraught at the time—"

"No. Mother, I wasn't distraught or delirious or dumbfounded or whatever other word you can come up with and *have* come up with over the past few years. I came to my senses. Father understood and supported my decision, and I would appreciate it if you would do the same."

"There's no call for such an attitude, Tayler Grace. It's time for you to settle down and stop gallivanting off on your ridiculous adventures." Mother looked to Mr. Dunham. "I do apologize for bringing you into the middle of this. I'm afraid my daughter has been allowed a rather unruly upbringing. As you know, my husband spoiled her."

Tayler put her hands on her hips. "I'm standing right here, Mother." She held in a groan. "While I mean you no disrespect, you know this has nothing to do with my being spoiled. And I don't go gallivanting off. I'm a naturalist." Trying to keep her voice calm, she felt the words gushing to the surface. "You also well know of Emerson's exploits and, dare I say, love affairs—while we were engaged—that were all over the papers? And that Emerson freely admitted to? And then, he didn't even bother to respond to the broken engagement, nor did he come to visit and apologize?" Her voice always rose in pitch when she was angry, and she fought against the squeaky childish sound. She was an adult and needed to be heard.

"But, darling, you know that he needed to go away for a while to let the gossip die down." Mother *tsk*ed at Tayler like she was a child.

Shaking her head, she took another deep breath. "No, Mother. It wasn't gossip. I'm done with all of this. I will *not* be marrying Emerson Pruitt. No matter what you say. I have a job to get to. A job I love."

"I've had quite enough of this, Tayler Grace Hale. You haven't listened to a word I've said all morning, have you? Besides, Emerson told us just now that none of it was true." Mother turned to the slimy weasel. "Isn't that right, dear?"

Tayler narrowed her eyes. Should she tell her mother once and for all that she witnessed it firsthand? In their own home, no less? Images flitted back into her mind. Images that had broken her heart. Of Emerson kissing that Wainwright girl behind the grand staircase. Then at the Stewarts' party the following month—a party he attended with *her*—she caught him in the gazebo with his arms around Mary Lou Stewart. Not to mention the dozen other episodes over that spring. The spring that Tayler had to grow up and face facts. While he'd been back in Denver and she'd been away at college, he'd apparently had plenty of *friends* to take her place.

Not that they'd ever had much time together for her to *have* a place. After their little mountaintop promise, he'd gone back to prep school and then went off to Harvard. By the time he came home to Denver, she was off to college. The few weeks they'd seen each other over the years had been few and far between. And it only proved to her one thing:

Men were liars and cheaters. At least Emerson proved to be.

She put a hand to her face and pinched the bridge of her nose. While Joshua had listened to her and comforted her before he went back to Harvard to continue his graduate studies in law, he'd also had to admit that his best friend of all these years hadn't been faithful to his little sister. And *everyone* knew it. Tayler refused to be the laughingstock. She was a child of God. And He had something much better for her. She knew that. Felt assured in that. If the Lord had a special someone out there for her . . . somewhere . . . then she would rest in that and wait for God to reveal him. She only knew for sure that it *wasn't* Emerson.

Emerson moved toward her. "Tayler, let's put all this behind us. I'm here now."

Tayler held up a hand to stop him. "No. I don't know what game you're playing, but I'm going back to my job in Yellowstone. There's nothing more to discuss."

Emerson had the gall to laugh. "Your *job*? As a tour guide?" He looked at her mother and simply shook his head.

Rage bubbled up to the surface, but Tayler clenched her teeth to keep from exploding. Measuring her words, she spoke in a controlled tone. "I'm not a tour guide, Emerson Pruitt, and you know that. I'm a naturalist and interpreter with a degree in botany. A well-respected one at that."

"Honey, I'm sure you are very well respected, and I wasn't trying to belittle you, I promise. But we both know that you are just doing this job until we marry. I'm sorry for my wayward behavior as a boy, although I assure you it was never as bad as the newspapers made out. I've come to my senses. You know me . . . I was just a silly young man." He stepped the rest of the way to her and put an arm around her shoulders.

It made her cringe. "Silly young man? For all these years? You expect me to believe that? No. Do not call me 'honey' and again, *no*, I'm not just doing this job until we marry." She lifted his hand from her shoulder and flung it back to his side with more force than was necessary, but she couldn't help it. Marching over to the window, she stomped her feet. Then she turned back to face the liar. If flames could shoot from her eyes, she'd want to aim them at him right now. "I will never marry you, Emerson."

"Let's not be hasty." He held up his hands and pasted that oily smile back on. "You made a promise to me, and I know I've been a little careless, but my heart is true."

An unladylike snort escaped at his ludicrous response. "A promise when I was a child, you big oaf. Just as you made mistakes as a . . . what did you call it . . . silly young man? I made mistakes as a silly young girl. A girl who believed the best of everyone—until they betrayed me. I have no feelings for you whatsoever . . . you . . . you womanizer."

"Tayler Grace!" Mother grimaced. "I will not stand for you speaking to Emerson in that manner, and in front of poor Mr. Dunham no less." She glided over the marble floor to stand in front of Tayler, but Tayler turned away. Her action did nothing to deter Mother.

"You made a promise and our families have invested heavily in each other because of that promise. You and Emerson have been best friends since you were little." Her voice turned calm and soothing. "Now, let's put all the past behind us and move forward, shall we?"

Tayler turned to look at her mother. "What has happened to you? Dad would never force me to marry this liar." Tears streaked down her cheeks, her emotion threatening to choke her. "Don't you care about me anymore?"

"Of course I care about you, dear. I want what's best for you. And this union between you and Emerson is just that. You're simply upset. Losing your father has been a terrible blow to us all."

Mr. Dunham stepped beside her mother. "Let's not forget the family ties, Miss Hale. Your mother simply wants the best for you and for the whole family. As she mentioned, investments have been made on both sides that would be irresponsible to dismiss when speaking of the future of your fortunes."

Mother nodded.

Emerson played innocent and stayed quiet, but all the while he watched her like a cat sizing up his prey.

Something wasn't adding up in her mind. Her mother's behavior the past few months. Mr. Dunham's visits. Hushed conversations in the study and private meetings elsewhere. If her heart could break again after Emerson's betrayal and then the loss of her beloved father, she was sure it would shatter into a million pieces on the floor. If she ever wanted her big brother to walk through the front door, it was now. Why couldn't Joshua put aside his own grief and help her?

"Tayler Grace, you must know that this is the right thing to do. For the Hale and Pruitt family legacies." Emerson simpered at her, a very unbecoming look.

Tayler turned to Mother and looked her square in the eye. "So let me get this straight. You want me to marry this *louse* because you have *invested heavily*? Isn't that how Dad built your precious empire—by investing? Is that what all this is about? Your precious money and family legacy? I don't care about who has invested in what or whom." She flung an arm out in front of her. "I doubt you even know all the companies that Dad built by investing, so why does this matter? You and the Pruitts can continue on investing however you please. What happened to the mother who cared about my hopes and dreams rather than marrying me off to a man who probably has five mistresses lined up already?"

Mother gasped and put a hand to her throat. "You will not speak to me in that manner, young lady!"

Dunham placed a hand on Mother's arm. "Henrietta, she's distraught. Let me." He turned to Tayler. "Your mother cares for you a great deal. But yes, your family has invested quite heavily in the Pruitts' businesses, and they have reciprocated. It's been ten years since you two pledged to each other, so quite an industry has been built. The two family holdings are quite intertwined now. Real estate, iron, steel, oil . . . many purchases and investments have been made together." He moved a step forward. "Your mother has so much weight on her shoulders. She simply wants you to be happily married and settled down."

Tayler couldn't believe it. The Hale family was extremely wealthy. What did a little investment in the Pruitts' holdings have to do with this? Why not just sell off the purchases they'd made together? Was it that big of a deal? Tayler didn't understand it and didn't want to. And now she was a burden to her mother? What was going on? And why was Emerson here all of a sudden? "But I broke off the engagement three years ago . . . why didn't Dad just adjust things if those investments were a problem?"

Mother swallowed. "Emerson's father came to us a few months after you broke it off—while Emerson was in Europe— and assured us that everything would go as planned and Emerson had changed his ways. . . . We all just thought you needed time. . . ." Her voice trailed off as if the excuse uttered didn't sound all that good anymore.

"But you've had plenty of time to grow up. We both have, my dear. Mistakes were made and now we must forgive and put it all behind us." Emerson finished and gave a small smile.

Tayler backed up a few paces and shook her head. Looking at the three people staring back at her—waiting for her reply— made her feel very alone. Had she really been this blind? All this time? Her own parents had thought she would *still* marry Emerson? Dad had listened to her time and again and consoled her. Why hadn't he told her the truth?

"So you all just thought you could plan my future without even consulting me?"

Mother sighed. "I'm sorry, Tayler Grace. I really thought you would be all right with this. It's been long enough. It's time for us to move forward with the wedding. You've loved Emerson forever." Her tone was sad and motherly. For a brief moment it reminded Tayler of the woman her mother had been. The woman Tayler wished she could see on a regular basis. The real lady underneath all the layers of aristocratic and rich nonsense. The woman who had genuinely loved her husband and not just his business dealings. Or were they ever his? Perhaps Mother had always orchestrated the business and this was all just an act. Oh, it was too confusing and too much to bear.

"Tayler, your father loved to talk about the camping trips and how well you and Emerson got along. We both thought you would be perfect for each other." Her mother looked out the window. "Your father even told me . . . that . . . well . . . he knew in time you would work things out, because your love was genuine and you had such a forgiving heart." She looked back at Tayler. "He said there were many people in the world who pretended to love, but he knew your heart would never allow for that."

Tayler felt the weight of her mother's comment. Had Dad really said that? If he had, then surely her mother understood why she couldn't play a game of loving Emerson.

Mr. Dunham cleared his throat again. "Maybe we just need to give Tayler some time to think."

Emerson held out his hand toward Tayler. "This isn't about time, it's about forgiveness. I thought God wanted us to forgive one another. I know I have His forgiveness, and if God can forgive me, then I know you will want to do likewise. After all, Tayler, it is about pleasing God, is it not?"

Tayler was never at a loss for words, but the fact that Emerson would bring God into the conversation when she knew full well he didn't have much to do with God, church, or even prayer was enough to momentarily stupefy her.

He took advantage of her silence. "Now, let's not delay things anymore. Everything is fine. Really. Isn't it, Tayler? We simply need to work through a few things. You know we've always been destined for each other, and I'm completely devoted to you."

That cleared the shock from her brain. "Completely devoted to me? When you were running around with other girls and getting into all sorts of trouble? Really?" Tayler could hardly believe her own ears.

"You know me . . . I needed to 'sow my wild oats,' as my dad put it. But now I'm ready to settle down and be respectable." His smile seemed pasted on. "I'm a new man."

What was his game? She knew that Emerson didn't care for her like a husband should for a wife, so why was he trying to convince her? Especially with an embarrassing explanation of sowing his wild oats. "No, Emerson. How many times can I tell you in one day? No. It's *not* fine. We're *not* going to work through anything. And I will *not* marry you." She put a hand to her stomach and took a glance around the room. A room that was filled with beautiful memories with her family. But today, it only felt cold and lonely. The marble floors and deep bookcases seemed sterile instead of inviting. There wasn't a fire in the fireplace to warm the chill from her bones. No tea or sponge cakes on the tray inviting her to stay and read a book. And Dad. He was gone. Forever. She'd never have the chance to watch him work at his desk again. This room had been her favorite.

Instead she wanted to run from it. And hope no one would follow. But she'd never been one to run from her troubles.

Until now.

"I leave in three days—as you all well know—and I've made a decision. I won't be returning in the fall."

Her mother gasped.

"Tayler." Emerson's voice cracked. "Don't make any hasty choices right now. If time is what will prove my sincerity, we can wait a bit."

As much as she wanted to honor her parents, since that was what the Bible said, and it was the good Christian thing to do, she couldn't abide by their decision to force her into a loveless marriage with an unfaithful man. It didn't make any sense. At all. She closed her eyes and tried to block out the people before her.

Lord, I don't understand what You want me to do. Help. Please!

How had things spun out of control so fast? When she'd awoken this morning, everything was normal.

While she didn't comprehend what was happening with her family, peace had washed over her. God would supply all her needs. She simply needed to trust Him. He hadn't brought her this far and through all that pain for nothing.

She turned to go, but Emerson stepped in front of her. "But my parents have had our engagement party planned for months. It's next week."

"Wait . . . what? Months? And I'm just now hearing about this *today*?" She furrowed her brow. Had they all gone mad? She glanced at her mother. "You knew about this too, didn't you?"

"Of course." Her mother sat on the couch, looking confused. "Honestly, Tayler Grace, it was what your father wanted."

Tayler shook her head. "Don't even attempt the guilt trip, Mother."

"I have no idea what you mean." Her expression turned stony—like she became unfeeling all of a sudden.

"How could you do this to me? *It was what my father wanted?*" she mimicked. Unbelievable. Maybe she was having a nightmare. How else could she explain all this? But as Tayler looked around the room, her eyes came back to rest on her mother, a woman she hardly recognized anymore. In her mind she longed to question the woman who'd given birth to her. *What have you done?*

But the question remained silent on her lips. With a deep breath, she tried to still the quaking that started in her hands. "I wish you would have told me, Mother." Tears pulsated behind her eyes, but she bit the insides of her cheeks to stop from breaking down and took another shaky breath. Raising her chin, she looked each one of them in the eye. "I don't understand what is going on here, but there will *not* be an engagement party next week. We are not engaged, Emerson. Now, or ever."

"But—"

"No buts, Emerson. It's over. Now leave me alone. Please." Tayler went around him and exited the study as fast as she could. Voices called out to her, but she ignored them. Running up the massive staircase, she felt the hot tears releasing, and they stung her cheeks as they rolled down her face.

Her parents weren't perfect, but they'd always been supportive and loving. Mother had her quirks, yes, but she'd never been like this. Where in the past she had merely been annoying, now Mother was harsh and unfeeling. The loss of Dad had put them all in a tailspin.

Trying to put the puzzle together, she attempted to get her breathing back to normal as she walked the long corridor in the east wing to her suite. The purple carpet had been her favorite, with the cream-colored wainscoting and gold wallpaper above it. Daddy had always called it her "royal pathway" because she was the princess.

Oh, how she missed him.

With her father gone, nothing seemed balanced. It was like her whole world had tilted on its side, and she didn't know how to set it right.

As she approached the door to her rooms, she turned and looked back down the hall. How she loved her home. The citrusy scent of the wood oil used to polish the furniture would forever be imprinted on her mind as a smell of home. It made her want to cry. It was all too much.

She couldn't stay here another night. That fact stabbed her in the heart. She hoped Millie wasn't in on the charade too, because Tayler needed her maid in this hour of madness. She'd always been independent and strong-willed, but she longed for someone to lean on. Someone to love her for being *her*. Longing for a bright future filled with adventure and love and family threatened to overwhelm her.

It all seemed unattainable now. With Dad gone, Mother's coldness, Joshua's absence, and Emerson's lies . . . her hopes and dreams lay dashed. . . .

Except for her job at Yellowstone.

She took a deep breath and stared at her door. She could

honor God with her talents and gifts. Maybe things hadn't turned out the way she'd wanted, but that didn't matter. Maybe she hadn't understood God's plans for her life, but she could move forward.

One thing was certain—she had her faith and knew that God loved her more than anyone on earth could. She'd have to rest in that.

Opening the door to her room, Tayler breathed in deeply. Millie stood at the foot of the bed twisting her hands. "I'm sorry I didn't tell you, miss. Your mother swore me to secrecy."

"So you knew about Emerson? About the engagement party?"

The maid nodded, tears streaming down her cheeks. "I'm sorry. Truly, I am."

"I'm surprised Mother didn't demand that you unpack all my things and put them back."

"She didn't. And I wouldn't want to, either." She swiped at her cheeks. "Look, I need to report back to Mrs. Henderson since I missed the evening check-in, but I'll be right back to help you finish your packing. Again, I'm sorry."

Numbness took over Tayler. She nodded and Millie left to find the housekeeper, while Tayler could only sit and stare at the room. Her room. All her life, she'd slept in this room. Read in this room. Dreamt of her future.

But in that moment, it no longer felt like home.

Rubbing her forehead with her hands, Tayler looked at her suitcase and focused on her packing. Thoughts of the past weren't going to help her move forward.

Inside the case, she'd packed three brown split skirts, six brown neck scarves, six olive-green neck scarves, three burnt-orange blouses, three rose blouses, three deep golden yellow blouses. Two pairs of sturdy hiking boots, her favorite wide-brimmed, Stetson-style campaign hat, and her three green split skirts lay on the bed—Millie must have found them. Her chosen uniform as a naturalist wasn't grand, but it was practical. Now she needed plenty of undergarments, and she'd be packed. When she glanced back to her closet, some of her gowns called to her. The sequins, lace, and frilly trim always made her feel like such a lady. And she indeed loved being noticed as a lady, but shouldn't practicality win out?

She shook her head and put her hands on her hips. A million thoughts tumbled through her mind. She couldn't wear her uniform everywhere. While she needed to be prepared for her job, she also needed to be prepared for . . . life away from home. As the weight of it all pressed into her thoughts, she knew her mind had been made up.

She wouldn't be coming back.

Decision made, she started making piles on the bed. It hurt to think she may not return to this house, but relief also filled her being. A heaviness felt like it had been lifted. This was the right thing to do.

Millie tapped on the open door. "I've returned, miss."

"Would you mind grabbing the rest of my cases for me?"

Her maid tilted her head for a moment and then nodded. "Of course, I'll be right back."

Tayler made a few more trips to her dresser and back, piling the rest of her things on the bed. When Millie returned with the other three cases that matched her luggage set, Tayler went back to the closet. "I need your advice, Millie. I need to be practical but need to pack for the long-term."

"You're not returning home after the summer, are you?" Millie put a hankie to her eyes. "I had a feeling."

Tayler walked over to her and grabbed her hands. "No, I'm not. And I need you to promise me that you won't tell a soul."

Her sweet maid nodded. "I promise."

"Anything that I tell you this evening?"

"I promise."

"You've always been a dear friend to me, Millie. Much more than just my maid. I hope you know how much I appreciate you."

Millie nodded and sniffed.

"I hate to create any problems for you when Mother finds out. . . . I'm sorry."

"When she finds out what, miss?"

Tayler bit her lip and then blurted it out. "I've decided that I'm not waiting to leave in a few days. I'm going to leave tonight. And I need your help covering for me."

Millie nodded with understanding in her eyes. No condescension. Just trust. And a bit of sorrow. "I can do that."

"Let them think that I'm pitching a fit, pouting, whatever. Just don't let them know that I've gone. I need to distance myself from it all and settle into my job. Who knows? Maybe it will all die down and they'll leave me be."

Millie chuckled. "I highly doubt that, miss."

Tayler sighed. "I know, but a girl can hope, can't she?"

2

Emerson Pruitt stood before the fireplace in his parents' home and thought of all that had transpired that evening. He hadn't seen Tayler Hale in some time, and it was most impressive how the period apart had added to her loveliness. With her dark, long, curly hair that begged to be touched, Tayler's beauty drew him like a moth to the flame. Her enviable hourglass shape needed no help from those pesky undergarments women used. Not that *he* knew anything about such things. A slight laugh broke the silence. Ah, the innocence of youth. Of which he had none.

Something Tayler knew all too well. He'd seen it in her eyes. Those eyes that he remembered most. The darkest of chocolate brown and so intense. He felt almost as if she knew every thought he was thinking. She'd been certain of his character . . . or lack thereof. Emerson smiled. Who would have thought that the sweet little playmate his parents had chosen for him to marry would turn out to be such a gorgeous dame? Unfortunately, convincing Tayler to forget the past and marry him hadn't been as easy as he had hoped. But it was necessary, and it would happen. Determination would win. It had to.

He paced in front of the fireplace and tried to figure out a way to convince Tayler. She'd always been headstrong. She was one woman who truly knew her own mind. When she was a child, it was amusing, but now it was threatening all of Emerson's well-laid plans.

Pop's ultimatum was all too real. And Emerson couldn't risk getting cut off. He was too accustomed to living in wealth.

It all seemed easy when he had Mrs. Hale in his corner. For some reason, she was just as convinced that the two should marry and soon. But Tayler was being stubborn. He'd have to figure out how to worm his way back into her affections.

A noise sounded in the hall and Emerson's father passed by the door. When he spied Emerson, he stopped. "Why are you back so soon?"

Emerson shrugged and put on what he hoped was a confident expression. "Tayler is still pretending that she's mad at me. You know how women can be. She's making me work to win her back. It's a game, nothing more."

Pop's eyes narrowed. "Are you sure? Martin Hale told me she was quite wounded by your escapades." The old man crossed his arms over his chest, his tone condescending. "I'm not surprised either. She's a smart girl."

The barb stung. "I know Tayler better than anyone in the world." Emerson pasted on a smile. "She'll come around."

"I'm beginning to doubt that." The look on his father's face was like steel. "You're reckless and pay no attention to the rules." To Emerson, those words were compliments. To Pop, however, it was the worst condemnation. His father moved closer. "We had a deal. You settle down and start playing by *my* rules and I bail you out . . . *again*—or I leave you to deal with your own mess. But it looks like you've failed." He turned on his heel and headed out of the room.

"Pop . . ." Emerson followed the senior Pruitt and tried to figure out how to weasel his way out of this one.

"Don't *Pop* me. You know I despise your lack of respect to begin with." The man marched into his study and went behind his desk. Pointing to a stack of papers, he narrowed his eyes. "You know what this represents?"

Emerson eyed the stack and shrugged.

"This is your legacy, Emerson. Your failures."

Another barb meant to wound him and put him in his place.

"I'm not going to bail you out this time, Emerson. I've thrown good money away just trying to help you keep your businesses afloat, but you have no understanding of sensible industry. Good grief, son, you've watched me and Martin all these years. We taught you better than this. Showed you how to find businesses to start, or businesses to invest in." He spread his arms wide. "How do you think all this was built? On my good looks?" Pop shook his head. "I refuse to allow you to throw away any more of *my* hard-earned money. You're just going to have to face this mess on your own."

Emerson grimaced. The old man was a product of the 1800s and old Victorian views that had no place in the 1920s. Emerson tolerated his father's rant, knowing that the only hope he had of getting more money was to allow his father the chance to berate him. But as he watched his old man's face . . . a deep dread built in his gut. This time was different. The look on the old man's face proved as much. Maybe the March stock upset had made him more cautious than Emerson had understood. That didn't bode well.

His father sat down. "We're done here."

"No . . . Pop . . . *Father*, please. I'm certain I can change Tayler's mind. I just need this one last chance. Mrs. Hale is behind the union as well—you know that. I just need to apologize and show that I'm sincere. Besides . . . haven't you always wanted the two fortunes combined? This is the only chance."

"Don't bring me into this, son. We might have wanted you to marry Tayler, but we also wanted you to make good decisions. Something you—"

"Sweetheart." Emerson's mother chose that moment to make her entrance—she must have been listening at the door—and approached Pop's side. "Let him try. Please? There's no harm in that. Let him prove he can make good decisions."

The old man swiped a hand down his face. "Don't you think he's had plenty of time? The only reason he's gotten serious about marriage is because I gave him an ultimatum."

"He's our son. Our only son." Mom was always good at sweet-talking. She laid a hand on his arm.

"I know that, dear." His father huffed. Time ticked by.

Emerson felt his hands go clammy. Maybe he had gone too far this time.

"Fine." Pop's word echoed through the room.

Mom leaned in and kissed him on the cheek. "We'll just postpone the engagement party while Emerson fixes all this." She walked past Emerson and shot an eyebrow up at him.

He got the hint. She'd come to his rescue, but it was the last time.

Silence permeated the room after she left.

Emerson stood there and waited for Pop to speak. He was on the proverbial thin ice, and he knew it.

When his father stood, he braced himself. The man was gearing up for another lecture.

Emerson tried not to let his expression show any disrespect, even though he'd prefer just about anything else at the moment.

After almost a quarter of an hour of Pop chiding him for his poor business practices, the old man crossed his arms again. "This is your last chance. You know how intertwined the Pruitt and Hale holdings are. You also know how much money is at

50

stake here." Pop narrowed his eyes. "And not just the money that you lost and that I'm sure you *owe* . . . I'm talking about your future."

"What do you mean?" Anger and fear fought each other in Emerson's stomach. Pop wouldn't do that? Would he?

"You know exactly what I mean. I saw it move across your face just now."

Emerson swallowed.

"That's right. If you don't marry Tayler Hale, straighten up your act, and stop gambling your life away, I'm cutting you off. Completely."

• • • • •

SATURDAY, APRIL 6

Emerson dressed in his favorite suit. After sequestering himself in his room, he'd finally come up with a plan. A bit devious, but it would work.

After he visited the Hale home today, he was confident he would have good news to share with Pop. With a quick glance in the mirror, he put on his most convincing smile. How could Mrs. Hale argue with that face? She'd shared her fears the other day before they'd attempted to convince Tayler. It wasn't *so* terrible that he'd be playing on those fears today, was it? He didn't feel a bit guilty.

Confidence in his step, Emerson headed to the Hale estate. Maybe fortune would smile on him today. If he could just see Henrietta without Tayler around, he could put his plan into place. All he needed to do was lie a little.

When he arrived, the new butler greeted him. "Mr. Pruitt." The man raised an eyebrow. "Miss Hale is not here."

"I'm not here to see Tayler but thank you." Emerson straightened his jacket. "I'd like to see *Mrs.* Hale, please."

Both eyebrows rose this time. "Of course. She's with Mr. Dunham at the moment, but you can wait for her in the formal sitting room, and I will let her know that you wish to speak with her."

"Thank you." Little did the man realize that Emerson knew every nook and cranny in this house as if it were his own. As soon as the butler left him, Emerson sneaked around to the study. It couldn't hurt his cause to eavesdrop on whatever the dandy lawyer had in cahoots with Henrietta. Why was he around all the time anyway? It didn't make sense.

The door was closed, but Emerson put his ear to it.

Mrs. Hale's voice sounded angry. ". . . if you hadn't made a mess of things . . ." Her voice trailed off.

Made a mess of what? Was she talking about Tayler? Or about business?

Dunham's deeper voice drew Emerson's attention. "It was your idea to create an alternate will. I simply complied with your wishes. I think we should just move forward with the plans we have."

Emerson pressed his ear a bit closer. There was an alternate will? Forged, obviously. It was almost too good to be true. Henrietta went on about Tayler and her tone rose. Dunham hushed her. The great Henrietta Hale had played right into Emerson's hands. Perfect.

The conversation in the study was now too quiet for him to hear. Stepping back, he leaned against the wall and thought it through.

An alternate will. It dumbfounded him. Everyone had been shocked when Joshua was given only a small inheritance rather than control of Hale Industries. Now Emerson knew why. There hadn't been any falling out between father and son, and certainly no scandalous behavior. Good grief, Emerson knew Joshua to be more of a teetotaler and church do-gooder than most so-called Christians. There'd never been a hint of cheating or ill-advised ventures in Joshua's business dealings—something that had separated the two best friends years ago. Joshua had always been conservative and Mr. Moral, whereas Emerson had chosen a life that wasn't.

Seemed as if Mrs. Hale was more like him. A grin split his face. Hurrying back to the sitting room, he decided to just wait for his turn and bide his time. This new information would help him gain the leverage he was looking for. Now he had an ace up his sleeve.

Only a few minutes later, the butler arrived for him, and Emerson obediently followed the man to the study.

"Emerson," Mrs. Hale crooned, "how lovely to see you."

"And you as well. You look lovelier every day."

She sent him a smile. "You forget I've watched you grow up, Emerson Pruitt. I recognize your smooth-talking ways, and I know you're up to something." Sitting across from him in a large wing-back chair, she gestured for him to sit as well. "Now, what can I do for you?"

Time to play the part. He let his congenial smile fall and furrowed his brow. "I'm afraid I'm here at my father's insistence. He wishes to dissolve the Hale-Pruitt family holdings. In fact, he wishes to do this immediately, since Tayler has refused to follow through with her commitment." He looked down for a moment, hoping he conveyed the expression of a devastated fiancé.

"How dare you come in here and play on my fears, Emerson!" Henrietta Hale stood and narrowed her eyes. "I told you my concern about your father pulling out in confidence just last week when you came to ask for my help in wooing Tayler back. What are you up to?" She closed the distance between them, and it reminded him of the scoldings she used to give him and Joshua when they were little boys and got into mischief.

Emerson held his hands out in innocence, even though he was far from it. "I had no idea. Truly, I didn't. Father is quite concerned with the economy and has been advised to dissolve all questionable holdings." He felt the weight of the blow almost as if he'd thrust a knife in her back.

"Questionable? There's nothing questionable about our business practices." Fire shot out of the older woman's eyes. "We've invested together for years!"

He wasn't ready to throw down his trump card. At least not yet. "My father would never dissolve the businesses if Tayler and I were married, but since she has refused, and Joshua isn't at the helm . . . well, he feels the investments are no longer valuable to him." Ah, this felt good . . . like he had pushed the blade in to wound her further.

"Are you saying he doesn't trust me?" Henrietta put her hands on her hips. "That insufferable man."

Emerson tilted his head. "You know my father. He is Mr. Conservative when it comes to money, and while he had complete confidence in Joshua, he's not quite as sure about a *woman* running things." Might as well twist the knife in the wound too.

Mrs. Hale sputtered and Emerson held up a hand to stop her. "As I'm sure you both realize, this will not work favorably for you in the long run. For instance, if you should choose to buy him out, you will expend most of your liquid assets. To avoid that, my father will insist on selling to whoever will purchase at whatever price can be had. He has no interest in any of your businesses any longer."

Dunham's jaw dropped and he looked at Henrietta.

Mrs. Hale's face was pinched with anger. "This is utterly ridiculous. I'm going to go speak with your father right now."

As she passed by Emerson's chair, he reached out and grabbed her arm. "That's . . . *not* a good idea."

"Unhand me. I will not allow for your father to do this . . . not after all these years."

Emerson stood. "Well . . . I'd hate to have to tell him the truth. Or worse yet, tell *Joshua* the truth. About the will."

The color drained from Henrietta's face. "What do you mean?"

"You know exactly what I mean. How you cheated your son out of his inheritance and lied to him about his father's displeasure in him."

Mrs. Hale gasped.

Dunham sat down, shock all over his face.

They had been found out, and they knew it.

Clasping his hands behind his back, Emerson lifted his chin. "So you see . . . we really are at an impasse." He sat back down and looked Henrietta squarely in the eye. "You asked for my help the other day because you wanted Tayler to stop traipsing off to her job. You said you always wanted us to marry. Now you *need* me to marry her to keep your companies all intact. *I* need her to marry me for other reasons. So why can't we work together on this?"

"Let me get this straight." Henrietta returned to her chair and smoothed her skirt. "You want my help convincing Tayler to marry you, and you'll keep our little secret?"

"Exactly."

"She didn't seem too willing to forgive you."

"I have a new plan. And I'm going to put forth every ounce of effort."

• • • • •

Later that evening, Emerson strode into his father's study. "Father."

Pop looked up over the glasses on the end of his nose. "Yes?"

"I'm confident that Tayler and I will be married by the end of the summer."

Both of his father's eyebrows rose. "Oh?" He leaned back in his chair and pulled off his spectacles.

"Additionally, I spoke with Mrs. Hale at length today."

"I hope you made more headway with her than I have. Things haven't been the same since Martin died." Pop looked interested at least.

Emerson nodded. "Martin's death was hard on them all." He sat down across from Pop. "I need to tell you something in confidence."

"All right."

"Something you can't discuss with Mrs. Hale."

"Go on."

"Well, you know that she has always wanted Tayler to marry me—I know we all have." He tried to give a smile that would convince Pop of his sincerity. "But she also shared that there was some sort of trouble with Joshua, which was the reason Martin entrusted her with the wealth and running of his estate."

Pop leaned forward. "Joshua? He's always been aboveboard in everything. . . . I find that hard to believe. Although Henrietta has been a take-charge woman . . . I admit I assumed she wanted control for a bit longer." Puzzlement covered his face.

"They haven't wanted anyone to know, so you can't discuss it with her. The problems with Joshua must be recent. But she took me into her confidence today, since she knows that I care for Tayler and for our joint interests."

"Since when have you been concerned about our joint interests? And why would she confide in you? All you've cared about is wasting your money—"

"Father. Please. That's behind me now." Emerson sat up

straighter. "Mrs. Hale and I both want what's best. I've turned over a new leaf, and she has admitted that she's noticed. Even if you haven't. She wants to make sure everything is in order for the future. She needs me."

Pop laughed. "Oh, I see. . . . So you think that once you and Tayler are wed, Henrietta will just turn over control to *you* rather than to her son and heir? That doesn't seem likely."

"Like I said, there were problems with Joshua." It wasn't the truth, but Joshua *had* been passed over after planning for years to step into his father's place at the helm of Hale Industries. Even if it was all concocted. "Look, he was my best friend, and while I hate to admit it . . ." Emerson paused for effect. "He has a drinking problem. His father had to keep him from ruining his businesses. That's the only reason you know nothing of it." He hoped his words made Pop feel guilty for threatening to abandon *him*. "The Hales were hoping to come alongside Joshua in his time of trial."

Pop studied him a moment longer and shook his head. "That's hardly the way to teach someone to change their ways. I know that from experience."

Emerson was in no mood for another lecture. "Look, this isn't about my investments and mistakes, it's about doing things exactly as *you* would prefer. I'm going to marry Tayler and then when Mrs. Hale is ready, I'll manage everything for her. You can pick out all the businesses you want to sell off, and we'll be done with that. You can hide in your conservative little cocoon and never take another chance so long as you live, for all I care. I just want to do the right thing by Tayler and our families."

Pop shook his head and headed back for the door. "I'll believe it when I see it, Emerson. My conditions still stand. Good night."

Emerson didn't bother to reply. Pop wouldn't care anyway.

All he cared about was having his way and having an upstanding and honorable son. Well, this time, he wasn't going to get it. Emerson smiled.

Crossing the room, he laughed out loud. "Fools." He poured himself a drink. As conservative as his father was, thankfully he still managed a bit of illegal liquor for "medicinal purposes." Emerson tossed back the drink and headed to bed.

No one was going to get the best of him. Not his father nor Mrs. Hale. And especially not Tayler. He'd make sure he was at her house well before the hour she'd leave to catch her train. If he had to, he'd drag her to the nearest judge and see them married.

3

Thomas Smith walked through the gleaming hotel lobby of the famous Curry Hotel to the manager's office behind the front desk.

It was good to be back. Good, too, to have a college degree in hand. Now he could be a real asset to the Curry's visitors as he led them on nature hikes and even mountain-climbing expeditions. He'd been a part of the Curry since it opened, but for the first time, he felt confident in what he had to offer. Memories drifted over him—all the years working for the railroad and then Mr. Bradley's taking pity on him and hiring him on for the new Curry Hotel. He'd gone from a gangly, clumsy kid to part of the Curry family. It made his heart proud.

Guests already dotted the landscape outdoors and filled the leather chairs in the sitting area, and the tourist season hadn't even officially started. They might be in the heart of the Alaska Territory, but the Curry Hotel was lush and elegant and drew the wealthy in large numbers.

Thomas had worked here since before it opened in 1923. They had started with little more than the hotel and a collection of strangers to run it. Now the hotel was better than the

59

day it had opened and those strangers were a family. At least as much of a family as Thomas had ever had. The polished wood and rich red carpets welcomed him into the lavish arms that were the Curry, just as it did the wealthy guests. But with one big difference. For Thomas, this was home.

Knocking on the side door to the manager's office, he straightened his tie with his other hand. As footsteps approached, he squared his shoulders and took a deep breath.

"Thomas!" Mr. Bradley's bright smile ushered him in. "Good to have you back, son. Our college graduate!" The man nodded, walked back to his desk, and rubbed his hands together. "As you can see, it's already busy, busy, busy. So I'll dive right in. Allan was just telling me he'd met with you already and caught you up on our goings-on. I asked you both here to talk about the situation with our calendar."

"Thank you, sir." Thomas let his smile broaden. "It's good to be back."

Thomas walked over to the large pine desk and glanced down at the schedule his boss, Allan Brennan, had laid out for the Curry Hotel manager. It was already filled to brimming and more reservations were coming in every day. The hotel would be running at full capacity all summer long.

He was anxious to get back to the routine and feel normal again. College had been great, but this was home and Thomas had missed it more than anything in the world.

Allan tapped the schedule and brought Thomas's attention back to it. "As you can see, Mr. Bradley, we have more outings booked than Thomas and I can handle. My father-in-law can help fill in when he can, but his knees have been troubling him greatly."

The manager nodded. "This is indeed a problem. Because we all know the schedule will only increase once the guests arrive.

I know John is willing to help, but let's not rely on that—he's become too large of an asset *inside* the Curry consulting with guests and advising about what excursions they should take, and we need him exactly where he is." He sat down in his chair and looked at Thomas, then at Allan. "What do you suggest?" He steepled his fingers and frowned.

"If I may be so bold, sir." Thomas stepped forward an inch. "I believe we need to hire another full-time guide. Someone who has been trained like we have and knows the terrain. The hotel is prospering, and we have a record number of reservations already."

Mr. Bradley bobbed his head and turned to Allan. "Is that what you think as well?"

Allan took a long, deep breath and tilted his head. "I hate to say that we can't do our jobs, but Thomas is right. There's not any way to coordinate all of this, especially for outings that take both of us and multiple days. If you will recall, we were swamped with John, Thomas, and me running things full-time. There simply isn't a way to do this without more help. Preferably young, experienced, and *knowledgeable* help as a full-time guide—just like Thomas suggested—and then we need a couple experienced hikers—young men—to assist with all the carrying and so on." He scratched his forehead. "With the new pool and golf course in, those activities will help give the guests other options, but even with that we're still overbooked.

"Not only that, but the attraction for visitors here is the aspect of camping in the wilds or at least hiking out into it. They can golf and swim back home, but only Curry has the High One."

Allan's reference to the mountain the natives called Denali or "the High One" made Thomas smile. The scenery in Alaska was all impressive, but the crowning jewel had to be Denali. At over twenty thousand feet, the mountain towered above them like a silent sentinel—watchful, but deadly.

Crossing his arms, Allan shrugged. "I think we'll disappoint a lot of people if we don't have extra help."

Bradley nodded and Thomas waited for the man's decision. Seconds ticked by as their manager studied the papers in front of him. Never one to be too hasty, yet a man of action, Mr. Bradley was wise in his running of the beautiful hotel. He stood again and walked to the window. "I'm not concerned with the finances of hiring on more workers, so don't worry about that. When Ivanoff told me about his knees last week and what the doctor had said, I knew this was coming. But I wanted your opinions, since you are both so knowledgeable regarding the details of what's needed and what's reasonable. Over the years, you've done a fine job expanding what Curry has to offer and getting everything to work like a well-oiled machine. My only real concern is how to find someone who's qualified at this late date. The season is starting for the whole country at all the national parks." He sighed. "But I will get to work on hiring another man straightaway. Just don't hold out hope that it will be fast. If we have to cancel some excursions, so be it." He went back to his chair and sat. "I'll see if I can get four more assistants as well."

Allan nodded. "Thanks, Mr. Bradley. We'd better get back to inventory."

Thomas followed his boss out the door and wondered what they would do if help didn't arrive in time. "This might prove to be a very challenging summer." He'd secretly hoped for a chance to get up to the national park himself. Denali was a mountain he'd love to climb one day. But with the schedule the way it was, he doubted there would be *any* days off for anything personal.

"Challenging indeed." Allan rubbed his head, then laughed.

"Not to mention my twin boys, who are getting into everything. This summer will be interesting. And exhausting."

"Cassidy definitely has her hands full." Thomas thought about Allan's wife—his friend whom he loved like a sister—and their twins, Jonathon and David. The past two and a half years had been full of joy for anyone living at the Curry. The two little butterballs had wiggled their way into everyone's hearts with their smiles and antics. Since they were twins, they were a bit small when they were born, but they made up for it within the first year. What a joy to have babies around!

Last summer was the first time they were mobile during tourist season, but Allan and Thomas had made special backpacks that each of them wore to carry the boys on most of the hikes all around the Curry. But this year—the twins were bigger and not just walking but *running*. They were indeed into everything. Over the winter months it had been a bit easier, since there weren't so many guests about, and the staff loved doting on the boys. But with the bustling tourist season upon them, it would be an adventure with two toddlers underfoot.

Thoughts of the Brennans made Thomas smile. Allan and Cassidy had been lifesavers to him. In more ways than one.

Orphaned as a child, Thomas was raised in an orphanage for a few years by overbearing missionaries. He didn't remember his parents but had been told that his mother died and his father simply didn't want to be bothered with him. Eventually, the missionaries didn't want him either. When they decided it was too expensive to feed him anymore, they kicked him out to find his own way. Had Joseph Carter not taken pity on him, Thomas wasn't sure he would have survived. And once the railroad was close to completion, he'd been out of a job, until Mr. Bradley hired him when the hotel was first opening. Otherwise, who knows what would have happened to him? But at the Curry,

he met Cassidy—at that point she was still Cassidy Ivanoff—
and then Allan Brennan. When Cassidy and Allan married five
years ago, Thomas couldn't have been happier for his friends.
They sacrificed a lot for Thomas. Even sent him to college in
Fairbanks and paid his bill.

He owed a lot to these wonderful people. His gratitude overwhelmed him. Thomas pulled on Allan's arm and stopped him
in the hallway. "Why don't you take a bit of a break and go let
Cassidy know what's happening, and I'll finish the inventory,
then go check on Mrs. Johnson."

Allan gave him a wide grin as he swiped a hand down his
face. "Are you sure?"

"Of course. I can probably get it finished in about an hour
and still have time to see Chef before the dinner rush gets too
hectic."

"All right, then." Allan placed a hand on Thomas's shoulder.
"I appreciate this. Especially since it doesn't look like we will have
much time to breathe this summer." He shook his head. "And I
think we need to ask Cassidy to pray so that we get some help.
Otherwise, this summer could well be a disaster in the making."

Thomas headed back down the stairs to their office in the
basement where they stored equipment. He owed so much to
Allan and Cassidy. And to John and Mr. Bradley. And, of course,
to Mrs. Johnson too. Goodness, if it weren't for his family at
the Curry, he'd probably be dead in a gutter somewhere.

The thought made him shiver. God had been good to him.

Taking the inventory sheets and pencil, he began to check
off lists and enter in the numbers. Memories of all his years at
the Curry flooded in.

His clumsiness for the first few years as he grew into his tall,
lanky frame and limbs. It was a miracle Mrs. Johnson hadn't
thrown him out on his ear.

The Fourth of July festivities each year with fireworks and cake were one of his favorite events. And he always ate too much of her famous flag cake.

Mrs. Johnson scolding him over and over again for dropping things.

The time he knocked over all the pots in the pantry.

And the time he tripped, fell on his face with arms spread wide, and dumped a shower of flour over the entire kitchen right before dinner.

Cassidy encouraging him and telling him that the *"floor must have needed a hug."*

Then John's taking him under his wing and teaching him. Allan's coming alongside him and encouraging.

His award for one hundred days without a mishap.

The certificate John and Allan had bestowed on him after he'd successfully completed his training.

The send-off to college and all the tears from the ladies who'd packed him up and sent him off.

Then the cheers each time he returned home from school.

The love and hugs from his Curry family as they welcomed him home from a job well done.

Now he was a graduate. A college graduate. Who would have ever thought that a clumsy, awkward, orphan boy could go this far in life?

They were all wonderful memories, but something kept bugging him. Something he couldn't quite put his finger on.

Why was he feeling this . . . restlessness? Even with all the beautiful memories that made him smile, something just wasn't right in his heart. He wanted to be here in Curry, didn't he? He'd tried to be positive about everything and his return— because it was true, he loved it here. He'd been so excited to come home—but there was this nagging in his gut that kept coming back. And it always felt a bit depressing—not at all joyful. What was this about?

Maybe he just needed to think of something else.

But the thoughts continued to pop up—whenever he had time to himself to think. Was this where he was supposed to be? His professors at college had encouraged him to apply to be a ranger at the national park—and he did—but was that what he really wanted to do? Everyone at the Alaska Agricultural College and School of Mines told him he needed to spread his wings and get as much experience in geology as he could. They encouraged him to go work in the national parks at Denali, Yellowstone, and even the Grand Canyon. They said he needed real experience and had to get away from the little town of Curry. He'd never go anywhere in a job like that.

But as much as Thomas wanted to excel in his field, he wanted to belong . . . somewhere. And Curry made him feel that way.

At least it used to. Until Caroline.

Caroline had been in his classes at school the previous semester. She immediately captured everyone's attention with her carefree and ambitious attitude. Not only that, she was the only woman in their classes. Thomas thought her most intriguing, and she gave him more attention than any other female did, save for Mrs. Johnson, the Curry's chef, and, of course, Cassidy.

Being with Caroline had made Thomas feel braver and more daring. He enjoyed working with her and listening to her stories of life in the States.

"Why did you choose to come here for school?" Thomas asked her one day.

She laughed and chucked him under the chin. "Because life is too short not to live to the fullest—and my big brother dared me to do it."

Her reason for being there was shallow and didn't speak at all of a passion for nature or a desire to learn, but Thomas enjoyed her company too much to question it, even when she wasn't all that interested in studying and following their instructor's directions. If only he had questioned it, or at least helped her to see the importance, things might have turned out differently.

He shook his head. These memories were getting him nowhere. They served no good purpose. Caroline had gone back to where she'd come from, and Thomas was where he belonged. Maybe he just hadn't been home long enough to really settle in. He'd be better off getting his mind back on his work.

It took less than an hour to finish up in the office. After the inventory was completed, he checked on Mrs. Johnson—she beamed him a huge smile, hugged him, gave him a cinnamon roll, then shooed him out so she could finish cooking. The roll was as good as ever, but an emptiness still left Thomas feeling unsettled. He headed to the tiny chapel. Cassidy had always told him when in doubt, seek God's direction. Perhaps a visit to the pastor would help him work through his odd feelings.

Hammering sounded from inside the small building, and Thomas walked in. "Pastor Wilcox?"

Henry Wilcox turned from his work on a pew and smiled up at Thomas. "Thomas, I didn't realize you were back. I understand you've finished school with a degree. How does it feel to have your life so well ordered?"

"That's why I'm here, Pastor."

"Surely you don't have troubles already." He put the hammer down. "Aren't you glad to be home?"

"Yes, it's been wonderful to return. But . . . I'm not real sure what's wrong. I mean to say . . . I can't even explain how I'm feeling. That's why I came to seek your counsel."

Brow furrowed, Pastor Wilcox walked over to Thomas. "Why don't we sit down for a few minutes?"

Thomas sat on one of the pews and looked at the beautifully hand-carved cross at the front of the sanctuary. He'd given his life to Christ years ago, but this was the first time he'd really struggled with his emotions and thoughts of the future. Being an adult was so much harder than what he'd imagined when he was growing up. "I don't even know where to start. I'm not feeling my normal joy. I know I just returned, but I've never felt like this before. It's almost like something needs to shake things up inside me. I tried to jump right back in to all that needs to be done, and my wonderful memories from here washed over me, but then I started feeling this . . . almost restlessness. Dissatisfaction."

Pastor Wilcox nodded. "I'm glad you're willing to be open and honest about this. So let me see if I can help you. . . . I take it you are feeling a bit melancholy as well?"

Thomas thought about that for a moment. "No . . . well, maybe. I guess it's a fact that I just don't know what I'm feeling. Kinda like I'm here but I'm not really here. Does that make sense?"

"You're feeling . . . *out of sorts?*" the pastor suggested with a small smile.

"That's a good description. But it seems like more than that. I'm questioning what I thought I'd always do. 'Is this what God wants me to do?' That sort of thing." He decided not to mention his encounter with Caroline.

"Have you prayed about it?"

Thomas nodded. "But I don't feel like I've gotten any answers. Not that God has to answer me right away. I know that. But I just thought I'd feel like I always did before."

Pastor Henry rubbed his chin with his hand. "Exactly what is that?"

"Like this is where I belong."

"And you're not feeling that anymore?"

"That's the thing. I don't know *what* I feel."

"It's no wonder that you're in a bit of distress over all this. You've had a lot of upheaval in your life, young man. And lots of changes with school and lots of changes here as well. My suggestion to you is to dig into God's Word and put this before God in prayer every day. If your focus is on Him, He will direct you. Find some time to spend just with the Lord and try to blot out all the other noise around you." Henry patted Thomas's shoulder. "I'm betting you had all kinds of advice at college and were surrounded by a lot more people. That's why I said it's probably good to try and blot out a lot of the noise. Man's advice can be good, but we must always seek *Him* first." He pointed to the ceiling.

Thomas tried to sound casual. "How did you know I'd been given lots of advice?" The truth was, much of that advice had come from Caroline. She thought Thomas was silly to be content with his life in Alaska.

"You have that overwhelmed look in your eyes, as if to say, 'I'm on my own and done with school. Now what do I do?' People love to give advice. And I'm sure there were lots of people up at the college who wanted to see you succeed. But remember that man's success isn't always what God calls success. Son, we all come to this place at least once in our lives—searching for our purpose and what God has for us. In fact, some of us old coots have to come to that place many times. It's part of being human and part of our search for God."

Thomas let the words sink in. Was he letting other people's words and advice cloud his judgment? Was he letting what Caroline said—what had happened—make things harder than they had to be? The more he thought about it, the more what the pastor said made sense. "Thank you, Pastor. You've given me a lot to think about. I'd better get back to work, but I'm glad I came."

"Anytime, Thomas. Come to see me anytime. I'll be praying for you, and I'll be here all summer."

Thomas stood and shook the man's hand. Maybe the man was right. Maybe there was just too much noise in his head. He needed to settle down and spend some time in the quiet with God.

With new determination in his steps, Thomas shoved his hands into his pockets and walked back to the hotel. His days were often extremely long, especially with the late hours of sunlight, but he could dedicate time to the Lord every evening. He could take a walk by the river and blot out everything else. Spend the time in prayer and reflection.

That was just what he needed.

4

Margaret Johnson placed her hands on her ample hips and felt the heat rising to her face. That man! After all these years, he *still* thought he could get away with the same shenanigans. "Daniel Ferguson, if you think for one minute I'm going to let you rearrange my kitchen *again*, you've got another think coming!"

The fiery, redheaded man stopped in his tracks. His eyebrows rose.

Cassidy brushed up against her side and said under her breath, "And possibly a cast-iron skillet upside his head?"

Margaret couldn't contain her laughter as the image formed in her mind of giving good ol' Scottish Chef Ferguson a wallop with her skillet.

This time, it was the large, bearded man's turn to put his hands on his hips. "And just what is so funny, lass? I'm just tryin' to be efficient."

Not about to back down, Margaret quieted her laughter and gave him "the look." The look that made every *other* person who had ever stepped foot in her kitchen obey. "The thought of my skillet swinging toward your head if you mess with my kitchen, that's what. Now get your ornery self back to work

71

and don't even *think* about rearranging anything. I don't care about your efficiency. It all works just fine the way it is."

The man's mustache twitched, and his eyes sparkled their merriment. "Aye, Chef." His brogue thicker than molasses, he bowed and went back to his station. Ever since he came to help in the Curry kitchen while Cassidy was laid up three years ago, he'd kept Margaret on her toes. For the longest time, she couldn't wait until the man left. Now she didn't know what she would do without him. Other than keep her sanity.

She turned to face Cassidy. "Oh, that man loves to get my dander up."

Cassidy just giggled. "You like it and you know it." She wrapped her arms around Margaret's neck. "I had to come down and see you for a minute. The boys are down for a nap and Collette came up on her break, so I thought I'd give you a hug and have two minutes of adult conversation."

This girl was so dear to her. Like a daughter. "What? You don't enjoy the babble of the boys?"

"I love it. But there are times I wish I understood what they were saying. They make all kinds of noises with their toys and jabber away to each other. They carry on conversations and understand everything. To me and Allan, well, if it isn't *mama*, *daddy*, *ball*, *dog*, *please*, *thank you*, or *toy*, the majority is gibberish. But *they* think they're making sense. One of these days, I'm sure it will all sound like words. Although, I'm pretty sure they're trying to master *Grandma Maggie*, but for now it just sounds like 'gammamag.'"

Margaret laughed—something that only ever happened when Cassidy was around. The rest of her crew knew she was no-nonsense and could bark out orders like an army sergeant. But Cassidy had been second-in-command for a long time—until she took a tumble down the stairs while she was pregnant and the doctor put her on bed rest. Even though Cassidy was no longer a full-time fixture in the kitchen, she made her presence known a lot, and Margaret could tell that the staff loved to see her.

Of course, Margaret also knew that her staff loved to see her loosen up—something reserved for a special few. Like Cassidy and the twins. And Thomas. Why, that boy had been such a thorn in her side for so long . . . but now? He was like a son to her as well.

"Penny for your thoughts?" Cassidy nibbled on a shortbread cookie, her eyebrows raised.

Margaret lifted her chin. "I was just thinking about how special it is to have family again. But don't you go telling anyone. I don't need them thinking I've gone soft."

Laughter filled the space around her. "Oh, there's not any chance of that." Cassidy moved in closer and spoke in a hushed tone. "But what about Mr. Ferguson? Any chance you'll soften toward him? I think he's interested in being more than your assistant chef."

"Now you hush, child. I won't have any of that." But her heart lifted a bit at the thought. Daniel Ferguson's attention was hard to ignore. But was she ready for that?

Cassidy smirked and lifted an eyebrow. "Uh-huh. I don't believe that for a minute." She leaned in and kissed Margaret's cheek. "I'd better get back to the boys. Laundry is never-ending with those two, but I'll be back to whip up the chocolate mousse when MaryAnn comes to watch the boys after their nap."

"Believe what you want, you cheeky girl." Margaret did her best not to smile. "But you best keep your opinions to yourself, or that skillet might come looking for *you*."

Cassidy's giggle drifted back as she headed out of the kitchen and waved.

"Don't forget to send Collette back down. I've got a ton of bread she needs to make." Shaking her head, Margaret thought of the joy that now filled her life. Ever since Cassidy had forced her way in and gotten her to open up. She felt a smile lift her lips.

"Ah, lass . . . it does my heart good to see you smiling." How Daniel had sneaked up on her, she'd never know. The man was as big as a lumberjack.

"Don't you have work to do?" Her tone held an edge, but he was used to it. At least he should be by now.

"I've finished it all, so I came to see if you needed my assistance." His mustache twitched.

Ban it all! That man got under her skin like no other. And he didn't have to seem so happy about it either. "There's puff pastry to be made. And the gratins need to be prepped for dinner."

"Pea?"

"Yes." Despite how much the man infuriated her, he was brilliant in the kitchen. But she wouldn't ever tell him that. He had a knack for always anticipating her next move. They worked well together.

"One of my favorites of your fine recipes, Chef Johnson." He moved around the kitchen with ease.

Margaret found herself watching him out of the corner of her eye. She had to admit, he *was* a handsome man. Even if he was Scots-Irish and meddled in her kitchen.

But there was no way she would open up her heart to a man again. No. Way.

•••••

Friday, May 3—Yellowstone National Park

The handwriting on the letter in Tayler's hand was all too familiar. Mother. Again.

74

With a sigh, she headed to her room and prayed for wisdom. Joshua had sent one letter to her apologizing for not being there and telling her it was fine to keep her job at Yellowstone, but he didn't think that marrying Emerson was a good idea. He was reserved in the note, and Tayler knew he was holding something back. Like he had been for months. She just didn't know what it was. But he'd always been there for her . . . that wouldn't change, would it? Or had it already? The thought made her sad.

Mother, on the other hand, had written daily—reprimanding her and scolding her for her behavior and for leaving without saying good-bye. And it wore Tayler down.

Why the push to come home?

While she didn't understand the motivation behind her mother's wishes, she knew that Mother loved her. At least she had. The woman who now ruled the Hale house was like a stranger. Tayler was glad her mother hadn't just wasted away after Dad's passing, but the creature who'd taken her place was hard-hearted and infuriating. Tayler wondered more than once if that person had always been there but was merely subdued. Now without Dad there to balance her mother's demands, Tayler was up against her mother's mandates that she marry and do so soon. Why the rush? That was what she couldn't figure out. And Emerson? Her parents had always wanted the two to wed, but her mother seemed fixated on it now.

Tayler's insides cringed every time she thought about marrying Emerson. The more she prayed about it, the more she felt at peace in her decision, but her spirit did urge her to work things out with her mother. But how? They were on opposite sides of the spectrum.

Yes, she was twenty-three years old and all of her friends were married. Yes, Mother surely wanted grandchildren. But what about Joshua? Shouldn't she be trying to marry *him* off before she did it to her? Tayler fisted her hands, then relaxed them again. Why couldn't she be left to live her life as she pleased? She had an inheritance from Dad, and she didn't ask for more. Let Mother run the family corporations and investments. Tayler didn't care who managed them or whether they were successes or failures. With Dad gone, none of that mattered as much.

As she unlocked her bedroom door, she shook her head. Weary from another long day of work, she wasn't sure she was up for reading the letter. She plopped down onto her bed and looked at the ceiling. *What do I do, Lord?*

With a sigh, she sat back up. Tearing into the letter, she decided to get it over with and then she would write Mother a simple note back. She could tell her that she was fine—very busy—but not respond to anything else.

But when she opened the sheets, she noticed it wasn't just a letter from her mother. There was one from Emerson as well.

A quick scan of Mother's letter showed her the same thing that had been in every other letter. Tayler needed to come home. Mother was very disappointed in her behavior and reprimanded her for the way she spoke to Emerson and the way she sneaked out of the house. She'd been very rude to the Pruitt family by leaving, and they'd had to cancel the engagement party. The list went on and on.

Tayler folded her mother's letter back up and sighed. There wasn't any way to please the woman, other than to go home. Something Tayler wouldn't do.

Then there was the letter from Emerson. Half tempted to burn it, or simply throw it away, she considered how foolish it would be to not read it. What if he realized the error of his ways and released her? Wouldn't that be a welcome word?

Shaking her head, she took a deep breath and opened the single sheet of paper.

Dearest Tayler,

I pray you've had time to calm down and think about your actions. My love for you hasn't changed. I'm sincerely sorry for all the heartache I caused you when we were younger. Please forgive me.

That being said, my desire—and the desire of your family and mine—is for us to marry at the end of the summer. I will be coming to Yellowstone at the end of the month. So please gather your things and make arrangements with your boss for a replacement. You will need to have your affairs in order so that we can promptly return to Denver. There is much to do.

I look forward to the future together.

With all my heart,
Emerson

Tayler wadded up the paper into a ball and threw it into the wastebasket. What was Emerson's game? It didn't make any sense. Why settle down when he was happy to chase other women and carouse around?

Well, it didn't really matter, did it? Because it sounded as if he was coming whether she agreed to it or not.

Tayler stood and paced the room. Time was of the essence. She stopped in her tracks as only one real option came to mind.

She needed to be gone before Emerson got here.

Tired of it all, she wanted to just leave without a trace. Maybe then, over time, the world would right itself—Mother would be back to her old self, Emerson would leave her be, and Joshua would return—and she could come back to her beloved job. Shaking her head, Tayler wondered if that future was even possible. But the fact remained: she had to leave.

Where could she go? An idea struck—maybe there was another national park she could go to. She wasn't hurting financially. She had her inheritance, and Joshua had promised she would be taken care of and insisted she should not worry about their mother's push to marry. And it wasn't like she didn't wish to marry one day—if God brought her the right man. A *faithful* one. But she did want to work. She loved what she did. Dad had encouraged her to follow her dreams and study what she loved, and so she did. She'd never known how he'd convinced her mother to let her attend college. Tayler could still remember her mother's unhappiness at her choice.

"This will be a terrible inconvenience and horrible embarrassment for our family," Mother had told her more than once. Tayler argued that lots of women were going to college and getting educations.

"It's not normal, Tayler. Others in our social status will consider it quite out of line."

It might have been out of the norm for a woman of her status, but what did social status really matter?

She shook her head to rid herself of the memory. Mind made up, she rushed out of her room and headed down to her boss's office. He always worked late, so hopefully she could catch him.

With a deep breath and a knock to his door, Tayler prayed for guidance. *Lord, I don't know what You want me to do, but I need You to guide my steps.*

"Come in." Mr. Cunningham's voice came through the door.

Tayler entered. "Sir, I'm so very sorry to come to you like this." She twisted her hands in front of her, but a calming peace flooded her and she put her hands at her sides. "But I have some extenuating circumstances . . . and I need to know if you've heard of any other national parks that need a naturalist like me." There. She said it.

Mr. Cunningham came around his desk and shook his head, crossing his arms over his chest. "Any other day, I would have thought you were joking with me because I know you love it here, but I just received a letter from your mother." He picked up the letter, waved it, and then dropped it back onto his desk.

A groan left her lips. "I'm sorry, sir. I can only imagine—"

He held up a hand. "No need to apologize. She might be a formidable woman, but she has no sway in my dealings here." He smiled and took off his glasses. Rubbing the bridge of his nose, he shook his head. "In fact, I must say that your timing is quite interesting, Miss Hale. As much as I hate to think of you leaving, I can't believe this happened by coincidence."

Tayler furrowed her brow. "What do you mean?"

He held up a small yellow slip of paper and put his glasses back on. "I was just reading a telegram from a friend of mine up in the Alaska Territory. Apparently, he sent this to his friends who work at the national parks. Bradley is the manager of a hotel up there, and they offer excursions and hikes to the tourists. Some even into the McKinley National Park. They are in desperate need of another staff member. A naturalist and interpreter just like you to help lead nature walks and hikes and to help with the larger trips."

Her eyes widened as her breath caught in her chest. Could this be? She closed her eyes and breathed a prayer of thanks heavenward. "Mr. Cunningham, do you think I would be a good fit for the job? Would you recommend me? How soon do they need someone?" Her words tumbled out.

He chuckled. "I've had ten more young men apply for jobs here, but I'm not sure any of them could fill your shoes. Like I said, I hate to lose you, but if you're of a mind to do this, I can send a telegram back to Mr. Bradley directly. Hopefully, before anyone else jumps at the position."

"Oh yes, please."

"Are you quite certain? It's a long way from home."

Exactly what she was looking for. "I'm sure. In fact, I wouldn't mind if you telephoned your friend right now."

Cunningham chuckled again and shook his head. "I would do that if the telephone lines were more reliable in Alaska. A telegram will have to do. I'm sure I'll receive a response in the next day or two. And I'm sure it will be positive. Bradley trusts me, and it sounds like they are in desperate need." He offered her his hand. "I've never had a staff member work as hard as you, or be as knowledgeable as you, Tayler. It will be a great loss to Yellowstone National Park, but I had a feeling I would lose you one day."

She took his hand and shook it. "Thank you, sir. That means a great deal coming from you."

"I'm serious. Don't let anyone doubt your talent or abilities. I will gladly write you a letter of recommendation."

"Thank you, sir." His praise gave her confidence that this was the right thing to do. "You've been an incredible teacher and mentor. Thank you for everything you've done for me."

"You are well deserving of the position you have here, and of my recommendation for this new job. I'll be excited to hear of your progress and how you change the world up in Alaska."

His words made her smile. He'd always been such an encouragement to her, challenging her to learn new things and giving her books on plant life around the country. "It will be hard to leave, sir, but thank you. Thank you *so* very much."

"You're welcome." Then the smile left his face and he looked thoughtful. "I know how difficult it has been to lose your father."

She nodded, fighting the sting of tears.

"Is everything all right? Your mother sounded . . . well, I'm not quite sure how to describe it."

"It's hard to explain. I understand what you're saying." Tayler looked out the window for a moment. The deep hues of the sunset were almost gone. "I'm not sure if everything is all right, but I know this is something I must do." She glanced back at him, and the fatherly way he looked back at her almost broke her heart. How she missed her father! "I need to ask you to keep my whereabouts a secret. Can you do that for me?"

His face softened even more. "I'll do everything I can. No one else needs to know where you've gone." He put his index finger to his lip. "But I would advise you to not keep it a secret from your family for long. Even in difficult situations like this, it's best to try to mend your differences."

Nodding again, Tayler swallowed. Unsure of the future before her, she prayed she would be able to. But how? "Thank you, sir."

"You will be greatly missed, Tayler. Please stay in touch." He gave her a fatherly hug and then patted her shoulder.

Afraid to say anything else and let her emotions get the best of her, she turned around and left his office, pulling the door closed behind her.

A few hours ago, she'd had no idea what direction her life would take. She'd had no idea about the letters, nor about the telegram her boss had received.

But now, here she stood. On the precipice of something new and exciting.

Tayler let that thought sink in. The fear and uncertainty she'd felt after reading Emerson's letter disappeared. God had given her a new path.

She was going to Alaska.

5

After a few days of prayer and lots of searching, Thomas felt he was back on sure footing. The restlessness was still there a bit, but for the most part, he felt like himself again. His new routine included getting up an hour earlier and reading his Bible, then discussing things with John Ivanoff over breakfast, then heading to work. When work was over, his favorite part of the day became his walks down by the river. Talking to God as he walked, he felt more connected and in tune. As he poured out his heart, he asked the Lord to help him keep his focus on Him and nothing else. Whenever the negative thoughts and doubts threatened to fill his mind, he determined to think of a Scripture to recite or a hymn to sing.

Tonight, the staff was gathering for a late dinner in the dining room after all the patrons were served. It was their annual special dinner at the beginning of the season where they would welcome the new hires and returning workers and discuss all the extra needs that came with the hectic pace of a new season, which was already upon them, as the number of guests arriving increased every day.

The annual dinner was always a joyous time, as everyone

was excited to be back together. About half of the staff lived here year-round, while the rest worked in Anchorage or Seattle until the tourist season.

But soon, they were going to need more of the staff to remain. Especially once the new ski lift was finished. With all the improvements happening in and around Curry, it wouldn't be long before the hotel was packed every month of the year.

He sneaked into the kitchen a few minutes early and came up behind Mrs. Johnson. Placing a quick peck on her cheek, he jumped back to avoid her wooden spoon.

"Thomas Smith, you sly young man. Sneaking up on an old woman like that! You just about gave me a heart attack," the chef scolded, but Thomas noticed the sparkle in her eye.

"Let me give you one proper, then." He kissed the other cheek.

"You do beat all." The blush that crept up her neck told Thomas everything he needed to know. She cared about him. A lot. She was the closest thing he'd ever had to a mother. "Now carry this into the kitchen, and don't you go snitching anything off that platter."

Thomas did as he was told and carried the overflowing platter of fried chicken into the dining room.

All the tables had been pushed together to make one long table, and the chatter around the room was warm and welcoming. This was one of the things he'd missed most about the Curry Hotel.

Several new faces peeked at him. A few young maids, and a couple of younger boys with their aprons tied around their waists. Probably all a bit intimidated by the fierceness of Mrs. Johnson. He remembered those days all too well.

Mr. Bradley entered the room and shut the large French doors behind him. Most of the chatter quieted as people took seats around the long table. Mrs. Johnson came in from the kitchen with Chef Ferguson behind her. The rest of the kitchen staff entered with plates and bowls and steaming platters. Allan and Cassidy entered with their two little boys in tow.

"Gammagammagamma!" the little cherubs chanted together as they ran to Mrs. Johnson, wrapping their little chubby arms around her legs. She laughed and hugged them both and then grabbed a hand of each boy and led them to their seats.

Allan and John had fashioned them special chairs that were just the right size, but at a height where they could reach the table. They were normally kept in the downstairs dining room the staff used during the season, but they must have brought them up for the special supper tonight.

Cassidy walked over and wrapped Thomas in a sisterly hug. "I believe you've gotten even taller. And look at how handsome you are. I bet you had all the girls of Fairbanks just fawning over you." She had to tilt her head up quite a ways to look at him.

Thomas forced himself not to frown as memories of Caroline came to mind. "I was too busy with my studies. Wanted to make sure you got your money's worth." She looked at him with a strange expression. It was almost as if she knew he was keeping something from her. "Oh, look, Mr. Bradley is ready to address us." Cassidy nodded and went to claim her seat, while Thomas planted himself at the table and sighed.

Their manager stood at the head of the table and cleared his throat. The crowd quieted and settled in. "Good evening, everyone. I hope you've all had a chance to meet the new members of our staff—if you haven't, make sure you introduce yourself tonight after supper."

Several people smiled and nodded.

Bradley continued. "It has been quite a busy winter season here at the Curry, and you've probably noticed the construction on the new ski lift. Which means, we will likely need to run at full capacity year-round from now on." He held up his hand as chatter started up again. "I will be meeting with each one of you to find out your schedules and discuss opportunities for the future.

"Now if John Ivanoff would be so kind, I'd like to ask him to say grace for our meal and then we will dig in." He held up his glass of water. "Welcome to a new season at the Curry!"

"Hear, hear!" Glasses were raised around the table.

John stood and smiled out at everyone. "Let's bow our heads. Thank You, Heavenly Father, for this feast set before us. We praise You for such bounty and for the hands that have so graciously prepared it. We praise You for the season ahead and ask Your blessings upon the time we have here to serve the guests. In Jesus' name we pray, amen."

"'men!" Jonathon and David called out from their seats, while Jonathon banged his fork on the table.

Laughter surrounded Thomas as platters were passed and everyone dug into the meal. He let the weight of his memories fall away. His heart already lighter, he glanced at each face. This felt right again. Curry was home.

John elbowed him from his left side. "What's got you smiling?"

Thomas looked at his mentor. "All this. It's good to be home."

The older man patted him on the shoulder. "It's good to have you home, son. And I agree with Cassidy, it looks like you've grown some more. How tall are you now, anyway?"

"The doctor measured all of us before our final assessments, and I must admit I was a bit shocked to learn that I was four inches over six feet now. But he thought maybe I was at the end of my growth spurt. After all, I'm twenty-three now. Most men are done growing by my age." A shock of hair fell into his face and he brushed it back.

"Your hair's gotten darker too. Cassidy is right, you're quite a handsome young man. We might have to spend all summer beating off your admirers with a stick."

The comment made Thomas blush. "Oh, I doubt that, John."

His mentor just chuckled. "You wait and see." He passed him a bowl of mashed potatoes. "I heard Allan complaining to Cassidy this afternoon that there were a lot of young ladies coming with their families this season. The moms and daughters all wanted to go on excursions."

Thomas moaned. That was all he needed. "Oh, great. A bunch of city girls with their ridiculous frippery and impractical shoes."

"Exactly." John laughed. "Can't say I didn't warn you."

"Well, Allan and I are already going to have our hands full. Maybe since we're shorthanded, we can conveniently cancel any hikes with the girls."

"What's wrong with girls who like to hike?" One of the new maids pointed her knife at Thomas from across the table. "I like to hike, and some of us actually know what we're doing." She tossed him a look and lifted her chin.

Thomas had heard that before. Caroline thought she knew everything about the great outdoors. He opened his mouth to respond, but an elbow in his ribs stopped him.

John leaned in and spoke in a hushed tone. "Don't make any enemies, my boy."

Thomas nodded and looked at the girl who'd spoken. "My apologies, miss. I'm sure you are quite adept at it. We've just had experiences in the past with some of the privileged ladies who've injured themselves with inappropriate footwear." He gave her a smile, hoping to soften his explanation.

She looked at him and her cheeks turned pink. A smile lit her face as well. "I understand now. Thank you for your input. I'd love to hear more about the work you do." The look she gave him across the table made his stomach uneasy. She maintained eye contact, increasing his discomfort.

"And so it begins." John's mumbled words drifted to Thomas's ear.

Thomas looked back to John and saw the man trying to contain his laughter. "All right, Mr. Ivanoff. I see we're going to have to talk about this later." He tried to compose himself, but he looked at Cassidy and saw her eyes were filled with mirth as well.

Heat crept up his neck. This was not what he was planning for his return. The years of embarrassing himself should be over, shouldn't they? Hadn't he made a big enough fool of himself in Fairbanks to last the ages?

Allan leaned his head toward Thomas from a few places down. "I received a letter from Jean-Michel today."

Cassidy's face brightened into a huge smile. "Oh, how is Katherine?"

Allan chuckled. "They're all fine keeping everything running down in Seattle. I tell you what—bringing him on as a partner for Brennan Outfitters was the smartest move I've ever made."

"And it's brought an incredible amount of tourists to the Curry as well." John nodded and took another bite of his chicken.

Thomas had gotten several letters from the Langeliers at school. Jean-Michel had hired Thomas to help him with his strenuous exercises to rebuild the muscles in his leg that first summer Jean-Michel arrived in Curry. They'd formed a close bond. "I hear that his leg is almost completely healed and that they are doing well in the Pacific Northwest."

"He told me he'd kept up with you at school." Allan speared a piece of asparagus with his fork. "And he sent a gift for you to congratulate you on your graduation."

"Which reminds me." John stood and lifted a knife to his glass. He clinked it several times to gain everyone's attention. "I believe we all know that tonight has another special meaning." Smiles rounded the table.

John put a hand on Thomas's shoulder. "We're also here to celebrate our very own Thomas's graduation with full honors from the Alaska Agricultural College and School of Mines." Applause surrounded him as everyone stood. Mrs. Johnson and Mr. Ferguson came in carrying a huge cake covered in candles.

Allan stood and came to stand on the other side of Thomas. "Our incredible young guide here is now also a geologist!" He lifted his glass in the air and began to sing, "For he's a jolly good fellow."

The crowd joined in. "For he's a jolly good fellow. For he's a jolly good fellow! Which nobody can deny!"

Thomas blew out the candles and smiled.

Cheers surrounded him as packages with bows and cards came out of hiding and were pushed toward him. The love that engulfed Thomas made him feel like he never had before. It also confirmed in his heart that yes, he might have had doubts, and they might still come, but this was where God had him for now.

He spent the rest of the hour opening gifts and cards and hearing everyone's congratulations.

As the kitchen staff began to clear the plates, Mr. Bradley approached him and Allan. "I have incredible news for you, boys."

"I don't know what could top this night, sir, but I'm sure Allan and I would love to hear it."

Their manager grinned. "Oh, you'll love this. It will be the 'icing on the cake,' so to speak—even though you've probably had enough icing." He laughed at his own joke. "I sent a telegram on Thursday to a good friend of mine down at Yellowstone

National Park—as well as a few other parks—asking if he knew of an experienced guide we could hire immediately. You won't believe it, but I received his response back today. Including a recommendation and qualifications. Our new guide will be here sometime in the next two weeks."

Allan released a huge sigh. "That's incredible news, Mr. Bradley. And quite a relief, if I may speak for all of us."

"I'm still in shock, but I replied immediately to send him up as soon as possible. He must have been waiting for my reply because he sent word back that our man is on his way." The manager looked quite proud of himself.

Thomas couldn't believe it. The good Lord above had given them a huge gift by answering their request so quickly. "What do you know about him?"

"Not much, other than he's highly recommended, has a degree in botany, and has been a naturalist and interpreter there for several years."

Allan patted Thomas on the back. "That sounds perfect. Exactly what we need to round out our expertise."

"Exactly what I was thinking." The manager took a sip of lemonade from his glass.

Thomas found himself getting caught up in the excitement. It would be a little difficult getting used to a new man around— and the fellow would have to get acquainted with Alaska—but it did indeed sound like the perfect fit. "God is good, Mr. Bradley."

"Yes indeed. Now if the rest of the season could run this smoothly, I'll be happy."

"Agreed." Allan nodded. "What did you say the man's name was?"

"Tayler Hale." Mr. Bradley turned to leave the dining room. "I'll see you all bright and early." With a wave he was gone.

Thomas turned to Allan, who was watching his boys play on

the floor with Chef Ferguson. It would definitely be a big relief for all of them to have the help of another experienced guide. The more he thought about it, the more excited he became. This season would be the best one ever.

He couldn't wait to meet Mr. Tayler Hale.

6

The train station in Gardiner, Montana, at the north end of the park, bustled with activity. Tayler sat on a bench waiting for her train to arrive. Excitement bubbled up out of every cell in her body. She'd never been this excited about anything before. Maybe this was exactly what she needed. Something new and fresh.

The air smelled of cigar smoke and the coal that powered the steam engines. Every once in a while, the faint scent of a woman's perfume would pass by and make the air a bit sweeter smelling.

The engines would allow steam to escape in great bursts, and the sound almost always made her jump. Maybe she needed to spend more time around trains to get used to the cacophony of sounds. Between the chugging of the engines, the steam releasing, and the oft-times squeaky brakes, it was amazing to her that the regular railroad employees weren't deaf.

People shouted over one another, and the long call from the conductor, "All aboard!" added to the mayhem around her.

She'd gotten here too early. Her anxiousness had driven her this morning. Now she would just have to deal with it and wait.

91

Pulling out her beloved sketch pad and pencils, she set to drawing the steam engine in front of her. Its round face had such a short, stumpy stack coming out the top. She attempted to count all the wheels, but several seemed to be hidden and there were different sizes. Tayler tilted her head and studied the engine carefully. She'd never drawn anything quite like it. It was pretty intricate now that she examined it.

"Miss Tayler, is that you?" A voice from beside her sounded awfully familiar.

Tayler turned and searched the crowd.

Millie, her maid and dear friend, ran toward her. "It *is* you!" She hugged Tayler and then sat next to her on the bench. "What are you doing here?"

Taken aback by the fact that her maid had shown up in Gardiner, Tayler pasted on a smile. "I think the question should be, what are *you* doing here?"

Millie scooted a bit closer on the bench, tucked a stray lock of hair behind her ear, and adjusted her hat. The lovely wide-brimmed silk hat had been one of Tayler's that she'd gifted to Millie last year.

"That color suits you." Tayler gave her friend a smile.

"Thank you, miss. Yellow is my favorite color, and when you gave me this hat—well, it's about the prettiest thing I've ever owned." She took a deep breath, reached into her purse, and pulled out an envelope. "As to why I'm here, your brother sent me. He wanted me to give you this."

Tayler took the packet and wondered what Joshua was up to. Tucking it into her bag, she looked back to Millie. "You came all this way just to deliver an envelope?"

Millie laughed. "Not exactly. Mr. Hale didn't want your mother to know that he'd sent me, so he told me I had to keep this a secret. He sent the telegram to my folks' place. Aren't you going to open it?"

"Where does Mother think you are?" Maybe she could divert the conversation. She didn't want to risk opening something that might make her cry in front of strangers.

"Visiting a sick cousin."

"Oh, Millie, I don't want you to lie to cover for my brother." Tayler felt horrible, but wasn't she lying by not telling her own family where she was headed?

"Oh, don't you worry about me. It's exciting to get to travel by train, and your brother is paying my expenses. Now, why are you here? I wasn't expecting to find you so easily and at the train station to boot!"

"Well . . ." Unsure of what to say, Tayler bit her lip. Especially after she'd just told Millie she didn't want *her* to lie. "I'm leaving."

A tiny gasp made Millie cover her mouth. She looked around. "This is because of Mr. Pruitt, isn't it?"

Tayler sighed but didn't answer.

"He's been telling everyone that he's coming to collect you and that the wedding will be this summer."

"I know. I received a letter from him. But I won't be here when he arrives." She reached toward Millie's lap and covered her friend's hand with her own. "Please. You can't say a word of this to anyone."

"I've always been true to you, Miss Tayler. I won't let you down. I promise."

"Thank you." Tayler's heart raced. What would Emerson do when he discovered she'd gone? "You didn't get in trouble with Mother when I left, did you?"

Millie shook her head. "No. She never even asked me anything. She's been so different since your father passed. Always busy with that Mr. Dunham. They're constantly discussing business and financial matters that go way beyond me. But your brother sent me a telegram after you left. My mother sent word for me to come home—that she had something for me. When I got there she gave me the telegram, and a packet followed after that."

Joshua had been wise to contact Millie's family instead of writing to her directly. Mother would never have understood the maid receiving personal correspondence from Joshua.

"I'm just so thankful I didn't put your job at risk. With Mother acting so strange, I wouldn't put it past her to fire the entire household staff."

"I appreciate your concern, Miss Tayler. But your brother has promised us that if anything happens, he'll help us. We have only to let him know."

Tayler remembered the horrible days after Dad's death. The reading of the will and all the technicalities that went along with the vast Hale empire of businesses. Everyone had presumed Joshua would be in charge of everything business related, but most of the family holdings had gone to Mother, with the exception of a small inheritance to Tayler and Joshua. Tayler had been surprised by this. Joshua too. Father had groomed Joshua for years. Of course, Joshua had businesses of his own and was financially independent, but he'd expected to step in upon Father's death. Instead, Mr. Dunham announced that the will had been changed and Mother was in charge. Joshua's hurt was clear to all, but Mother assured him it wasn't a slight on him, but rather Father's yielding to her request. It made her feel more secure. She tried to smooth things over, telling Joshua and Tayler it would all be theirs one day and that in the meantime, Joshua would be needed to help her manage it all. Joshua left after that, much to their mother's disapproval, but little else had been said on the matter.

"Where will you go?" Millie's question brought Tayler back to the present.

"A good distance from here. If I don't tell you, then you won't have to lie. If anyone asks, you don't know where I'm going."

Millie nodded and bit her lip. Her head ducked for a moment as she fiddled with a string on her skirt. "What if I were to go with you?"

The sweet offer touched Tayler. No one had ever done anything like that for her before. "Oh, I wish you could go with me. Truly I do. But I don't have the funds to take you with me, nor do I have a place for you to stay . . . or employment for you, for that matter. I'm so sorry, Millie, but I'm touched that you offered." Tayler wanted to cry. She looked toward the trains, then peered back at the woman who'd practically grown up beside her. Only three years her senior, Millie was the closest thing Tayler had ever had to a best friend. "I'll write often—I promise—and once I'm settled, if there's employment and housing for you, I'll let you know. Would you come then?"

"Of course."

Most young women of Tayler's age and societal connections didn't think of working or even going to college. But Tayler did both. And Millie had quietly cheered her on. What must she think of her? "May I have your folks' address to send letters?"

"Of course." Millie sniffed and pulled out a pencil. "I'll write it on the back of this train schedule."

"And you promise you won't tell anyone about this?"

"I promise, miss. Only your brother, and I'll tell him that I found you and delivered his packet. He was expecting me to be gone a few days."

Tayler put her sketch pad and pencils back into her bag and

then reached for her purse. Pulling out a crisp twenty-dollar bill, she handed it to Millie. "This is one of the new bills. You've probably seen them, but they're smaller. I just didn't want you to think it was counterfeit. Please, take it. You're going to need a place to stay and food to eat."

"Oh no, miss, I couldn't take your money. That's far too generous. Your brother gave me plenty of funds."

"Well, then, you should explore the park. It's absolutely breathtaking, Millie. You've never seen anything like it. Buy yourself and your family some souvenirs, or a new outfit, or a hat. Please, I insist." She tucked the money into her friend's lap as another train pulled into the station. This time, it was hers. "I've got to go, Millie." She hugged her maid and grabbed her things. Thankfully, her cases would all be checked and loaded for her. The thought of wrangling all her luggage was a bit daunting.

"I'll be praying for you, Miss Tayler."

"And I you, Millie. I will be in touch."

She waved good-bye and headed to the train just as the conductor shouted his "All aboard!"

Tayler boarded the train in her blue suit jacket, blouse, and matching skirt, feeling quite smart in her t-strap shoes and cloche hat. Instead of being the wealthy socialite, she was simply Tayler. Headed for an adventure in Alaska.

It had been so nice the past couple weeks to wear her plain uniform rather than change clothes several times a day to abide by all the rules of society. While she appreciated her family's wealth and their impact on the world, she found she really didn't care for all of the rules.

When she settled herself into a seat, she peered out the window and saw Millie waving. Tayler waved back and hoped her friend would be all right. Prayerfully, she hoped Millie wouldn't divulge her secret. Her boss at Yellowstone was the only one who knew where she was headed, and he'd sworn himself to secrecy when she left.

Finally, the train started moving forward, and Tayler released a long sigh. Remembering the packet from her brother, she reached into her bag and pulled it out. Since there wasn't anyone around her, she opened the top of the envelope and peered inside. A large stack of bills greeted her and a folded paper.

She pulled out the paper and tucked the envelope back into her bag.

My Dear Tayler,

I've had a lot of time to think since you left, and I'm realizing that I've made some missteps. I'm so sorry for Mother's encouraging you to marry Emerson. While it is true that Dad invested heavily in Pruitt companies, that doesn't sway me in my thinking. Money doesn't mean anything if I lose my family over it. And I fear I have lost you. I know my absence has been difficult, but there are things I can't tell you right now. Please know that I'm doing everything I can to bring the truth to light and to be here for you. It devastated me to lose Dad, and the change of the will was like a betrayal. I know you're grieving as well, and you probably feel as though you've lost your big brother in the midst of it all.

I don't know how Mom will deal with your prolonged absence, but I've sent Millie to you with this note so you know that I am behind you. I know you want to make your own way, but please, allow me to help provide for you. It will comfort me to know you have enough in case of any emergencies that should arise. I've also set up a private account for you at our bank. I will place funds in

*there monthly, and should you need anything, just contact
the bank and they will wire it to you, no questions asked.*

*I know Mom loves you. She has dreamed of this wed-
ding between you and Emerson for many years. When you
broke off the engagement, I thought she would get over
it. But once Dad was gone, something snapped inside her.
Many of her decisions have been strange, to say the least.*

*So now she's focused on this union for you and Em-
erson. And you know her, once she gets attached to an
idea, it's hard for her to let it go. But I pray I will be able
to convince her in the time to come.*

*Please accept my apology for my absence. I know it is
too late for that, but I wish you well, my darling sister.
Believe and know that I am here for you. I promise.*

Please let me know how you are doing.

Love,
Joshua

Tayler folded the paper and put it in her bag with the envelope. Wiping a tear from her eye, she knew that only time
could heal these wounds. Her heart felt such a sense of relief
in hearing from her brother. Joshua had been grieving just like
she had, so she really couldn't blame him for his absence from
her life, but now she understood there was more to the story.

The burdens he must have had to carry alone all this time!
It made her sad. And made her determined to send him a long
letter in response. A small spark of hope started in her chest.
Maybe there was a chance of a renewed relationship.

She eased back in her seat and watched the world go by. Her
family had once been such a comfort. How she longed for that
again. Even Mother with her quirks and concerns about what

society thought weren't such a bother with Dad to balance things out.

She thought back to that day so long ago in Estes Park when Emerson had asked her to wait for him. She genuinely thought herself in love—thought he had been as well. He even wrote her dozens and dozens of letters talking about how much he cared, how wonderful their future together would be. But then the letters were fewer and fewer as the years went by. Then comments were made at social events about his antics, and it wasn't long before the truth came out about his affairs.

It was like the entire bottom of her world had fallen away, and Tayler was falling without hope of something to hang on to.

God is always there to hang on to, a voice seemed to whisper.

It was true. She knew that well enough. God was the only one who had gotten her through these difficult times.

Why must these things be, Lord? Why must Mother push me to marry a man I don't love and can never respect?

Tayler sighed. What had happened to her family?

•••••

CURRY

Margaret Johnson slid into a pew in the little Curry chapel, hoping Cassidy would arrive soon with the twins. She looked forward to seeing them every day.

Footsteps sounded behind her, but when she looked up, it wasn't Cassidy Brennan and her little family. It was none other than Bertram Wilcox—the railroad man who was brother to the pastor—along with Daniel Ferguson.

Both men grinned down at her.

"May I?" Bertram held his hat in his hands.

"May you what?" Margaret sent him a frown.

"Sit in this pew?" The man wouldn't stop smiling.

She shifted in her seat and shrugged her shoulders. "It's no matter to me where you sit, Mr. Wilcox."

"Please, call me Bertram." The man stepped out of the aisle and sat on the end of the pew right next to her.

Bothersome man. She scooted more toward the middle and hoped Cassidy would hurry up and get there. What could be taking so long?

"Ahem." Chef Daniel winked at her.

She rolled her eyes. "What is it you need, Mr. Ferguson?"

"I'd like to sit in this pew."

"Good heavens, there's plenty of open seats. I don't know why you two insist on invading my pew," Margaret barked at him.

But it didn't faze him. He was used to her bite. "I'll just scoot in, if that's all right."

Before she could say anything to stop him, the big man pushed his way past Bertram on the end and squeezed his way past her. "Ow!" Nothing like getting her toes stepped on by that big lug.

"Forgive me, lass. I didna mean to step on your foot."

"Oh, just sit down," Margaret huffed.

"You're glad that I'm sitting with you, aren't you, dearie?" Daniel wiggled his eyebrows and then his mustache.

Piano music fluttered over them. "Shhh." Bertram leaned around her and frowned at Daniel. "The service is starting."

"Don't be shushing me, Mr. Wilcox. It's simply the prelude." Daniel frowned.

Margaret looked to the ceiling for rescue as words flew between the two men, but none came. So there she sat. Sandwiched between two men who seemed determined to sit with her . . . if not on her lap.

"Hush, both of you. I'll not have you arguing during church."

For a moment, she thought they'd be quiet, but then one of them asked the other about his favorite Bible passage and if he'd been reading his Bible every day. Then the other asked how it felt to be a heathen, and the argument continued.

Margaret tried to tune them out and listen to the piano, but to no avail. Finally, she stood to her feet before it went any further. "Enough!"

Everyone in the little church looked at her.

But she didn't care as she wiggled her way past Mr. Wilcox—you'd think the man would make it easy for her to move, but no—and she prayed for a way of escape.

"Gammagammagamma!" chimed two little voices from the back.

Margaret turned and saw the Brennan family entering the door of the church. "Praise be to God." She looked to the ceiling and several chuckles sounded around her.

Opening her arms to the toddlers, she embraced them and then let them lead her to the front pew, where she sat with one cuddly boy on either side.

Cassidy and Allan joined them and the pew was full. Thank goodness.

Margaret smiled down at each of the boys nestled by her side. "Now, these are two men that I will allow to fight over me."

Cassidy gave her a puzzled look.

"Don't worry. I'll tell you all about it after church." Margaret snuggled with her two favorite boys and wondered what she would do about the two *big* boys who were in the back, probably fuming.

She didn't have enough energy for this. At her age, she shouldn't have men squabbling over her. It was ridiculous.

Although she had to admit, the attention from two men was

heady. The thought made her smile as Pastor Wilcox walked up to the pulpit. But a scuffle in the back made the pastor's eyebrows rise. "If everyone would take their seats, please? Let's open our hymnals to 'Blest Be the Tie That Binds.'"

Voices in the back continued in argument.

Margaret didn't have to turn around to see who was involved. Maybe if she ignored them, it would all just go away.

But it didn't.

"Gentlemen!" The pastor never raised his voice like that. Silence filled the room.

Pastor Henry cleared his throat. "As I was saying, let's all turn to the hymn and sing together." He lifted his book as the piano played an introduction. "A song that seems very appropriate for this morning." His eyes focused on the back.

Margaret knew exactly who was arguing. She was pretty sure the whole congregation knew.

Voices rang out together in their little chapel. A bit louder than normal.

> "Blest be the tie that binds
> Our hearts in Christian love;
> The fellowship of kindred minds
> Is like to that above. . . ."

If only Daniel and Bertram got the point.

•••••

WEDNESDAY, MAY 8—CHICAGO, ILLINOIS

Greg DeMarco knocked on his boss's door.

The door opened a crack and Bucko gave him a nod. The bodyguard was almost as large as the doorway, but that's how Charlie hired them—big and intimidating.

Bucko allowed him entry, and Greg walked to the desk. "You wanted to see me, boss?" The boss's chair was facing the other wall. So Greg straightened his suit, took his stance, and clasped his hands in front of him.

The large leather chair turned around. A fat puff of smoke floated into the air. Charlie "the Chisel" Lorenzo held a cigar to his lips and squinted at Greg. "Greg-o. I got another job for ya."

"Whatever you got." Greg lifted his chin.

"Good. I like a man who's eager to serve."

"You know me, boss. Just your average public servant."

His boss almost grinned. "This kid"—Charlie slid a folder toward him on the desk—"is overdue. *Way* overdue. And my patience is runnin' thin." He leaned back and took another puff of the stogie. The gold rings on his fingers clanked together as he knocked off the ash. "I need you to take care of it."

Greg nodded. "What means?"

"Any means necessary." Charlie nodded to his bodyguard.

Bucko held out a case.

Greg took it. "You got it, boss."

"This one might take some time, and I don't care how far you have to go. I want what belongs to me, and if I can't have that . . . I'll take his life. Make it clean. Some kind of accident." Charlie pointed his cigar at him. "Obviously, I'd prefer getting what's mine . . . but sometimes, *examples* need to be made. Understood?"

"Yep."

"Good." Charlie turned his chair back around.

Greg took the cue and exited the office. When Bucko closed the door behind him, Greg glanced at the file.

A curse left his lips.

This one wasn't going to be easy. Why did these rich kids think they could play with fire?

Shaking his head, he let out another curse. He'd have to get creative. Rich and famous families tended to have more attention in the public eye. Well, it was a good thing he knew how to make people disappear.

7

THURSDAY, MAY 16—CURRY

The rocking of the train slowed as they approached Curry station. Tayler couldn't believe she was finally here. After days of train travel and delays, she'd boarded the ship to Alaska in Seattle. The seas hadn't been kind, though, and Tayler found out firsthand how horrific seasickness could be. Weak and weary, she was grateful when she made it back on land. But this morning when she'd discovered there weren't any roads to Curry, she raced to catch the train. This last leg of her trip had been beautiful, but she was ready to be done with travel. For a long time.

Added to that, she needed a nap. An extended one. She hoped no one expected her to work the day she arrived. She simply didn't have the brain power or physical energy.

As she stepped off the train onto the wooden boardwalk, the bustling activity around her welcomed her to Curry. Young men in their spiffy hotel uniforms and caps greeted passengers and took their bags.

One approached her. "May I help you with your luggage, miss?"

Tayler gave him a smile. He barely looked old enough to

shave. "I would love to have your assistance, young man." She handed him the tickets for her checked cases. "Would you point me to the manager's office?"

He took the tags and then pointed to the door underneath the canopy that read Curry Hotel and Depot. "If you go to the front desk, I'm sure they will direct you to Mr. Bradley's office. I'll meet you there with your luggage and you can check in."

"Thank you." Tayler handed him a large tip. The young man didn't know she was an employee of the hotel. At least not yet. Some days it was hard to remember there were lines between the working class and the wealthy. Today, she needed lots of help, and a worker was due his wages and more. "I'd appreciate it if you could help me get it all to my room after I've spoken to Mr. Bradley."

He looked down at the bill in his hand and his eyebrows shot up. "I'll be waiting for you, miss." He gave her a huge smile.

She smiled back, though she grimaced inside. Hopefully her tip wouldn't spark gossip with the workers. But she couldn't take it back. Besides, the boy would earn it with all her luggage. There was always a chance he wouldn't say anything. Tayler took a moment to get her bearings and looked down the boardwalk. Buildings stretched in both directions, making up this little town of Curry. But it was the wild flowers on the hillsides that spoke to her. She couldn't wait to pull out the new books she'd purchased in Seattle and get a closeup view of the plant life. While her studies in college had given her a good background, she found that a lot of Alaska's plants only grew here, and she'd never seen them in person.

A group of young socialites interrupted her reverie.

"Heavens. Is this where we are supposed to stay? All summer?" The tallest of the group turned her nose up at the hotel. "What an ugly brick building."

An impeccably dressed man walked up behind her. "Esmerelda, my dear, this is an extremely highly rated and luxurious hotel. The only of its kind in all of the territory. The President even stayed here when it opened." The man puffed out his chest. "I've asked to be placed in the same accommodations." The man must be her father. He walked a few steps ahead, and a woman tucked her hand in the crook of his elbow.

The woman looked over her shoulder at the girls. "It may not be up to our usual standard, but please, be courteous."

The couple walked into the hotel while the three girls stood and chattered. Dressed in their finery, the girls stayed on the platform and looked among the crowd, whispering to one another.

Probably about their clothing and station in life.

Tayler shook her head. She knew all too well—because she came from that crowd. The elite. The spoiled. The group that Tayler never wanted to fit into. She'd discovered years ago that most young women her age were caught up in material things, and while she had plenty of money and material things to her name, Tayler wanted so much more than the shallow life her peers yearned for.

Shaking her head free of those thoughts, she decided it was time to meet her new boss.

Following the crowd of passengers through the front doors, she couldn't help but gasp at the interior of the hotel. It was lovely! Gleaming dark wood framed the entire lobby, and the red carpets were beautiful. Her favorite color.

Delicious smells assaulted her nose. Some type of bread was baking and it made her mouth water. Looking to her left, she noticed an elegant dining room. That must be where all the guests ate their meals. As Tayler Hale, the socialite, she'd eaten many fine meals in dining rooms like that one, but as Tayler Hale, the hardworking naturalist, she'd have to find where the staff ate their meals. As long as it smelled as good as what was wafting her direction just now. Her stomach rumbled.

The line at the desk moved at a nice pace as boys brought luggage to the passengers and then escorted the people to their rooms. The staff seemed incredibly efficient. And a well-run hotel meant the manager was top-notch.

Excitement filled her even as exhaustion pulled at her mind. Mr. Cunningham was wonderful to have told her about this opportunity and given her the recommendation. It seemed the perfect place for her. Now as long as Emerson didn't get word of where she was, maybe he would leave her alone for a while and things would settle down. She could only pray.

"Welcome to the Curry Hotel. How may I help you?" The pleasant young woman behind the counter gave her a big smile.

"My name is Tayler Hale. I believe you have a room for me? And I will need to speak to Mr. Bradley."

The young woman looked down at her ledger and then quirked an eyebrow in her direction. "I'm so glad you're here. Why don't you speak to Mr. Bradley first and then I will get you settled?" She came out from behind the counter and led Tayler to a door behind the reception area. She knocked and opened the door. "Mr. Bradley, Miss Hale is here to speak with you." The receptionist looked back to Tayler and smiled. "I'll be at the desk when you're done."

The manager sat behind his desk, with his head buried in a ledger. "My apologies. I've only got a few minutes, Miss Hale. I'm waiting on a new employee to arrive." He looked up and stood. "How may I help you?"

"*I'm* your new employee."

"I'm sorry, but if you've been hired for kitchen work, you need to see Mrs. Johnson. Let's head down there and I will introduce you."

"No, I'm not here for kitchen work. Please." She stuck out her hand. "Mr. Bradley, it's a privilege to meet you. I'm Tayler Hale."

The manager blinked rapidly.

Tayler tilted her head. Was she not the employee he was waiting for? Had he forgotten she was coming? "You hired me through Mr. Cunningham? I'm from Yellowstone. You needed another guide and lecturer—a naturalist and interpreter?"

"*You're* Tayler Hale?" Mr. Bradley shook his head and ran a hand down his face. "Please have a seat."

"Is there a problem, Mr. Bradley?"

The man paced behind his desk with his hands on his hips. "Um . . . well . . . My apologies once again, Miss Hale, but to be blunt, we were expecting a man."

"A man?"

"Yes. Cunningham didn't mention that you were a woman . . . and he sent your name and stellar recommendations. I just assumed . . ." He let the words fall and straightened. "My apologies, but your name is quite unusual for a woman."

"Sir, I promise you that I'm more capable than most of the men I worked with in Yellowstone. Not that men don't do a good job—I didn't mean that—but I've got a great deal of experience and expertise. From the time I was a young girl, my father had me camping and exploring the Rocky Mountains. I graduated college at the top of my class. I had to work with men who had little more knowledge than the ability to set up their tent. If that." Tayler felt the heat rising to her face. This couldn't be happening. "As to my name, it's unusual for a woman, yes, but my father gave me my name. It was my grandmother's middle name and has been passed down through our family for some time."

Mr. Bradley cleared his throat and pointed to a chair. "Why don't you have a seat?" He sat in the chair behind the desk.

"Sir, I came a long way for this job, and I know you need the help."

He held up a hand. "Oh, I'm sure you're quite capable. Cunningham wouldn't have sent me anyone less. But the other guides are men and I'm not sure . . . well, I just wasn't planning on hiring a woman for this position."

"But, sir, if I may be so bold, this is 1929. Women have the vote and are even serving in Congress. I've worked for Yellowstone for *five* years. That's got to tell you something of my abilities."

He chuckled. "Well, you've got spunk, I'll give you that. And I'm sure you were wonderful at your job in Yellowstone—"

"Please"—she couldn't let this opportunity pass—"will you allow me the chance to prove myself?"

Mr. Bradley leaned forward and put his elbows on his desk. "I don't think you need to prove yourself, Miss Hale, but I do need to speak with the other two men who run all the outdoor programs. I'll leave the decision up to them."

He stood and walked toward the door.

Tayler stood and felt a bit defeated. Surely she could prove to these men that she was capable.

"Now, if you'll follow me, let's go find Mr. Brennan and Mr. Smith."

Without any other options, she followed him out the door and prayed that Mr. Brennan and Mr. Smith would have compassion.

•••••

Thomas wiped the sweat from his brow as he handed Allan another of the crates shipped from the mountaineering store in Seattle. It still amazed him that a man with such a large amount of money would work side by side with him every day. Yet Allan and Cassidy Brennan treated everyone the same and lived simply. Although, this past winter, they did spend a good bit of money to build a larger house. It seemed the twins were taking up a lot of space. The thought made Thomas laugh. Who knew that two toddlers could turn the world upside down?

"What's so funny?" Allan's face was red as he smiled. "Wondering if this old man can keep up with you?"

"That's not at all what I was thinking. But I was thinking about your twins and how they take up a lot of space."

Allan rolled his eyes. "You're telling me. If you ask Cassidy, she says they'll soon take over the world with all their blocks, toys, and balls. And the fact that we've been acquiring two of everything." He sighed. "It's no wonder I can't keep up with a young college graduate like yourself. You still get your sleep."

Thomas laughed. "I didn't say you were old. Just for the record."

"You didn't have to. I'm feeling my age today."

"Only because of all the hefty crates. Good grief, how much stuff did you order?"

Allan smiled. "Perks of owning the company. I can get whatever I want." He winked.

"Well, next time, why don't you have them send a guy to do all the heavy lifting while you're at it."

Mr. Bradley rounded the corner at quite a pace. His face looked flustered, like he was upset about something, but the man was on edge most of the time trying to keep the hotel running at the highest of quality. A small, shapely woman was several steps behind him. Someone Thomas didn't recognize.

He straightened and wiped his face and neck again with his handkerchief. They must look a sight, all sweaty with their sleeves rolled up and their jackets tossed on one of the crates.

"Gentlemen, I'd like you to meet someone." Bradley held out his arm and watched as the lady caught up.

Now that she was closer, Thomas got a better look at her. Her brown hair was curled, and most of it was tucked up into her hat, except for the few curls that escaped on the sides. She smiled at them. And when her dark-eyed gaze met his, Thomas's heart did a little flip.

Dressed in a stylish suit, she exuded confidence. The closer she got, the more Thomas noticed that she was . . . short.

"This is *Miss* Tayler Hale." Their manager's lips were a tight, thin line. "She's come to us from Yellowstone as the new naturalist and guide."

That name? It hit Thomas in the gut. They'd all been expecting a man. And here stood a woman. A short woman at that. No wonder Mr. Bradley looked upset.

Allan held out a hand to Miss Hale. "It's a pleasure to meet you. I'm Allan Brennan, and this fella is Thomas Smith." He elbowed Thomas.

Sticking out his hand, Thomas nodded. "Nice to meet you, Miss Hale."

Mr. Bradley walked over to Allan and whispered something in his ear. Then he turned on his heel. "I'll be up in my office, Miss Hale." Then he walked away.

Thomas looked to Allan.

But his friend just smiled and motioned for them all to sit on the crates. "So, Tayler, tell us about yourself."

She lowered her brows. "If you don't mind my being direct, didn't Mr. Bradley tell you his concerns?"

"What? That you're a woman, and we all thought you'd be a man?" Allan laughed and crossed his arms, looking relaxed and calm. "I'm not worried about that. Tell us what you did at Yellowstone and a little about your experience."

Thomas wasn't sure what to think as Miss Hale told them about her experience in the Rocky Mountains as a young girl and then studying for her degree in botany. Apparently, she'd been working at Yellowstone in the summers for the past five years, guiding tourists in a better understanding of the park and even saving a few from bear and moose attacks. Impressive. If the stories were true. But could she do the job here? There wasn't much to her. Short and pretty, she definitely was a woman with plenty of curves, which made Thomas blush that he was even sitting here thinking about it. It was all a bit too much like with Caroline. And that had ended in disaster. Thomas shook his head to get rid of the memory.

"I'm impressed." Allan slapped Thomas on the back. "What do you think?"

Not ready to be put on the spot, he cleared his throat. "Well, um . . . it sounds like you indeed have a lot of experience, but Alaska is a whole lot different from Colorado or Yellowstone—at least as far as I've heard and read."

Miss Hale just gave him a sweet smile. "Yes, I can see that for myself. I'm willing to learn. And as soon as I heard of the position, I started doing extensive research."

Allan looked back at him as if he was expecting Thomas to say something profound. His friend raised his eyebrows. "Well, Mr. Bradley asked us to make the decision about Tayler, since we weren't expecting a woman."

"And?" Thomas wasn't sure what he was supposed to say. He swallowed.

Brennan just laughed again. "And . . . so I'm asking for your opinion. What do you say?"

It was almost like the breath had been knocked out of him. Looking at Miss Hale, he had to admit she was attractive—very attractive, which could be a problem—but it embarrassed him to voice his thoughts about her working with them. How could he do that in a professional manner? The memory of

Caroline's antics, promises, and accident couldn't be easily forgotten. Her screams as she fell with the landslide—of her own making—were still easy to recall. She too had come with promises of her abilities and knowledge, but those had been lies or at best exaggerations. How could he trust that Miss Hale wouldn't be the same?

"I . . . that is . . . well, as much as I respect women's rights to hold different jobs and to vote and all that . . . I'm concerned that the conditions up here may be more than she can manage." And that she might be too distracting. But he shook his head of that thought.

Miss Hale stood.

Thomas stood. He towered over her by a good foot.

All smiles gone, she placed her hands on her hips. "Have you ever scaled a fourteener, Mr. Smith?"

"No." He swallowed again, but his mouth had gone suddenly dry.

"I have. Have you ever spent the better part of a summer living completely off the land?"

"Well . . . uh . . . no."

"I have. Have you ever had to rescue one of your hikers— single-handedly, mind you—because they ventured too close to the dangerous hot springs?"

"No, miss, I haven't."

She stepped closer and tilted her head back to look up at him. "Well, I have. I have faced down mama bears and angry moose on multiple occasions and had to keep tourists from getting trampled by the buffalo. I'm an excellent shot with a rifle and a pistol. Not only that, I'm not so prideful of my abilities that I don't realize there's always something to learn." Her eyes sparked with intelligence. "I've come a long way for this job, and I was recommended by one of the top men of

114

the field in this country." She lowered her arms and stepped back a pace.

Thomas was instantly sorry. Not for how he felt about her working with them, but that he missed her presence as soon as she moved.

"I'd be forever grateful if you all would allow me to do my job here. It's hardly fair to judge me by my appearance or because I'm a woman. God looks at the heart. I can assure you my heart is to be the best naturalist and tour guide I can be, and I'd appreciate your at least giving me a chance to prove myself."

Allan walked over and winked again at Thomas. "I like your attitude, Tayler Hale. As far as I'm concerned, you can stay. Of course, if you fail to learn, can't keep up, or cause any upheaval, we'll have to find someone else. That would go for *any* new employee. You will come to find out that safety is our utmost concern here. Not just for the guests, but for all of us as well. We have strict guidelines and rules that we expect to be followed."

Her smile was back and her shoulders lifted. But she didn't look at Thomas. Her attention was all directed at Allan. "Thank you, Mr. Brennan. I won't let you down." She shook his hand again.

Allan turned to Thomas. "What do you say?"

He nodded his head and swallowed. Allan was his boss and his friend. He couldn't argue with him. At least not here. Maybe he could voice his concerns later—tell him about Caroline and how her lies nearly got an entire group of field researchers killed. "Of course, everyone deserves a chance." He tried to give her a smile, but it felt lopsided. What was wrong with him?

Tayler Hale shook his hand too, but her smile had dimmed. "I'd better get back to the lobby. I had a boy watching all my luggage, and I don't want to keep him waiting any longer."

Allan held up a hand. "Dinner is at eight thirty for all the staff in the downstairs dining room. You go ahead and get settled. We will see you at dinner and then you can meet us back here at seven sharp tomorrow morning."

She beamed another smile toward Allan, then turned and walked back the way she'd come.

Thomas watched her for several moments. They'd just hired a woman. Somehow it felt like a catastrophe in the making. And not just for the Curry Hotel.

8

The Curry kitchen bustled with the finishing touches for the dinner hour. Margaret watched over all of her workers to make sure that the meal would be up to her high standards. After all these years running the Curry kitchen, it never ceased to thrill her to put out fine, exquisite meals.

Collette Langelier walked over to her with a tray in her hand. "I've finished the *canapés*. You would like for me to put the *hors d'oeuvres* on the platters now, Mrs. Johnson?" The young lady's English was much improved, but the French accent was still strong. The summer she'd come with her brother to the Curry was quite memorable. Was that really three years ago now? Margaret shook her head. Time flew by.

"Yes, that would be excellent. Thank you for offering. Please tell Chef Daniel I'd like to speak with him too."

"*Oui*, Chef." The beautiful French girl glided away. Why she wanted to stay and work under Margaret's drill-sergeant ways was definitely a puzzle. But she wouldn't complain. Collette was a huge help.

Chef Daniel appeared at her side. "I hear ya be needin' me, lass?" His face was all smiles as he crossed his arms over his broad chest.

Margaret shook her head at him and tried to contain her

grin. She never knew whether she should just laugh in his face at his attention-grabbing antics or get angry with him. "I need you to do your job, Daniel Ferguson."

"Aye. And what is it that ya be needin' done now?" He gave her a wink.

She looked toward the ceiling. That man. What was she supposed to do with him? At least he no longer tried to take over her kitchen. After his near-death experience the year influenza had come to the Curry, he'd been changed . . . well, at least a bit softened. Toward her, anyway. Especially of late. No matter how gruff she got with him, he always seemed to take it in stride. Infuriating man. Sometimes she missed the days when he would argue with her and their hollering could be heard all the way in the lobby. But he still tried to get under her skin—especially when it came to how she organized her kitchen. "What I *need* is for you to prepare those chops for tomorrow."

"Bone in or bone out?"

"Bone in. It will make a beautiful presentation."

"As you wish, Chef." Ferguson bowed his large frame to her, which made the young girls washing dishes giggle.

After he walked away, Susan—one of the youngest—looked at her and smiled. "You know he's sweet on you, don't you, Mrs. Johnson?"

"Oh, hush. I'll have none of that sappy talk in my kitchen." The girls just giggled some more.

"Heavens, how am I supposed to get anything done around here?"

Collette walked over with the tray filled and began helping with the shortcakes. "With lots of help from me." She grinned and then leaned in and lowered her voice. "But the girls are correct, yes? Chef Daniel is . . . what is the word . . . *smitten* with you."

"Oh, stop. I don't need you starting in on me too."

"Starting in on what?" Cassidy appeared at the workstation.

"Chef Daniel is smitten with Mrs. Johnson. No?" Collette's whisper was a bit too loud for Margaret's taste.

Cassidy simply laughed and gave Margaret a kiss on the cheek. "Along with Bertram Wilcox." She snatched up a strawberry from the counter. "You would think Mrs. Johnson was sixteen and the belle of the ball." She shrugged. "I've never seen anything quite like it. They're like two lovesick teenagers. I fully expect them to appear beneath her bedroom window with singing and poetic readings."

"Oh, *oui*," Collette agreed. "Like Romeo and Juliet." She put one hand to her chest and stretched out the other. "'What light through yonder window breaks? It is the east, and Juliet is the sun.'"

"No." Cassidy shook her head. "It is the east, and Margaret Johnson is the sun."

The other kitchen girls worked hard to suppress their giggles, which only made them laugh all the harder. Cassidy winked at her mentor.

Margaret felt a blush rise in her cheeks. "You two need to stop. There will be no more talk of who is smitten with whom." Her tone had gotten snippy. "Aren't you supposed to be somewhere?"

Cassidy grinned and didn't seem to mind Margaret's terse attitude. "I checked on the mousse, and now I'm going to get the boys." Snickering, she walked backward toward the dining room. "I'll see you later at dinner, and we can discuss how you *don't* have two men sweet on you . . . Juliet." Turning, she waved over her shoulder and shook her head.

"Look at what you started." Margaret leveled her gaze at Collette.

"*Moi?*" The French girl looked from side to side. "It wasn't me, as I recall." She shrugged. "You know . . . this English language is so confusing." Collette lifted a spatula. "Is it who is smitten with who, or whom is smitten with whom, or who is smitten with whom?" She shook her head and went back to spreading the whipped cream over the shortcakes. "I'll never understand it."

Margaret felt the tension in her shoulders ease. Collette had taken the spotlight off of her. A complete change of subject would be a relief. What was it about men's attention that made her feel out of control? And she was not a woman who was used to things being out of her control. Never mind. In all her forty-six years, she had never felt quite so helpless. She needed to focus on something else.

As she finished her tray of shortcakes, she watched Collette. At ease and comfortable in the kitchen, the sweet girl had changed so much since she first came. That summer could have spelled so much trouble had Collette not given her life to the Lord. She was still vivacious and larger than life many times, but she was no longer self-focused and oblivious to those around her. In fact, she'd become one of the most caring people Margaret knew. Her brother, Jean-Michel, had so many wounds from the war that he hadn't known what to do to help his sister. The memories flooded over her. Interesting how God had done a lot in her own life that year. She shook her head.

It had been a while since the other Langeliers had visited. "How is your brother doing, Collette?"

"He is very happy working with Allan's business. Their . . . what is the word? Partnership? In business has done well."

"Katherine is well?"

"Oh my, yes. She writes to me the most beautiful letters. I love having a sister."

Margaret's heart twinged. Family was a wonderful thing. She stole a glance across the room at Daniel. Would it be so bad to open her heart again?

Ridiculous thoughts. Yes. Yes, it would. She'd loved deeply, and she'd lost. It had been hard enough letting Cassidy in . . . and oh, how she loved that sweet girl and her family. But when Cassidy came down with the influenza during her pregnancy, it had just about broken Margaret. Could she allow her heart to be that vulnerable again with a man?

Margaret shook her head. Daniel was a good man. And they got along just fine the way they were.

Collette wiped her hands on a towel and lifted another tray. "*Voilà!* This tray is *fini!*"

"Thank you, Collette. They look *magnifique.*"

The young woman chuckled. "You make my heart happy when you use French. I'm curious, have you met the new girl?" She started working on the next tray of desserts.

Margaret looked at Collette. Then around the kitchen. If there was a new girl in here, surely she would have been the one to hire her. "What new girl? Is she French too?"

"*Non.* Forgive me, I changed directions too quick. The one who came from another national park. She is to work with Thomas and Allan to guide the people on their outings."

"They hired a girl?"

"*Oui!* And she's enchanting. I like her a lot." Collette made a peak in the cream for the top of each cake on the next tray. "It will be nice getting to know her. I believe she is around my age in years."

Susan came up to Margaret, twisting her hands. "Mrs. Johnson?"

"Oh, goodness. What happened this time?" The poor young girl had broken at least five dishes since this morning.

She shook her head. "Don't worry. I haven't broken anything. But there's a visitor at the dining room door for you."

"Oh, bother." Margaret wiped her hands on her apron. "Who would be visiting in the rush of dinner?"

The young girl smiled. "It's the railroad man. Mr. Bertram Wilcox."

All the other young helpers in the kitchen started up their giggling again.

"I will have none of that, now!" Margaret eyed the young girls. Turning to Collette, she huffed. "Would you mind asking Mr. Wilcox if he will kindly leave me alone during the busiest time of my day? If I have time to speak with him later, I'll come out." Picking up the towel again, she slung it over her shoulder and grunted.

"Of course, Chef." Collette curtsied and went to the door.

Margaret couldn't hear the man's response, but she heard the tone. It would seem she made the man unhappy.

Collette appeared in front of her again. She leaned across the table a bit. "He brought you flowers."

"I have no need for flowers in my kitchen." What was wrong with these men? Didn't they understand she had a job to do?

"Maybe he wants to let you know that he cares. Bring some beauty to you." Collette shrugged. "He probably wanted you to take them to your room and think of him."

"Oh, bother. You're hopeless, Collette."

"I am French, you know . . . yes?" Her young assistant said some flowery French phrases that Margaret didn't understand. "Isn't it wonderfully romantic that you have two men vying for your hand?"

Margaret glanced around, glad to see Daniel was nowhere in sight. "The *back* of my hand is what they'll get if they don't knock it off."

The girls started giggling again.

Margaret shook her head and sighed. So much for the change of subject. *Lord, help me.*

•••••

Tayler found herself hungrier than she was tired. And that was saying a lot. She felt like she could sleep for days.

When she'd first entered her room, she found it was a generous size, quite a bit larger than the one she'd had at Yellowstone. And she'd been very tempted to try out the comfort of the bed but made herself unpack instead. The dresser and wardrobe were roomy, and there was even a desk and chair situated beneath the window. It would be a great place to journal, sketch, and write letters.

The thought of letters made her miss her family. Alaska was indeed a long way from home. Shaking her head, she forced herself to think of the adventure ahead.

After getting settled in her room, she cleaned up as much as she could in the few minutes she had and determined that she wanted a decent meal and then needed to meet the other staff. No matter how unprepared she felt. At least she'd been given the chance to stay. The misunderstanding with Mr. Bradley had made her feel quite nervous about the whole thing. Something she wasn't used to. She'd never been doubted for being a woman. But then, her father had probably had quite a bit of influence when she first started out. Now she was completely on her own. A very long way from Colorado and Yellowstone.

She ventured down the stairs and saw the same group of girls who were on the platform sitting around the lobby, giggling and whispering to each other. For some reason, Tayler's spirit felt like something wasn't right. Those girls could cause problems.

She'd have to keep an eye out in the coming days. Maybe she was just oversensitive right now. She didn't know anyone and she was too tired.

Tayler headed down the other stairway that led into the spacious basement of the hotel, which housed the laundry, section gang kitchen, overflow bunkroom for the railroad, storage, provisions rooms, and the large dining area for the staff. Her tour earlier had been a bit overwhelming. The building was well thought out, however, and kept in pristine condition, so she was pretty confident she wouldn't get lost.

As she stepped into the staff dining area, the comfortable chatter and tantalizing smells greeted her. She stood on the edge of the room for a while and just watched. It appeared as if the staff here was like one giant family. That was encouraging. With great anticipation, she hoped they'd welcome her into that family.

Allan Brennan—her new boss—walked over to her. "Tayler, it's so good to see you. I was hoping you'd make it for dinner. Let me introduce you to my wife. She just ran to get the boys' bibs . . . wait, here she comes."

A lovely, dark-haired woman with a brilliant smile walked toward them with twin boys in tow. She was the most beautiful woman Tayler had ever seen. Tall and thin with dark eyes that sparkled in merriment. She seemed so . . . exotic.

And it made Tayler feel frumpy and . . . short.

"Hi, Tayler, I'm Cassidy—Allan's wife."

"Hello. It's nice to meet you." Crouching down in front of the boys, Tayler smiled. "And who are these handsome young men?" She loved children.

"These are our sons." Allan patted the boys' heads.

"Jonathon and David"—Cassidy leaned down—"this is Tayler. Can you say Tay-ler?"

"Tay!" the boys chimed.

It made Tayler laugh. "I'll take that. It's nice to meet you both." She tickled each of the boys' bellies. Little childish giggles followed. "Who is David and who is Jonathon?"

Cassidy laughed. "Most of the staff can't tell them apart. Especially since we dress them alike. But if you look closely, you'll notice that David's hair is just a shade darker than Jonathon's."

Tayler looked back and forth. She raised her eyebrows. "No wonder people can't tell them apart." After looking at the boys for several seconds, she pointed to one. "Are you David?"

The little boy nodded.

"And that means you are Jonathon." She tapped the other boy's nose.

He nodded.

"Jonathon." She winked at him. "And David." She winked at the other adorable brother.

"Tay Tay!" they chanted and clapped their hands.

"I think you have new friends." Cassidy grinned. "Why don't you come sit next to me so we can visit? I can't promise it won't be an adventure with the twins, but hopefully you can leave the table unscathed."

Allan snorted. "Or covered in mashed potatoes. You pick."

"They're not that bad." Cassidy rolled her eyes. "But that's why I wear my apron during dinner."

"They should make full-body aprons for parents of small children." Allan chuckled.

The banter made Tayler feel more at ease. "Thank you, I'd love to sit with you, and I don't mind getting covered in mashed potatoes." She followed the little family to the long table. Allan pulled out a chair for her, and she took a seat next to Cassidy. Little David sat next to her and then Allan took a seat on the other side of the table with Jonathon.

Cassidy leaned toward her. "There's less mess when we split them up."

Tayler nodded. "Ah, I see." It made sense. As she watched the people settle she studied the Brennans. Maybe it wouldn't be so difficult after all—maybe only Thomas and Mr. Bradley had doubts about her being a woman and doing her job. There were lots of women who worked at the Curry Hotel. In fact, she'd heard the head chef was a woman and had another chef—a man—as her assistant.

It took a little time for everyone to take their places, but then Mr. Bradley walked in and the room fell silent.

"Good evening, everyone." He smiled. "Before we eat, I'd like you all to meet our newest staff member. She comes to us highly recommended from another of our beautiful national parks—Yellowstone."

Several oohs and aahs were heard around the table.

"Please welcome Miss Tayler Hale, an expert in botany, a naturalist, and an interpreter."

Hearty applause surrounded her. Mr. Bradley grinned from ear to ear. Maybe he was on board after all. The applause made her feel appreciated—something she desperately needed after the long journey here.

"She joins the team for our outdoor activities led by Allan and Thomas. Please stand, Miss Hale, so everyone can see you."

Tayler scooted her chair back and stood. Not that it helped a whole lot. She always told her father she was height impaired. But at least most of the people could see her. As she gazed around the table, she tried to connect with each person. When her eyes landed on Thomas, her stomach fluttered. He didn't seem pleased to have her aboard, and she wasn't sure if she should try to fix that or not. Maybe it was best that he didn't seem to care for her, because Thomas was a good-looking man, and she didn't need any interest in men right now.

"Let's say grace." Mr. Bradley bowed his head and led the table in prayer.

As Tayler settled back into her chair, the chatter picked up around the table. Once again catching Thomas's eye, she gave him a smile. But he just stared back.

Great. He really didn't like her. It made her wipe the smile from her face.

Cassidy nudged her. "What's that frown for?"

Tayler shook her head. "I'm sorry. Is Thomas always so . . . brooding?"

Cassidy laughed. "Thomas? You mean the Thomas who works with Allan?"

She nodded.

Her new friend looked at the object of their conversation and then looked back. "No. That's not like Thomas at all. I wonder if something is bothering him." She looked a bit worried.

"I take it you are close?"

"Oh yes. Thomas is like a little brother to me. We've known each other ever since we came to the Curry."

Maybe it was best to keep her mouth shut about her thoughts of Thomas around Cassidy. She didn't want anyone to think she was difficult.

But Cassidy pressed. She lowered her voice. "Has Thomas done something to upset you?"

She tightened her lips. She didn't want to start off at a new place with issues.

"Come on, Tayler. I can see something is bothering you. We don't like to keep things bottled up here—we all have to work together."

With a sigh, she ventured forth. "I'm guessing you haven't

talked to your husband about our meeting this afternoon. It's nothing big. I just get the feeling that Thomas thinks I can't do my job."

Mrs. Brennan looked puzzled. "That's not like him at all. I wonder what brought that on. I'll talk to Allan about it." Cassidy patted her hand. "Don't worry about Thomas. He's the sweetest and kindest soul around here."

Sweet and *kind* weren't the words Tayler would have used to describe the man she'd met this afternoon. In fact, she didn't know what she thought of him. He'd seemed aloof and untrusting earlier. Was she going to be able to work with a man like that?

With a sigh, she watched the food platters being passed around. She'd have to work with him. It couldn't be any worse than her situation with Emerson. At least Thomas had no need to lie to her or pretend to be in love with her. Tayler would just have to make the best of it.

Her stomach rumbled right as Cassidy held out a platter to her.

Tayler leaned forward and took a sniff. "What is it?" She'd tried to keep her voice low.

"It's salmon. Fresh, caught right here. It's one of our kitchen's specialties. This is salmon with dill sauce."

Taking a slow inhale, Tayler closed her eyes for a brief moment. It smelled heavenly. "I can't wait to try it." She scooped a large portion onto her plate. "But wait, didn't I read that the salmon run later in the summer?"

Allan nodded from across the table and swallowed the bite he'd taken. "That's when they spawn. They travel back to where they hatched and lay eggs. Good observation. But there's plenty of salmon in the rivers and streams from May until November, since there's several species to fish. But we have plenty of other fish year-round. Dolly Varden are one of my favorites."

Several other platters passed, and she took generous servings of each. She hoped no one would think she was a glutton, but she felt half starved. Besides, she'd always been able to eat more than her share. Dad used to say she was trying to keep up with the boys and trying to grow taller. But it never seemed to work. At least she didn't have to worry about getting fat. No matter what she ate, she always seemed to work it back off before the next meal. She was fortunate that way. So often she heard her mother's friends bemoaning their weight and whatever new diet they were trying. Of course, if she ever stopped hiking for miles every day, she might find herself in the same boat.

The man next to Allan pointed his fork in the air. "I'd like to take you fishing sometime if it's something you enjoy." The man nodded in her direction. "I guess I should introduce myself before I jump into your conversation. I'm John Ivanoff. That beautiful young lady next to you is my daughter, so this lug next to me is my son-in-law, and the two miniature rascals are my grandsons." He puffed out his chest just a hair.

"Big lug, huh?" Allan eyed the older man. "And here, I was about to tell her how you were the best fisherman around these parts."

"All said in love, my boy. All said in love." John elbowed Allan and the two laughed. "Besides, it's the truth about who's the best fisherman. I won the contest, remember?"

The easy banter between the family soothed Tayler's soul. Maybe she would be able to find the same comradery soon. Mr. Ivanoff's dark complexion made her wonder if he was native Alaskan. She'd read about the different tribes but was hesitant to blurt out anything at the dinner table. One day, she'd have to ask Cassidy. Taking a bite of her salmon, she couldn't believe how it just melted in her mouth. "Mmmm." The creamy dill sauce was the perfect complement to the fish. Next she took a bite of her chosen vegetable. The glazed baby carrots were sweet and caramelized, an absolute delight. "Oh, my goodness, these are divine." She couldn't help sharing her thoughts.

"Wait until you taste the rolls." Cassidy winked at her while she popped a bite of roll in her mouth.

Tayler went for hers next. The aroma alone just about did her in. But when she separated the layers of the steaming roll, she didn't even put any butter on it, just placed half of it into her mouth and savored the light and soft texture. "This must be what heaven will be like." She let a soft moan escape her lips.

"Don't worry, we've all had that same thought over the years. Mrs. Johnson is incredible in the kitchen." Cassidy handed a roll to David. The little boy clapped his hands when his mother set it down in front of him.

"You'll really enjoy the chocolate mousse for dessert. It's Cassidy's masterpiece," the man on Tayler's right spoke up. "I don't believe we've officially met. I'm Matthew Reilly. The resident doctor." He wiped his hand on his napkin and held it out to her.

Tayler shook it. "How exciting that there's a doctor in the hotel. And I absolutely adore chocolate mousse."

"Well, I don't live *in* the hotel, but in the town." He went back to his food as if he were done talking.

Interesting man. Tayler guessed him to be older than her brother, Joshua. With blond hair and blue eyes, he was a striking man but didn't seem to say a lot. She looked across the table to the pretty blond woman who was seated next to Mr. Ivanoff. The lady appeared to be around Tayler's own age.

The woman noticed Tayler's scrutiny and smiled. "Good evening, *mademoiselle*." She put a hand to her chest. "I am Collette. I work with Mrs. Johnson and Cassidy in the kitchen. We met briefly in the lobby."

"Yes, I remember. I love your accent. You must be from France?" Tayler took another bite of her salmon.

"*Oui*. Cassidy taught me how to cook when she was laid up, and now I cook with Mrs. Johnson."

Tayler took a sip of water, then switched from English to French. "I have been to France and loved it there—especially the cooking. Not only that, but my grandmother was French-Canadian."

Collette clapped her hands. "Oh, how I miss speaking my native tongue. You must promise me long conversations."

"I promise." Tayler changed back to English.

Allan leaned over and gave Collette a smile. "That ought to make you happy. Someone to talk to when you want to share secrets."

"I can share secrets in English," Collette declared, "but sometimes I do long to speak my native language."

"You're full of surprises, Miss Hale," Allan said in an approving tone and offered Tayler a smile.

"I know several languages. Something my parents insisted upon. It helped a lot at Yellowstone, where we had visitors from many countries."

"I can imagine." He nodded toward Collette. "I'm glad you two have a connection. Her brother, Jean-Michel, helps run my mountaineering business in Seattle."

Tayler took in a sharp breath. She patted her lips with her napkin and looked at Allan. "You mean, you're the Brennan behind Brennan Outfitters in Seattle?"

The man shrugged and nodded. "That's me."

"My boss in Yellowstone introduced me to your store. He refused to buy anything from anywhere else, saying you had the best gear."

"Ah yes. Mr. Cunningham. We send several orders to him every year." Allan took a sip from his glass.

Tayler couldn't believe it. "It really is a small world, isn't it?" Feeling more at home already, she dug back into her food and found she couldn't wait for dessert.

But when she looked down the table she noticed Thomas staring at her. And he didn't look happy.

9

Thomas watched Allan give Tayler the explanation of all the supplies and equipment they used. She appeared to be very knowledgeable, but was it all an act?

He couldn't bear for something to happen to Tayler—or anyone else for that matter—like what happened to Caroline. All because he never spoke up. He'd have to keep a close eye on her. Which wasn't a problem, because he felt drawn to the new employee. Another reason why he would need to guard his heart. He'd also trusted Caroline all too soon.

But just because Caroline had been false didn't mean that Tayler was. He really wanted Tayler to be all that she seemed.

As Allan and their new co-worker rounded the room, Thomas listened to their conversation about the equipment while he sorted all the ropes. Maybe he should ask Tayler about her knot-tying capability when Allan was done. They had to tie a lot of ropes for all their camping and hiking excursions, and it would be better if they found out now if she was capable or not.

"I noticed you have downhill skis as well as cross-country skis." Tayler nodded to the pile of skis in the corner.

Allan nodded. "We've had a lot of interest in skiing, but the lift this year will make it even more popular."

"Won't these get in the way stacked like this?" She pointed to the corner Thomas had sorted them in.

His boss chuckled. "I have to admit, I've almost caused them all to tumble at one time or another."

"Have you thought of hanging them from the ceiling?" Tayler looked up and tilted her head to the side. "I organized our equipment room in Yellowstone and used a simple Plank Sling knot system to suspend all the skis from the ceiling. Of course they were organized by size and type as well."

"That's a brilliant idea. Why don't you show me what you envision? I don't know if I'm familiar with that knot system." Allan grabbed skis out of the corner.

Thomas kept checking all the ropes for flaws while he watched them out of the corner of his eye. Did Tayler even know how to tie a Plank Sling? That must be what Allan was up to—he must be testing her.

"It's quite simple, really." She took the end of a long rope and placed it under one of the skis. "You just push an extra bight under the ski here to make an *S* shape. Bring this end over the ski and tuck it through the bight on the other side." She demonstrated the skill with ease. Maybe she did know what she was doing. "Then take the other end of the rope and go over the ski, tucking it through the opposite bight." Lifting the ends of the rope, she adjusted it. "Then you simply tighten or loosen the sling so the tips of the bights are just above the edge of the skis, and there you have it." She placed her hands on her hips and looked back up to the ceiling. "Back at my old job I used rings and two round turns and two half hitches at the top to hang them."

"Wonderful, Tayler. Let's do it." Allan looked toward Thomas. "Won't it be nice to not trip over those skis anymore?"

Tayler looked to Thomas for approval. The look on her face made him squirm. She was very cute, which made her very distracting.

"Um, yes, that will be great." He licked his lips. But his mind was screaming for him not to trust her. It was too dangerous. He couldn't let it happen again. What if she was just playing a charade like Caroline?

Tayler pulled a chair over to the east wall and climbed up on top of it to stand. "Thomas, I need you to come here for a minute."

"Why me?" His confusion must surely be apparent on his face.

She laughed and put her hands on her hips. "Because you're the tallest, and unless you want me to hang these where you're going to knock your head on the skis, I need you for reference."

Allan chuckled along with her and brought over the ropes and rings. "I've got a few sturdy hooks upstairs in the utility closet that we can screw into the beams. The rings can hang from those." He headed out the door. "I'll be right back."

"Thanks, Allan!" Tayler called after him. She then turned back to Thomas. "Now will you please come over here so I can mark the wall with your height?"

Thomas walked over. With her standing on the chair, she was actually about a head taller than he was. Her orange blouse made the pretty brown of her eyes sparkle. And she smelled really good. He shook his head. What was he thinking?

"Stand up against the wall, and I'll make a pencil mark above your head." And she was bossy for a short little thing too.

"You know, this isn't exactly how we've done things at the Curry." His mouth spit out the first words that came to mind. He winced. Probably not the best idea to criticize her. But it was true.

"I know. But it will give us a bit more space in here." She

leaned in and marked the wall above his head and then leaned back. "Although not as much as I originally thought."

He frowned. "What do you mean?"

A smile split her face, and she looked down at him. Those big brown eyes invited him to laugh along with her. "What it means"—she hopped down from the chair—"is that if we were going off of *my* height, we'd have a lot more storage space above our heads."

•••••

Denver

Emerson Pruitt tapped his fingers on the desk. Things had not gone as planned.

Tayler had grown into a beautiful woman—one who he'd gladly add to his entourage of women on his arm. He was even willing to take her as his wife. Because it would benefit him.

But to his surprise she wasn't taking him back. It was possible she was just toying with him—punishing him for what she perceived as his wrongdoing. She'd been lovesick over him since they were children, so what was going on in that smart little mind of hers?

Tayler had a mind and strength of her own. Always had. But for as much as she *had* been devoted to him, she was even more devoted to her belief in God and all those pesky rules that religious sorts burdened themselves with.

When she'd broken off the engagement, she declared she'd had enough of his philandering. Pop berated him to such a degree that Emerson was ready to come home and apologize, beg Tayler's forgiveness, and then be more discreet. But Pop had other ideas. Send a large bouquet of roses along with a flowery letter of condemnation toward his behavior and his deep regret for having hurt the only woman he truly loved. After that, lie low, put his nose in his books, and let it all die down, fully expecting that she would take him back.

But it hadn't worked.

Had it been a decade or so ago, Tayler would have been made to obey and overlook her almost-husband's indiscretions. Now women were being empowered by getting the vote. Goodness, but did anyone honestly believe they were capable of valuable decisions? Handsome politicians merely appealed to their easily distracted nature and *bam*! Those men became senators, congressmen, and even presidents. It had given him the idea of running for office, and once he managed to get his other issues in order, he just might. After all, the Pruitt name got him whatever he wanted.

Except for Tayler.

Stubborn girl.

If he hadn't had his own calamities to take care of, he would have gone straight to Yellowstone after she ran off for her silly job. But he hadn't invested the last of his fortune wisely, and it was coming back to haunt him. Apparently, there were plenty of people who wanted to dupe the rich and were good at it. And then there were the gambling debts.

Forgiveness wasn't exactly the Mafia's strong point.

Another thing he couldn't let Pop know. So that left Emerson either at his father's mercy and demands or with the need to come up with a better plan.

He needed to act fast. The only thing to do would be to bring Tayler home. Marry her and dig himself out with her fortune. Let Mrs. Hale think whatever she wanted. As long as she helped him tie the knot, after that he could use his leverage to get what he wanted as to the businesses.

Pop could rot for all Emerson cared.

"Emerson." Speak of the devil. Pop chose that moment to appear in the library. He stared at Emerson sitting there and scowled. "I thought you would be doing some more to bring the Hales in line. Sitting here hardly seems beneficial."

"Yes, well, that is where you are wrong. I'm making travel arrangements. Tayler is playing a game, pure and simple. She's punishing me for embarrassing her and making her feel less than important." He smiled and gave a little shrug. "She's a woman."

"Yes, and that demands a bit more of your respect, young man."

Emerson let out an exasperated sigh. "Yes, I know that. I'm building her trust, Pop."

"Don't call me Pop. You know I despise it."

"Very well—Father." Time to put out the bait. "I'm also quite concerned for Mrs. Hale."

Pop's brow furrowed. "Why is that?"

Emerson knew he'd set the hook. Pop and Martin Hale were best friends. He wouldn't want to hear of Martin's wife going through difficult times. "She's not even a full year widowed and that ubiquitous lawyer of hers has been giving her bad advice."

The older man gave a curt nod. "What makes you think this?" Father took a seat at one of the library tables and motioned Emerson to join him.

With reluctance, Emerson left the comfort of his leather wing-backed chair and took one of the wooden seats at the table. "I know because I make it my business to know. I've had several conversations with Mrs. Hale, and Dunham is usually close at hand. There are also some things she has shared with me that give me great concern."

The older man's shoulders straightened. "I'd better go see Henrietta straight away."

"No. You can't. I promised I would keep her private matters

confidential. As her future son-in-law. She would be devastated and embarrassed if you got involved at this point. I've already offered your assistance and she declined."

"But you'll let me know if I *need* to get involved? Do I have your word?" Worry etched Pop's face.

"I promise."

Pop stood. "I'm trusting you, Emerson. You'd better not be playing games."

"No, sir. Like I said, I'm making travel arrangements."

With narrowed eyes, the elder Pruitt assessed him.

Emerson smiled at his father and tried to look the obedient and changed son.

"Let me write you out a draft. I want you to bring Tayler back in style and apologize to her profusely. You do whatever it takes to win that girl. She's the best thing that's ever happened to you. I promised Martin I'd look out for her. . . ." His voice cracked almost as if the old man was choked up. "I'll go get the draft."

Emerson stood and wanted to pat himself on the back. Now all he had to do was go after the wayward Tayler. But the pursuit could provide a great deal of entertainment. He'd at least have fun bringing her home. Especially if this was going to be his life sentence.

A smile split his lips as he thought about getting away from the stresses in Denver. This trip to Yellowstone could be just what he needed.

10

TUESDAY, MAY 21—CURRY

The trek back down Curry Ridge had given Thomas plenty of time to think. The five-mile hike was pleasant and one he knew so well he felt he could do it without even looking. The young boys Allan had sent with him had done a good job helping him the past few days, but Thomas had allowed them to run on ahead when they got close to Curry. Their energy seemed unending. Had he been that way when he was younger? Good grief, he was only twenty-three. It wasn't like his teen years were *that* long ago. But at times, he felt like they were. Being an adult brought on the weight of the world. Or at least some days it felt that way.

The time alone gave Thomas some good stretches to sort things out and talk to God about the issue at hand.

Wisdom on Allan's part had sent Thomas up to the Regalvista lookout for a few days. Every season, they went up with a crew to clean up the lookout shelter and prepare campsites and fire pits for the coming influx of tourists. It had been good timing for Thomas to get away. Even though he hadn't talked to Allan about his doubts, the older man unquestionably knew that Thomas had qualms about their new hire, Miss Tayler Hale.

As his steps took him closer to the hotel, Thomas wondered what to do about the dilemma. Should he tell Allan the truth?

It didn't help matters that Tayler was very pretty. He felt drawn to her at the same time that he was aggravated at her doing such a risky job. In fact, she was all he could think about at times. He told himself it was just because of the working situation, but he knew better. Thomas found himself watching her—memorizing her. He wanted to know her better, while at the same time he feared knowing.

What if Allan noticed Thomas's attraction?

He walked along the suspension bridge that took him across the Susitna River. Maybe he should talk to John about this before he talked to Allan. The older man was always full of insight, and he understood Thomas better than anyone.

The worry of the situation weighed him down almost as much as the pack on his shoulders. Just because she knew how to organize the equipment and tie knots didn't assure him that Tayler could handle all they needed to do. He didn't mean to be so pessimistic . . . but he'd learned a hard lesson, and now it occupied his mind. A lot.

Childish laughter floated to him on the wind. It sounded like the Brennan twins.

A smile lifted Thomas's spirits. It would be good to see the boys. As he rounded the corner of the bridge, he spotted them playing in the field where they held baseball games. Cassidy was tossing a ball to her sons and then chasing them in a circle. Whatever game they had made up, it was obvious the toddlers thought it great fun.

Cassidy spotted him first and waved him over. "Thomas, it's so good to see you. I was just thinking I'd find you today so we could have a chat." Hands on her hips, she had that mother-hen look about her.

"What have I done now?" Thomas set down his pack and then joined the boys on the ground. The little tykes climbed on him and tried to feed him grass. "They definitely take after you, Cassidy. They're always trying to feed me. But their offerings aren't quite as yummy as yours." Usually it was dirt, a bug, or a worm. Thomas allowed the happiness of the moment to wash over him.

Patting him on the shoulder, Cassidy sat on the grass while Jonathon and David played. "It's about Tayler."

His mood instantly sank. Thomas looked to the ground. "What about her?"

"Allan told me how it went the day she arrived."

Great. "And you agree with your husband."

"Well, of course I agree with him. But what I don't understand is why you *don't* agree with him." She quirked an eyebrow at him. "You worked with me for a long time in the kitchen. And I'm a girl. You've worked with lots of women, so what's the big deal about hiring a female guide?"

"She's a naturalist."

Cassidy rolled her eyes at him. "Okay, so what's the big deal about hiring a female *naturalist*?"

He sighed.

"Come on, Thomas. This isn't like you, and poor Tayler thinks that you're brooding and untrusting."

His head popped up at that.

"Yeah, you didn't give the greatest first impression."

"It's a lot more complicated than just her being female."

Cassidy crossed her arms over her chest. "All right, then. Enlighten me. Why is it so complicated?" One of the boys plopped in her lap and stuck his thumb in his mouth. Pretty soon, the other one joined his twin, and she had her hands full rubbing their backs.

If anyone would understand, it would be his longtime friend

and supporter Cassidy. Thomas chose to tell her everything. "Do you remember me mentioning Caroline?"

She tilted her head and furrowed her brow. "Was she the one you were thinking of asking to dinner last Christmas?"

Thomas nodded. "Yeah. I met her the school term prior. She was on a study team with several of us, and she was chosen for one of the field trips we took to study volcanic activity in areas where ash sediment had been discovered. It was well into the wilds, and while the hikes weren't all that strenuous, my professor kept mentioning that he didn't think Caroline should be along. Thought it was too dangerous. He'd never had a female student studying geology before." He hesitated and took a deep breath. "I guess none of us fellas thought she should be with us. Having a woman along just complicated things . . . for a lot of reasons."

"Go on." She glanced down at her sleeping twins. "You have my undivided attention."

"Caroline was a consummate actress and deceived all of us into thinking she was more capable and knowledgeable than she really was. She assured everyone that she knew what she was doing, but it just wasn't true. Not only that, but she was careless and loved to show off."

"That never bodes well."

Thomas looked at Cassidy and shook his head. "No, it didn't. You see, Caroline had assured everyone that she was fully qualified by previous experience to be with us. She provided all sorts of references and had been admitted to the class at the request of several important men."

"Surely her actions would have given her away." Cassidy shook her head. "A person can only pretend so long."

"Exactly. She was actually able to pull off quite a few assignments, but other times she'd make major mistakes. Always gave one excuse or another. She even went so far as to say that she often tried a different approach to prove or disprove particular theories. I saw this early on, but she was intriguing and . . . well . . . she always managed to charm me one way or another. I ended up covering for her on more than one occasion." He looked away, embarrassed by his confession.

"It's all right, Thomas. I've made my share of humiliating mistakes."

He looked up and nodded. "Well, this mistake almost cost us our lives."

"Goodness, Thomas, now you really have my attention. Please continue."

"The last day of the trip we located a previously unknown deposit of ash. We were trying to map it and figure out exactly how long ago it might have been made. We spread out across the valley with the professor's strict instructions not to climb the ridge because of loose rock. Caroline, being true to her nature, didn't listen. She wandered off, and in truth, I think most everyone else was relieved to be rid of her. Then a horrible rumble sounded and a massive rockslide started above us.

"The two classmates closest to me saw it all like I did. It looked like the mountain was raining down rocks and boulders above us. Caroline was right in the middle of the slide, and we couldn't do anything. We heard her screams, and it made me sick to my stomach."

"Heavens, you never told me this! Did she *die*, Thomas?" Cassidy put a hand to her stomach.

"No. Praise God, she didn't die. But by the time it stopped and we got down the mountain and found her . . . she was pretty hurt. Her leg was broken and the professor feared she had internal damage as well."

"Oh, Thomas. I'm so sorry. I didn't know." A tear slid down Cassidy's cheek. "What happened?"

"We rushed her back to Fairbanks for care, and thankfully she suffered only lacerations and the broken leg. But the school told her she couldn't come back."

"Did you *like* her a great deal?" Cassidy tucked her chin and bit her lip. She always seemed to guess his deepest feelings.

"Yes, I did. I hadn't gotten up the nerve to tell her how I felt, for which I'm now quite glad. Even though she'd tried to deceive me several times, I still felt attracted to her." He paused for a moment and shook his head. "Once she was bandaged and her leg cast for the trip home, she had the nerve to make light of the entire situation. The professor confronted her, and she admitted she didn't have half the experience she claimed. She was there only for the thrill of it and to fulfill a dare."

"A dare?" Cassidy asked.

"Yes, apparently she'd been challenged by her friends and older brother to come all the way to Alaska and put herself in a place and situation she knew nothing about. It was a game of theirs. A stupid game that had been concocted by bored rich children. Caroline cared nothing about any of us, nor what we were doing. She laughed it all off. Thought it was funny that she'd been able to pull the wool over our eyes. She was still making sport of it when she boarded the train for Seward. In fact . . . " He fell silent, not sure he wanted to admit the most embarrassing part of all.

"Thomas?" Cassidy smiled. "You know you can tell me anything. I'm not going to betray your trust."

He nodded. "She said she knew she could get whatever she wanted from me because I was in love with her."

"And were you?"

"I liked her a great deal, but I don't think it was love. Especially now."

"What do you mean?"

Thomas wasn't really sure what he meant. The statement actually surprised him. "Well . . . I suppose . . . having had time to think about it . . . it's just clear to me. I liked her and wanted to know her better, but . . ."

"And you now think Tayler is going to turn out to be the same way?"

"Yes . . . no. I don't know. Don't you see? I don't know what to think. Tayler comes with all these recommendations and supposed experience, but Caroline came with hers as well."

"Thomas, I can understand why you'd be skeptical after that, but I think Tayler deserves a chance to at least prove herself." His friend's tone was reproving.

"But even if she is telling the truth, there are some very real dangers out there. This area is difficult enough for a man, but much more so for a woman. Take, for instance, the ridges around here."

"Yes, and I've climbed all of them." Cassidy's sarcasm couldn't be missed. "I'm a girl too, you know."

"But you grew up with all this."

"And Tayler grew up in Colorado. Last I heard, she's climbed mountains pretty much her whole life."

Exasperated, Thomas huffed at her and plucked a few blades of grass. "Or so she says. You don't understand."

Cassidy raised her eyebrows and gave him that big-sister look. "Oh, I think I understand just fine. You can lash out at me all you want, but you know I'm pressing you because I care about you. Good grief, Thomas. Allan has great discernment, and he thinks the world of Tayler already. Says she's more skilled than anyone else he's ever worked with. And her education is top-notch.

"This is more than Tayler being female. And I think it's more than what happened with Caroline. But I'll come back to that another time. *You're* the one who doesn't understand. I'm not trying to say that women should be doing everything that men do. You know that I believe God made us all different, with diverse strengths and abilities. But I *am* saying that it sounds like Tayler really knows her stuff and has a lot of experience. Allan has made her prove herself. She's not lying like Caroline. So why are you not supportive of that?"

"I don't know." He shrugged his shoulders.

Cassidy gave him that look. The one that said he was an idiot. "Ugh. Men."

"She's too short?"

Her expression turned to confusion. "What? Oh, now you're just being ridiculous. Well, how about this, Mr. Know-it-all? Maybe you're too tall!"

He chucked the grass at her.

Squinting her eyes, she leaned back on her hands and then nodded. "Oh, I see . . ."

"You see what?"

"You like her." Her face changed from anger to amusement.

"What? I don't even know her."

Cassidy bit her bottom lip—something she did when she was thinking. "Now it's beginning to make sense. You had a horrible experience and a woman got hurt, I get that. Then you all were waiting for someone to help here at the Curry. You thought it would be a man. No problem. Then Tayler arrives and you find out your new expert isn't a man, but a *short*, and very pretty woman. And of course, being the gallant gentleman that you are, you don't want her to get hurt . . . because you're attracted to her just like you were to Caroline. Partly because she is quite lovely, but also because she has an interest in the same work and could be a potential mate who shares your love of Alaska and nature."

The flood of information caused Thomas to become flustered. "Maybe . . . it's . . . because, because I don't want to get hurt." The words were out before he could even think of the repercussions.

But true to her nature, Cassidy wasn't condemning or judgmental. Especially since she'd already come down on him pretty hard. "I can't say as I blame you there. You started to like someone, and she proved to be false. Now you feel attracted to another young woman, and you're afraid the same thing will happen."

Thomas knew it was foolish to deny the attraction. "Well, it's possible."

"Yes, Thomas. It is possible. Perhaps even probable that you will give your heart and get hurt. But that happens, and we shouldn't be afraid of it. Otherwise, we miss all the blessings that come with giving our heart."

Thomas looked away across the field. "It's just such a risk to care."

"No less than climbing Denali." She leaned in and whispered, "But every bit as rewarding."

Thomas looked back at her and felt the weight of what really troubled him most. "I don't like being made the fool."

"No one does, Thomas." The boys were beginning to stir and Cassidy shifted her weight. "But I'd rather know love and be made a fool than to never know love. What Caroline did was deliberate and wrong. She didn't make a fool of you, Thomas. She made one of herself. Don't put the actions of one misguided woman onto another who is innocent of wrongdoing. If Tayler is lying, it will prove itself soon enough, but let her stand or fall on her own merits or the lack thereof. And, Thomas, if Tayler is the right woman for you, trust God to show you the best way to deal with the relationship. He won't fail you, and He certainly won't make light of your feelings."

•••••

The long daylight hours took a bit of getting used to. For the sixth night in a row, Tayler had fallen into bed exhausted, and yet she couldn't go to sleep. Granted, she was trying to go to bed early so she could catch up on much-needed rest, but why couldn't her body simply adjust and give in to sleep?

After wrangling with her covers and shifting from one side to the other, she yanked her pillow out from under her head and put it over her face. She let out a frustrated shout. "Why can't I go to sleep?" Good thing the pillow muffled her voice or someone would have probably come running to her rescue and busted the door down, wondering what the ruckus was about.

Tayler sat up in bed and pulled her Bible off the nightstand. It had been hard lately to know what to read, as she was so unsure of what the Lord wanted her to do. She hated the thought of defying her mother, but she also knew she couldn't marry just to please her. And what was there to gain? A lifetime of misery? A broken heart because her husband couldn't be faithful? And then what if they had children?

But maybe she was being unfair. Maybe Emerson really had changed. Was she simply unwilling to forgive? The Bible said that if she didn't forgive others, God wouldn't forgive her.

The thought was horrifying. Had she done Emerson wrong by refusing to reconsider marriage? Was she being unforgiving?

She settled back against the pillows and searched her heart. No, she forgave Emerson as far as she understood forgiveness. To her way of understanding, forgiveness wasn't approval or acceptance, but rather giving up your right to seek revenge. She had definitely done that. She didn't even wish Emerson ill. He was young and foolish and gave in to sinful temptations. Tayler herself was no less a sinner. No, it wasn't about not *forgiving*

149

him. It was about not *loving* him. Seeing him for who he really was hadn't made her feel superior or less of a sinner, but it had proven to her that she didn't love him in the way a wife should love her husband.

Tayler knew she'd done the right thing. She felt certain God had wanted her to end the engagement, just as she felt certain God had led her here. But she was having a tough time getting past her own doubts, especially when she was so tired.

Opening her Bible, she turned to First John, chapter four. Before she'd left Yellowstone, the pastor of the small church she attended had started going through the first, second, and third letters of John. It was the first time she'd paid much attention to the three small epistles in the New Testament, and she wanted to finish going through these tiny powerhouse books. She could finish studying them on her own and make lots of notes. Maybe she could talk to the pastor here in Curry about her thoughts.

Decision made, she started reading in verse seven, where they had left off.

Beloved, let us love one another: for love is of God; and every one that loveth is born of God, and knoweth God.

He that loveth not knoweth not God; for God is love.

In this was manifested the love of God toward us, because that God sent his only begotten Son into the world, that we might live through him.

Herein is love, not that we loved God, but that he loved us, and sent his Son to be the propitiation for our sins.

Beloved, if God so loved us, we ought also to love one another.

Twice in five simple verses it mentioned loving one another. She had to admit, her anger toward Emerson had taken over her emotions. There hadn't been a lot of "loving one another" going on in her mind. Just grief from her dad's passing and then escape as the pressure to marry her former fiancé flew at her from Mother.

150

She knew she could still love her mother through all this, but was she showing others God's love? And how could she love Emerson the way she should, even though he'd been a complete louse?

That was a tricky question. Something she'd really need to mull over for a while. She could forgive him and had, but could she love him? And when God spoke of loving one another— exactly what did that entail?

She continued reading, and when she made it down to verse eighteen, tears pricked her eyes.

There is no fear in love; but perfect love casteth out fear: because fear hath torment. He that feareth is not made perfect in love.

We love him, because he first loved us.

If a man say, I love God, and hateth his brother, he is a liar: for he that loveth not his brother whom he hath seen, how can he love God whom he hath not seen?

And this commandment have we from him, That he who loveth God love his brother also.

This whole time—all these years—she'd struggled with the thought of not being loved. Knowing that her love for the outdoors made her an oddball in her little circle of society. She'd always been loved by her parents and brother, and then there had been Emerson. Even though he'd been flirtatious with other girls at first, he still told her that he loved her. Tayler had basked in that.

Until one day when she'd turned sixteen, she didn't feel like he really meant it. Maybe ever. His attention to other girls upset her and made her feel like she wasn't good enough. As she matured and grew up, she realized that Emerson talked a good talk, but he didn't actually follow through with anything. If he truly loved her, wouldn't things have been different?

Tayler gently ran her finger along the edge of the delicate

page in her Bible. She felt guilty for a moment. She was holding Emerson up to a very high standard. God's standard. But shouldn't that be the standard that girls hoped their future husbands would attain? Dad had always strived for that standard, and he had continued to love Mother, even when she had belittled him. Still, men were only human, and while they should strive to live up to God's standards, was it fair for others to put those standards on them? Was it right to put expectations on someone else and then judge and condemn them when they fell short?

But shouldn't she want to find a man who loved her the way God instructed husbands to love their wives? She sighed and let her hand drop. Could she ever hope to really understand love?

What amazed her the most was that God loved her so much He gave His only Son up to be the sacrifice for the whole world—including her. Now that was love.

The last verse in the chapter had reiterated once again Jesus' command. If Tayler loved God, she had to love her brother also. Even if he didn't love her. But then—who *was* her brother? Was it anyone—everyone? Or was a brother someone who was of like mind and believed as she did? Hadn't she once heard that references to brothers in the Bible meant fellow Christians? Her mind whirled with unanswerable questions.

Instead of her thoughts constantly going to Emerson and her woes with him, this time they went to Thomas. She'd heard Cassidy mention Thomas to be a man of faith. Maybe that was where she could start. Maybe there was something she could do to win over the tall guide she needed to work with. Maybe she just needed to show him God's love. But that made her nervous. It seemed pretty obvious that Thomas didn't like *her*.

Wanting to clear her muddled mind, Tayler got up and walked to the window. The sun still lit the day, making her chuckle.

Here she was in her nightgown, praying for sleep, and the sun was still shining.

But she needed this time in the Word. Time to gather her thoughts and get her perspective back in the correct place. It was time to cast her burdens and cares and worries upon the One who could carry them much better than she could.

Lord, I hope I haven't made a huge mess out of everything. I truly wish to seek You and You alone. Help me to do that here. Show me how to love as You love—to forgive as You forgive. Help me to make the choices You would have me make, rather than be embarrassed or hurt because of the choices of someone else. And, Lord, please guide me in this new job. Help me to be a light for You. In Jesus' name, amen.

Her heart lighter, Tayler knelt on the floor by the window and laid her arms on the windowsill. Resting her chin in her hands, she watched the river roll by. She loved that her room in the staff dormitory overlooked the river. It was more peaceful than the train side.

Movement out of the corner of her eye grabbed her attention.

A tall, familiar figure walked at a slow pace, chucking a rock into the river here and there.

Thomas.

Her heart dropped a little. How could she fix this misunderstanding with him? She didn't even know how she'd offended him. He obviously didn't care for her—nor did he care to have a woman on staff with him. But Tayler wanted his approval. Deep down, she knew she'd have to work hard to prove she could do this job and do it well.

With a sigh, she watched him sit on a bench and lean his forearms on his legs.

What or whom was he waiting for?

11

Emerson Pruitt sat across from Tayler's mother in the Hales' formal receiving parlor. Henrietta Hale was a beautiful woman. She had been refined with age and yet maintained a youthful appearance that could have allowed her to easily pass for a woman ten years her junior.

"She's not responded to any of my letters," she told him. Sipping tea from her Haviland china cup, Mrs. Hale gazed at him over the rim.

"Yes, well, she'll respond soon enough to all of our wishes."

Mrs. Hale lowered the cup. "And you're sure your father will wait? I can't risk losing everything."

Emerson smiled. "I assure you, my father is quite busy with other things at this time, and he gave me his word. If Tayler and I marry, then he'll be content to keep things as they are. His biggest concern is that the families be as committed to one another as they were in the past."

"Of course we will remain committed."

Emerson couldn't help bringing up the matter of the will. "And what of Joshua? Is he any wiser to the terms of the will?"

She paled. "No."

"You do realize you hurt him very much by telling him his

father didn't believe him ready to take on such a large responsibility." Emerson pretended to pick lint off the cuff of his suit coat. "I know how I'd feel if my father treated me in such a way." No need to tell her that Pop had made clear his lack of confidence in Emerson's business practices.

"It was never about hurting Joshua." Mrs. Hale was clearly uncomfortable with the topic. She lowered her voice. "I would rather we not discuss this matter."

"I'm sure you'd prefer that, and I'm certainly not trying to be a cad. I just want to be assured of your assistance."

"I already told you I will support the marriage. I am doing all I can to force Tayler to comply."

"And I appreciate that." He stared at her and then raised his eyebrows. "Ah, Mrs. Hale. I believe I understand you now. . . . It's all about control, isn't it?"

The silence stretched as she stared back. Then with a quick move, she stood. "So I don't want my son running my life. There's no shame in that. I helped Martin build this empire, and of course I want control. I've lived my whole life watching women not have any say. Well, that's not going to work for me." She took a deep breath, and an expression Emerson couldn't decipher washed over her face. As quickly as she'd stood, Mrs. Hale sat back down. "I'll hand things over to Joshua in due time. Now, if you will be so kind, I don't wish to speak any more on the subject, young man." The look she gave him was final.

"Well, then. Discussion closed. However, I am hopeful you might assist me in another matter."

She looked confused. "What matter?"

Emerson put on his most charming smile. "All of my funds are tied up at the moment, as I explained. Still, there is an opportunity I have to get in on the ground level of a new promising industry. I need five thousand dollars."

Mrs. Hale straightened. "Five thousand?"

Emerson nodded. "And I need it today. . . . I won't be able to see you again before I leave to go get Tayler."

She took a long drink from her tea as she appeared to consider his request. Emerson knew she didn't want to part with her money, but she would. She knew she had no choice. Either she did as he asked, or she and Mr. Dunham would end up in jail.

• • • • •

Saturday, May 25—Curry

Collette Langelier pounded out the dough onto the bread board. What she wouldn't give to be able to stomp her feet and have a little tantrum right now. But grown women didn't throw tantrums. Sadly.

"*Pouah!*" she huffed as she slammed the dough down one last time. She blew a tendril of hair off her forehead.

Mrs. Johnson walked up to Collette's station with her brows raised and hands on her hips. "Exactly what has got you all in a dither this morning?" She pointed to the lump of yeasty dough. "I'm sure the bread doesn't deserve your wrath." Her boss leaned in and whispered, "That wasn't a French curse word, was it? Because I do not allow any such talk in my kitchen."

Collette began to giggle and put a flour-covered hand to her face. The back of it hit her nose. "*Non*, Chef Johnson. It was simply the equivalent to your . . . *moan* . . . ummm . . ."

"Ugh?" Chef Daniel supplied as he walked by.

"*Oui!* That's it." Collette pointed to him and smiled.

Mrs. Johnson nodded. "Good. Now, why don't you tell me what's got you so riled up that you're pounding my dough to kingdom come?"

Collette sighed. "You won't tell anyone?" Keeping her voice low in a bustling kitchen was difficult.

"Of course not. Who am I going to gossip to? The utensils?"

"I would like to know how you have managed to gain the attention of two men."

Mrs. Johnson frowned. "I haven't *gained* all that attention on purpose, and you know it."

"But how did you do it?"

The older woman gave a slow nod. "Oh, I see. You're interested in someone."

Collette felt her cheeks warm. "*Oui.* And I don't think he knows I am even here."

"Well, if it's any consolation to you, I haven't done anything, and I don't want their attention. But I can give you some advice."

"Oh, Mrs. Johnson, *s'il vous plaît.* Please."

"If you really like this someone, you should do what you can to win their affections—make yourself useful to them, but don't force your interests on them."

"I think I understand." She bobbed her head. "You think that will work?"

"A man appreciates a woman who goes out of her way trying to help make his life easier. A woman who notices things." Mrs. Johnson accentuated her point with a wooden spoon raised in the air. Then she went back to the stove.

"Notices things . . ." Collette murmured to herself. But what could she notice? The man she admired more than anyone was Dr. Reilly. He was quite a bit older than she was, but his blond hair and blue eyes made her melt every time she saw him. She'd kept her feelings under wraps for so long because she was afraid it was just a silly crush. But when they stayed with her for more than a year, she knew it was serious. The problem was, she had no idea how to catch a real man. In her younger years, she'd been an outrageous flirt, but she'd never actually cared for anyone. Now that she cared, she found herself tongue-tied. Which was quite an achievement for her.

Determination in place, she realized she'd just have to find ways to observe Matthew Reilly and find out how she could help him. Then maybe he would notice her.

The smooth dough beneath her fingers smelled heavenly, and Collette breathed in deeply. Mrs. Johnson was just as Cassidy said—a big softy, once you got to know her.

"Mrs. Johnson?" The recognizable voice made Collette freeze in place.

When did he come into the kitchen? He hadn't heard anything, had he?

"I need to make a poultice with these ingredients." Dr. Reilly held a paper up to the chef. "Would you happen to have any extra available? It's not things I normally keep on hand."

Mrs. Johnson wiped her hands on a towel and glanced over at Collette with a quizzical look. "I certainly do. Let me get them for you."

Matthew saw her and gave her a little smile as he walked over to her station. "Miss Langelier, how are you today?"

She blinked several times and then realized she hadn't answered. "I'm quite well, Dr. Reilly. And you?"

"Please call me Matthew." He rubbed the end of his nose and looked at her. "I'm doing very well, thank you."

Silence stretched for a moment as she couldn't think of one thing to say. She just stared at him.

He rubbed his nose again, and the right side of his mouth tilted up into a half smile.

"Here you are, Dr. Reilly." Mrs. Johnson returned with the ingredients.

"Thank you, Chef." He took the packet, gave Collette one last smile, and walked back out of the kitchen.

Collette watched him walk away, then realized she was still holding the dough in her hands.

Chef Johnson chuckled. "So he's the one, is he, now?"

Her shoulders sagged. "Yes, and I couldn't think of anything to say." She thumped the dough down again.

"Well, at least he knows you are here. I noticed that he spoke to you."

"*Oui*. He did." Oh, but how she wanted so much more. Collette sighed.

More laughter from her boss. "Well, let's get back to work." She leaned in and winked. "But first, you might want to wipe that flour off your nose."

• • • • •

WEDNESDAY, MAY 29—YELLOWSTONE

The train had been adequate transportation for Emerson, but now he wanted to see Tayler for himself and then get some much-needed rest. The train's berths were not only uncomfortable but too short to accommodate Emerson's height. A real bed and bath would be his goal once he had Tayler in hand.

As he walked into the lodge where he had his reservation, Emerson thought about his future. At first, he'd been angry at Pop for his demands, but then he realized it could be much worse. He'd always had great affection for Tayler, and Josh had been like a brother. The solution really could be quite simple. But, of course, Tayler got the wild notion to run away, which amused him. Leave it to Tayler to throw them all off their game. He liked her spirit.

Maybe that fondness could at least turn into some sort of love. They could be happy together. At least he'd have access to the Hale money, thanks to knowing what Mrs. Hale had done to her son.

Shrugging his shoulders, he made his way to the front desk.

"How may I help you, sir?" The young lady behind the desk looked at him over the top of her spectacles. In spite of her eyewear, she was a cute little thing.

Emerson turned on the charm. "They certainly have hired the prettiest of clerks."

The girl blushed and looked at the ledger in front of her.

"I have a reservation and some business to deal with."

"Name?" She opened the register.

"Emerson Pruitt."

"Please sign here." She turned the book toward him. "Your room is number twenty-one. Up the stairs and down the hall on the right." She handed him a key.

"Thank you. Now, might you tell me where I can find Miss Tayler Hale, please?" He tried not to sound impatient. "Her mother has sent me here on business," he added, just in case he wanted to pursue something more with the girl at a later time.

"Miss Hale isn't here, sir."

Infuriating woman. "Do you know when she will be back?"

"No, sir. But Mr. Cunningham might know." The lady pointed. "He's just over there at the fireplace talking to some new lodge workers."

"Thank you." Emerson glanced down at his luggage. "Will you have someone take my bags up?"

She nodded and smiled. "Of course, sir."

Emerson squared his shoulders and walked over to the gray-haired gentleman. The man was dressed neatly in a brown tweed suit. His handlebar mustache was perfectly curled on the ends.

"If you have further questions, you can find me in my office over by the registration desk."

The workers nodded.

"Now go to your duties."

The ladies scattered in different directions.

"Mr. Cunningham?"

The man turned toward him with his hands clasped behind his back. He raised his eyebrows. "Yes, how may I help you?"

"I'm Emerson Pruitt. I'm looking for Miss Tayler Hale."

The man looked bored and turned back to the fire. "She's not here."

"Yes, I've been told that." Emerson's patience was growing thin. "Do you know when she will return?"

"No, I do not." The man looked over his shoulder. "And who, pray tell, are you to be asking after her, Mr. Pruitt?"

"I'm her fiancé."

The man didn't look impressed. "Well, as I said, she isn't here."

"Good heavens, man, don't you keep track of your employees? Do they simply come and go as they please? What kind of a place are you running here?"

Cunningham lifted his chin and turned very slowly to Emerson. "I do not appreciate your tone of voice. This is a national park with the finest employees in this great country."

He'd offended the man. Great. Now Emerson had to win him back over. "I apologize. I'm just tired and would like to find my fiancée. I'm certain she's expecting me."

"You won't find her here, Mr. Pruitt, so you'd best be on your way. Miss Hale left Yellowstone for parts unknown." The man almost smiled under the mustache.

"What do you mean she *left*?" He was practically yelling, but the thought of having come all this way only to find her gone was too ridiculous to believe.

"Exactly what I said, Mr. Pruitt. Now unless you'd like to be escorted *out* of our fine establishment, I suggest you lower your voice and behave like a gentleman." The man squinted at him and then walked right past.

Rage boiled inside Emerson. How could she leave? And where on earth would she go? Stubborn woman. Apparently, Mrs. Hale's letters *hadn't* done the trick. He replayed the conversation with Cunningham over in his mind. That man knew something, and Emerson intended to find out exactly what it was, but first he had to get some sleep.

He fingered the room key and made his way to the stairs. Tayler couldn't have gone all that far, could she? She loved her work, and it would be impossible for her to leave it for long. Chances were better than not that she was still working for the national parks. Maybe he could get someone to check their records.

Perhaps the little clerk who'd checked him in. She'd known that Tayler wasn't here. Maybe that wasn't all she knew. He smiled to himself. After a bit of rest and a bath, he would explore that avenue and see if perhaps she might recall something more about Tayler's absence.

12

The past week had flown by for Tayler. Allan immediately took her out on every hike and outing they offered. He said the best way for her to get acclimated would be to dive right in. Some of the outings were pleasant hikes—nothing arduous— while a couple of the others were more strenuous. It didn't bother her at all. She'd enjoyed each one of them, and she'd already filled an entire notebook with everything she'd learned.

Though some of the flora and fauna were different from what was found in Yellowstone and Colorado, they were still her expertise. What she didn't know from personal encounters, she had learned from books. She had a knack for providing information to the guests that Allan said *he* didn't even know. She also spoke three additional languages—French, Spanish, and Italian—thanks to her mother's insistence on the high-society tutor. All three languages had come in handy at different times.

The animals they encountered provided some of her favorite experiences—especially the hard-to-find caribou, who were rarely spotted. No matter what, each day, Allan had congratulated her on her knowledge and a job well done.

But the same couldn't be said for her interaction with Thomas.

He'd been guiding other outings so they could keep up with the schedule. She knew that soon she'd have to work on her own or even with Thomas on other events, but he still hardly even spoke to her. Not that there had been much of a chance, but still. She didn't know what to do about the situation.

The end of the workday was upon her and she sighed. Was there anything she could do to gain Thomas's respect?

The object of her thoughts walked into their shared office at that moment. He went straight to Allan. "Only one sprained ankle today." He wiped a hand down his face. "I really wish some of these people would listen a bit better to the precautions."

"Was it another woman in fancy shoes?" Allan shook his head.

"No, this time it was a man. But his shoes were definitely *fancy*." Thomas's face lit up in a smile. It made him very attractive. "When I informed him that he'd stepped in a pile of moose scat, he had a fit and took a tumble down the hill. And it wasn't even much of a hill. . . ." Thomas shook his head and laughed. "And then the ladies all wanted to examine the droppings. Lots of giggling ensued as they examined the pellets and talked about how uniform their shape and size were. You know how it goes."

Allan laughed along with him. "Unfortunately, I do. Everyone is fascinated with moose scat." He looked back down at the papers he'd been working on. "Tayler, would you join us over here?"

She walked over and stood next to Thomas. "How can I help?"

Allan looked at both of them and put his hands on his hips. "We have two camping excursions scheduled for the middle of June. These are the first overnight trips of the season, and they will be going on at the same time. I'm taking a group of men up to the Ruth Glacier, and you two will be taking a group up to Curry Ridge."

Tayler felt the tension in the air increase. Maybe if she stayed positive and professional, she could defuse it. "I saw those on the schedule. I'm happy to do whatever you need me to do." But was Thomas willing to work with her?

"Well, I just saw the list of members of the excursion to Curry Ridge." Allan sighed. "I'm sure you've seen a group of young ladies around who will be here all summer?"

Oh, great. The snobbish socialites who always seemed up to no good? That wouldn't make for a fun time at all. They'd complain about everything—Tayler was sure of it. "Yes, I've seen them on several occasions."

Thomas sighed. "They took a hike with me yesterday."

"Well"—Allan shook his head again—"they are part of the group going camping. I hope there won't be any problems, because their families are going along, but this is not a group of rugged outdoorsmen like the ones I'm taking up to the glacier. These are people who will probably have a difficult time with the length of the hike to the Regalvista lookout. I just wanted you to be aware." Allan took a deep breath and crossed his arms over his chest. "I also think it's time to let you spread your wings, Tayler. You are more than qualified, and I'm confident in your abilities. Maybe some of these young women can learn a thing or two from you on the trip."

His praise made her heart soar.

"And it's high time that you two work together as well. We're a family here, and you should probably get to know each other." With that, Allan patted her on the shoulder and headed to the door. "I'm going to check on my wife, and then I'll be back to finish the paper work before we have dinner. If I don't see you both before then, I'll see you in the dining room."

Then he was gone.

And Tayler was left standing next to Thomas.

He turned and gave her a small smile. "Sounds like we should plan plenty of things to keep the guests occupied on the camping trip." He headed off into the corner where he kept his things.

Tayler put her hand to her stomach and took a deep breath. Maybe this was the opportunity she needed to bridge the gap between her and Thomas. "Thomas, could I speak to you for a moment?"

He turned back around and his brow furrowed. "Sure."

Best to just blurt it out. "I know you feel that I'm not good enough for the job and that you have a problem working with a woman—specifically me—but I just wanted to apologize. I'm sorry if I offended you with anything I said the first time we met. I was a bit hurt and surprised when I arrived that you didn't think a woman could do the job, and well, I was very defensive, and I'm sorry. But if you would just give me a chance—I'm sure you'll see that I'm very qualified and know what I'm doing." Her courage was bolstered a bit. "I think you just need to get used to the fact that a woman is fully capable of doing this job."

He blinked and his expression was hard to read. "Allan has said that you've done a great job." Thomas went back to what he'd been doing.

That was it? That was all he was going to say? More frustrated than ever, Tayler walked out of the room. What was she supposed to do now?

Fuming, she stormed out the back door and walked toward the river. Cassidy and Mrs. Johnson sat on a bench on the pathway with a little boy in each of their laps. She stopped in her tracks and tried to make a quick getaway before anyone noticed her.

"Tay!" the boys called out to her.

Too late.

"Tayler, come on over here for a minute," Cassidy's voice called to her.

Working to control her foul mood, Tayler turned back to her new friends.

The boys clapped and smiled at her. "Tay Tay!" Her name had become a new chant for them as they said it over and over, and she had to admit, she liked it. A bit of her frustration slid away, and she smiled at the sweet toddlers.

"Oh boy, did you see that face?" Mrs. Johnson laughed. "Someone has a storm cloud over them."

Tayler grimaced. "Is it that obvious?"

"Yes."

"Yes." Both women laughed at their simultaneous response. "So you might as well just spill the beans, Tayler."

Plunking herself down in the grass in front of the women, she huffed. "Thomas is a thorn in my side. Or maybe I should say that I'm a thorn in his. I don't know. He's snooty and hardly speaks to me, and I don't think *he* thinks I can do my job!"

The two looked at each other and laughed.

Cassidy's expression of unbelief was obvious. "Thomas? The Thomas who works *here*?" She pointed to the ground.

"Of course. What other Thomas is there?" Tayler didn't understand. Why were they laughing?

Mrs. Johnson just shook her head. "Young lady, I can say with absolute honesty that a long time ago, Thomas was a thorn in my side too. That poor young kid couldn't keep his feet under him if he'd put glue on his shoes. But now he is the sweetest and most accepting person I've ever known." She looked down at Tayler with a protective look.

Cassidy laid a hand on the chef's arm. "What I think Margaret is saying is that Thomas is the least 'snooty' person we've ever known."

Tayler groaned. "Then what is it with men thinking women can't do the same job?"

"Tell me about it, Miss Hale. I've been dealing with that my whole life." Mrs. Johnson didn't look very sympathetic. "The question is, How are you handling it?"

With a hand to her forehead, Tayler let out a long breath. "Well, I even asked to speak with him just now. I apologized to him if I offended him, and he didn't say anything other than 'Allan said you've done a really good job.'" She mimicked a lower voice. "But then nothing. Not another word." She watched the two women for their response.

Cassidy and Mrs. Johnson shared a look.

Cassidy turned back to Tayler. "Have you thought about the fact that maybe Thomas is nervous working with a pretty girl?" Her voice was softer now.

"Because he doesn't think I can do the job?"

"No, because he thinks you're *pretty*."

The words sank in. "You think Thomas thinks I'm pretty?"

Mrs. Johnson laughed. "Of course, dear. You're a very attractive young lady. I've seen you turn the heads of many of the men as you walk by."

Tayler felt herself frown at that. "Really? But my uniforms aren't very pretty. . . ." She looked down at her clothes. "I don't dress to lure men to look at me. And I'm not . . . well . . . I am not at all ladylike when it comes to things like sitting and sewing and making polite conversation." None of this made sense to her. She wasn't here to attract men. "In fact, I've had some ladies say that I'm rather . . . boyish."

Cassidy reached a hand out to her. "Tayler, you are really quite beautiful, and even if you were wearing a potato sack, the men would notice you. There's nothing boyish about you."

"But I don't understand. Why do you think that's the problem with Thomas?"

"Because we know Thomas." Mrs. Johnson smiled. "He's

not snooty or aloof or against working with women. Goodness, he has worked with the two of us for years."

"And she's really good at bossing people around." Cassidy pointed at the chef.

The older woman gave a nod. "Yes, I am, thank you very much. I just think maybe you need to get to know Thomas a little better. He's not at all like what you're judging him to be."

"Besides"—Cassidy winked at her—"I've heard you are absolutely amazing at your job. Thomas knows that . . . he's just got some things to work through."

At that moment, Thomas rounded the corner of the hotel and headed toward the men's dormitory. A couple of the young socialites were sitting on the grass, and they called out to him.

"Yooo-hooo. Thomas!" The girls waved their handkerchiefs.

He turned to them and waved. "Good day, ladies."

"Won't you come and play with us?" one of them called in a simpering way. "We do miss you so very much. Don't you like our company?"

Thomas smiled. "That's very nice, but I have work to tend to. Maybe later." He turned back around and slammed into one of the maids carrying a large basket of linens. The two bounced off each other and landed on the ground.

Giggles from the girls on the lawn followed as Thomas and the maid both turned red and got back up. He leaned down and tried to help pick up the sheets but ended up yanking on the one underneath the maid's feet and she went down again.

Tayler watched as he reached down and helped the young girl back to her feet as the gaggle of socialites made comments from their seats.

Mrs. Johnson grimaced. "Looks like Thomas hasn't completely gotten over his old ways."

Cassidy laughed. "Poor guy."

The chef stood and set one of the twins down on the bench. "I left Chef Daniel in charge of dinner this evening, and while the break has been nice, I need to make sure he hasn't made a mess of my kitchen." She winked at Tayler. "Now, don't you worry about a thing. It will all work out."

"Bye, Gamma!" A chubby little hand waved.

"Bye-bye, my darlings. I will see you in a little bit." She walked back to the hotel.

Cassidy turned to Tayler. "I never divulge confidences, Tayler, and I don't mean to start now, but just remember everyone has things from the past that trouble them. Thomas is no different. He's going through a big transition in his life, having just graduated. You also went to college and graduated, if I remember right."

Tayler nodded. "I did."

"Well, then, you know how it can be. I would imagine after years of going to school and knowing exactly what was expected of you with classwork and such that after it came to an end, you were probably questioning the future."

Tayler was amazed by her insight. Could Cassidy know more about Tayler than she let on? No. That was silly. No one up here knew about her past. "I knew what I wanted to do, but I had already been warned that it was a very difficult field for women and that jobs would be scarce."

"I'm not sure what Thomas plans. I think he's going through a time of trying to sort out the details. Everyone has to grow up and embrace the future, but that means leaving behind the old ways. I don't think you have anything to worry about. Let's get together and chat again soon, but right now, I need to get these boys cleaned up."

"Thanks." She watched the beautiful young mom walk away. Maybe she didn't have anything to worry about. But then Mrs. Johnson's words came back to her mind.

"Looks like Thomas hasn't completely gotten over his old ways."

Great. The thought hit her square in the face. Could Thomas be another Emerson? A man who played upon the affections of young ladies and used them to his advantage? Maybe he was even hired to do such a job or at least encouraged to carry on in such a way. Entice the women young and old to better enjoy their stay at the Curry. No doubt the gratuities he'd receive would be well worth his efforts. Hadn't she been encouraged at Yellowstone to do the same?

"Always make the tourists feel special, Miss Hale. They come here for excitement and adventure. Some might even hope for a little summer romance." She remembered Mr. Cunningham's words and shook her head.

Tayler sighed. Thomas was certainly handsome enough for the job. Oh, it all made so much sense now. Of course he wouldn't spend time talking to her or even befriending her. It made her sad to see the truth of it because she was hoping they could become friends.

But Cassidy and Mrs. Johnson thought very highly of Thomas. Allan too. In fact, it seemed that Thomas was beloved by most of the staff at the Curry. Could Thomas truly be a shallow cad and fool all of these people?

She sighed again. It wasn't worth getting hurt. Tayler decided then and there she'd just have to learn to work with him and keep him at a distance.

"Guard your heart," Dad had often advised after she'd learned the truth about Emerson. And so she would.

13

A breeze fluttered through his open window and pushed Thomas's hair over his forehead. As he sat on his bed, embarrassment washed over him. He just had to knock Lucy down, and then to make everything worse, he'd knocked her down *again*. In front of an audience that included Tayler Hale.

The past week had been really trying. While it had been a shock to meet the new guide and find out she was a woman, it was even worse that simply being in her presence was doing strange things to him. Anytime Tayler came near, he seemed to lose the ability to put his thoughts together.

And she was really pretty too. Those thoughts invaded his mind on a regular basis.

Now they were going to lead an excursion up Curry Ridge together. Could his life get any more difficult?

The biggest problem right now was that Tayler thought he didn't like her. She thought she had offended him and was kind enough to offer him a sincere apology.

And what did I do?

Nothing. He hadn't even really responded to her apology. He'd made some comment about how Allan thought she'd done a good job. Why didn't he just tell her she had no need to apologize—that she was proving her merit and that he . . .

that he . . . What? That he liked her? That he spent way too much time thinking about her?

He let out a moan. She thought he hated her, when the opposite was true. At first, yes, he hadn't been sure of her abilities. But unlike Caroline, Tayler Hale had proven more than once to not only be knowledgeable about nature but sensible about it too. And the fact that Allan thought highly of her wasn't lost on him.

Yes, he liked her, what little he knew of her. They were usually working apart, but when they took meals together or attended staff meetings . . . well . . . there were a lot of things about Tayler that drew his attention.

In fact, there were many things to like about her. The way her nose turned up at the end in such a cute way. The freckles on her cheeks, and the sparkle in her eyes as she talked about the plants and flowers. The way she could make the twins laugh whenever she saw them, and in return, they called her TayTay.

Even the fact that she was short drew him in. She was feisty and stubborn. And she loved what she did.

All of this he'd realized in the past week, but he'd done nothing to earn her friendship or trust. He hadn't said more than a few sentences to her.

Then this afternoon's conversation was a disaster, followed by his clumsiness coming out once again. He thought he'd conquered that, but sadly, Lucy would probably have the bruises to prove otherwise.

What was he going to do?

A glance at the clock told him he'd better get cleaned up and back to the office to meet with Allan. Maybe he could hash it out with him if Tayler wasn't around. And then, maybe he could make a difference at dinner.

As he entered the dining room, Thomas looked around until he spotted Tayler.

Perfect. No one was sitting beside her yet. He took long strides over to the table and pulled out the chair next to her.

She turned to him, a frown on her face. Her dark eyes bored into him as if to assess the danger of the situation.

"Is this seat taken?" He gave her a smile.

"Um . . . no." She blinked and her expression relaxed a bit.

Thomas sat down and took a deep breath while he shot a prayer heavenward. Conversation drifted around him. He turned back to Tayler. "I need to apologize for my behavior earlier."

Her brows sank down. "I don't know what you mean."

"I just want to make things clear between us."

She sat up a little straighter and turned to face him. Keeping her hands in her lap, she looked him in the eye. "All right."

"I know you've proven that you are more than qualified for this job, and I don't want you to think otherwise. I don't have any qualms about working with you."

Her face relaxed a bit, but she bit her lip before she spoke. "Thank you."

What should he say now? The pink of her blouse brought out the pink in her lips and it distracted him. "Good. I just wanted to make sure you knew."

She nodded. "Good."

The awkward moment stretched.

Tayler reached for her napkin and laid it in her lap.

Thomas took a drink of water.

Then she turned back to the table.

Good grief. This was ridiculous. He was a grown man. He put his arm on the back of his chair and pasted on a smile. He could do this. "I hear you're quite good at fishing."

She turned her head back to look at him. A smile lifted the edges of her lips. "Where did you hear that?"

Thomas laughed. "John told me that you two have gone twice now."

Her body shifted on the chair to face him again. "John's a fascinating man. I learn something from him every time we talk."

"I know. I feel the same way, and I've known him for many years. He's an amazing man and has such a wealth of knowledge."

She nodded. "So . . . I've been wondering this but didn't want to sound presumptuous."

"What is it?"

"Is John an Alaskan native? You know, like one of the tribes of Indians?"

It was Thomas's turn to nod. "Good observation. He is. In fact, he's half-Athabaskan and half-Russian." He smiled again. "But all American."

"How interesting." She looked around the room. "I'll have to ask him about it next time I see him. Does he speak the language? And do you know which tribe?"

She was even smarter than he gave her credit for. "He does. Ahtna. I asked him once to show it to me in writing, but he said there's not a lot of it actually written down. He's got trusted friends who still live with the tribe and come through here and advise us on the movements of the wild herds, weather, poachers, things like that."

"Oh, I would love to meet them."

"I'm sure you will. They come to Curry a few times a year."

The conversation dropped again for a few seconds. Thomas wasn't about to let this chance pass him by.

"Tayler? I really would like us to be friends. Do you think we could start over?"

She squinted her eyes at him. "I don't know . . . how do I know you are capable of filling that role?"

For half a second he was nervous, then he noticed the sparkle in her eye. She was joking about when they'd first met. "I don't know, you might have to let me go through a probation period. See if I'm worthy."

Her face broke out into a full smile and then she laughed. A beautiful sound. "I think I can handle that." She held out her hand. "Hi, my name is Tayler Hale."

He took her hand and shook it. "Thomas Smith. It's nice to meet you."

· · · · ·

Tayler was glad to finally have Thomas treating her in a friendlier manner, but she wouldn't forget her resolve to guard her heart. The folks here at the Curry were like a family, and Thomas could surely fill the role of cousin. That was safe, wasn't it? A nice distant cousin.

She thought about him throughout the meal. It was hard not to with him sitting right there beside her. At one point he'd invited her to go fishing with him sometime, when the workload would allow for it. Cousins went fishing . . . didn't they?

As they ate and conversed with the others around the table, Tayler couldn't help feeling quite conflicted over her earlier conclusions. Thomas didn't act at all like a womanizer. When Collette came to join them, he stood to help her with her chair, but he hadn't been flirtatious at all. Emerson wouldn't have missed an opportunity with such a beautiful young woman.

"How are you settling in?" Collette leaned forward to speak across Thomas. She switched to French. "Have you managed to get used to all the sunlight and mosquitoes?"

Tayler laughed and kept to the French. "You mean those aren't hummingbirds?"

"No, but they do occasionally fly together," Thomas interjected, also in French.

Tayler's eyes widened in surprise, and she reverted to her native language. "I didn't know you spoke French."

"You never asked," Thomas stated matter-of-factly. "Collette's brother taught me some, and then Collette helps me keep it up from time to time."

"You're doing very well, I must say," Collette offered. "I'm making it my goal to teach everyone French. I even gave Mrs. Johnson a little lesson."

"Oh, I can't imagine her caring much for that." Thomas shook his head. "She can, however, rake a fella over the coals in her Scottish tongue."

"And don't I know it," Collette replied. "You should hear how she and Mr. Daniel argue. Although it is calmer now."

Thomas chuckled. "I have. I've learned it's best to back away slowly and clear the area. They throw things."

Tayler laughed and continued to enjoy their stories. Collette, she learned, had also been raised in wealth. The two had a great deal in common, so they just might get to know one another better.

She glanced around the table. Truth be told, she hoped she would get to know them *all* a lot better, because—for reasons she really didn't understand—this place was starting to feel like home.

That evening as a group of employees walked back to their quarters, Tayler decided to approach Collette. She kept to the French language, knowing it would please the petite blonde.

"It still feels like it's the middle of the day."

Collette nodded and surprised Tayler by looping their arms

together. "It took forever until I got used to it. In fact, sometimes it still fools me. I get caught up in doing something and think, oh I should go to bed. But it's so light outside, and I convince myself I have plenty of time, only to look to the clock and find it's much later than I expect."

Tayler had fallen victim to that as well. "It is beautiful here, however. I grew up with the mountains. Beautiful, large mountains. But everything in Alaska seems so much bigger."

"*Oui*, it is like nothing else on earth. People are always saying it is heaven, but then I think to myself that heaven will be even better and . . . well . . . it is more than my mind can imagine."

"Mine too." Tayler glanced out across the river. "I have enjoyed talking with you, Collette. I hope we will be good friends."

"Oh, but we already are." Collette gave her arm a squeeze. "I like you very much."

"Thank you. I feel the same about you."

"So why did you come all this way to Alaska when you had plenty of mountains and wild lands to see in Yellowstone and your Colorado?"

Tayler hesitated. Should she tell her the truth? They were friends, but perhaps an abbreviated answer would do. "I needed a change. Life in the States had become . . . complicated."

"*Oui*, I can understand that."

"How about you? How did you end up coming to Alaska?"

Collette smiled. "My brother. He needed a change. His life had become very complicated too. And then there was Katherine—his long-lost love. She was here. For me, I just wanted to see the world and experience everything. But when I got here, I fell in love."

"With a man?" Tayler hadn't remembered there being anyone in Collette's life—no one she had talked about anyway.

"*Non*, at least not then," Collette said. "I fell in love with

God and then with Alaska. Suddenly, I didn't want to travel. It is strange, yes?"

Tayler shook her head and gazed across the panorama of beauty. "No. Not strange at all. There's a peacefulness here I've not encountered elsewhere. A sense of something I've never really known. A feeling of . . . coming home." She looked at Collette and hoped she would understand.

Collette's expression confirmed that she did. "*Oui*. It is like suddenly all the pieces have come together."

"Yes." Tayler sighed. In Colorado her life was in pieces and none of them seemed to fit together to make sense. Especially since Dad died. But here, they were falling into place. The same pieces were making an entirely different picture, and with it came a peace of mind Tayler hadn't known since childhood.

She imagined Dad smiling down from heaven on her—his little girl, finding her way.

•••••

Saturday, June 1—Denver

Greg DeMarco took his jacket off and hung it up in the closet. His room at the Brown Palace was nice enough. Being on Charlie's payroll always got him the best, and he deserved the best.

Stretching out his arms and neck, he thought about his next move. He'd sent a note to the kid. The question was, Would he show up?

Sometimes these rich and spoiled little brats didn't understand who they'd tangled with. But it was Greg's job to show them. It might take a little time to extract what he needed, but he'd get it. He always did. And the kid would learn a lesson.

It was totally up to him whether it would be the hard way or not. Greg wasn't *completely* heartless.

14

Collette sat in church and wondered how she could do something for Matthew when the man clearly didn't need anything. He kept to himself about anything personal, didn't talk a lot, saw to his patients, and spent his free time hiking around or reading books.

Alone.

It was enough to drive her mad, because while she had plenty of ideas of what she'd like from him in the future, she had no clue what to do *for* him now.

After the embarrassing flour-on-the-nose incident, she'd thought maybe it was hopeless until last night at dinner when Tayler struck up a conversation with her. Then they walked together after the meal and got to know each other better. Collette felt that Tayler was a kindred spirit. Collette had shared the story of the flour humiliation, as she had come to call it. Tayler laughed with her but pointed out that at least Matthew *had* noticed her. He'd even spoken to her. Which was a very good start.

So here she sat in church, next to Tayler, trying to figure out what to do for a man who didn't seem to need anything.

If he was so self-sufficient, maybe he didn't want anyone in his life.

The thought made her heart sink and she sighed.

Tayler elbowed her, and Collette turned her attention back to the front. The pastor was about to start.

To her right, she heard a scuffle.

Then Mrs. Johnson's all-too-loud whisper, "If you two can't behave, then I refuse to sit with you." It obviously wasn't the twins giving her fits, so Collette didn't need another guess to figure out who was in the pew with her.

Chuckles echoed throughout the room.

Pastor Wilcox stood at the podium and eyed Mrs. Johnson's pew. "I'll wait until you gentlemen decide."

More chuckles. Especially since everyone knew that one of the men was the pastor's brother.

Collette got up the nerve to glance over there and saw Bertram Wilcox and Daniel Ferguson straighten in their seats and smile at the pastor. Mrs. Johnson sat between them, looking completely and utterly miserable. The poor woman.

The pastor then cleared his throat. "This morning we have the privilege of using our brand-new hymnals. They were donated to the church anonymously, and I have enjoyed perusing the pages. What a wonderful gift for our little church body."

Several *amens* and *thank-you*s were heard throughout the room, and several people clapped.

"This morning, I thought it appropriate to begin our service with a poem I read recently by Rhea F. Miller. It's entitled, 'I'd Rather Have Jesus.' The words brought tears to my eyes the first time I read it.

"I'd rather have Jesus than silver or gold;
I'd rather be His than have riches untold;

181

I'd rather have Jesus than houses or lands;
I'd rather be led by His nail-pierced hand.

"Than to be the king of a vast domain
Or be held in sin's dread sway,
I'd rather have Jesus than anything
This world affords today.

"I'd rather have Jesus than men's applause;
I'd rather be faithful to His dear cause;
I'd rather have Jesus than worldwide fame;
I'd rather be true to His holy name. . . ."

Collette allowed the words to wash over her as the pastor read the rest of the poem.

At this point, she realized the pastor had been correct. She had tears in her eyes and prayed that the longing of her heart would always be for Jesus first.

"Now please turn in your hymnals to Fanny Crosby's hymn 'Give Me Jesus.'"

The pastor led them into the song.

Take the world, but give me Jesus,
All its joys are but a name;
But His love abideth ever,
Through eternal years the same.

Oh, the height and depth of mercy!
Oh, the length and breadth of love!
Oh, the fullness of redemption,
Pledge of endless life above!

After the first verse, Collette wanted to sing this song from the hilltops. She ventured into verse two and sang along with the congregation.

Take the world, but give me Jesus,
Sweetest comfort of my soul;
With my Savior watching o'er me,
I can sing though billows roll.

Oh, the height and depth of mercy!
Oh, the length and breadth of love!
Oh, the fullness of redemption,
Pledge of endless life above!

She felt a tap on her right as the congregation continued. Looking up from the hymnal, she looked into the eyes of none other than Matthew Reilly.

"Excuse me. It's quite full. Might I sit here?"

"But of course." She nudged Tayler to move over so there was room for Matthew. Since there wasn't another hymnal, she offered to share with him.

Matthew's deep bass voice singing out sent shivers down her spine. This must be what heaven was like. To sing praises to their Savior all day long.

Oh, the height and depth of mercy!
Oh, the length and breadth of love!
Oh, the fullness of redemption,
Pledge of endless life above!

As they finished the song, Collette swiped a tear off her cheek. The hymn had moved her beyond words, and she felt refreshed and joyful. Take the world, but give me Jesus! Yes, she would rather have Jesus. More than anything.

Then Matthew moved next to her, and she realized that the man she'd been thinking about more than anything was right beside her.

Her heart felt instantly convicted. All this time, she'd been thinking of Matthew left and right, but if she truly was following Christ, then she would have the attitude of the hymn she'd just sung.

Maybe she needed to spend a little more time in prayer and a little less time obsessing over the good doctor. And she could start right now—by sitting in church and listening to the pastor preach the Word and completely ignoring the fact that the man she was attracted to was sitting with her. On the very same pew. Right. Next. To. Her.

She shook her head and focused her attention forward. *Lord, I need Your assistance here. Help me to pay attention to You rather than the handsome man next to me.*

As the congregation rose for the benediction, Collette let out a slow breath. That hadn't been so hard. And she'd learned a great deal. But now that the service was ending, she didn't want Matthew to leave. What could she do?

Pastor Wilcox said an amen, and then Tayler saved the day. "Dr. Reilly, it's so good to see you again." She spoke around Collette, successfully sandwiching her between Matthew and herself.

Matthew smiled at them both. "And you as well. How's the new job coming?"

"Quite well, thank you." Tayler laughed. "I'll try to stop sending you so many patients."

The handsome doctor shook his head. "If the people would simply read the instructions about sensible footwear and appropriate clothing, I'm sure we would avoid many of the mishaps."

"Indeed."

Collette tried to think of something to add to the conversation, but it was as if her mind was void of thoughts.

"Will you be joining us for lunch today at the hotel? I understand Collette had a hand in the preparations. She has been making some of the most amazing lunches for our picnics, so I'm certain you won't want to miss lunch."

Matthew looked at her. "I've had many of your fine meals, Miss Langelier. They are indeed fabulous, and I wouldn't miss the opportunity for another."

"Thank you, Dr. Reilly." Now what was she supposed to say? Should she mention she was starting to feel a little light-headed? He was a doctor after all.

Tayler jumped in again. "I hear that you have a new building for your home and clinic?"

The handsome doctor gave a smile. "Well, yes, it's new to me, one of the buildings they moved in from Chickaloon, but it hasn't been used. So I've been taking the time to get it into shape before I bring patients over there permanently. It's ready, but the windows are so dirty, I can't even open them. At least not yet." He stepped out of their pew and into the aisle. "But it's a much bigger building than the small room I used in the dormitory, so I'm happy they saw fit to allow me to use it."

"I'm sure as more people come to Curry, they will be so grateful for your services." Collette gave him a smile.

Dr. Reilly nodded at them and bid them good-bye.

Tayler leaned in close. "I heard him tell Allan yesterday that he was going to hike this afternoon."

Exactly the opportunity she needed to serve the man she admired. An idea took root. "And you think that would be a good opportunity to clean some windows, yes?"

Tayler nodded.

Collette hugged her friend. "That is the perfect idea!"

15

ayler held Collette's hand as they sat in the new clinic office. Dr. Reilly began stitching Collette's other hand and she winced.

Why did she ever tell Collette about Matthew's hiking plans? Maybe she was trying to help her friend, but the results had been a disaster.

A broken window and Collette's cut hand.

The dirty windows were painted closed and covered in soot from the trains. No wonder the doctor hadn't messed with them yet. The inside of the clinic was pristine—evidence of his diligent work—but he was probably waiting for someone to help get the windows open before he tackled the project.

Which should have been what Tayler and Collette had done.

Dr. Reilly tugged on another stitch. "I'm sorry, I'm all out of my numbing powder. I don't want to hurt you, Miss Langelier."

"*Merci*, I am fine. And please, you can call me Collette." She sniffed and turned her face toward Tayler.

Tayler watched her friend's eyes glisten with tears. Getting stitches wasn't a pleasant experience. Collette was such a lovely and dainty little thing. When they'd both pushed on a window to try to get it open, it hadn't ended well, and the sweet girl had almost fainted from all the blood gushing from her hand.

Dr. Reilly finished the stitching and wrapped a bandage around it. "You must keep it clean and covered if you work in the kitchen. Perhaps you could wear a glove of some sort? That would be best." He put away the supplies. "The pain will probably persist for a few days, so no heavy use of that hand. Mrs. Johnson will have to keep an eye on it for me." His look toward Collette was tender, but she probably didn't notice, as she seemed so embarrassed by the whole thing.

Collette nodded.

The doctor continued, "You know, perhaps you should let me check it every day after work. To make sure there isn't any infection and that it is healing properly."

"If you think that's best. I will come." Her head drooped a little.

"Exactly how did this happen?" Dr. Reilly crossed his arms over his chest.

Collette looked to Tayler and then back to the doctor. "I heard you mention that your windows were dirty, and I just thought it would be a kindness to you to clean them."

"And you ran into the same problem I did—the windows are all stuck."

Collette nodded. "I am sorry to cause you more work, Dr. Reilly. You probably didn't want to be disturbed on your hike, especially to come back and stitch up my hand. And now you have a broken window to contend with." Tears trickled down her face.

"It's all right, Collette. And please, call me Matthew." He gave her a smile. "But perhaps you should stick to the kitchen from now on, since that is where you excel."

Collette stood and nodded again. "Thank you, Matthew." She wiped her cheeks with her uninjured hand.

Poor Collette, she'd tried to do something nice for the man, and it had ended in disaster.

They left the clinic, and Tayler put an arm around her friend's waist. "Does it hurt?"

"*Oui.* More than I can describe in words." She shook her head. "Tayler, why do I get myself into these things? I didn't even get to accomplish what we set out to do. In fact, I didn't help him in any way, just caused him more work."

"That may be true"—Tayler leaned in close—"but look on the bright side. Now you have a reason to go see him every day."

Collette giggled. "*Oui.* That is true. Thank you, Tayler. For being my friend."

$$\bullet\bullet\bullet\bullet\bullet$$

Collette's words had touched Tayler's heart in an unexpected way. For the first time, she had friends. Real friends. Not social acquaintances, or peers, or co-workers. But friends. After spending some time with Collette and Mrs. Johnson—who fussed over her young charge—Tayler wanted some time to think, so she decided to take a walk down by the river. It was a beautiful day and the lupine were beginning to bloom. The velvety blossoms had just started opening. In the coming weeks, she imagined the beauty she would behold in this field of periwinkle. As she walked past the end of town, she followed a path by the railroad tracks. The peace and quiet around her soothed her weary soul. It had been two months since she left her home under circumstances that were not the best. In time, she would need to mend things with her mother, but this separation had been good for Tayler.

In Denver, she'd grown up with the same girls, but they didn't share any interests at all. Most of them were boy crazy when they were younger and only cared about catching the richest one. Then at Yellowstone, there weren't many women employees.

And she rarely saw any of them, since her job kept her extremely busy during the summer season.

But now, things were different. Coming to Curry had been a fresh start. There were no high-society expectations of her here—in fact, no one knew she came from a wealthy family. And the more she got to know people, the more she realized she could be a part of the group, no matter what. Just look at the Brennans. They owned a very successful business in Seattle that was known nationwide. Then there was Collette. Her friend had shared in confidence about her background as well. She had a substantial inheritance but chose to work in the kitchen with Mrs. Johnson. It was unheard of.

The only thing she could attribute to all this was the fact that each one of them had God as the center of their lives. Not money. Not wealth. And they were happy and content right where God had them.

That was what Tayler wanted. But when she thought of how she'd run away from her problem, guilt threatened to overwhelm her. Then there was Joshua. What had happened to her beloved sibling?

One thing was certain. She'd really have to pray about how to deal with the situation at home. Maybe Pastor Wilcox could give her some sound advice once she knew him a little better.

Her heart constricted a bit. It would be nice to be loved for who she really was—just Tayler. The longer she spent with these people in Curry, the more she longed for a loving relationship like Cassidy and Allan had. Their marriage had been an inspiration and encouragement to her. And a reminder that she didn't want to settle for an arranged marriage with an unfaithful husband.

A tall figure approached her from down the tracks. Her heart did a little jump as she recognized Thomas. His long legs ate up the distance between them.

"Good afternoon, Tayler." He tipped his hat at her and gave her a smile.

"Hello." She noticed a string of fish in his left hand. "Looks like you have had a very productive fishing trip."

"That I have." He looked down and then back at her. "Would you perhaps like to try your hand at it for a bit? I've still got plenty of bait." He smiled and lifted an eyebrow.

"Oh, my goodness, I would love to!"

His grin widened. "Why don't we go back to Deadhorse Creek where some of the others are fishing? We could probably catch a few and then be close enough to make it back for dinner."

"Couldn't we just fish right here?"

He grimaced. "That's not a good idea. I wouldn't want your reputation to be at risk." His cheeks turned pink.

Tayler felt herself warm on the inside. He was being cautious, and that made her feel cared for and protected. She hadn't even thought about the fact that they were out here alone. But he had. Her respect for him rose. "Thank you. Lead the way." They walked back toward the hotel and made it to the creek in just a few minutes.

"John tells me you are quite good at fishing . . . so how would you like to make it a bit of a competition?" He squinted at her. "Let's say whoever loses has to wash dishes at the campsite when we take the group up to Curry Ridge?"

She stuck out her hand. "Deal." It was a no-brainer. She could beat him at fishing. She hoped. Besides, she'd always won out and made the boys wash dishes on camping trips. She couldn't lose now. She hated washing dishes.

After they shook on it, she rubbed her hands together. "So what are the rules?"

"Easy." He handed her a pole. "Whoever catches the most fish in the next thirty minutes wins. And we have to be fishing

190

in the same area. No cheating." He walked up the creek a bit. "This looks like a good place."

Tayler smiled. She could see the fish in the water. This would be an easy win. "Okay, when do we start?"

"Do you need help getting the bait on the hook?" Thomas's expression told her he was teasing her.

"No. Do *you*?" It was fun to banter with him.

"Now that you mention it"—he held out his hook—"I really don't like to touch—"

"Oh, stop." Laughter bubbled up and spilled out. "Ready, set . . . go!" She cast her bait into the stream. Within seconds, she had a fish on the line. She jerked the pole just a tad and set the hook. As she reeled it in, she gave Thomas a smug smile. "That's one for me."

Thomas caught one in a matter of seconds after that and the game was on. "So . . . what's your favorite thing to do?"

"Pretty much anything outdoors." She cast her line out again. "Hiking, fishing, exploring, mountain climbing . . . I love all of it. But I also love to sketch and paint."

"That sounds like me. I hadn't expected this would become a love of mine until John took me under his wing." He paused and looked down at the water. "I didn't know you were an artist. Would you let me see some of your work sometime?"

"Of course." His interest seemed sincere. "What did you do before that?"

"I was the lowest of the low men on the totem pole in the kitchen." He laughed. "I took scraps out to animals, fetched things, and generally ran up and down the stairs a lot. Mrs. Johnson wouldn't let me do much else. I think I gave her patience a good testing when I was younger."

"And you've been at the Curry Hotel all this time?"

"Yep. Since it opened in 1923. Of course, I went off to college in Fairbanks, but returned here on holidays and for the summer seasons." He reeled in another fish. "Two for me! So how about you? What did you do before Yellowstone?"

"Well, I spent my growing-up years in Colorado climbing mountains, fishing, and doing camping expeditions with my father and brother."

"Do you still take trips with them?"

"My dad died last year. And I don't see my brother much anymore." It sounded so pathetic and sad, but the words were out before Tayler could get them back.

"I'm so sorry." Thomas watched the water for a few moments. "I never knew my parents. I was raised in an orphanage by missionaries, and when they decided they couldn't afford to feed and clothe me anymore, I was out on my own."

Tayler reeled in another fish and looked at him. "I had no idea."

"It's okay. I'm not embarrassed by it. At least not anymore." He shot her a grin. "I guess that's two for you. We're tied."

Tayler took her fish off the hook and baited the hook once more. She sneaked a glance at Thomas. Maybe she had misjudged him in more ways than one. Granted, their first meeting hadn't been stellar. And their second and third hadn't been glorious either . . . but now she was seeing a totally different man. Kind of like the one Cassidy had described to her.

She put her line out in the water again and a fish hit it almost immediately. Laughing as she reeled in another, she glanced at Thomas. "Look who's got three."

He moaned. "I do *not* want to do dishes. Here fishy, fishy." He whistled at the water.

Tayler laughed at his antics, and it made her feel joyful. Something she hadn't felt in a long time. The simplicity of life here really did suit her. She turned back to him as she baited her hook again. "I don't think they come when you call them."

"Hey, it's worth a try." The smile he gave her warmed her all the way to her toes.

The air around her suddenly felt sucked away and then pushed at her face as a rush of wings bombarded her ears. Ducking out of instinct, Tayler hit the ground while Thomas did the same.

Before she could catch a breath, an eagle swooped down and took off with two of her fish. As it flew away, Tayler couldn't believe she'd been that close to a bald eagle. The majesty of the massive bird enraptured her.

Thomas stood back up and brushed off his pants. "Well, at least you still have one."

She blinked several times. "Do they normally come this close?"

His chuckle broke her fascination of the moment. "Yeah, if you're fishing. Guess we gave him an easy lunch."

Even though she'd never seen an eagle up close before, her mind shot back to the competition. "Let's just remember that I had three. An eagle taking off with two of mine doesn't count."

Thomas's laughter was contagious. "Okay. You had three. But it's not over yet."

Female voices reached her ears. It made Tayler want to groan aloud. It was none other than that group of girls who stuck to each other like glue. They seemed to complain everywhere they went—when they weren't fawning all over the men.

Unfortunately, the group was headed straight for them.

She let out a sigh and breathed a prayer heavenward. Her peaceful afternoon would be gone now.

"Oh, Thomas! Is that you?" The tallest of the group waved to him with her handkerchief in the air.

Clearly it was him. Good grief. Tayler pulled in another fish as the girls approached.

"Oh, look. He's fishing." One of the girls giggled.

How observant. Well, at least they had evidence of brains. Tayler scolded herself for her ugly thoughts. "Four for me." She looked at Thomas and raised her brows.

But his gaze was fixed on the girls. She couldn't tell what his expression meant. But he was staring.

"Good job." His answer seemed absent-minded.

The group of socialites reached them and stood on the other side of the creek. The tallest one had reddish brown hair that was stylishly done in finger waves. She had a hard look about her, but the way she sauntered and stuck out her hip made her look very sultry and seductive. A fact that Tayler didn't like at all. How old were these girls, anyway?

"Thomas," the red-haired girl purred, "I would simply love to learn how to fish. Won't you teach us?"

His expression still indefinable, he pulled in another fish. "It's my day off, ladies."

"Oh, pretty please? My daddy will pay you whatever sum of money you require. We're bored." The girl pouted and lifted her skirts—entirely too high—to walk across the stones in the creek.

The other girls followed their leader.

Thomas looked perplexed.

"Please?" The redhead sidled up next to him and looped her arm through his. "I really want to learn."

The group of other girls was behind Tayler now. "He's so cute," one of them whispered.

"He is. But he's no match for Essie. She always gets what she wants," another voice replied.

Tayler couldn't help rolling her eyes. She glared back at Thomas.

He looked at her and half smiled. But not a mention of how they were fishing together or of their competition. It made her fume. Well, if that was how it was going to be, fine.

194

Tayler reeled in yet another fish. "That's five." She glanced at her watch. "Looks like I win, Mr. Smith." Her tone had turned cold, but she couldn't help it. She handed him the pole and picked up her fish. "I'll let you get to your fishing lesson."

She eyed him one last time and saw a moment of hesitation cross his face. Then Essie had her hand all over his arm again, and he smiled down at the alluring redhead.

Tayler walked away without another word. Seemed like she'd misjudged him *again*.

He *was* just like Emerson.

•••••

MONDAY, JUNE 3—DENVER

Emerson hung up the phone and swiped a hand down his face. Nothing was going as planned.

Absolutely nothing. And Pop wasn't going to help him. No matter how much he begged and pleaded. The old man thought that Emerson needed to earn things the same way he had—the hard way. The only option he offered was to marry Tayler and bring the family fortunes together.

Well, Emerson was trying. But nothing had gone right with that plan either.

One thing after another had proven his luck was bad.

First Tayler had disappeared . . . then he got home and received an ominous note about his debts . . . then this phone call about the airplane manufacturing company he'd bought in Ohio. It had been hit by a tornado and completely wiped out.

Another investment washed down the drain. And he had no money to cover any of it.

His debt soared, and he owed way too much to Charlie the

195

Chisel back in Chicago. If Emerson didn't recoup his losses soon, Charlie would chisel him up too.

The infamous crime boss was known for carving up people and leaving them for dead when they owed him money. And Emerson had gambled too much at Charlie's gambling emporium. His name might have saved him for a while, but not for long.

Especially if that note meant anything.

Charlie had sent someone after him. To get what he owed. And Emerson owed a lot.

Maybe that was his saving grace. If he could find a way to convince Charlie's man that he would get the money, then maybe he'd buy himself enough time. The Chisel surely wouldn't pass up the opportunity to get his money back.

He'd have to make the call and meet to try to hold off the dogs.

Only problem was, he had no leads as to Tayler's whereabouts. Every private investigator he'd hired had come up empty. And Mrs. Hale hadn't heard a word from her daughter.

Well, he'd just have to lie about that . . . for now. It was the only way.

Then he'd have to do everything in his power to find her and bring her home.

It was the only option left. Unless he wanted Charlie the Chisel to take his payments via pounds of flesh. And with as much as Emerson owed to the crime boss, once Charlie took his share, there wouldn't be anything left of Emerson Pruitt.

That wasn't an option.

Tayler was his only hope.

16

The kitchen was always teeming with activity, but today had been crazier than most. Margaret shook her head. This day felt like it would never end. And they still had dinner for the guests and an elaborate birthday party after that.

Mr. Bradley thought it would be wonderful for the hotel to offer such events when a guest asked for one. He thought that they could eventually host weddings and anniversary parties, and the hotel would become a special event location.

As if they needed more business. It felt like they were busting at the seams already.

Cassidy entered the kitchen and put on her apron as she walked. "I'm here."

"Thank goodness. I'm about to lose my mind." Margaret patted the young mother.

"That bad, huh?"

"Oh, I don't even want to talk about it. But do you think there's any chance you could help a little longer tonight? I've got dinner and this birthday party, and we're behind schedule. Collette has done amazing, even with her injured hand, but we'd both need four hands to keep up at this pace."

Cassidy frowned. "I'm not sure. Allan is out on an overnight hunting trip, and I'd have to find someone to watch the boys. But if you give me a minute, I'll run upstairs and see what I can do. Mr. Bradley might be able to lend me one of the hotel maids."

"That would be wonderful."

The rain outside had put several of the kitchen workers in foul moods and too many people underfoot inside the hotel. There had been more requests for hot chocolate, hot tea, and hot cider than they'd ever had before. You'd think these poor people didn't know what cold was like. They should come back in the winter, then they'd find out what cold *really* meant in Alaska.

Margaret shook her head. Some of these tourists were quite silly. But she reckoned that most people wouldn't know what to do with Alaska's weather. It was definitely different from anywhere else in the world.

The soufflés wouldn't make themselves, and since Cassidy was off finding somebody to watch the twins, Margaret might as well get them started.

A scuffle sounded over by the back door. Margaret looked to the ceiling. *Lord, if there's one more problem today, I just might have to throw someone out of my kitchen.*

Susan appeared at her side. "Mrs. Johnson, I tried, but he wouldn't take no for an answer."

"What are you talking about, young lady?"

The young kitchen maid opened her mouth, but big and burly Bertram Wilcox stepped next to her. "Now, don't you go getting your knickers in a knot over this young gal. It's my fault that she's got to deal with your wrath, but I'm tired of being kept away."

"Mr. Wilcox, I do not have time for any shenanigans today. You shouldn't be in the kitchen. Now get."

"No, I won't 'get,' Mrs. Johnson, not just yet. I brought you a present, and I aim to give it to you." The big man laid a box of chocolates on the worktable in front of her. "These are for you."

"I don't care if they are for a queen in Africa, you are interfering in my kitchen." She went back to work and ignored the box.

"You are a handsome woman, Chef Johnson, and I aim to call you Mrs. Wilcox before too long. I've been trying to get to know you for a year now. That's long enough to make a man wait."

Amazingly, the entire kitchen went silent. "You can call me whatever you wish, Mr. Wilcox, but that won't make it so." She cracked eggs into a bowl with one hand and refused to look at the man. "And just because women your age are scarce up here doesn't mean that I'm going to go weak in the knees from flowers and chocolates."

"You may be stubborn, Margaret Johnson, but you've met your match. I'm mad with love for you, and I want you to marry me."

"You're mad with something all right, but it's not love for me, you big oaf. You've been breathing too much locomotive smoke." Shaking her head, she wiped her hands on a towel and pushed Mr. Wilcox out of the kitchen. "Do not come into my kitchen again, or I'll have to call the manager."

As she turned around, she noticed that every member of her staff was standing there gawking at her like she'd come to work in her nightdress or something. "Get back to work, or I'll fire the lot of ya."

Cassidy walked up to her at that moment and grinned. "You know, it wouldn't be so bad to see you married and happy."

"Oh, stop it. I'm perfectly happy without being married." The reply was stiff.

"All right." Cassidy held up her hands in surrender. "But maybe you could be *happier*."

Margaret remembered days that were the happiest. Before

she'd lost her husband and children to the influenza eleven years ago. But being happy also meant risking her heart. When you love, there's a greater risk of being hurt.

She shook away the memories and turned back to the girl who felt like a daughter. "Did you find someone to help with the boys?"

"I did. I asked Thomas first, but Mr. Bradley needed him for something. Then I found Tayler. Even though the rain just stopped, the rest of the hikes for today were canceled. She said she was glad to help, and the boys just love her."

"Perfect, thank you. I need all the help I can get. No one seems to be able to stay focused around here today."

Chef Daniel chose that moment to invade her space. *Dear Lord, another one. Help.*

"What do ya mean, lass, letting that railroad man come into the kitchen? Why, just look at the chaos he's created. The whole place smells of soot now. And I bet he left some dirty footprints too." The man spotted the box of chocolates, and his cheeks turned a shade of red that matched his hair. "Chocolates? He brought you chocolates? Why, that . . ."

Margaret chose to ignore the rampage and walked over to the stairs to head down to the provisions rooms. But Daniel Ferguson bellowed about her gentleman caller and followed. Rolling her eyes, she sighed. *Lord, now would be a good time for that help.*

●●●●●

Tayler walked to the Brennans' little house at four thirty so she'd have plenty of time to get all the instructions for the twins tonight. She had no illusions that babysitting toddler twins would be easy. She needed a plan.

"Tayler, wait up!" That sounded like Cassidy's voice.

She turned and the young mom ran toward her from the hotel, her apron still tied around her waist.

"I saw you walking toward the house and figured I could chat with you while we walk."

"That sounds great."

Cassidy took a few deep breaths. "The boys have been a little out of sorts today since their dad is gone on a hunting trip. The weather was uncooperative earlier, and we couldn't go outside to play, and well, they're rambunctious and active little guys."

Tayler nodded. "Since it's stopped raining, do you mind if we go outside now?"

"There's plenty of daylight, so I'm not worried about that. Just know that it's always a challenge to keep up with two of them if they go in different directions, and it's sure to be muddy. But I'll make sure everything is ready for a bath, and I think it will all be fine." Her friend gave her a smile. "Just remember, I warned you."

"Warned me about what?"

"Twins." Cassidy just laughed. "And their uncanny ability to thwart you."

"Oh boy."

"You'll do fine. They adore you."

As they entered the Brennan home, Tayler heard the incomparable sound of little running feet. The boys charged their mother and she hugged them, and then they spotted Tayler.

"TayTay, TayTay!" they chanted. She hugged the little guys and tickled their bellies.

The older lady behind them came forward. "I best be going, Cassidy. The morning starts early in the laundry. I'll see you tomorrow afternoon."

"Thank you, MaryAnn, for watching them. Tayler will take over now."

"And don't forget me." Thomas appeared out of the kitchen. The boys jumped up and down. "Yay!"

Tayler wasn't sure what to think. "Is Thomas babysitting?"

Cassidy laughed. "Well, I asked him too"—she turned toward him—"but I thought Mr. Bradley needed you for something else."

Thomas shrugged. "We finished early and I thought I'd come over to see if you still needed help." He looked so relaxed with his hands in his pockets and a shock of hair falling over his forehead.

Cassidy glanced between her two guests. "It would definitely be easier with the two of you working together. Like I said, they're a handful."

Tayler stared at Thomas. She hadn't said much to him since their little competition the other day. It still irked her how those girls intruded and he'd allowed it. "I can leave if you think Thomas will be better suited. . . ." She followed Cassidy to the bathroom.

"Heavens no. To be honest, I would be worried about either one of you trying this alone." She pulled out towels and soap. "Here's the things for the boys' baths. They like to take one together, but don't let them play too long, or there will be water covering everything. Their pajamas are under their pillows." She glanced down at her timepiece. "I'd better get going. Mrs. Johnson seemed fit to be tied."

Tayler followed Cassidy back out to the front door, where she passed Thomas on the floor with Jonathon and David climbing all over him. "Maybe we'll go on a walk and expend some of this energy."

"Sounds like a great plan." Cassidy looked back at the boys. "I'll be home as soon as I'm done helping with the birthday party. It should be in plenty of time for me to get them fed and into bed at nine o'clock."

"Don't worry. We've got it all under control." It was easy to say it, but she wasn't sure it was true.

As soon as Cassidy left, Tayler turned back to the living room. The boys saw her and started chanting "TayTay, TayTay" again and tackled her to the floor.

Thomas reached a hand down and helped her up. "I have a feeling we're going to be exhausted after just a few hours of this. I don't know how Cass does it." He grinned at her. "So what's the plan, boss?"

Tayler straightened her blouse. "Well, I thought we could go for a walk and get them to run off some of this energy. Then we could pick salmonberries. Some of them are already ripe."

"I noticed that this afternoon." Thomas shook his head. "It normally starts a couple weeks later than this, but we've had lots of sunshine and warmer temperatures. I'll go see if Cassidy has any small buckets we can use."

Tayler looked down at her charges. "Who wants to go for a walk?"

They giggled and jumped up and down again.

"I'll take that as a yes from both of you." She leaned down and looked at them real close. "Jonathon?"

The little guy nodded.

"So you must be David?"

His twin giggled. "TayTay!" He pointed at her.

"You're right. I'm TayTay." She reached down and took one of each of the boys' hands in her own. "All right, so one of the rules is that we have to hold hands while we're walking so you don't lose me, okay?"

"'Kay."

"We would never want to lose Tayler, now, would we?" Thomas came back with a few small buckets in his hands.

"TayTay!" the boys shouted at Thomas.

"Forgive me, Miss TayTay. It seems I mispronounced your name." Thomas bowed gallantly, which sent the boys into a fit of giggles. He walked up to her and whispered down into her hair. "I kinda like your nickname."

Tayler did too. Especially when Thomas said it.

With him so close, a shiver ran down her spine. Tonight was going to be very interesting.

• • • • •

Cassidy wasn't kidding when she warned that the boys would keep them running. Putting on their rubber boots had been an adventure in and of itself, and then it took them thirty minutes just to get to the ball field because the boys had to investigate every bug, leaf, and rock that crossed their path. Thomas enjoyed watching Tayler trying to keep hold of each of their hands, but she was smart. After the first few minutes, she passed one off to him. That way they each had two hands to keep track of one boy.

Even that had been difficult.

But then they'd spent the better part of an hour chasing the boys in a circle as they ran and ran and ran.

At that point, Tayler announced it would be a good time to pick some berries. That would be a nice treat for them, and then they could walk home and build with blocks and read stories after a bath.

It sounded like the perfect plan.

Thirty minutes later Thomas wondered what would have happened if only the perfect plan had gone the way she intended. Walking back to the Brennan home, Thomas couldn't believe he'd been bested by a two-year-old. He sighed.

Tayler muttered something to herself behind him. He didn't even want to look. He was already in enough trouble with her.

He held Jonathon in his arms because the boy had gotten both of his boots stuck in the mud. He'd finally pulled the shoes loose only after Jonathon had fallen onto his backside and spread mud over his hair and face. Amazing how two seconds was long enough for a little guy to make a huge mess. He hadn't even made it to the salmonberry bushes. By the time he'd rescued the boots *and* the little boy, they were both covered in mud. From head to toe.

Tayler wasn't in much better condition, but she had salmonberry juice mixed in with the mud all over her. Apparently, she'd started off strong with David, and they had been happily picking berries together. Until Thomas showed up with Jonathon. Complete messes.

David—obviously not wanting to be left out of the fun—ran to Jonathon and tackled him in the mud. By the time Tayler had the boys apart again, they were *all* covered in mud, and their berries were squished. All of them except the ones the boys managed to eat along with a little of the mud.

So now here they were, traipsing back to the Brennan house for all to see, each of them carrying a toddler, and each of them covered in mud and berries.

Thomas attempted to hold his head high, even though there were plenty of guests outside tonight since the weather had finally broken. His only hope was that no one would recognize them.

"If you would have just listened to me, this wouldn't have happened," Tayler hissed from behind him.

"Exactly how could I have kept this little guy from getting stuck in the mud?" Thomas shook his head.

Tayler walked up beside him. "Need I remind you that I warned you to stay on the path?"

Oh, that. "Well, yes, I see how that was a mistake on my part.

But the flowers *were* pretty, and Jonathon wanted to see them." Thomas tried to lighten the mood. Maybe if he could make her laugh, things would be better. "As a graduate of botany, I would think you would want to encourage that in the little guy."

"I can't believe you're blaming the two-year-old. What is Cassidy going to say? We've made a mess, and not just of her children but of ourselves. How are we going to get cleaned up and not drag all of this through their home?"

Thomas thought about that predicament. Tayler was right. This was going to be a nightmare to clean up. And not just the mess. She'd probably never forgive him.

17

The little white church sat in the midst of the hustle and bustle of Curry. As Tayler walked to the building, she soaked in the beauty of the mountains rising around her. Covered in lush green grasses with carpets of purple, blue, pink, and white wild flowers, this place was a dream come true. Everything she'd discovered so far had been enchanting.

Except maybe for Thomas.

Well, maybe he *was* enchanting—with his sweet smile—but their situation was *not*. Why was it that everything ended in a mess between the two of them? It was too simple to say that they'd had a rocky start. The thought of working closely with him excited her and then also made her stomach churn. She'd never dealt with this before. But she felt bad for how she'd treated Thomas. None of her reactions to him of late had been very nice. What was that all about? He'd really put forth an effort to be friends, and she kept shutting the door in his face.

The real crux of the matter? She'd been hurt. By a man. But not all men were like that, were they? Allan wasn't that way. Neither was John. So why was she giving Thomas such a hard time?

207

Then there was the guilt she felt about leaving things estranged with her mother. And she felt abandoned by her brother. The more she thought about it all, the more she realized it was just one big pity party for Tayler.

Thoughts of Joshua made her heart ache. They'd always been so close. Certainly she could have dealt with Dad's death and Mother's demand for control a bit better if only she'd had her brother. But he'd left her to fend for herself. Frustration fought with her sadness and won out. If Joshua were here, she'd give him a stern talking-to.

But he wasn't. And it hurt. Plain and simple.

So many reasons why she wanted to speak to the pastor. She let out a sigh.

"Something bothering you, Tayler?" Mrs. Johnson's gruff voice broke the silence.

Tayler looked to her side and saw the head chef walking next to her. "You caught me deep in thought. But in answer to your question, yes, a number of things are bothering me. Mainly my own actions with certain people. I need to work on that so much."

"Dearie, if you only knew how I treated people before God and I had a come-together meeting. You think I'm harsh now? You should've known me a few years ago. It's a good thing God never gives up on us."

The thought made Tayler smile. "I'm so thankful for that. But why can't I handle things correctly the first time?" She sighed. "You'd think as an adult I would be better at this and would know how to control my tongue."

Mrs. Johnson laughed. "Oh, child, if only it were that easy. I outnumber your years—probably even double them—and I've still got a long way to go. But you know what? Cassidy shared a Scripture with me last year that has become my favorite verse." The older woman smiled.

"Would you mind sharing it with me?"

"Certainly. It's found in the book of Philippians, chapter one. 'Being confident of this very thing, that he which hath begun a good work in you will perform it until the day of Jesus Christ.'" Mrs. Johnson nodded emphatically. "It comforts me to know that God isn't finished with me yet, He'll keep working on me until the end. Which doesn't mean I don't need to keep trying, but I need to keep growing and letting Him prune me along the way."

"That's a wonderful verse to remember. Thank you for sharing that." Tayler thought about the older woman next to her. She seemed so rough around the edges—with her gruff and terse ways—and yet it was apparent that she had a heart of gold. "Why are you headed to the church so early this morning?"

Mrs. Johnson chuckled. "You'll probably laugh, but I don't care." She looked around her as if to make certain no one was listening. "I need to beat those two men to the church. Cassidy said she'd bring the twins early so I don't have to sit with two buzzards fighting over their last meal."

The picture the woman painted did make Tayler laugh. She put a hand to her mouth. "Oh my, that is definitely an interesting way to put it."

"Sorry to be so blunt, but that's how they make me feel."

"Do you truly not care for either one of them?"

"Bother, I don't know. Neither one of them has given me a chance to find out because they're always aggravating me. I'm always breaking up fights between them or telling them to get out of my kitchen or worse yet having to get them to behave themselves in church."

Tayler found herself giggling at that last part. "Well, why don't I sit with you until Cassidy comes with the boys? I'll be your bodyguard."

Mrs. Johnson laughed along with her. "That would be a sight—you up against those two large men. How tall are you anyway?"

Tayler stopped and put her hands on her hips, chin in the air. "I'm over five feet. I know that. And with my shoes, a couple inches taller."

Chef Johnson patted her arm. "You do beat all, Tayler. And I mean that as a compliment. I used to say that to Cassidy all the time." Her smile got brighter. "But you remind me of myself—stubborn, self-sufficient, short, and . . . well . . ." She looked her up and down and put her hands on her hips.

Tayler had to hold back the tears she started laughing so hard. "I believe 'well-endowed' is the word you're looking for. My mother used to use it all the time and I hated it. When all the styles were calling for flat-chested figures with the drop waists and tall, willowy lines. Yeah, that wouldn't work for me."

"Don't you worry one bit about that. You look absolutely lovely just *exactly* the way you are. Most women would pay any amount to have your figure. Besides, the men I know don't want a bunch of stick women wandering around."

"Thank you, Mrs. Johnson." Tayler grinned. "You've made this morning very cheery for me." She squinted her eyes as she thought of something. "But you mentioned that you had to tell *them* to get out of your kitchen. Doesn't Chef Daniel *work* in the kitchen?"

"Of course. I didn't mean him." She put her lips together in a fine line and waved off Tayler's question as they entered the little church.

Ah, so that was it. "So maybe you've just answered your conundrum for yourself."

"What on earth do you mean, child?"

"Maybe there *is* a certain man you do like attention from—

you just haven't admitted it." Tayler quirked an eyebrow and hoped the woman wouldn't kick her out of church for her words.

"Gracious, young lady, I . . . I . . ." The woman's words dropped off as the pastor approached them.

"Good morning, ladies. It's a beautiful day to worship the Lord, isn't it?"

"Yes, sir. It certainly is." Mrs. Johnson's face was a little red from Tayler putting her on the spot, and it made Tayler feel instantly sorry.

They shuffled into the pew together. Tayler had left early to speak to the pastor, but this probably wasn't the time. She didn't want to abandon Mrs. Johnson.

"Gammamag! TayTay!" The voices signaled the entrance of Cassidy and her crew.

Two little guys ran to their pew and gave out hugs and slobbery kisses to them both. Mrs. Johnson's laughter filled the air, and then she placed one boy on each side of her.

She gave Tayler a wink. "Now, this is how I want to sit in church."

Tayler stood and went to the next pew as Cassidy and Allan filled up the pew with Mrs. Johnson. "I'll just sit here so you have enough room."

"TayTay!" David clapped his hands.

"I'll be right here, David." She gave the boy a smile.

"Ahem."

She turned to see Thomas, holding his hat and his Bible in his hands.

"Would you mind if I sit with you?"

His words caught her off guard. "Not at all." Embarrassment flooded her as she realized how she'd treated Thomas this week, and yet he still treated her kindly. She scooted over.

Someone tapped her on the shoulder from behind.

She looked over her shoulder and saw Allan leaning toward them.

"I just want you to know that the boys can't wait for the next time the two of you babysit." Allan chuckled.

Thomas groaned next to her. "I was still finding mud in my hair and ears the next day. Are you sure you want me to watch your boys?"

It made Tayler laugh. Even after the scolding she'd given him, he was still able to laugh over the whole situation. The past few days had been tense, but mainly because she didn't know how to let Thomas know she'd gotten over her fury with him. Maybe he hadn't listened to her, but she'd been far too angry. The whole thing had been a disaster when all she wanted to do was give Cassidy a good impression. Once again, she'd been trying to prove herself capable.

"We'd love for you to watch the boys. But next time do it when I can get some quiet time with my wife. Not while I'm gone on a hunting trip. Even a simple walk together where we can hear ourselves would be wonderful. And at that point, I don't care how muddy you get."

Tayler watched as Cassidy beamed up at her husband. Obviously in love with him, she looked so content and peaceful. Something Tayler longed for.

She turned back to the front and looked at Thomas. He gave her a slight smile.

"I'm sorry—"

"I'm sorry—" The apologies came in unison.

He held up a hand. "Why don't you go first?"

Tayler shook her head and smiled. "I'm sorry for being so angry with you the other day. And I was too bossy as well. I'm sure I would have had the same problem had our roles been reversed."

"Well, there's no doubt I should have listened to you. I'm sorry I didn't." Thomas stuck out his hand. "Why don't we start again?"

She covered a laugh and took his hand. "How many times are we going to need to start over?" The pews filled up quickly around them.

"As many times as it takes for us to get it right." He shook her hand and nodded.

She opened her mouth to respond but closed it again when Pastor Wilcox walked to the pulpit.

The service started and Tayler tried to put forth all her attention. She desperately needed guidance in so many areas of her life.

It had thrilled her to find out that the hotel didn't offer any guest services during church times. That way, everyone had the chance to attend and worship. It was encouraging and none of the staff felt guilty for neglecting their duties.

Tayler had to work at focusing while they stood together and Thomas shared a hymnal with her. There was something thrilling about his nearness that she couldn't quite put into words. What did it all mean? After her years of engagement to Emerson—that all seemed false—she didn't know what to think. She'd been terribly hurt by him, but had she ever truly *loved* him?

The more she thought about it, the more she realized she hadn't. What started as a young girl's crush never blossomed into anything real.

As the voices of the congregation rose in worship, her heart felt lighter.

A rush of relief flooded her. The guilt she'd poured onto herself all these years was for naught. Why had she tortured herself?

She sighed as the answer washed over her. Because she was loyal. She'd always been that way. And loyalty wasn't a bad thing, but maybe God wanted to teach her something through all this. She just wished He would hurry up and tell her what it was.

They sat as Pastor Wilcox asked them to open their Bibles.

"As you all know, we've been in the book of Matthew, and today we are going to attempt to finish chapter five. There's such wonderful truth in every passage of Scripture, so I urge you all to continue studying throughout the week. Let's pick up in verse twenty-three:

> "Therefore if thou bring thy gift to the altar, and there rememberest that thy brother hath ought against thee; leave there thy gift before the altar, and go thy way; first be reconciled to thy brother, and then come and offer thy gift. Agree with thine adversary quickly, whiles thou art in the way with him; lest at any time the adversary deliver thee to the judge, and the judge deliver thee to the officer, and thou be cast into prison.

"Friends, this is something we ignore all too often. We carry grudges, we keep the truth from people, and we don't forgive. And it's got to stop right now. Especially in a community as tight-knit and close as we are, it grieves me to hear of the squabbles and fights that are brought to my attention."

Pastor Wilcox paused as a hush fell over the room.

Tayler felt her heart pounding in her ears. Thank goodness she'd resolved things with Thomas this morning. But she'd held a grudge against Emerson . . . and struggled to forgive him. Same with Mother. Except it was even worse—she hadn't told Mother the truth.

Lord, what do I need to do to make this right?

Pastor Wilcox continued with his passionate plea for them

214

to reconcile with their brothers, sisters, and neighbors. But all Tayler could think of was everyone she'd left behind in Colorado and the wrong she'd done them.

The more she thought about it, the more she realized there could be some serious repercussions. And the fact that if she told the truth and stopped hiding, Emerson would know where she was.

Could she deal with that?

She argued with herself for a while. A little more time to herself would be really great. And what was she hurting by keeping her whereabouts to herself for a while longer?

But then she thought of how quickly she'd lost her father. What if something happened to Mother or to Joshua and they didn't know how to reach her? What if something happened to *her*? Her family would be devastated.

Tayler turned back to the passage in the fifth chapter of Matthew and realized that God was asking her to be reconciled to her family. Not next month, or next week, but now. She needed to do it before she did anything else.

Closing her eyes, she prayed for the Lord to guide her. She needed forgiveness, and she needed healing. More than anything, she needed strength to do what was to come.

When she opened her eyes, she realized she had missed a good portion of the sermon. The pastor was already down to verse forty-three.

> "Ye have heard that it hath been said, Thou shalt love thy neighbour, and hate thine enemy. But I say unto you, Love your enemies, bless them that curse you, do good to them that hate you, and pray for them which despitefully use you, and persecute you; That ye may be the children of your Father which is in heaven: for he maketh his sun to rise on the evil and on the good, and sendeth

rain on the just and on the unjust. For if ye love them which love you, what reward have ye? do not even the publicans the same?"

More convicting thoughts churned in her gut. Thoughts of the young socialite group who were never positive. She'd looked down upon them for their behavior just as much as they looked down on others for their attire or station.

If Tayler wanted to truly live like Christ, she'd need to take captive those thoughts. Perhaps those young women didn't know God. Perhaps Tayler could be a light to them.

Thomas shifted next to her.

And then there was *him*. Her feelings had flipped about the handsome guide several times—almost as if she rode a giant pendulum. That wasn't fair to him. She was all judgment one minute and guilty conviction the next.

Maybe after she took care of her problem with her family, she should talk more to Thomas as well. After all, she wanted Thomas to give her a chance. Shouldn't she do the same for him?

Everyone stood and Tayler realized she'd missed the end of the sermon. *Lord, help me to be a better steward and pay attention next week.*

But she'd been so convicted this morning. That was good, right? God had been working in her. The verse Mrs. Johnson had shared with her earlier popped back to her mind. *Being confident of this very thing, that he which hath begun a good work in you will perform it until the day of Jesus Christ.* There was hope for her. God wasn't finished with her yet.

The pastor dismissed everyone, and Tayler couldn't get back to the hotel fast enough. She excused herself from Thomas and told him there was something she simply must do. She'd have to apologize for running out later, but her heart was convicted, and she couldn't wait any longer for relief.

As she ran to the hotel, she pondered what she would say. An apology and the truth seemed to be the best ideas.

Racing her way across the lobby, she headed straight for Mr. Bradley's office. The manager wasn't back from church yet, so she sat in a chair and waited.

"Miss Hale." The manager sounded surprised as he walked in. "I wasn't expecting to see you here."

She stood. "Mr. Bradley, I'm sorry to intrude, but I have something very important I need to do. Could I perhaps make a call on the telephone?"

He removed his hat and rubbed his head. "If you're needing to call anywhere other than Anchorage or Seward, I'm afraid it won't work. But I can make sure a telegram gets out for you right now if it's urgent."

A telegram was better than nothing, and it was definitely faster than a letter. She took the slip of paper the manager handed to her and began writing in pencil.

I am safe and well (stop)Working in Curry, Alaska (stop)
Will write soon (stop)Please forgive me for how I left (stop)
I love you (stop)
    Tayler

18

Thomas walked next to Mrs. Johnson as she held the twins' hands and they stepped out of the church. It was such a beautiful day. He'd hoped to ask Tayler for a walk, but something had upset her in church and she'd run off. Maybe he could ask Mrs. Johnson's advice. She was like a mother to him.

"Mrs. Johnson, do you have a minute?"

She turned and smiled at him. "Of course. I will always have time for you, Thomas. What's on your mind?"

"I'm afraid I've not handled a situation very well and I need a woman's advice."

Her eyebrows shot up. "Could this be about a girl?"

"Yes." He smiled at her.

"Perhaps the girl you sat with this morning?"

He felt the heat rise up his neck. "You know me too well."

They started walking back toward the hotel at a slow pace so the boys could keep up.

"So are you going to make me guess?" she prodded.

Thomas opened his mouth, but Bertram Wilcox walked up and blocked their path. "Mrs. Johnson, might I walk you back to the hotel?"

"It's a free country, Mr. Wilcox. You can walk wherever you like."

The poor man held his hat in his hands. "What I meant was, I was hoping we could take a walk and talk to one another. Just you and me . . . as we walk . . . back to the hotel." His face turned red, and Thomas wanted to take pity on him as he stumbled over his words.

"Well, if we're walking in the same direction and you happen to be near, then, of course, we can have a discussion. That's what normal folks do. But I was already having a discussion with Thomas." Mrs. Johnson wasn't going to make this easy for anyone.

Thomas held up his hands and backed away a step. "Don't mind me. We can chat later." Maybe he should just try to have a conversation with Tayler, if he could do that without ruining everything. Better yet, maybe he should just talk to the pastor again.

Mrs. Johnson gave Thomas a look, and he tried not to laugh. She took a few steps forward with the boys, making Mr. Wilcox walk backward. He asked if they had to go straight back to the hotel.

"Where else would we go?" Mrs. Johnson shook her head.

Thomas stayed in his spot. Over the years, he'd faced plenty of Mrs. Johnson's wrath. He did *not* want to get in the middle of this.

Cassidy joined Thomas and whispered to him, "I'd better go retrieve the boys. I'll be back."

He did his best to cover his mirth. Mrs. Johnson would not appreciate his laughing. But the expression on her face when Cassidy took the twins from her and she was left alone with her suitor! Heavens, if only he had a camera to take a picture of that.

Cassidy stepped back toward Thomas with her sons and Allan followed.

Thomas wanted to ask Cassidy what this was all about, but

Chef Daniel walked up to the other chef and her admirer and started walking on the other side of Mrs. Johnson.

Allan chuckled. "Well, that's one way to keep an eye on the competition."

They watched as the trio walked back to the hotel, and Thomas couldn't believe it. "Do those two men have any idea what they're getting into?"

Cassidy patted him on the arm. "Bertram and Daniel have both been sweet on Margaret all winter long. Daniel probably a good deal longer than that. She's done a good job avoiding it, but apparently, neither one of those men is willing to be silent any longer."

"You think either one of them has a chance?" Thomas shook his head. Mrs. Johnson was very dear to him, but she was a wounded soul. Ever since her husband died, a little piece of her had died as well. It was almost her undoing when the influenza struck Curry a few years back while Cassidy was pregnant with the twins. But anyone who knew Mrs. Johnson knew that behind her hard shell was an amazing woman. She was tough to crack, however, and not a lot of people had the opportunity to see her heart.

"Oh, I'm pretty sure that one of them is bound to win her over."

Allan grunted. "You really think so?"

"I'm pretty positive." A nod accompanied Cassidy's grin.

Thomas elbowed Allan. "So which one do you think it will be?"

"My money is on the chef." Allan shrugged. "He has the opportunity to spend more time with her."

Putting a hand to his chin, Thomas thought about that. "I think you're right. Although, a few years ago, I thought those two were going to kill each other."

"Goodness, I'm still amazed anyone survived that summer."

Allan put an arm around his wife's shoulders. But then had to lean down and pull dirt out of Jonathon's hand as it was headed to his mouth.

"Let's not eat dirt, all right?" Cassidy rolled her eyes. "I think we should get these two home and feed them. Would you like to join us for dinner, Thomas? It's nothing fancy, just roast beef sandwiches." Most of the time the staff all ate together, but the Brennans often hosted Sunday dinner at their home.

"Not this time. I'd like to speak to the pastor, but thanks." He waved to his friends as they headed back home and he returned to the church.

A few people still milled about outside, but Pastor Wilcox was heading back into the building.

Thomas caught up with him on the steps. "Do you have a minute to talk?"

"Of course, Thomas. Come on in."

The pastor closed the door behind them, and Thomas strode to the front, sending a prayer heavenward.

"What's bothering you, son? Still feeling out of sorts?" The pastor sat on the front pew.

Thomas sat as well and faced the pastor they were fortunate enough to have during the tourist season. Curry had gone too long without a church. "I've battled a lot of emotions these past few weeks. A lot of doubts and wondering where my place is in all this."

The pastor nodded.

"I've put more time into my study of the Bible and prayer and have spent a lot of time with the Lord in the evenings, but there's one question that keeps plaguing me. Where do I belong?"

"You don't feel that you belong here?"

Thomas thought about that long and hard. "I do and I don't. I *want* to belong here. This has been the only real home I've

ever known. But I see Allan and Cassidy's family and get letters from Jean-Michel and Katherine and their family, and I
see all the families that come through here. Good grief, even
Mrs. Johnson has two suitors trying to win her affection right
now." What was he trying to say?

"Ah. I think you just explained what you haven't been able
to put into words."

"What?" He thought through what he'd said and still didn't
follow.

"You want a family of your own. You ache to belong to someone who is just for you."

Thomas blinked. The truth hit him. All his life he'd wanted a
family—and he'd found that at the Curry Hotel. But the pastor
was right . . . in his heart, he longed for love. The husband-
and-wife kind of love.

The pastor chuckled and looked down at the floor for a moment. "Is there anyone special in your life?"

The first person who came to mind was Tayler. Was that what
this was all about? After his youthful crush on Cassidy, he'd
learned to take his time with his feelings. Then when Caroline
came along, he'd fallen for her when it had all been just a game
to her. But Tayler was different. Special. "I can't say that there's
anyone *yet*. Well, at least . . . she's special to me, but she doesn't
know it. And I have no idea where I stand with her."

"But it sounds like you'd *like* there to be something, that
intimate connection that God calls for a man and a woman
to have."

Again, Thomas didn't know what to do with that information.

"There's nothing wrong with you, Thomas. And you're not
doing anything wrong. Keep seeking God, and He will bring
the right person to you." The pastor leaned in again. "I re-

member when I first met my wife. She couldn't stand me, but I was smitten. It took a lot of patience and a lot of seeking God, but eventually He brought our paths together." The older man smiled.

"Thomas, you're a young man who loves the Lord. All this doubt and confusion around you is an attack. If you truly believe that Christ died for you and paid your ransom, then you are whole and complete in Him. You don't need anything else to make you feel complete or to help you feel like you belong. Before you seek out a relationship, I suggest you deal with the doubt in your heart."

He blinked. "Yes, sir."

"Once you can rest in the fact that you are whole and complete in Him, then you'll be ready for a helpmeet. And I'm sure God has just the one picked out for you." The pastor stood and gripped his shoulder. "Why don't you give it some thought and prayer and come see me again this week if you need to talk?"

The man walked away, and Thomas felt more confused than he had before he came in. He thought about all the negative thoughts and emotions he'd had the past few weeks. All the doubts. Was it true? Was it all just an attack? To make him feel worthless and unloved all over again? To make him doubt his identity in Christ?

Shifting his thoughts, he focused on all the wonderful things God had done in his life.

He *did* want to be in Curry.

This was home and he wanted to belong here.

But he also longed to belong to someone special.

Truth be told, he wanted it to be Tayler.

The thought hit him between the eyes. Maybe the pastor was right. He needed to take some time and pray about it and think it through. He couldn't be a part of another disaster like his relationship with Caroline. But if he admitted it, he'd have to say that he'd taken his focus off of God during that time and put it on her. That was the truly disastrous part.

Right now, he needed to focus on the fact that God had him exactly where he was supposed to be. He would rest in that fact and be confident he was complete in Christ.

And if God saw fit to give him the blessing of a helpmeet like Tayler, he would rejoice and shout it from the mountaintops.

•••••

MONDAY, JUNE 17

The day was perfect . . . crisp, cool air that was refreshing for this time in June, a brilliant blue sky, and a camping trip.

Thomas was ready for a week up on Curry Ridge. Especially since Tayler was along.

They'd had some time to talk this past week. Not of anything important, but it made him feel like their friendship had at least grown. And they worked together quite well in a comfortable, easy manner. She'd proven she wasn't like Caroline—Tayler hadn't lied about her experience—and she was as adept as he or Allan. It was impressive.

With all their duties of leading the expedition, he doubted he would have much time to speak with her alone, but at least he would get to see her a lot this week—to soak in her presence and, with God's help, show her who *he* really was. He so wanted to be a man devoted to God. Complete in Him and Him alone.

So far, the trip had gone as planned. Sixteen guests had set out with them. Three families—which included the four girls who wouldn't seem to leave him alone—and three married couples. Tayler led the hike with the families behind her, the couples following, then Thomas and their assistants bringing up the rear.

Thankfully, John had found four young Athabaskan men who wanted to work for the Curry. On John's recommendation, Mr. Bradley hired them on immediately. That meant Thomas could let them carry the majority of the loads so he was available to help the guests and to lead, answer questions, and do anything else the group needed from him.

He remembered the days when he had been the young guy in training. He'd loved every minute of the trips, no matter how strenuous they were. There was always something exciting to see and interesting to learn. Alaska was unlike any other place. And seeing it through the visitors' eyes helped him to appreciate the beauty he took for granted.

Before they'd set out, there'd been quite an upheaval about which girl would get to follow Thomas. He'd had to quickly nip that in the bud and insist that none of them would, as he would be taking up the rear. Thankfully, the girls' fathers had been eager to step in and keep the pouting to a minimum. But it didn't bode well for the rest of the week. Maybe he and Tayler needed to sit down tonight and discuss how they were going to handle these types of conflicts.

Shaking his head, Thomas determined to think positive. This was the day the Lord had made, and he *would* rejoice in it. He was thankful for everything he had. A wonderful job, the opportunity to serve the Lord in the most beautiful place on the planet, and his Curry family.

It seemed to take forever to reach the top of Curry Ridge, but once they did, several gasps were heard throughout the group. Everyone set down their packs so they could take in the view. The guests stood in awe.

Denali stood tall and fierce in the distance. Covered year-round in snow, today was a rare day when the High One allowed people to see him in his glory. A thin halo of clouds wrapped around his crown. The contrast of the massive mountain against the brilliant blue of the sky was glorious.

The air was still as everyone took in the grandeur before them. Lush valleys lay below them, covered in grasses of varying shades of green, the deep, almost black color of the spruce, and a riot of colorful wild flowers. Rivers snaked their way through the landscape like pathways leading to the great mountain. Thomas spotted the area where the Kahiltna Glacier cut its way down the mountain. Was there anywhere on earth that could compare to this? Was this what heaven would be like?

"Mr. Smith"—Mr. Bolans interrupted his thoughts—"I hear you have a hankering to climb the mountain one day." The older man stepped next to him.

"That I do, sir."

The older man just shook his head. "After this climb today, I'm pretty sure I'll forego anything more rigorous." He laughed at himself. "How tall is it?"

Thomas laughed along with the gentleman. "Denali is over twenty thousand feet high. The tallest mountain in North America. And yes, this five-mile hike is a bit strenuous in places, but nothing like climbing a glacier-covered mountain. I look forward to the challenge one day."

"I guess we all have to dream big while we're young." Mr. Bolans patted him on the back. "Well, we anticipate a wonderful week up here." He leaned in. "Including the trek back, which I'm assuming will be easier since we're going *down*."

"Yes, sir, and I'm glad, sir. We aim to make it as enjoyable as possible."

Thomas sneaked a glance in Tayler's direction. She stood facing the mountain, her hands on her hips. He wished he could see her face. He bet she shared the same awe he felt every time he got a glimpse of the High One.

Giggles sounded off to his left. He turned and spotted the four girls who were a constant nuisance to him this summer. Bother. He fought the urge to roll his eyes. What could they be up to now?

Still aggravated that they'd interrupted his fishing with Tayler, he'd thought for sure the new naturalist wouldn't speak to him again for weeks. Thankfully, they were past that and on friendlier footing now. But how could he get past all this nonsense with those silly girls?

"Put your focus on the Lord. Keep it there." Pastor Wilcox's words came back to him.

The tug in his heart was to get to know Tayler better. But it seemed like everything else was trying to pull them apart.

Ignoring the younger girls, he didn't know what to do with his thoughts, which volleyed back and forth. If he kept his focus on God, did that mean he had to ignore Tayler? Or did it mean he should feel confident enough to talk to her?

He could have the argument in his mind all day.

Lord, show me what to do. Should I talk to her?

As soon as he'd lifted his heart in prayer, a peace washed over him.

Walking toward Tayler, he smiled. "It's a beautiful sight, isn't it?"

She released a huge sigh. "Yes, and I'm amazed that God has been so gracious to me . . . to allow me to come here and work, and then to see this."

"I agree. The mountain is one of my favorite things about Alaska. So many different views of him. Crazy weather around him. But when you get to see him, it's breathtaking. The entire range is something to behold. Denali, the husband, with his wife and child."

"I find it interesting what I've read about the different names for the mountains. I don't understand why people thought they needed to change them. The native names are so beautiful. And I just adore that the meanings are the High One, the Wife, and the Child. They're so fitting."

He watched her face light up when she talked. He loved her inquisitive mind. Her thirst for knowledge. Even at meals, she grilled John with questions, and he found her more times than he could count studying one of the many books she'd brought with her. Everything from facts on native tribes to plant life, mountain climbing, and survival.

"What?" She tilted her head. "Why are you staring at me like that?" Her eyebrows rose, and she swiped at her face. "Do I have something on me?"

"No, I'm sorry. I was just admiring your hunger to learn. I'm the same way." He turned and gazed back toward the mountains. "Even at college—the place where everyone is supposed to be learning—I got teased for always having my nose in a book."

She took in a big breath and gave his arm a little tap with her hand. "Me too!" She shook her head and smirked. "I was called bookworm way too often."

Something else they had in common. It made his heart sing when she smiled at him. "You'd think that would be an honorable title in school."

"Exactly." She shrugged and sighed, then patted his shoulder. "It's nice to know another book and knowledge lover. Maybe I could show you this new book I've been reading. It's fascinating. About—"

"Thomas!"

Thomas inwardly cringed. He knew that voice. Esmerelda.

"Thomas! I need your help."

His gaze stayed on Tayler, but her expression wilted. *She's been hurt*, a voice seemed to whisper in his heart. Like him.

Thomas hesitated. Maybe that was something else they had in common. Was it possible someone had betrayed Tayler, just as Caroline had betrayed him?

"Thomas! You promised," Esmerelda whined in a voice much more childish than normal.

"You'd better go. You're being summoned by your fan club." Tayler gave him a sad smile, turned, and walked away.

19

Greg DeMarco watched the crew tie up the ship to the dock in Seward. He'd send a telegram to Charlie to let him know he'd made it to Alaska, and then he'd make his way to Curry.

The kid thought he could sneak past him, but it hadn't worked. Hadn't bought him any time either. The boss was even more convinced the kid couldn't follow through with his outrageous claims that he could get his hands on the money he owed.

Charlie had been more than generous. And he wasn't a generous guy.

Greg adjusted his cuffs and pulled out a cigar.

At least up here, it'd be much easier to dispose of a body. No one would ever know.

He couldn't resist the smile that split his lips. But it wouldn't hurt to play with Pruitt for a while. Make him think he had a chance . . .

•••••

Curry

Collette tied her apron around her waist, put the protective glove over her injured hand, and went looking for Chef. She'd gotten here two hours before her shift was to start, and she prayed Mrs. Johnson would accept her reason for being so early. She found the lady in question by the pantry, holding a clipboard. Collette took a deep breath. "Mrs. Johnson?"

The older lady turned, a quizzical look on her face. "Collette, you're here awfully early." There was a question behind her statement.

Collette wrung her hands and sighed. "*Oui.* I'm hoping to achieve your permission for something . . . er . . . special."

One of Chef's eyebrows went up, a sure sign Collette had used an interesting word or phrase. "Does this have anything to do with our fine doctor?"

She nodded. "I want to make a treat for him."

"Do you have anything in mind?"

"He mentioned at dinner the other night that he loved chocolate cake. With an abundance of chocolate icing."

Mrs. Johnson set her clipboard down and chuckled under her breath. "I know just the thing. And if you get started right away, you should be able to finish it before I need you for your other duties."

Relief filled her insides. "So you will allow me?"

"Of course, you silly girl. I aim to see you catch your man." Mrs. Johnson winked, and Collette almost fell over with surprise. "Well, don't just stand there . . . we've got a cake to make!"

Seven hours later, Collette suppressed a yawn. The cake was beautiful and the morning shift had flown by. Now, she only had a brief break to bring Matthew the surprise before she had to return to her afternoon baking duties.

As she walked to his clinic, she prayed that he would be pleased. Her mouth watered just smelling the divine concoction. Mrs. Johnson had insisted they make it seven layers, with a decadent chocolate buttercream between each layer. The heady aroma of deep, dark chocolate made Collette want to eat a piece right now.

The door to the clinic opened and made her jump. Thankfully, the cake didn't fall.

"Why, Miss Collette! How lovely to see you today." Matthew's eyes fell to the chocolate surprise and widened. "Oh, my . . . is that for me?"

"*Oui.*" She curtsied. "I thought you might like a nice treat after all your hard work. Especially after you mended my hand so beautifully."

"Goodness gracious, that smells delicious. I love chocolate."

"I heard you mention that the other night." She couldn't contain her smile.

"Please, come in." He took the cake from her and ushered her in the door. "How's your hand?"

"It feels almost . . . what is the phrase?" She tapped her chin. "Good as new."

"I'm so glad. That was a nasty cut."

Silence stretched between them. What should she do now? "Would you like to try a piece?"

"I thought you'd never ask." He went to another room and came back with two plates and two forks. "Oops, I'd better get a knife to cut it." He disappeared around the corner again.

Collette took the moment to try to calm her breathing. He'd brought two plates! He was going to sit and eat it with her. The thought thrilled her more than she could have imagined.

"Here we are." Matthew gave her a smile. His cheeks turned a bit pink. "I hope it's okay . . . I mean . . . are you able to stay a moment and enjoy this with me?"

"I'd love to. Thank you." If only he knew how she'd been hoping he would invite her.

Matthew cut them two generous slices of the cake. He didn't hesitate to try it, and he closed his eyes with a groan of pleasure. "This is by far the best chocolate cake I've ever tasted."

"*Merci.* I'm so glad you like it."

Matthew gave her a grin before he took another large bite. "I *love* it. Thank you. I don't remember the last time anyone made me something special like this."

His words of gratitude made her heart soar and gave her confidence. "Matthew . . . would you like to . . . perhaps take a walk with me this evening?"

He polished off the rest of his cake and leaned back in his chair. A soft smile spread across his face. "That would be lovely, Collette. Thank you for the suggestion. In fact, I've been wanting to gather some plants that Cassidy told me about. Her father has a vast knowledge of the native growth here and the herbal remedies."

"I would love to help you gather." Trying to remain calm, Collette wanted to run all the way back to the kitchen and hug Mrs. Johnson's neck. It worked! She stood. "I need to get back to the kitchen, but I will meet you after dinner?"

"I will look forward to it for the rest of the day." He stood with a smile and bowed to her in a very courtly manner.

"I will as well."

"Thank you for the cake."

"It was my pleasure." She turned for the door.

"Collette, would you mind asking Cassidy if she can join us tonight? That way she can show us the correct plants."

Her heart sank. So much for a quiet walk alone. Was she really so inept at this? Or was he simply not interested and trying to be polite? Oh well, it didn't matter now. "*Oui.* Of course." She tried to keep the disappointment from her voice.

Next time, she would think twice before she sacrificed her sleep to make a man a cake.

•••••

Wednesday, June 19

The train jostled Emerson around as they headed into the Curry Depot. This trip had not been the most pleasant. He found out quickly that he didn't have sea legs. At all. His stomach could still attest to that fact.

What luck that he'd been at the Hale home about to discuss things with the matriarch—actually, it was just to pick up his money—when a telegram from Tayler arrived.

Apparently, she'd felt guilty about leaving without a word and thought she should let her mother know her whereabouts. Well, that sure played into his hand.

Mrs. Hale wanted her daughter back in Denver and for her wealth to continue to grow. Emerson wanted the same. There were different reasons for each of their wishes, but if bringing Tayler back meant that it achieved both of their goals, then Emerson would gladly do it. Besides, now Mrs. Hale offered to pay all his expenses. So did Pop. That meant there was plenty of extra. He couldn't pass *that* up.

He glanced down at his watch. Perhaps they could catch a train back today. If there even was one. It seemed he had journeyed to the end of the world.

Surely Tayler was ready to listen to reason—she had apologized to her mother, after all, and sent that telegram. It must be a cry for help. She needed rescuing, and he was the man for the job.

If his luck held out, he could be back in Denver and married before the middle of July.

Now *that* would be the answer to all his problems.

•••••

THURSDAY, JUNE 20—CURRY RIDGE

Tayler stood in front of their little group with several samples of Alaskan wild flowers in her hands. Every evening, they'd decided to give some informative lectures for their guests. Thomas handled one evening and she took the next and so forth. He talked about the native culture and survival, while Tayler talked about the flora and fauna. All the guests seemed to really enjoy these times in the evenings after dinner while the sun still shone brightly overhead. They were normally full of questions and quite generous with their compliments about what a wonderful trip it had been.

All of them except for the four girls.

They weren't a problem while Thomas was speaking. They all acted as if every word he spoke was divine revelation from God. Quite a contrast from when she spoke. The first night she'd lectured, they'd acted mildly bored and did a lot of sighing. Tonight, however, they giggled, whispered, and pointed at her from the back of the audience and made Tayler feel like she was standing in front of all of them in her undergarments.

What shocked her most was that the parents of these young ladies simply rolled their eyes and cast backward glances every now and then. Thomas even frowned back at them, which made the girls smile and wave and sit a little straighter. But they continued on with their antics.

She tried not to judge them as being spoiled and snobbish, and instead wanted to think of them as God did. But that was much harder than she anticipated. They truly tried her patience. Reminding herself that God loved them just as much as He loved her, Tayler took a deep breath. What could she do to reach them?

An idea took root, and she walked to the back of the group

as Mrs. Bolans asked a question. "The lupine are one of my favorites, but how do they stand so tall against the wind?"

"That's an excellent question. And it's one I think we can answer by examining these flowers a little more closely." She held up a sturdy lupine stalk. "But first, I need a volunteer." The girls looked at her with disdain as Tayler stepped up to them. "Can I get one of you to volunteer to help me?"

They all shook their heads, and the redheaded girl, Esmerelda, gave her a bored look as she leaned back on her hands.

Tayler stood and stared each of them down while everyone waited.

After several awkward moments of silence, Tayler gave up. Walking back to the front, she sighed. "Well, I guess—"

"I'll be your volunteer." Thomas jumped to his feet.

In less than a second, the girls in the back raised their hands. Esmerelda stood. "I'm sorry we gave you a hard time. We'd love to volunteer."

But Thomas looked at them and back to Tayler, and he gave her a wide grin. "That's okay. I think I can handle it."

Tayler's stomach did a little flip.

She handed him several different flowers and then picked up the rest. His nearness was very distracting, but she reminded herself she could do this. "All right, so we're going to talk about each flower, and I'll let you all touch them as well so you see for yourself the different textures. One thing I've learned about the Alaskan wildlife and plant life? It's all unique and hardy. We'll start with the lupine Mrs. Bolans asked about and compare it to the beautiful fireweed. They both have tall stalks with the blossoms moving up in a cone shape, but if you'll notice, the fireweed blossoms seem more delicate, while the lupine are a bit more bulbous."

The ladies stood and gathered closer to inspect the flowers.

After they'd all oohed and aahed for several moments over each one, everyone took their seats again.

Tayler's plan was to also talk about berries tonight, but as she handed all the flowers to Thomas, she looked toward the back of the group and the four girls were gone. She shot a look to Thomas and nodded to the absent row.

He closed his eyes for a moment and shook his head.

"It seems as if we've lost a few of our audience." She smiled at everyone. "I hope I'm not *that* boring." Trying to laugh off the inadequacy she felt, Tayler hoped their guests wouldn't be upset.

The parents all turned to look for their daughters, but no one seemed too worried.

One of the mothers picked flower petals off her skirt. "I'm sure they've probably just gone to one of the tents. Please continue. It's fascinating."

Tayler nodded and decided she couldn't let herself get discouraged over a bunch of ninny socialites. No matter how much she tried to think of them as God did, the thought of them leaving her lecture still aggravated her. Why were they so preoccupied with Thomas? It seemed odd that a group of wealthy young girls would cast their sights on him.

Even though he was devastatingly handsome.

Tayler shook her head to dismiss the thoughts. The guests were waiting, so she started by explaining that a lot of plants were poisonous, and that even included some berries. "In Alaska, don't eat any berry that's white—"

A scream split the air.

People jumped up and turned toward the sound.

Thomas took off running and grabbed a rifle on his way.

Tayler followed with the rest of the crowd. *Lord, please let them be okay.*

It didn't take long to find the source of the scream. One of the girls—Mary—was thrashing in the water while the others stood on the bank.

"Oh, please help! I can't swim!" Mary's voice carried on the breeze.

Tayler made it to Thomas's side just as he let out a huff.

"Thomas, help, oh, please help!" Mary bounced up and down.

Mary's parents made it to Thomas's other side. "Aren't you going to do something?" Her father pointed, a stricken look on his face.

Thomas took off his shoes.

"You're wasting time!" Mary's mother put a hankie to her face.

Thomas strode into the water and reached out to grab the girl, but she yanked on him and he fell into the water. He came up sputtering while the girl clung to his neck and practically threw herself into his arms.

"Oh, thank you for saving me."

The dramatics of the young lady were so overboard that everyone realized at the same moment she was faking. A couple of moans were heard from a few adults, and as Mary continued her acting, Tayler tried not to laugh. No wonder Thomas had sighed and taken the time to take off his shoes.

"You didn't need saving, Mary. The water's not even up to your waist. You were clearly jumping up and down off the bottom to thrash around." His words held a bit of scolding.

But then the girl clung tighter. "I was so scared."

Whispers sounded behind them. "What a terrible prank to pull. Don't these girls know better?"

More comments from the others reached them.

Mary's father bolted to the front, his face red as he obviously heard some of the comments. "You're fine, Mary. Enough with the melodramatics."

The girl gave up her ploy and dropped her arms. "We were just having a little fun. Weren't we, Thomas?" Mary beamed a coy smile up at her rescuer.

"No. This wasn't fun, Mary. It will never be fun for someone to risk their safety—and others' safety—to play a trick to get attention." Thomas took her elbow and escorted her to the grassy bank. "You know, if you cry wolf too many times, you may not have the help you need in the time you need it most." Even though he scolded her, he gave her a smile. Tayler assumed it was to soften the blow.

Mary crossed her arms and pouted. Her friends circled her, and Tayler didn't even want to know what was going on in their silly little heads.

One thing was certain. This trip would be a learning experience for them all.

• • • • •

"Welcome to the Curry." The lady behind the desk offered him a smile. "How may I help you?"

"I'd like a room, please."

"How long will you be staying?" She examined the register.

"Oh, I don't know. It's such a lovely area."

A large smile spread across her face. "Yes, it is." She turned the book to him. "You're in luck. We're almost full up, but I've got a cozy little room for you on the second floor. If you'd please sign in, I'll get your room key ready for you."

"That sounds lovely, thank you." Greg DeMarco signed the ledger as Fred Jones. He'd just be another tourist and guest at the hotel.

As the bellhop carried his bag up the stairs, Greg followed behind. It was a wonderful day to be alive. Too bad Pruitt didn't have many of those left.

20

E smerelda curled a lock of her hair around her finger. Mary
stood there soaking wet, looking like a fool. "Exactly what
did you think you would accomplish?"

Mary shot her a scathing look. "You aren't the only one who
can get the men's affections, you know." She wrung out her hair.
"I'm tired of all your flirtations. Frankly, it's making me sick,
and I don't want to spend the rest of the summer watching you
make a fool of yourself."

Esmerelda put her hands on her hips. How dare she. "Fool
of myself? I'm not the one soaked to the bone."

"Well, at least I managed to get into his arms." Mary stepped up
to her until they were toe-to-toe. "That's more than you can say."

"Is that a challenge?" Could this drowned rat actually be serious? "We've been friends since before any of us can remember.
Have I *ever* not gotten the guy I wanted?"

"I, for one, don't want to just watch you play your games all
summer. Maybe you need a little competition." Mary crossed
her arms over her chest and walked toward the others. Her
sister, Martha, jutted out her chin. Obviously those two would
stick together.

"Is this how you feel too, Alice?" Esmerelda stared down at
the shorter girl.

"Oh, Essie, is this really necessary? Why can't we just enjoy the summer together? In a few years, we'll all be married off to a bunch of stodgy, rich men and be expected to start families. Why do we need to chase boys now?" Alice sighed.

"Thomas isn't a boy, Alice. He's a man." Mary snorted. "I bet that I can win Thomas's affection before Essie can."

Esmerelda stepped toward her so-called friend. "Oh, really? You think so? With more childish behavior like you demonstrated tonight?"

Mary huffed at her. "Think what you want, Esmerelda. I *know* so. He'll see straight through your simpering façade to the cat beneath."

She let the insult slide off her back. This would definitely make the summer a bit more fun. Esmerelda stuck out her hand. "It's a bet. But what will we win?"

Mary squinted at her. "If you win, I'll give you the diamond headband I wore to the Clemsons' party that you were so envious of."

Esmerelda let another insult fall, hiding her delight at the offer. The diamond headband was indeed a generous prize. One Mary's parents would be shocked to know that their darling daughter had wagered. "All right, then, if *you* win, I'll give you Marigold's foal."

The other girls gasped. They all knew the foal would be worth a small fortune, since the sire was none other than Esmerelda's father's champion steed.

Alice covered her mouth and then uncovered it. "What will your father say?"

Esmerelda shrugged. "What *can* he say? The horse belongs to me." She tilted her head to the other girls and raised her eyebrows. "You're witnesses. You must swear to tell the truth."

Alice and Martha nodded.

Mary grabbed her hand and shook it. "We have a bet. And witnesses."

Esmerelda couldn't help the smirk that lifted her lips. "May the best woman win."

•••••

FRIDAY, JUNE 21

Tayler walked to her new favorite spot atop Curry Ridge. The early morning hours were her favorite, the calm and quiet to gather her thoughts before the day began. Someone had placed several stumps on the side of the Regalvista lookout for seating, and it was the perfect place to watch the great mountain in the crisp and sunny morning. Even though a crystal-clear blue sky was above her, a large ring of clouds wrapped around the mountain's shoulders in the distance, keeping the peak covered and giving him an air of mystery and majesty. He wasn't called the High One for nothing. His reign over this terrain was undisputed.

She'd come here to think each morning and each evening, and it had done her spirit a world of good to pray and lay her burdens at the Lord's feet. But today it wasn't her own issues with Emerson, or even her mother, that captured her thoughts and prayers.

Today it was Thomas.

And the fact that she'd overheard two of the girls whispering about him last night as they walked around the edge of the camp.

Tayler hadn't caught the whole conversation, but it was worrisome. Apparently, there was some sort of a competition to win his affection. While she allowed herself to admit that winning his affection would be a glorious thing, it was only that for a girl who truly cared for him in return. It didn't make sense that these wealthy young women would go after a man who was of the working class when none of them showed any interest in being in the "middle of nowhere," as they had mentioned on numerous occasions . . . *unless* . . . it was just for sport. It crushed Tayler to think of it. Nothing good could come out of it, and Thomas was at risk of being humiliated.

What if they turned on the charm and he actually began to care for one of them? Tayler's heart twinged. That thought was horrible. The more she thought about it, the more she became jealous. Which only meant one thing: *she* cared for Thomas. Much more than she was willing to admit.

Sitting on the stump, she weighed all her options. Should she confront the girls with her knowledge of their competition? They'd probably lie their way out of it—none of them had any respect for Tayler. Maybe she should talk to the parents. Not that it would do any good. None of the parents seemed too concerned about the girls' antics so far.

Another option flitted through her mind. Maybe she should tell Thomas. At least give him some knowledge of what the girls might be up to. He'd obviously seen through Mary's farce before anyone else did. Maybe he wouldn't reject Tayler's concern. And hopefully he wouldn't think *she* was jealous and being silly. That would be mortifying. Perhaps she should just wait.

Lord, I have no idea what to do. Should I stay quiet so I'm not a gossip? Or should I warn my friend? And I don't have any idea what to do with these feelings either. Thomas is the first man I've felt attracted to since Emerson broke my heart. I'm . . . afraid to care for him.

As soon as she lifted the prayer heavenward, she realized the depth of her fear. All this time, she'd been independent and had taken care of herself, covering up the hurt and fear she'd held inside. She hadn't come to Alaska looking for love. She'd come to follow her dreams and to be respected for it. As Tayler Hale. Naturalist. Not the daughter of Martin and Henrietta of the Hale empire. But she also had to admit that she'd come to escape. To run away from her problems.

Footsteps sounded on the grass behind her. Tayler turned to see Thomas walking toward her, his hands in his pockets. She shot him a smile and watched his long legs eat up the distance between them. Her heart beat faster, and she looked back to the mountains. God was going to have to do a mighty work in her heart because she felt incapable of handling any of this.

"Good morning." Thomas gave her a lopsided grin.

"Good morning." She sighed. If only she knew what to do.

He sat on a stump next to her. "I noticed you like to come here in the mornings. Am I intruding on your private time?"

The fact that he'd noticed made her feel special, and it was really kind of him to ask. "No. It's nice to have some company." She stared straight ahead so he couldn't see her eyes. She couldn't trust herself right now, her emotions were too raw and skittered all over the place. Should she tell him?

"This has always been one of my favorite places." He turned toward her, and she could feel his gaze.

Was it rude to keep staring ahead?

"Did I mention that Cassidy and Allan had their wedding up here?"

"That's quite a hike for a wedding." She bit her lip. Not only was she undecided about her quandary, but his nearness made her feel even more attracted to him. And that wasn't something she could deal with right now.

He laughed. "Yeah, but none of us minded. We love it up here. And we love Cassidy and Allan. If you haven't figured it out, Curry has been like a big family for many of us."

"I like that." A family she'd already begun to care for . . .

He leaned his elbows on his knees and clasped his hands in front of him. "You know, I don't know anything about your family. Would you tell me about them?"

His question made that all-too-familiar twinge in her heart hit full force. She couldn't lie to him—she really did want to get to know Thomas better, but there was so much that was a mess in her life right now. There hadn't been a telegram back from Mother, and that meant only one thing—her mother was seriously angry with her.

"I'm sorry. Is it too painful for you?" Thomas's voice held so much sympathy.

She shook her head. "No." Pasting on a smile, she looked at him. His eyes drew her in. "My mother is in Denver, and my brother is in New York. Last year, I lost my dad and that was really hard. But I have amazing memories to hold on to." She couldn't bear to look at him anymore for fear her feelings would betray her.

"I bet your mother is very proud of what you do."

While she was sure he meant his words to be encouraging, Tayler couldn't help but cringe. "No. She's not."

He frowned at her answer. "Are you not close to your mother?"

In that moment, Tayler wanted to tell him everything, but there didn't seem to be a good place to start. She longed to have someone to share it all with—all her longings, dreams, hopes, and fears—but she just couldn't bring herself to do it. Not with everything that she'd gone through with Emerson. But he waited for an answer, so she gave him the easiest one. "We were . . . but losing my father was tough on all of us."

"I'm sorry, Tayler."

"Me too." And she was. If only Joshua were here. He could fix everything.

But he wasn't. And Tayler wasn't sure she'd get to see him ever again. The thought broke her heart.

Thomas shifted next to her. "Do you think you'd like to stay here . . . up in Alaska?"

The question brought her back to the moment at the top of Curry Ridge. As she gazed around her, she knew her answer. "You know, I think I'd like to. It's an amazing place."

"I'm glad. It's really great to have you here. A lot of people don't appreciate the isolation and lack of amenities."

She stole a glance at him. It seemed like he wanted to say more, so she waited.

He looked down at the ground, and that shock of hair he was always pushing back fell over his forehead. It made him even more handsome.

Lifting his head, he turned and caught her staring at him. He gave her a smile. "I'm not too good at this."

"Good at what?"

He sighed. "I know we've had to start over multiple times already, and I haven't been myself. There was the whole misunderstanding at the beginning, and well, I wasn't the perfect gentleman. But I hope you can see now that I really respect you, Tayler . . . and . . . I'd be honored to get to know you better."

The simple words were so sweet. Nothing arrogant about them. Not at all like Emerson. The comparison sprang to her mind too quickly. "I'd like to get to know you better too, Thomas." The words were out before she could snag them back. So much for guarding her heart. But getting to know one another was what friends did, right?

"Do you think maybe we could take a walk together when we return to the hotel? You know, when we're not working?"

"I'd like that very much." She felt heat moving toward her cheeks. A walk sounded nice. Innocent and sweet. She could handle that. And as much as she wanted to be careful about her feelings, she couldn't deny what she felt for this man next to her.

He looked forward and cleared his throat. "Tonight and tomorrow night we need to have late lectures. It's the time of year for the midnight sun."

Tayler clapped her hands in front of her. "I know! I'm so excited. I can't wait to see it for myself—"

"There you are!" Esmerelda's too-sweet voice bounced off the lookout structure.

Thomas swiped a hand down his face and sighed.

Tayler tried not to groan. What did *she* want?

"Thomas, I've been looking all over for you. You said we would take a walk together!"

He stood and stared down at the redheaded girl. "Exactly when did I agree to a walk?"

"Last night, silly. You haven't forgotten, have you?" She batted her eyelashes and pouted.

Tayler's stomach plummeted. No. He couldn't have done that.

Thomas shook his head. "I did not say we were going on a walk like that. I said the whole group was taking a walk."

"Well, I already told my parents that you invited *me* for a walk, and they were quite pleased with the notion. Can't we go? No one needs you right now." Esmerelda shot a scathing look at Tayler.

"That's where you are incorrect, Miss Esmerelda. The only walk I will be taking is when we go back to your parents so I can clear this up immediately."

Thomas gave her an apologetic look, and Tayler tried to give him an assuring smile.

Esmerelda grabbed his arm in a very possessive manner and sashayed away with him. She looked over her shoulder at Tayler, and the meaning of the glare was undeniable.

In that moment, Thomas removed her hand from his arm and stepped a couple paces to the right.

The breeze blew over Tayler, and it all became clear. Esmerelda had been listening to their conversation. She must've heard Thomas invite Tayler on a walk, and she couldn't have that, now, could she? Not with her bet in place with her little friends.

The pure conniving of the young woman baffled Tayler. Sure, she'd seen enough behavior like this in the wealthy circles, but these girls were doing this for sport. There wasn't an advantageous marriage at stake. It was only winning and plain, pure spite—out to hurt someone else.

Thoughts tumbled around in her mind, and she put a hand to her forehead. She should've told Thomas what she'd overheard. This game could get far too risky for him, and he was probably too sweet to notice.

Maybe they'd have another chance to speak alone later.

Hopefully nothing would happen that would hurt him before then.

21

"Couldn't you send someone out to find her?" Emerson gave the hotel manager his most concerned expression. "I've been waiting for days as it is."

"Mr. Pruitt." The manager sighed. "Miss Hale works for the Curry Hotel. She is leading an expedition, and I won't interrupt the paying customers' trip just so you can let her know that you have arrived." He turned away and waved over his shoulder. "Good day, Mr. Pruitt."

What was going on at this place? As soon as he'd announced that he was Tayler Hale's fiancé, everyone had treated him like the plague. Had she possibly told them all the truth?

No. He shook his head. She wouldn't disparage his family name.

He walked into the dining room and sat at one of the tables. Drumming his fingers on the cloth-covered tabletop, he thought about his next move. There had to be a way to get someone to talk. Someone had to know where Tayler was.

The train whistled in the distance. He glanced at his watch. Already time for the evening train. Emerson shook his head. Another day wasted.

A waiter came by the table. "Would you like coffee or tea, sir?"

249

Emerson dismissed the man with his hand. "No, I'll return for dinner in a little while." Exasperated, he stood up and stormed from the room. But as he reached the doors of the dining room, a familiar face stood out in the crowd.

One of Charlie's goons.

The man who'd sent him the note in Denver.

The man he'd tried to convince to give him more time so he could get the money.

The man who would surely kill Emerson if he couldn't convince Tayler to marry him right away.

He was here. And that only meant one thing. . . .

•••••

Only two more days.

Two more days before they would be back at the Curry and Thomas could talk to John and Allan about these young girls. Never in his life had he dealt with anything of the sort. He'd never thought he had much of a temper, but those socialites brought out the worst in him. He'd almost exploded at Esmerelda earlier in the day. Her conniving and catty ways were a nightmare. How would Allan deal with this?

The facts of the matter were that the girls wouldn't leave him alone, and two of them especially seemed determined to touch him constantly and vie for his attention. So he'd spent much of the day praying about keeping his mouth shut and trying to avoid the girls. Which proved impossible.

At dinner around the camp, they'd decided to take a nature hike, since the weather was so perfect. Maybe another activity would keep the girls occupied.

As he crested another ridge, he looked back to see the girls all huffing and puffing after one another to see who could make it to the top first. He'd intentionally led, and with his long legs he could gain quite a lead. It wasn't exactly the best for the rest of the guests, but he could use the excuse that he was scouting ahead.

Poor Tayler was left at the rear of the group, and it looked like she was herding cattle. Several of the adults were dawdling and probably struggling with the strenuous hike.

Mary reached where he stood a step ahead of Esmerelda. "Oh, what a lovely view!" She put her hands to her chest and gave him a coy smile.

Thomas rolled his eyes and looked back down the hill.

Esmerelda grabbed onto his elbow. "What a romantic spot, don't you think?"

Thomas raised his eyebrows. What were they up to?

Mary grabbed his other elbow. "I could just stay here forever."

"No, you couldn't. You hate camping." Esmerelda gave her friend a dismissive look.

Lifting her chin, Mary stepped forward and placed her hands on her hips. "Yes, I could. I love everything outdoors." She gave Esmerelda a glare and then shot Thomas a smile. "I think it's a magnificent job you have here, Thomas." She turned and looked back to the scenery. "Oh, look!" Mary took off down the hill in the other direction.

Esmerelda moved closer. "Good, now we have a few moments alone." She leaned and brushed her body up against his.

Alarm bells went off in Thomas's mind. He stepped away. "We don't need any moments alone, miss. I'm not sure what you're trying to do, but it's not going to work."

"Oh, isn't it?"

Before he could stop her, she flung herself at him and pressed up against him. Wrapping her arms around him, she hugged him tight. If he hadn't been so tall, she probably would have tried to kiss him.

Untangling himself from her grasp, Thomas once again

stepped away. "Don't make me speak to your parents about your behavior, Esmerelda."

"You wouldn't say anything." She moved toward him again. "You like it too much . . . you like *me*, don't you, Thomas?"

The brazenness of the young girl made him sad. What had turned her into this . . . ?

He shook his head. "No. I don't." He walked toward the path and looked down at the others still hiking. If only they would get here sooner.

"Thomas!" Mary's voice echoed up to him.

He ran to the other side of the ridge and looked toward where Mary had gone. There she stood, a huge smile on her face, pointing at a baby moose.

"No, Mary. Don't go near it!"

But, of course, the young woman did exactly the opposite. As she got closer to the moose, Thomas realized a new disaster was at hand. He raced down the hill to try to keep her from touching the baby.

All too soon, Mary seemed to be enjoying the chase, and she sauntered closer to the gangly animal.

When Thomas reached her side, she giggled. "I just want to pet him. He's so cute."

"Mary, no, that could get you seriously hurt."

She shrugged. "What could possibly hurt me? You're here to keep me from harm."

The young animal darted off into the distance. Mary took off after it.

Thomas looked to the sky. "Lord, I could use some help here." He ran after Mary.

Within a moment, he watched her tumble to the ground.

Wincing, she grabbed her ankle.

He caught up to her in a few long strides and knelt before her.

"I think I twisted my ankle," she moaned.

"You shouldn't have been chasing that moose, Mary. I warned you."

"I know, and I'm sorry, but I really think I'm hurt."

Thomas took compassion on her. "Can you put any weight on it?" He helped her to her feet.

She put the injured foot down and cried out in pain. "No. It hurts too much." She bit her lip and a large tear rolled down her face.

Goodness, this was going to be the longest summer ever if he had to put up with these girls much longer. "All right. I'll have to carry you back to the camp. This isn't going to be easy, and your ankle will most likely throb."

She sucked in a breath. "Okay." Mary looked miserable.

Guess he couldn't blame her. Getting injured on vacation was no fun.

He lifted the young woman into his arms and started the long trek back up the ridge.

"What is it like living here all the time?" Mary laid her head on his shoulder.

"If you don't mind . . . I need to focus on my steps. Not talk."

She whimpered and shifted even closer.

As if he needed her any closer. Inside, his temper flared. If the girl had simply listened to him to begin with, they wouldn't be in this mess.

An hour later, the weary hikers all returned to their camp. Thomas plopped Mary on a stump—a little harder than necessary—and waited for everyone to gather around. Hands on his hips, he paced the area.

Once everyone was back and seated, Thomas looked at the group. Esmerelda had her arms crossed over her chest in clear agitation while Tayler looked as if she could strangle any one of them at any moment. The adults all seemed weary and worn. Good. He hoped none of them would complain about what he had to say.

"Folks, I'm sorry to tell you that we will need to cut our camping trip short. Mary has managed to hurt her ankle and needs to see the doctor. We need to pack up as quickly as possible and get back to the hotel tonight."

Several moans were heard through the crowd.

"I don't want to be the cause of everyone missing out on the rest of our camping trip. I'm sure it will be fine in the morning," Mary piped up, giving him a smile.

Thomas narrowed his eyes at her. "This is serious business, Mary. You couldn't put any weight on your foot . . . it could be much worse than a sprain—your ankle could very well be broken, and we can't take the chance. Besides, no one has time or strength to carry you around."

Her cheeks turned red as she glanced at all the guests. "No, really. I'm feeling much better. Let's not go back early."

In that instant, Thomas knew. His stomach churned. He reached out and brought Mary to her feet.

She stood without any hesitation. "See? I'm feeling better already."

"You lied." Thomas said the words through gritted teeth.

"It was just a little fun. . . ." Mary giggled and looked out to the rest of the people. The smile slipped from her face as she looked at her parents. "So, see? There's no reason to return early." She shrugged her shoulders.

Thomas looked at Tayler and took a deep breath to try to calm himself. Her face went from anger to pity. Shaking her head, she looked down at the ground.

He put his hands on his hips, then held up one hand. "Folks, again, I apologize." He took another long, deep breath. "But we will be leaving the camp first thing in the morning. I cannot abide by any breaking of the rules. Rules we have in place for the safety of you all." He turned and looked at Mary. "You were all supposed to stay with the group, and you didn't." He gave the other girls a glare. "You were also supposed to listen to instructions, and you didn't. Then you were told time and again to stay away from the wildlife . . ." He looked back to Mary. "And you didn't."

Several of the adults nodded at him as he glanced at the group.

"I'm sorry to cut the trip short, but I have no choice. Make sure you pack everything up tonight so we can leave early. I won't tolerate any excuses."

Without looking at anyone else, he walked back to his tent and hoped that he hadn't sounded too angry, but that his words had sunk in. Especially to those silly girls. When they returned, Thomas would have to speak to John, Allan, and Mr. Bradley about the situation. Those girls couldn't be allowed to continue to ruin everyone else's summer.

• • • • •

Margaret sat at her desk in the corner of the kitchen. The day had been extremely long, but most of them were that way. Especially during the summer months.

She liked it when she had time to gather her thoughts. Tonight it seemed that instead of the kitchen duties, she couldn't keep her mind off a particular kitchen staff member and Tayler's words from a couple of weeks ago.

"Maybe there is a certain man you do like attention from—you just haven't admitted it."

Until the young naturalist had spoken up, Margaret had

pushed aside any thoughts of her own feelings. But now? She couldn't stop thinking about it. At least it felt that way.

As much as she hated to admit it, and after the years of his getting under her skin about every little thing . . . she enjoyed Daniel's company. The chef from Seattle had been her nemesis that first summer. But after he almost died and she'd prayed with him . . . well, things had changed. She knew that.

Almost three years had passed, and she didn't want to think about working without him. And if she were truly honest with herself, she didn't want to think about not having him in her life at all.

Then there was Bertram. Maybe at another time, the interest from him might have been reciprocated. But deep down, she had to admit that his pursuit had only helped her realize whom she really cared for. She didn't want to think about hurting the man, but eventually, she'd have to tell him the truth.

Footsteps sounded behind her. "Margaret." Daniel's husky voice made her heart pick up its tempo. How had she deceived herself for so long?

She turned.

In his hands, he held a bunch of wild flowers. "I know I'm not much good at courtin' you proper, lass. But I would like to ask ya for a walk."

Margaret stood and nodded. "I'd love to take a stroll with you, Daniel." She clasped her hands in front of her and gave him a smile.

The shock on his face was enough to make her chuckle.

Taking the flowers from his hands, she held them in her right hand and tucked her other hand in his elbow. "Shall we?"

22

The hike back down to Curry took entirely too much time. With pouting girls slowing them down at every turn and weary adults who didn't want to carry their loads for long, it was a wonder they'd even made it back in one day. Tayler was ready to run away and hide from them all. She'd often had difficult tourist guests at Yellowstone, but this group gave *difficult* a whole new meaning.

As they made their way across the suspension bridge, Thomas caught her arm. "Would you like to take that walk tonight? I don't think I'm up for seeing anyone else after our little fiasco."

Even as weary as she felt, she nodded. "I'd love to."

"All right. I'll meet you down by the creek where we went fishing. Is that okay?"

"Sounds lovely."

"In an hour?"

She looked at her timepiece. "That should work for me. I wanted to get cleaned up, but that can wait."

"Well, you know what? Don't worry about the gear. I'll take care of everything from here and that way you can do whatever

257

you need to do before we take a walk." He shot her a smile and went on ahead.

His thoughtfulness made her smile again.

After she crossed the bridge, she went straight to her room. A quick bath would be wonderful and would clear her mind. She had a lot she needed to tell Thomas. Too much had happened on this trip that made her worry about his getting hurt. Those girls were taking things too far.

She grabbed clean clothes and headed to the washroom she shared with the girls on this floor of the staff housing. Everyone was probably at dinner, so this would be a great time for her to be alone with her thoughts.

As the hot water helped ease away the dirt and grime, it also helped to make her next steps clear. Maybe it was time to let Thomas know about her life back in Denver. Everything. Including Emerson.

Maybe it was time to start fresh and get rid of all the shackles of her past, all the walls she'd built up, all the things she'd kept hidden. The people here at Curry deserved more from her. They'd taken her into their family.

After getting cleaned up and putting on fresh clothes, she felt completely refreshed. She went down the back staircase and out the door, heading for the meeting spot.

Tayler checked her timepiece and realized she was a bit early. She hoped Thomas hadn't had to deal with too many headaches after getting back. Mr. Bradley was sure to want a full report, since they'd returned early.

When she rounded the bend and spotted the creek, Thomas was already there. His hands in his pockets, he stared out at the river.

"Hi." All of a sudden, she felt unsure of herself.

"Hi." He turned toward her and smiled. "I told Allan where

we were, and we're still visible from here. I didn't want you to think anything untoward. I'd never want to put your reputation at stake."

Just like the time they'd gone fishing, he always wanted to make sure they were visible to others. The thought made her proud of him and also made her feel protected. That he cared for her reputation when most men would love to take a girl out of sight nowadays. The world was changing. "Thank you, Thomas."

"I take a walk every evening." He looked back to the water. "It's my time I spend talking to the Lord."

"I watched you once from my window." Tayler chuckled. "I wondered who you could be meeting out here. That was before I knew you."

He gave her a smile. "Well, now you know. I'm having my meeting with God. It gives me peace of mind."

An easy silence spread between them. Tayler wasn't sure where to start, but she felt the prodding to open up to him. "Thomas, there's something I'd like to tell you about."

Turning back toward her, he nodded. "Would you like to sit and talk or walk?"

"We can walk. It's a beautiful evening." She fidgeted with her hands. Something she only did when she was nervous. As they stepped along the path together, Tayler watched Thomas slow his long stride so he wouldn't get ahead of her. Which was quite a feat, since his legs were so much longer than hers. His character made her respect him even more, and it made her feel the need to tell him the truth.

"It is . . . but not as beautiful as you are, Tayler." His words were soft. "I've been wanting to tell you that for quite some time now." He stared ahead, but she noticed the smile that lifted his lips.

"Thank you." All of a sudden she felt very feminine. "I didn't think you liked me at all."

"I can understand why. I wasn't the most gracious to you and I'm sorry. But even though I was shocked that a woman had come to fill the position, I still found you quite stunning, and it did funny things to my heart."

"Why are you telling me all this now?" She ventured a look in his direction.

Thomas shrugged. "I figured it was time for us to be completely honest with each other. As much as we have to work together, and as many times as we've had to start over, it's hard to deny that I want to spend more time with you."

Her heart was thrilled with the thought of Thomas caring for her. But then it sank. There were still her mother and Emerson to consider. She had a mess on her hands. "I haven't been honest with everyone here."

"Oh?" He didn't turn or sound too shocked.

"When I came here . . . I was . . . well, I was basically running away."

Thomas didn't say anything. He just kept walking and listening.

"After my dad died, my mother really changed. And I mean *really* changed. She pressured me to quit my job and submit to high society's expectations. Nothing felt right, so I asked my boss at Yellowstone if there were any other positions available that he had heard of. He had just received Mr. Bradley's telegram and so that's how I came here."

Thomas nodded.

"There's more. My family is quite wealthy. I know I haven't told anyone that, and it's not like it needs to be a secret, but I just wanted to be me. Tayler Hale. To prove that I could do all this on my own and that I was good at it."

"You *are* good at it." His tone had changed, but Tayler thought maybe he was disappointed that she was just now telling him the truth.

"Thank you, Thomas. That means the world coming from you."

He stopped and turned toward her. "What about your brother?"

"I don't really know what is happening with him right now. We were always very close—but again, after Dad died everything changed. I miss him."

"Does it bother you that I'm an orphan? That I don't have any social standing or money behind my name?"

She frowned. "Of course not. Why would that matter?"

His brow furrowed. "I thought maybe that was what you were trying to tell me . . . in a nice way."

Tayler shook her head. "No, Thomas. I'm not telling you any of this to try to push you away. I want to be honest with you. That's all. Because to get to know me means you have to deal with all the problems that come along with me."

He reached out and pushed a stray curl of her hair behind her ear. "We've all got baggage, Tayler."

She reached up and covered his hand with her own. She didn't want to break the moment, but she had to tell him the rest. "Thomas, I don't want you to get hurt, and I'm worried about you."

"What do you mean?" He pulled his hand back.

"Those girls—Esmerelda, Mary, Martha, and Alice—I heard them talking the other night. They've started—"

"There you are! I've been looking all over for you." Emerson's voice made Tayler shudder. No. He couldn't be here. Not now.

She turned.

Thomas stepped closer to her.

She felt safer with him near. Taking a deep breath, she crossed her arms over her chest. "What are you doing here, Emerson?"

"Why, I'm here to take my fiancée home." The smug smile on his face made her sick.

"Fiancée?" Thomas sounded so hurt.

"We are *not* engaged, Emerson."

"Tayler, it's time you stopped this little charade. We've been engaged for ten years." Emerson directed those words to Thomas, then he grabbed Tayler's arm. "Now, come on. It's time to take you home."

Tayler yanked at her arm but he held tight. She tried to wriggle from his grasp again and screamed as loud as she could. "Unhand me!"

Thomas jumped between Tayler and Emerson and looked down on her former fiancé. "Let go of her . . . now." His voice was calm but more serious than she'd ever heard.

Emerson squeezed her arm extra hard and then let go. He leaned to see her around Thomas and pasted on that slimy smile. One she would never trust. Not in a million years. "Tayler, I don't think you need a bodyguard with you. We have things we need to discuss in private."

She rubbed her arm with her hand. She'd never known Emerson to be violent, but she'd definitely have a bruise later. "We don't have anything to discuss, Emerson. You are not welcome here. You are the one who needs to go home." She felt her cheeks flame with heat. What would Thomas think of all this? She hadn't had time to tell him everything . . . in fact, she hadn't told him anything about Emerson.

"I'm not leaving here without you." Emerson jutted his chin out. "Let me at least escort you back to the hotel. We really do need to talk."

"No." She shook her head. "No, we don't. I'm done talking to you."

Emerson pushed toward her but Thomas blocked him.

"I don't think so, Tayler." That weasel-like smile was back. Emerson straightened his jacket. "You need to hear what I have to say. Especially when it comes to your family and Joshua."

Heat filled her face as her anger built. "Fine. Say it."

He laughed at her. "Um . . . no. I don't think so. Not like this. I want a private audience. Just you."

Everything swirled around her. He had to be lying. Again. This couldn't be happening. Why was he here? "I can't deal with this right now."

Emerson stepped back, his hands up as in surrender.

It gave her the opportunity she needed, and she took it.

Running for all she was worth back to the hotel, Tayler couldn't contain the tears that streamed down her cheeks. Emerson would surely fill Thomas's mind with lies now. She should have never left them alone, but she had to escape. *Lord, what have I done? What do I do now?*

·····

Collette knelt on the floor in the clinic and sorted the new medical supplies. When she'd volunteered to help Matthew after church, she'd assumed she'd at least get some time with him to talk. But so far, hours later, they'd only spoken a handful of sentences to each other. He'd left the clinic a half hour ago, and she hadn't seen him since.

This was not how she'd imagined it would go.

Footsteps sounded on the steps outside. She hoped it wasn't anyone looking for the doctor because she had no idea where he'd gone. Praying it wasn't an emergency, Collette stood and went to the door.

As she opened it, Matthew's face registered shock. "Hi. I wasn't expecting you to open the door."

She laughed and looked down at the box he carried. Putting her hands on her hips, she lifted one eyebrow. "Let me guess— more supplies for me to organize?"

"Not this time." He gave her a smile that she thought for sure would melt her insides.

"Well? What is my next task?"

Matthew opened the box and delicious smells wafted toward her. "It's dinner! I realized how late I had kept you and that it was very ungentlemanly of me to do so. I thought to repay your kindness with a picnic." He looked at her a bit sheepishly. "I know it's very late, but it's still light out. Would you like to sit on the lawn with me?"

She felt the smile ease onto her face. "*Oui*. I would love to."

He carried the box out to his small front lawn and set it down. They sat on the grass together, and he pulled out the dishes. "I'd enjoy hearing about France—your homeland—and the things you loved the most."

Collette grinned. He was actually asking her questions. That had to be progress. If there was one thing she'd come to learn about their good doctor, it was that he was a man of few words. "I miss the beauty of France's countryside, and I miss my *mère* and *père* very much, but I hope I will one day see them in heaven, *oui*?" Her heart raced. She had come to love this man so much, but of course she couldn't tell him that. "I . . . uh . . . I have come to love it here. Alaska is so beautiful, *non*?"

"Yes, it is. I can see myself settling here in this land. It has adventure and the best of all the seasons." He buttered his roll. "And you probably know that I enjoy hiking. I will never run out of places to explore."

"*Oui*." Dare she dig a little deeper? "What is it that you like most about hiking? Do you wish for solitude?" She tilted her head and hoped to understand this man who intrigued her more than anyone ever had.

He leaned back on his elbows and crossed his legs. "You know"—he looked toward the river—"it's not as much the solitude. I would enjoy hiking with a companion, but I find it difficult getting to know people as someone other than their doctor. I find it refreshing to hike, and it's a good way to work through anything I might need to think through."

For a moment, Collette watched him. She'd never thought about having to keep his work separate from his friendships. With what she did, it didn't matter. But matters of health had to be in strict confidence. She found that she admired him even more.

He glanced at her. "I see I've made you think."

Realizing her brow was scrunched up as she'd been thinking, Collette relaxed and smiled at him. "It is true that there is much I didn't understand about your work."

Matthew sat up and smiled back. "You're a good friend to me, Collette, to help me like this. I appreciate that very much."

Overwhelmed by her feelings for him, she leaned forward a few inches as well and blurted, "I would like very much to be more than friends."

His eyes went wide.

She'd shocked him. Of course, she'd shocked herself, but her brother had always chided her for speaking before thinking things through.

He opened his mouth.

Lucy ran up at that very moment. "Dr. Reilly, we need you. One of the women burned her hand on the steam down in the laundry."

He blinked several times at Collette—his shock still apparent—and then jumped up and turned to Lucy. "Let me grab my bag."

In a matter of seconds he was gone, and Collette sat on the lawn, wondering what he'd thought of her outburst and wishing she could take back her words.

23

MONDAY, JUNE 24

Thomas paced the office in front of Allan. He wasn't sure what to think of any of this. But one thing had become very clear to him—he cared about Tayler. "I just don't get it. She didn't say anything about being engaged."

Allan remained calm and leaned on the edge of the desk. "But she told this other fella that they *weren't* engaged."

"Yes, she was quite adamant about that." That thought made him feel a lot better, but he wished he could talk to Tayler about it right now.

"Maybe there's something else we're missing, Thomas. I think it's dangerous to jump to conclusions."

He stopped in his tracks and looked at the man he respected like an older brother. Thomas sighed. "I'm sorry. I don't want you to think I'm jumping to conclusions. I'm not. At least, I pray I'm not. But after our rocky start, we were just beginning to find sure footing together. She told me a little bit of her past last night, but it was all very vague." He started pacing again. "I really thought we had the beginning of something. . . ."

"And you're worried that this Emerson bloke is going to

whisk her back to Denver and her life there and you'll never see her again."

He stopped again and crossed his arms over his chest. Leaning his head back, he looked to the ceiling. "Yes. Well . . . no. Maybe, I guess. But I'm more worried about *her.*" He shook his head. "You should have heard her voice, Allan. There was something in it that . . . frankly . . . made me think she was scared."

Allan sighed. "I trust your instincts, Thomas. I do. And maybe there's something else we need to do to help Tayler right now."

"I just wish I could talk to her. Clear the air. Something's not right."

A knock sounded at the door.

Thomas took a deep breath as Allan went to answer it. Probably a guest wanting to request another outing. With so many beautiful days, everyone wanted to explore.

"Mr. Lancaster. What can I do for you?" his boss asked.

The rich man exuded confidence everywhere he went, probably because he always got what he wanted. When he entered the room, he nodded to Thomas and then looked back to Allan. "Mr. Brennan, my daughter Esmerelda would like to go on a horseback ride. The one along Deadhorse Creek I believe is the one she'd like."

Thomas had to force himself not to moan out loud. But he'd let Allan handle it.

"Will this be for her friends as well?" Allan queried but kept a stoic face.

"No, she's getting quite tired of some of the group's immaturity. She's been impressed with Mr. Smith here and his knowledge of the area and said she'd like some peace and quiet."

Peace and quiet. Sure. That's exactly what Esmerelda wanted.

How could her father be so blind? Thomas inhaled and held his breath as he waited for Allan to look at the schedule.

His boss frowned. "Hmm . . . My apologies, Mr. Lancaster, but Thomas isn't available. But I think Miss Hale would be able to squeeze that in this morning."

Thomas could have hugged Allan right then and there, but he refrained. He'd have to thank his friend and mentor later.

Tayler walked into the office. She looked at each man. "Good morning, gentlemen." With a nod, she straightened her pink blouse and adjusted the green scarf tied at her neck. "Did I hear my name?"

For a brief second, Thomas forgot about everything else. Tayler had chosen a simple and practical uniform for her duties as a naturalist and guide, and yet she made it look so beautiful. The long split skirt fell below her knees and covered her boots. Her clothes were much more modest than what the other young women were wearing these days. Besides, they were feminine yet practical, especially for hiking and riding horses. Thomas knew he shouldn't be staring, but he couldn't help himself. Tayler was beautiful.

". . . sure, that will be fine." Mr. Lancaster was talking, and Thomas forced himself to pay attention. "She's expressed the need to distance herself from the other girls and their silliness, which her mother and I respect. I'm positive Miss Hale will be a wonderful influence on her."

Tayler's features were pale this morning, and she nodded with a slight smile.

Thomas felt bad for her and the situation. No one wanted to deal with Esmerelda Lancaster.

Mr. Lancaster left the room, and any relief Thomas felt at not having to take Esmerelda on a ride disappeared as he looked into Tayler's eyes. Thomas walked up to her side. "Are you all right?"

"I don't know. I mean, yes, I'm physically fine . . . but . . ."

Allan closed the office door and pointed to a chair. "Sit down, Tayler. Thomas told me about Emerson's words yesterday, but we'd like to hear from you about what is really going on."

"But what about the schedule today?" Tayler sat in the chair and twisted her hands before laying them in her lap. "I know you just had to book something else, and I don't want to be the cause of the guests being unhappy."

"Well"—Allan shut the schedule book—"I won't lie to you and tell you that you'll enjoy taking Esmerelda out on a horseback adventure, but the young woman has been throwing herself at Thomas, and we can't abide by it. Besides, we need to keep propriety intact. The best way is to distract her with something else."

Thomas watched Tayler's face. She didn't even seem fazed about this. Normally, she'd get fiery about the young women and their behavior, but today was different. "Tayler, we want to help you." He swallowed. "Did Emerson hurt you yesterday when he grabbed you?"

She sniffed and slowly started to roll up her right sleeve. An ugly bruise emerged in the shape of a man's grip. Thomas tried not to react, but he wanted to punch the man who did this to her.

Allan came around the desk and crouched down in front of her. "I don't know what is going on, but let me tell you this right now: Thomas and I will make sure you are never alone if you fear for your safety."

She nodded and lifted her chin as she put her sleeve back in place and buttoned the cuff. "I'm really all right." The spark was back in her eyes as she swiped at a tear. "I've been able to handle Emerson for a long time, I just wasn't expecting him to be so pushy. There's got to be something behind it." Tayler sent Thomas a look he couldn't decipher and turned her attention back to Allan. "I went and spoke with your wife this morning. Cassidy prayed with me and helped me to see that I needed to tell all of you the whole truth. She said that we're a family here, and I'm now part of that family. I *want* to be part of that family."

"Why don't you start at the beginning?" Allan stepped back and leaned on the desk.

Thomas pulled the other chair up across from her so he could see her face.

"When I was thirteen, we all went on a camping trip. It was something I did often with my dad, my brother, and his best friend—Emerson. We grew up together climbing mountains, fishing, and camping. This particular trip was bittersweet because we all knew it would be the last one before the boys went to Harvard. They still had another year of prep school and after that, their futures were mapped out. Harvard and then law school after that . . ." She sniffed and looked at her hands. Shaking her head, she sighed. "I was young and foolish and after an incident with a bear, Emerson told me I was the one for him.

"He asked me to promise that I would wait for him."

Thomas raised his eyebrows. "And you did?"

Tayler nodded. "Yep. That was the dumbest thing I ever did. What you should know is that our families had been wanting this for a long time—the joining of the Hale and Pruitt enterprises was to be a wonderful thing. But it didn't take long for my young heart to be crushed. By the time I was sixteen, I'd heard numerous accounts of Emerson's . . . exploits." Her cheeks turned pink and she ducked her head.

Thomas wished he could take away the pain he read in her posture.

When Tayler lifted her head, there was fire in her eyes. "Over the next few years, I asked my brother about it, and he had to be honest with me. But I wanted to see it for myself. Emerson told me he loved me in his letters, but we rarely saw each other. He was at Harvard and I was in Denver. He stayed away."

Thomas disliked the man even more. Who could stay away from Tayler? He could hardly stand it if he didn't get to see her every day.

Allan crossed his arms over his chest. "I can tell you right now that this man isn't deserving of you. But why don't you tell us the rest of the story?"

Tayler sighed. "As you both know, I know my own mind and I'm independent. And not to sound as if I'm bragging, but I'm also intelligent. I graduated high school very early and talked my father into letting me further my education. He agreed, and I went to college to study botany. I was given the job at Yellowstone when I was eighteen years old, so I spent my summers up there and then attended college the rest of the year. It was incredible for me. I tried to ignore the drama at home until I had to return, and I'd have another letter from Emerson apologizing for any rumors I'd heard. By the time I was almost twenty, I'd had enough. Our families had invested in each other's businesses, but I didn't think that mattered, because our parents had been friends since long before we were born. That spring, I witnessed firsthand Emerson's unfaithfulness. Numerous times. I broke off the engagement."

Shaking her head, she released a heavy breath. "But apparently, our families just thought things needed to die down, because in the background everyone except for my dad and me thought that Emerson and I would eventually still get married. And then Dad died." She choked a bit on the last words.

Thomas handed her his handkerchief.

She took it and wiped at a tear. "Everything changed. I came home from Yellowstone to be a support for my mother, but she didn't need me. She'd turned into someone I didn't even recognize anymore, and when I was about to leave for my work again this past April, she brought Emerson and the family lawyer in to try to convince me we should set a wedding date. I couldn't take any more. I refused to marry him and ran away to my job. Emerson sent a telegram to say he was coming to collect me from Yellowstone, so I asked my boss for a recommendation somewhere else. He'd just heard from Mr. Bradley about the opening here, and so I ran again. And here I am."

Allan nodded and appeared to be mulling it over. "Did your family know where you went?"

She shook her head. "Not at first . . ."

Thomas took in a deep breath. "But after the pastor's sermon that Sunday about reconciling . . . the Sunday you ran out . . ." It all fit together now.

Tayler nodded. "I couldn't bear to be dishonest with my mother. I knew it wasn't honoring to her to not even let her know where I was."

Allan walked behind his desk and sat down. He shook his head. "So that explains Emerson's appearance."

"I'm afraid so." Tayler looked at Thomas. "I'm sorry." Her eyes begged for his acceptance.

"You don't need to apologize, Tayler. Remember, I didn't give you an easy time of it to start. But we're in this together."

"Most definitely." Allan pulled the schedule book back out. "I don't know what we will have to do, but I'm going to make sure that there aren't any opportunities for you to be cornered by him. That's my first objective. After that, we need to know how we can help."

An hour later, Thomas watched Tayler walk to the stable to prepare for the ride with Esmerelda. Her shoulders didn't have quite the lift they normally did, and it made him concerned. How had things changed so rapidly? They hadn't had a chance to really discuss anything privately, and he felt an urgency to protect Tayler and to tell her how he felt. But how could he? Their relationship had been . . . interesting, to say the least. Thankfully, John had volunteered to go with her this morning on the outing so she wouldn't be alone, and hopefully Emerson wouldn't find her. He looked back to the hotel. There was an incredibly full schedule today. He didn't have time to worry, but he couldn't help it.

Tayler had become his number-one priority.

•••••

"Mr. Pruitt." Greg found the man sitting in the dining room, reading the paper and drinking coffee. How quaint. "Nice to see you again."

The kid glanced up and didn't look a bit shocked to see him. "Good morning, Mr. DeMarco."

"Why don't you look surprised to see me?" Maybe the little weasel had someone tip him off.

Pruitt folded the paper and laid it on his lap. Leaning back in his chair, he gave Greg a smile—one that in some circles could be charming, but not today. "I'm sure you have a job to do, and Charlie is a smart man."

Greg narrowed his eyes at him. "What are you up to, Mr. Pruitt? You know why I'm here." He lowered his voice and took a seat at the table. No sense alerting all the little vacationing tourists to any trouble.

"Same as you, Mr. DeMarco. I'm here to get Charlie's money." The kid leaned on the table and spoke in a hushed tone. "We're out for the same objective here."

Greg couldn't help laughing at that. Pruitt had no idea. "I highly doubt that."

Pruitt raised his brows.

"You know why I'm here . . . you've had your chance. *Multiple* ones."

"But you want Charlie's money, don't you? It's within my grasp. I think that's worthy of another chance." The kid was arrogant. And a good actor. But Greg could see the tinge of fear behind his eyes. "Besides . . . you don't want me to call the press about an unsavory character who's threatened me."

Lowering his voice, Greg spoke in an even and controlled tone. "You can't very well call anyone if you're dead."

Emerson leaned back and laughed like they were old friends catching up. Then he leaned forward again. "But if anything happens to me, I have a courier with instructions to deliver a letter containing information about Charlie's business dealings that I'm sure he doesn't want the authorities to know about."

Probably a bluff. But Greg would humor him. "Ten days, kid. That's it." Greg stood and straightened his suit jacket. "I'm not leaving. I'll be watching every move you make. Remember that."

He walked away from the table and smiled. The kid was blowing smoke, and they both knew it. He'd string him along for the ten days . . . but that just gave him a little more time to plan and to see if there was any truth to the kid's threat. His job was always to protect the boss.

Charlie's nuisance would be gone soon. And as the story broke in the papers, everyone would see once again that no one crossed Charlie the Chisel. No one.

• • • • •

Esmerelda sauntered over to the stables. Today she would put the rest of her plan in motion. Daddy had arranged it, and she would get what she wanted. She always did.

As she walked the final steps, she noticed that annoying Miss

Hale leading two horses out of the stables. An older gentleman she'd seen around the hotel said something to Miss Hale, and it made her smile. No one seemed to have noticed Esmerelda yet.

She cleared her throat.

The man turned and smiled. "Miss Lancaster, how lovely to see you today. We were just preparing for your outing."

"Hello." She lifted her chin in the air a bit higher. "I'm here for a ride with Thomas." She pulled on her riding gloves. "I believe my father arranged it earlier."

"Thomas was too busy with other outings, so Mr. Brennan scheduled you with Miss Hale. Didn't your father inform you?"

Anger bubbled up inside her. Too busy? These working people needed to be put in their place. She was in charge here. She put her hands on her hips and scowled at them. "That is unacceptable. I requested Mr. Smith, and I expect to have my wishes respected."

"Well, the scheduling isn't up to you, Miss Lancaster." The older man walked toward her and had a very fatherly look about him. She didn't like it at all. It was as though he regarded her as a child.

"I'll complain to the manager," she huffed.

"I'm afraid that won't do any good. Miss Hale is an excellent guide and is ready to take you on your outing."

She stomped her foot. "I refuse to go anywhere with *Miss Hale*. I ordered Thomas and I expect to have him!"

Miss Hale stood by her horse and shook her head. When she stepped forward, her face held a look of pity.

It only served to enrage Esmerelda more. "I demand to see the manager right now." She spat the words.

The older man stepped closer to her again. "Miss Lan—"

"John, please, let me." The short little thing in her quaint and completely unstylish uniform put a hand on the man's arm.

She came close enough to whisper to Esmerelda. "I'm sure

you don't want to make a scene, Esmerelda, and embarrass yourself. That isn't proper for a young lady. Now, why don't we just go on and enjoy our ride?"

"What would you know of society rules, Miss Botany Expert? I don't have to listen to you, and I'll make a scene if I wish to make a scene."

Miss Hale stepped back and gave her a sad look. "Well, we are ready to go, and we do have a schedule to keep."

"I'm not going with you." Esmerelda crossed her arms over her chest.

"That's fine. But Miss Hale is your only option, and Mr. Bradley will not hear any complaints about the scheduling when the excursion you requested has been offered. This is your only choice." The man named John held a firm tone to his voice.

It might be her only choice for the moment, but Esmerelda didn't have to let these people tell her what to do. Fury burned through her. She wanted Thomas.

And Thomas she would have. She never lost. She wasn't about to start now.

24

Avoiding Emerson hadn't been as difficult as Tayler had imagined. For one thing, her schedule was jam-packed. For another, he was a guest and she was staff. A fact she'd pointed out to him twice already. As dinner rolled around, she went down the staircase to the staff dining room. In here she felt safe. It wasn't a domain that Emerson was welcome in, and she loved that fact. But the thought still niggled at the back of her mind about his words. What could he possibly have to tell her about Joshua?

Gazing around the room, Tayler thanked the Lord for putting these people in her life. She'd been told by numerous members of the staff that as soon as Emerson had told them he was her fiancé, they went into protective mode. He'd been so pushy and all fired up about finding her that most of the people realized something was up.

Another reason to realize that God had brought her here for this specific time to these specific people. She needed them. For an independent person to admit such a thing astounded her, but God had done a lot in her life lately. She shouldn't be surprised.

Mr. Bradley entered the dining room and headed straight

278

for her. "I'm sure you can guess who this is from. He asked me to deliver it to you."

Heat filled her face—the embarrassment of Emerson using the manager that way. "You don't need to do anything for him, Mr. Bradley. Emerson needs to give up and go home."

"He's a paying guest, so I do need to treat him like I would any other guest, Miss Hale, along with providing the amenities the others enjoy . . . but it is also encouraging to hear that you aren't planning to leave. We've had an extraordinary season so far with you on board, and I don't plan on letting you go that easily. Besides, I heard that you know how to ski. We're going to need you this winter." He gave her a smile and went to his seat at the head of the table.

Many of the others began to take their seats, and Tayler took that moment to open the envelope while no one sat next to her. She pulled out a small piece of paper and read:

My Dearest Tayler,

I'm not sure what game you are playing, but it really is getting tiresome. You have no need to be a part of the working class. Good heavens, what your mother would think if she saw you dining in the basement with them! Tomorrow evening, you will join me for dinner upstairs. Like civilized people of our station. Then we can discuss why you are hesitant to return home. I'm willing to listen to your reasons and wait a few days if necessary. Before you think about refusing, remember that there are things about your family you don't know. It's time for the truth to come out.

Yours always and forever,
Emerson

Food began to travel around the table, and she realized she'd missed the prayer. Shaking her head, she couldn't believe Emerson's newfound attention to their relationship. Or his domineering way of ordering her around. That wasn't like him. But that note was full of demands. And what sounded like a veiled threat. There must be something behind it. She just didn't know what. At least not yet.

She took another glance at the letter and decided then and there that she wouldn't even acknowledge it with a response. He could wait for her at dinner for all she cared. Tayler Grace Hale wouldn't kowtow to his whims. She tucked the paper back in the envelope and then shoved it in her pocket.

Thomas pulled out the chair next to her. "Penny for your thoughts."

"You do *not* want to know what's going through my mind right now."

He laughed. "Ah . . . I see the steam coming out of your ears. Must have something to do with Mr. Pruitt, I presume?"

She groaned. "Yes. But I am so grateful for everyone here. I've been constantly surrounded and protected. I can't tell you the last time I felt so . . . so . . ."

"Loved?" Cassidy piped in. She reached across the table and patted Tayler's hand as she held one of the boys on her left hip.

Tayler nodded. "You know. Yes, that's it. Like a family should."

"Good. Because that's how we want you to feel." She settled into her chair and put a sleepy-looking Jonathon in his seat next to her. "Sorry we're late. The boys didn't get their naps, so they're cranky. And when they are cranky, we are late."

"We're late when they're in a good mood," Allan said as he approached with David in tow.

Cassidy shrugged. "I feel like we're always late to everything with these two."

Tayler watched Cassidy care for her son as Allan placed David in his seat. No one minded that they were late. The table was huge, with room for all the staff, and everyone was welcoming. They all chatted as they ate and discussed their days and some of the antics of the guests.

Allan didn't hesitate to get started. Tayler noticed that parenting twins meant you had to eat and drink as fast as you could in between watching the toddlers like a hawk. He took a bite of his chicken with creamed spinach and pointed his fork in her direction. "So, Tayler, I hate to tell you this, but a certain someone managed to sign up for *two* of your events tomorrow. The hike up Deadhorse Hill and the lecture on the wild flowers."

Moaning, she leaned back in her seat and slouched. Had Mother seen it, she would have scolded Tayler until a month of Sundays had passed, but she didn't care. "I was wondering how long it would take him to figure out how to see me."

Cassidy gave her a smile. "Just be yourself, Tayler. But there's no problem in ignoring his advances. He's a guest and that's it." She took a drink of water. "Who knows? Maybe he will actually get the hint after a few days and decide on his own that it's best to leave."

If only things would be that easy. But Tayler feared there was no chance of that. Emerson didn't seem willing to give up this time. Which was a bit unnerving.

"I'll be on the hike with you." Thomas leaned toward her. "I'll see if I can keep him away."

His words made a little chill race up her arms. If Thomas was trying to keep Emerson away, that meant he would be with her . . . next to her . . . all day. Even in the midst of this turmoil, she looked forward to it.

"And I'll be along for the lecture." Allan nodded.

"How are you two managing this? You both have your own

schedules that are quite full already." A twinge of guilt hit her chest.

"We won't be able to keep it up for the long-term, but we've devised a system for now." Allan winked at his wife.

"And you don't need to worry about it. We've got it under control." The nearness of Thomas as he spoke made her smile. He leaned closer and whispered, "I'd really love to take a walk with you tonight, but I'm afraid that your admirer will try to follow us."

She smiled into his eyes. "You're probably right, but I appreciate the thought."

"We'll get through this, Tayler."

Nodding at him, she believed it. Especially since he'd said *we*.

• • • • •

FRIDAY, JUNE 28

The redhead he'd watched the past couple of days came out of the hotel.

Emerson had left her a note, and he hoped that his plan would work.

Tayler had become adept at ignoring him and making it impossible to talk privately. It was quite annoying. So he'd made a decision. If she was going to continue to play her little game, he would up the stakes. Time wasn't something he had in abundance. Sometimes someone just needed a little . . . push.

As soon as the young woman spotted him, he jerked his head toward the suspension bridge and walked to the meeting place.

The evening was getting on in hours, even though the sun didn't show it. Most of the good folks were tired from their days filled with activities and excursions, and there wasn't anyone else outside on the lawns that he could see. Good.

A few minutes later they met in the middle of the bridge. It would be very difficult for anyone to eavesdrop on their conversation here.

She gave him a flirtatious smile and leaned her hip toward him in a seductive manner. "How can I help you, Mr. Pruitt?" She tapped the note up against her hand.

"I believe we can help each other, Miss Lancaster."

"Oh?"

"I understand you have a little competition going on with your friends."

She frowned at him. "How did you—"

He held up a hand. "That's not of consequence. But you winning your competition could help me greatly. So I have a plan."

After he whispered a few things to her, she stood back and put her hands on her hips. "Why do you want *her*?"

"She's worth a large fortune, that's why."

"Seriously? That uniform-wearing botanist?" She turned to the water. "Well, even if she is rich, she isn't very congenial. It seems to me a handsome man such as yourself would rather have a woman who's willing to show you . . . special attention."

"Who said that I'm not looking for that too? I only said she was worth a large fortune. . . ." He let the sentence hang. From what he'd observed of the bored socialite, he knew exactly how far he could push. She wanted to win. Always. And she was bored. Always. And she liked to break every rule she could to get what she wanted. A lot like the flapper girls he knew in the city. He let a finger trail down her arm before turning to look at the water as well.

"So do we have a deal?"

"You need to make this worth my while, Mr. Pruitt. And I'm not just talking about winning my little bet. I want . . . compensation . . . and while we're at it, let's talk about your own family fortune. What are you planning to do for me long-term? A girl has needs, you know. And I need substantial promises of . . . fun . . . for the future. Not my parents' type of fun either. I'm a modern girl after all." She sidled up next to him and rubbed her body up against him. It was obvious she wasn't new at this type of game.

She leaned close and whispered things in his ear. Things that would make his own mother blush. Modern girl indeed. *This* was a long-term attachment he could deal with.

He nodded to her.

"It will be fun . . . and I'm always looking to have fun." She stared at him until he looked at her, ensuring that he got her hint. Yep, she was a pro.

Then she walked away.

Emerson couldn't help admiring the young woman as she did so. If he weren't so busy trying to get Tayler, he'd have a little fling with that one on the side right now. But there'd be plenty of time for that soon enough. Esmerelda had made herself quite clear.

Looked like his future wasn't going to be so boring after all. They were all about to have a lot of fun.

• • • • •

SATURDAY, JUNE 29

Thomas took three stairs at a time to make it to Mr. Bradley's office. The young messenger had told him to hurry and so he did.

Taking a deep breath, Thomas straightened his jacket and knocked on the door.

Mr. Bradley opened it, his complexion ashen. An expression Thomas had never seen covered his face. "Come in, Thomas. Thank you for coming so quickly."

Thomas stepped into the room, and the manager closed the door behind him. John and Allan stood against the far wall, their faces grim.

"Thomas . . ." Mr. Bradley rubbed his head. "I don't know quite where to begin, but I need to ask you a few questions."

He felt his brow furrow. "Of course. Anything, sir."

"Have you been sneaking off at night with one of the guests?"

"Of course not." Where was this coming from?

"So you're telling me you haven't been outside walking in the evenings?"

"No. I mean, yes, I've been out walking, but I haven't been sneaking off with anyone."

The manager sighed and looked to the other two men.

Allan stepped forward. "Thomas, I know you've talked about taking walks later in the evening and that you spend that time praying. Is that still true?"

"Yes." Thomas tried to swallow past the lump in his throat. The air around him was charged with foreboding. "What does this have to do with anything?"

"Gentlemen, I think it's best to just come out and say it." John walked over to Thomas and put his hands on Thomas's shoulders. "Thomas, you know I love you as if you were my own son."

All Thomas could do was nod.

John squeezed and then let his arms drop to his sides. "But there's been a serious accusation leveled against you. None of us want to believe it, but we have to investigate."

His brows shot up. "What?" He choked out the word. "What is the accusation?"

John Ivanoff—the first man to truly mentor him and show him what it meant to be a godly man—looked to Allan and then Mr. Bradley. "That you've been sneaking off at night with

Miss Esmerelda Lancaster and that she now believes herself to be in the family way."

The words dropped into the room like a lead cannon ball and exploded.

Feeling light-headed, Thomas stepped to a chair and grabbed the back of it. "Why? Why . . . would she even think to accuse me of this?"

"Are you saying there is no truth to it?" Mr. Bradley was stern.

"No, sir. No truth at all. I adamantly deny this. I've never been . . . never ever been . . . intimate with a woman. Never in my life, sir. And that's the God's honest truth. I can't believe she would make up this falsehood! Especially after she's been chasing me practically all summer and flirting and trying to get me alone." He couldn't stand on his shaky legs any longer. Thomas rounded the chair and sat down hard. Putting his head in his hands, he felt hot tears spring to his eyes.

"I believe you, Thomas." The manager leaned back on his desk. "But we have a serious situation on our hands. We need to discuss how we are going to handle this and try to keep the rumors at bay. The parents have agreed to keep this quiet for right now—out of respect for their daughter's reputation."

"Reputation? Forgive me, Mr. Bradley, but it seems it's *my* reputation that's on the line here. And I haven't done what I've been accused of doing. She could ruin me!"

"That's what I'm trying to avoid, Thomas."

"We all are," Allan added.

"But there's a big dilemma here. The parents believe their daughter is telling them the truth . . . and they are insisting that you marry their daughter immediately."

25

The drizzling rain and cold temperatures tried to convince Tayler that it wasn't almost July. She'd put on an extra sweater this morning knowing that the walk to church would be cold, but now she wished she'd grabbed her heavy coat. Shivering from head to toe, she climbed the steps to the little white church.

"Tayler!" Cassidy's voice made her turn.

"TayTay," the boys chanted.

It made her smile. But the look on Cassidy's face made her think of impending doom. "What's wrong, Cassidy?"

Her friend had a toddler on each hip and ran toward her.

Tayler looked for Allan but he wasn't anywhere to be found. "What is it?" Her heart pounded in her chest.

"We need to talk, right away."

"All right, do we need to go into the church?"

"No. Why don't you come back to our house real quick?"

"All right."

Cassidy went to turn, but Tayler stopped her and took David in her arms to help lighten her friend's load. They both carried a boy and walked briskly back to the Brennan home.

As soon as they entered the warm home, Cassidy plunked the boys on the floor with some toys and motioned to the small table in the kitchen. "Have a seat."

Tayler sat down and the chill in her bones from the rain made her feel numb. "Please. Tell me what's going on."

"It's Thomas."

"Oh no! Is he hurt? Where is he?" She jumped to her feet.

Cassidy grabbed her hands. "No. No . . . good heavens, your hands are like ice." She went to the stove and put the kettle on. "Last night, Allan came home and shared with me some horrible news. It appears that young socialite—Esmerelda—has accused Thomas of . . . well, of . . . inappropriate behavior and believes that she is now in the family way."

Not sure what she'd been expecting to hear, Tayler was at a loss for words. "But . . ." was all she could manage.

Cassidy went on. "She said they'd been sneaking out at night to take walks together."

The information sank into Tayler's brain. She'd seen Thomas go off by himself many times. *No, no, no!* her brain screamed. Everything swirled around her. Thomas walking down the path. His smile. Esmerelda's constant attention to him.

Then images of Emerson professing his love to Tayler, warring with Thomas, and Thomas taking other girls into his arms. Pretty soon it all meshed into one big cacophony of sound and images in her mind.

Tayler gripped the sides of her head with both hands. No. This couldn't be. Not Thomas.

Cassidy put a cup of hot tea in front of her. "Tayler, please . . . talk to me."

She shook her head. Ten years she'd been made the fool by someone she'd known all her life. How could a man she'd known less than two months be any different?

Her friend laid her hand on Tayler's knee. "Tayler, look at me. Thomas didn't do this. You know that, don't you?"

Tayler closed her eyes. "I . . ." She took a deep breath. All the time she'd spent with Thomas, working alongside him and simply watching him, made her realize one very important fact. He wasn't Emerson. Especially now that Emerson had come here to Curry—comparing the two men side by side showed with clarity the complete difference between them. Opening her eyes, she looked at her friend. Thomas was too honorable—she knew his character. "I know that. Deep in my heart . . . I do."

Cassidy let out a long exhale. "Good. You had me worried there for a moment." She pointed to the cup. "Drink the tea. I don't think the chill today is helping any. The reason I brought you here is to first tell you, and then to let you know that Allan and John are trying to figure out a plan of action with Mr. Bradley. Things might get a little difficult the next few days."

"Oh no," Tayler gasped. "The Fourth of July celebration is coming up."

"Yes, and Mr. Bradley fears that if we don't get this cleared up soon, we could have a disaster on our hands. Rumors are fast to fly in a small place like this."

The tea had a citrusy scent as Tayler lifted it to her nose. As she took a sip, the warm liquid soothed her nerves. "What are they going to do?"

"I don't know. But be prepared for the days to be difficult. We don't know what repercussions will come out of this."

Even though the tea was warming her insides, Tayler still felt the chill in her hands and in her heart. An accusation like this could destroy a man like Thomas. Especially since his accuser was wealthy and he . . . wasn't. As her fear and doubt disappeared, a new emotion emerged—anger. Esmerelda was doing something horrible to a good and decent man. Why? As her brain churned for answers, she realized she needed to go to Mr. Bradley immediately and tell him what she'd overheard. It could possibly prove Thomas's innocence. She rose from her chair. "Cassidy, I just realized I've got information that could help Thomas. I think—"

The door opened behind her and Allan entered the room, water dripping from his hat. "Tayler, Mr. Bradley asked me to fetch you. There's an urgent telegram for you."

• • • • •

Margaret whipped butter for her famous buttercream to prep for the monstrous flag cake she made for the Fourth of July celebration they had every year at the Curry Hotel. Church this morning had been lovely—even including the two men sitting on either side of her . . . again—but it was back to work for her. As usual.

Collette was working on the cake layers at the table across from her. Amazing the change in that beautiful girl over the years. She'd become an incredible cook, and a precious woman who loved God. Now if Margaret could just get Dr. Reilly to see all that as well. Pity he'd hardly spoken to Collette since their little picnic. She hoped the French girl hadn't run him off, but Margaret was determined to see this through. She'd never been a matchmaker in the past, but she realized that she enjoyed seeing the people she loved being happy. Why shouldn't she play a part in that?

The thought made her giggle to herself.

"Why, Mrs. Johnson. I do believe I heard ya laugh just now." Daniel's brogue washed over her. "It's a lovely sound."

"Go on with you. Don't you have dinner to be preparing?" She tried to scowl at him as she gently poured powdered sugar into the bowl, but she just couldn't do it. Yes, she was a hard woman. Yes, her staff didn't get to hear her laugh very often. But she'd run this kitchen for years with her brusque style, and it had gone just fine.

"Don't look now, but you just might be smiling." Daniel stuck his finger in the bowl and then lifted it to his mouth. "Yum."

She swatted him with a kitchen towel. "That better have been a clean hand, Chef Ferguson, or you will be facing my wrath!"

"Just washed, Chef. I promise." He sneaked back around the corner to the stoves.

She continued to stir the buttercream and added another splash of vanilla, then realized she'd left the cream on the other side. "Collette, would you hand me the cream?"

"*Oui.* Of course." She passed the pitcher of cream to her.

"This is normally the time that Thomas comes down and steals a bowl of my icing." Amazing how the clumsy boy had grown into such a wonderful man. She adored him and had an idea. "Collette, can you manage for a few minutes? I think I'm going to bring him a little surprise."

"*Oui.*" Collette winked in return.

Margaret lifted a spoonful of the tasty buttercream and placed it in a small soufflé dish. She added another spoonful on top. "Keep Chef Daniel out of the rest of this." She gave her assistant the eye and headed out to the office.

When she made it to Mr. Bradley's office, the manager was on his way out. "Can I help you, Mrs. Johnson?" He stopped in his tracks.

"I'm just looking for Thomas."

"Well . . . he's in his quarters."

She gave him a quizzical look. But the man didn't explain.

"I really need to be going. I'm sorry." The manager walked away.

Margaret shrugged and figured it wouldn't hurt her to run to the men's dormitory. She'd brought plenty of soup and bread to the workers when they'd been laid up. The least she could do was bring Thomas some icing. Wouldn't he be pleased.

She made her way to the dorm building and then headed up the stairs. "There's a woman on the floor, so behave yourselves," she bellowed down the hall.

Several chuckles were the only response she received, so she just walked down to Thomas's room and knocked.

It took a few seconds before she heard the door unlatch, and it only opened an inch. Thomas peered down at her, his face almost haunted.

Margaret didn't need any more. "What's wrong, son?"

He shook his head. "I can't talk about it."

"That's hogwash." She pushed her way into his room and put her free hand on her hip. "Now close the door so you can tell me everything. I'm not leaving here until you tell me what's got you so upset."

•••••

Tayler took the telegram from the front desk and went to the fireplace to read it. There wasn't time to go to her room. She wanted to be able to speak to Mr. Bradley about what she'd overheard.

Unfolding the paper, she read:

```
Will was forged (stop)Dunham involved (stop)
Investigators have evidence (stop)Do not marry
Emerson under any circumstances (stop)Going to
Denver to clear this up (stop)Watch for letter
(stop)

Joshua
```

She read through it three times to make sure she understood what was happening. While her heart was so grateful to hear from her brother, it also hurt to realize there was something terribly wrong. Probably what had kept him out of her life this past year. Was this what Emerson was trying to tell her? Or did he have a hand in all this?

The weight of it hit as thoughts tumbled in while she sat in one of the leather chairs. Was her mother involved in forging the will? What would this mean for her family?

The line about Emerson sealed in her mind that he was motivated by something other than love to marry her.

Was he trying to steal her family's fortune? Could this all be about money?

Her mind began to spin in so many different directions she couldn't think straight. Then she remembered Thomas's plight.

She couldn't do anything about whatever Joshua was facing except pray. But she *could* do something to help the man she'd come to love.

26

Thomas waited inside Mr. Bradley's office. The manager had called him here for a special meeting. He hadn't seen anyone—except for Mrs. Johnson—since they'd all decided it was best for him to be confined to his quarters. That way, no more accusations could be made. The past two days had been the hardest in his entire life.

Did Tayler know? That thought plagued him. What if she didn't believe he was innocent? What if no one did?

Heavenly Father, I know I've spent more time pleading with You the past couple days than I ever have, but I desperately need You to intercede. Help the truth to come out and for it not to tarnish anyone's reputation. And, Lord, help me to forgive Esmerelda. I don't know what has made her do this, but I know she is just as deserving of forgiveness as I am. I know I can't forgive her in my own strength, but You can help me.

The door opened and Thomas bolted to his feet.

Mr. Bradley entered the office, followed by Allan, John, Mr. and Mrs. Lancaster, and Esmerelda. "Please, everyone, take a seat." He closed the door behind the group.

Esmerelda kept her eyes down.

Thomas couldn't do anything to will her to tell the truth, so he would have to wait to see what God did.

A knock sounded on the door. Bradley looked at the clock on the wall. "Right on time." He went to the door and opened it.

Thomas's heart soared when he saw Tayler. Then it plummeted. What must she think? Obviously, she knew something. Otherwise, the hotel manager wouldn't have her here.

"Thank you for coming, Miss Hale."

Esmerelda squirmed a bit in her seat. "I don't think it's wise to have her here. This makes me very uncomfortable."

Mrs. Lancaster put an arm around her daughter's shoulder. "What is this all about, Mr. Bradley?"

"I've asked you all to be here so that perhaps we can get to the bottom of this."

"There's nothing to get to the bottom of, Mr. Bradley," Mr. Lancaster growled. "My daughter wouldn't make up such a humiliating claim. Her reputation is at stake here as well."

The manager tilted his head. "While I understand exactly what you are saying, sir, there is some information I believe you all need to hear." He turned to Tayler. "Miss Hale, do you mind?"

There weren't any chairs left, so Tayler stood beside Mr. Bradley and cleared her throat. "While we were on the camping trip up Curry Ridge, I overheard a conversation between Esmerelda and her friends. They made a bet about who could win Thomas's affections first. Your daughter made it very clear that she would do whatever it took to win."

Mrs. Lancaster gasped and turned to her daughter. "Is this true?"

Thomas couldn't believe his own ears. That's what Tayler had tried to tell him. No wonder she had been trying to warn him.

Esmerelda immediately burst into tears. "I can't believe you would even ask me that . . . this is so hurtful. . . ."

Thomas wanted to vomit over the dramatics taking place across the room.

"Esmerelda. Answer your mother," Mr. Bradley prodded.

The redhead lifted her matching red-rimmed eyes and sniffed. She stood up and pointed at Tayler. "Of course she's going to defend him and make up some outlandish tale about me. She wants Thomas for herself! Because she's in love with him." She poured on the waterworks again. "But I'm the one who has to deal with the consequences of my undying love for him . . . for the rest of my life and the life of . . ." She put a hand to her belly and eyed the adults in the room.

Thomas stood up, his hands fisted at his sides. How dare she lie like that?

Tayler stepped forward, a head shorter than Esmerelda, and spoke. "I am speaking the truth." Her voice was calm as she looked at the Lancasters. "I think if you examine your hearts, you'll know that your daughter has done this out of selfish motives, and it isn't fair to accuse an innocent man of anything as heinous as this."

"I would never!" Esmerelda's voice screeched.

"I believe there's a diamond headband at stake . . . and a foal sired by your champion steed, Mr. Lancaster?"

Esmerelda's face reddened and she sat in the chair.

"You wouldn't." Lancaster turned to his daughter.

She sobbed. "It's all a lie, Father. She's horrible. I would never do something like that."

Voices rose in the room as all the Lancasters started talking at once and Mr. Bradley tried to get them all to be quiet.

Finally, he found a moment to speak. "I think we have a clear choice in front of us."

Mr. Lancaster raised his brows. "What would that be?"

"We have a wonderful doctor here in Curry. If your daughter

has truly been compromised, there will be physical evidence. Dr. Reilly will be able to easily ascertain this and confirm her condition."

•••••

Stomping her way to the power plant, Esmerelda wished they'd never come to this awful place. What a waste of a truly beautiful summer. Her only hope now was for Emerson to have some way for her to get back to the city and be free of her parents.

No one knew how to have fun here, and she was tired of playing the good little girl for Mommy and Daddy. She just needed to make a clean break—as soon as she had some way to support herself in the style to which she was accustomed. Daddy would eventually forgive her and give her the trust fund she'd been promised when she turned twenty-one, but that was so long from now.

She wanted to dance and party with her friends and entertain men however she pleased. That was the modern way of doing things, and she was a modern girl. It was ridiculous to go on living by standards put in place by a bunch of Bible-pounding religious ninnies.

When she reached the building, she slipped behind it and found Emerson waiting for her.

"What is so urgent?" He looked a bit peeved.

"I'll tell you what's so urgent. Your little fiancée has got me in a pickle. She overheard that we had a bet and told my parents and the manager. So now they're demanding that I have a doctor examine me to make sure I'm not lying."

"What?" He crossed his arms and said a few nasty words under his breath. "I thought you said you could carry this through and convince them all?"

"I didn't know she was going to get involved," she spat at him. "You made a promise, so you need—"

"Nope, that's not how it works." He shook his head. "You haven't followed through on your part of the bargain. You don't get anything unless you get that useless guy out of the picture. That's the only way Tayler is going to leave with me."

"I can't have a physical examination. I'm not pregnant!" She waggled her finger at Emerson. "This was your idea. Now you tell me how to resolve the matter."

He leered. "Well, if I had more time . . ."

She gave an exasperated sigh. "Well, I guess we're at an impasse."

"Maybe you are, sweetheart, but I've got bigger fish to fry." He gave her a derisive look. "Such a shame too. You would've looked good on my arm."

"At least give me enough money to get out of here. I don't want to become the laughingstock of this godforsaken place."

Emerson brushed at his lapels. "My dear, I have a feeling you're too late to prevent that." He shrugged. "You wanted to play with fire. Now you have to deal with the consequences. I doubt you'll be down for long." He turned to go, then paused. "I've found it best," he said, looking over his shoulder, "to never let them know you care. Showing emotion will just give them power over you."

"Stop. If you don't help me, then I'll tell Miss Hale it was your plan all along."

•••••

TUESDAY, JULY 2

Tayler sighed in relief as the last of her group made their way into the hotel. She'd been busy with hikes and lectures all day long, and all she wanted now was to be with Thomas and assure him that she believed in him and that everything would be all right.

Mr. Bradley had restricted him to his room until after Esmerelda's examination—if her parents even agreed to it. They had been less than supportive of the idea, and Esmerelda had absolutely refused, saying it would be too great a humiliation. Tayler figured it would only be such because the truth would be known.

She glanced down at her uniform. It was filthy and she was sweaty and in need of a bath, but her desire to know what the Lancasters had decided was too great. She would go and speak to Mr. Bradley and then get cleaned up.

Tayler made her way into the hotel, and as she hurried past the dining room, shrieks stopped her in her tracks. She glanced into the room and saw the other three girls yelling at Esmerelda. Quite a crowd had formed, so Tayler drew closer to find out what was going on.

Mary slapped Esmerelda at that moment and gasps were heard throughout the room. "You little hussy. I can't believe you would make all this up just to win the bet! And all because you wanted my diamond headband."

Tayler noticed Mr. Lancaster marching over from where he'd been conversing with another guest. "What bet?" He looked at his daughter and then to her friend.

Mary put her hands on her hips. "To win Thomas's affection." She looked at Esmerelda. "But she doesn't know how to win without cheating. She never has. I can't believe you would stoop this low. When we get back to the city, I'm going to ensure that all the society pages hear about your little stunt here. Let's see how much they fawn over you now!" Mary marched off with the other two girls following.

Mr. Lancaster stumbled into the chair beside his daughter, his face registering shock. "So Miss Hale was telling the truth." It was more a statement than a question.

The room was silent.

Mrs. Lancaster appeared at her husband's side. She patted his arm, then turned to their daughter with a scowl. "I think we've heard enough." She grabbed her daughter by the arm and practically dragged her out of the chair. "Go pack your things. I warned you what would happen if I found out you were lying."

Tayler stepped back as the Lancaster matriarch marched her daughter out of the dining room and straight to Mr. Bradley's office. Mr. Lancaster followed behind, his face unreadable.

Could it be? Would Thomas be cleared of any wrongdoing?

Tayler felt a wave of relief wash over her. It seemed that it might be a happy Fourth of July after all.

"Tayler Grace."

She cringed, knowing that only one person would call her that, besides her mother. She turned and found Emerson only inches away. "What do you want, Emerson?"

"I want you, of course." He smiled. "Honestly, Tayler, I want you to sit and talk to me."

"If I do, will you go away? Today even?"

"Only if you come with me. You see, in losing you, I've come to realize just how important you are to me."

"That's funny, because in losing you I came to realize I hadn't really lost anything."

He had the good manners to look hurt, but Tayler didn't think he really felt anything at all. Unless it was frustration. Emerson Pruitt was used to getting his own way, and now it was being denied. Frustration and anger were all that he probably knew at the moment.

"Just talk to me."

Tayler had had enough. "Very well. Come with me." She marched across the busy hotel lobby and outside onto the train platform. "You have exactly ten minutes. No more." She held up her pocket watch. "Say what you want."

Emerson frowned. "I thought perhaps we could sit somewhere quiet and more intimate."

"Well, you thought wrong. You have nine minutes and forty-five seconds."

"Tayler Grace, doesn't the past mean anything to you? We had such good times, and I know you cared for me. I was wrong. I understand that and I've changed."

"I'm glad to hear it. The life you were leading was sure to cause you nothing but sorrow." Tayler could see he wasn't pleased with her comment.

Emerson moved toward her, and Tayler quickly sidestepped him. "You're wasting time."

"I love you. You know that, but it's more. I need you, Tayler Grace. Without you . . . well . . . my life isn't worth living."

"Are you implying that if I refuse you, you'll harm yourself?" She raised a brow. "Really, Emerson, we both know that isn't going to happen. You love yourself far too much."

"You won't even give me a chance." He sounded pathetic.

"I gave you several years of chances, Emerson. I even refused to believe the first stories I heard about your escapades. But seeing it firsthand convinced me that those stories were probably true. Even if they weren't, what was happening in front of me was most certainly true."

"But they meant nothing."

"That makes it even worse, Emerson. You took advantage of young women purely to gratify your desires." She shook her head. "Emerson, you need to turn to God . . . not me."

"I will. I have. I'll go to church with you every day if that will show you how much I love you. Tayler Grace, you can't leave me to face the future alone."

She shook her head sadly. "You wouldn't be alone with God. Emerson, I'm not talking about merely going to church. I'm talking about a real relationship with Jesus. Without Him, you're bound for hell. It's just that simple."

He looked stunned by her comment, and Tayler found herself feeling great pity for him. "The choice is yours, Emerson. It always has been, and so far you've lived for yourself and your pleasures."

"But I promise, from now on I'll live for you." He reached out quicker than Tayler could move. He gripped her wrist so tightly that Tayler nearly dropped the watch.

"I don't want you to live for me, and I will never live for you. Now unhand me." She fixed him with a stern look and waited.

For a moment it seemed as though Emerson would ignore her demand, but finally he released his hold and stepped back. "Isn't there anything I can do to convince you of my love?"

Tayler nodded. "Yes. Let me go."

•••••

With his long legs eating up the distance, Thomas went to his favorite place atop Deadhorse Hill. It had been here that Cassidy had challenged him to seek the Lord and dare to be like Daniel in the Old Testament.

It had been here that John had guided him in his faith and strengthened him as a man.

It had been here that Allan had taught him about being a man who followed after God with all his heart.

And it was here that he wanted to praise the Lord for his redemption again. God had seen fit for the truth to come out. While his heart ached for the Lancaster family having to deal with the deception of their daughter, it also rejoiced in the fact that he was proven innocent.

Thank You, Father, for interceding on my behalf.

He knew he was undeserving, but he was covered by the blood of Christ. And it was a beautiful thing.

Scripture flooded his memory, and he wished he could shout from this mountaintop about how amazing God's grace was. If only everyone could know this.

His heart ached for a moment. Had anyone ever told Esmerelda about God's grace? She was obviously miserable living the way she had been, and she seemed broken when her parents apologized to him for the accusation. What would happen to her now? The Lancasters said they were leaving Curry despite having paid for the summer. Would they send Esmerelda away? Would they go so far as to disown her? He knew what it was to be deserted by his parents.

Kneeling beside one of the rocks they used as seats at the top of the bluff, Thomas closed his eyes and lifted his face to the heavens, thanking God for all He'd done, and then he prayed in earnest for the Lancasters . . . Esmerelda in particular.

After relishing the wind on his face and feeling his whole soul washed clean, he stood and opened his eyes. Sitting on another rock in front of him was Tayler.

"How long have you been here?" He felt his smile lift his lips.

"Long enough to know I didn't want to interrupt your time with the Lord." Her voice was quiet.

Thomas stepped forward, his heart overflowing. "Tayler . . . is it all right to tell you how much I care for you?"

She smiled. "Yes."

"Well, I do. And I'd like to see what the Lord will do with this relationship."

"Only if you promise me one thing. . . ."

"What is it?"

"Promise me that we'll keep Him first in our relationship. I've seen firsthand what happens when people take their eyes off Jesus."

Thomas nodded. "I agree. But we both know it won't be easy. I may need you to remind me from time to time."

"I think I can do that." She stood and walked over to him. "But only if you do the same for me."

He opened his arms and embraced her. Even with their difference in height, he felt like she fit perfectly, and if he wasn't careful, he'd be tempted to stay here forever. But he'd made a promise to keep himself pure until marriage, and he was committed to seeing that through.

Stepping back, he held her at arm's length and looked down. It made him chuckle. "You know, you're really short."

She walked right back into his arms and laid her head on his chest. "I don't think so. See, I'm just the right height to be near to your heart."

•••••

WEDNESDAY, JULY 3

Emerson sat in the dining room alone. Life at the hotel went on full speed, and no one seemed to even care that he wasn't a part of it. In fact, the entire world seemed unconcerned by his absence.

Things had not gone as planned, and tomorrow the deadline would be up. Why had he ever enlisted the stupid girl's help? That had blown up in their faces. But at least she hadn't talked about his involvement. He hoped her little plan had worked, and she'd taken the stack of cash he'd given her and run.

But there was always the chance she'd come back for more.

He could just imagine her telling her father, and he in turn contacting Emerson's father. There would be no end of trouble if that happened. Of course, he wasn't sure there would ever be an end of trouble at any rate. He needed enough money to keep her quiet.

He looked at the empty cup in front of him. That was his life. Empty. Tayler said he needed God, but Emerson had a feeling even God had no use for him.

Now Thomas and Tayler seemed closer than ever. They'd been holding hands on a walk earlier, and it made him fume. How could she prefer Thomas over him? Emerson could show her an amazing life of luxury. Sure, it would come from her coffers, but he'd let her have a big opulent house with all the rich furnishings money could buy.

But she didn't care about those things. She had all that money at her disposal, and she didn't even care. She never had. She'd always been content with her paints and her nature walks. Emerson shook his head. Why couldn't she be more like her mother?

A thought came to mind. Her mother. He knew the truth about what Mrs. Hale had done. She had deceived them all. She had lied about the will. He grinned. All he had to do was go back to her and threaten to reveal the truth. She'd have to pay him. The Hale matriarch would never let it be known that she'd duped her own son out of his rightful place.

It was really quite simple. He'd return to Colorado and make his demands. But exactly what demands should he make? He could hardly suggest marriage, although that would be the optimum way to give him control. But no, that would create much too big a scandal. And his father would cut him off for sure.

He would simply go back and demand she pay him monthly to keep his mouth shut. He would get her to first give him a large enough sum to pay off his debts and then a monthly stipend to allow him to get back on his feet. Perhaps, he'd even force her to sign over a few well-placed stocks. It was all coming together. He could see this working out just fine. If he could get away from Charlie's goon.

"So I don't hear any wedding bells ringing." Greg took a seat opposite Emerson.

"Maybe not, but I've figured out another way." Emerson could see the man didn't appear convinced. "I promise you, I have. And I still have twenty-four hours." The very real fear that he'd denied all this time started to build in his gut. His name and family money meant nothing to the Mafia.

Greg shook his head. "I doubt it would help even if you had twenty-four years. You're a loser, Pruitt. You had a fortune, and you lost it because that's all you know how to do."

Emerson's anger stirred. "I'm not a loser, and I'll prove it to you. I just need time."

"But time isn't something I'm willing to offer."

27

Independence Day at the Curry put everyone in a celebratory mood. Well, nearly everyone. Earlier, Tayler had seen Emerson moping around the hotel lobby and dining room and knew that he wasn't going to be swayed into happiness even with a big helping of Mrs. Johnson's flag cake. She felt sorry for him but had no idea how to help him except to pray for him. He had, after all, once been a good friend. Very nearly a family member. She had even spoken to Thomas about their discussion, mentioning that she felt sorry for him because if he had truly come to realize his love for her . . . it was too late. Thomas hadn't held much sympathy for Emerson, but he suggested that Tayler pray for him. She couldn't help thinking, however, there had to be something more she could do. Maybe she could seek her brother's advice on the matter.

Walking across the lawn through the festive guests, Tayler caught sight of Dr. Reilly and Collette. They were strolling arm in arm—their heads close together as they whispered. The French girl had confided to Tayler about her boldness with the doctor. She had feared her words had been too much and that Matthew Reilly would run for the hills. But instead, it had served to give him the courage he needed to declare his interest. Mrs. Johnson said there was no living with Collette now. Her mind was never on her work.

She searched through the crowds for Thomas, knowing he had promised to meet her in time for the evening meal, which was to be served buffet style outdoors. He and Allan had been busy with several outdoor activities, but all arrangements were to come to an end by five o'clock in order for everyone to have time to ready themselves for the evening's events. It was possible they were already back and inside the hotel. With that thought in mind, Tayler made her way around back.

"And, I'm tellin' ya, she's made her choice!" The boisterous voice of Daniel Ferguson could be heard.

"Until I hear it from her, I won't give up," Bertram declared.

Tayler could see Margaret Johnson standing in the back door watching the entire affair. Making her way over to join the cook, Tayler gave a wave. Bertram and Daniel didn't even notice her as they stood nose to nose.

"What's going on?" Tayler asked as if she hadn't already figured it out.

"What do you suppose?" The older woman shook her head. "I know I have to stop this."

"So what's stopping you?"

Mrs. Johnson sighed. "I suppose I don't like hurting a good man's feelings."

"But you have to tell Mr. Wilcox the truth."

The older woman looked down at her. "Aye. I have to."

Tayler smiled and leaned in to whisper. "I'm glad Daniel won. You two just seem to belong together."

"It's a curse and a blessin', I'm sure." Mrs. Johnson shook her head.

"As I said, I'm not going until I hear Margaret tell me herself!" The railroad man pushed up his sleeves, and Daniel took off his chef's hat.

"Well, I'm telling you now, Bertram."

The men stopped bellowing and turned to face Mrs. Johnson as she made her way to where they stood. "Bertram, you're a fine fellow and I'm glad to call you friend, but that's all I have to offer, and if friendship isn't good enough, then I suppose you'll be needing to avoid the hotel."

The Scotsman threw the other man an "I told you so" glare and crossed his arms. Bertram looked as if he were going to say something, then began rolling his sleeves back in place.

"Now, there's no need to be fighting anymore," Mrs. Johnson continued. "I've a fine meal for everyone to share and tonight is a celebration, in case you've forgotten. I'll expect both of you to be civil and enjoy our Independence Day celebration." She turned to Daniel, who was grinning like a wayward child who'd managed to steal cookies unnoticed. "And you . . . get back to the kitchen. You've got work to do."

This caused the Scotsman to roar with laughter. "Aye, indeed. I've got me work cut out."

Tayler moved on as Bertram ambled away, his shoulders a bit slumped. Mrs. Johnson and Daniel disappeared into the kitchen. Tayler couldn't help smiling. Those two were meant for each other.

The encounter had made her forget momentarily about finding Thomas, and when she started back for the hotel, she caught sight of a big, beefy man and Emerson. A chill went up her spine, but she didn't know why. Something just didn't seem right. The big man's demeanor was threatening. He pointed to the forested hillside across the tracks, and Emerson seemed to be arguing with him.

Emerson held his hands up and started walking.

What was that other man doing? Would he hurt Emerson?

She didn't know why, but Tayler couldn't help following after them.

They seemed to walk forever, going deeper into the trees and farther away from the hotel. Tayler was careful to keep her distance in the seclusion of the trees. The closer she got, however, the more her stomach became unsettled.

Maybe she should go get help.

As she turned to go, the big man pulled an enormous knife out of his coat. There was no time! She had to do something. But what?

"Time's up." The large man sneered.

Emerson whimpered and put his hands out in front of him. "No. Please . . ."

"This is your fault, Pruitt, so don't go trying to plead your case to me. You owe Charlie and you can't pay with money, so you pay with your life. You always knew the arrangement."

"But just give me another chance. I have a new idea of how to get the money. I might not have been able to convince Miss Hale to marry me, but I have something on her mother, and I know I can get the money from her."

"It's too late for that." The man pushed him to the ground.

"But just hear me out." Tayler couldn't see Emerson, but his voice made it clear he was begging for his life. "See, I know that she forged her husband's will. I have proof."

Tayler felt as if a knife had been plunged in her heart. She clutched her hand to her throat to keep from gasping. Could Mother really have done such a thing?

"See, everything was to go to the son," Emerson continued to explain, "but she and her no-good lawyer fixed the will so that she got control of everything. She'll never want that to be known. She'll give me whatever I ask. You can even accompany me back to Colorado."

"Pruitt, like I told you before, you're a loser. Nobody is ever going to do anything for you."

Tayler had heard enough. She was heartbroken at the thought of what her mother had done, but she wasn't going to allow this man to murder Emerson.

"Stop!" She stepped into the small clearing. "How much does he owe? What if I gave you the money?"

The big man turned to look at her. He wasn't in the least bit unnerved by her appearance. "Why would you help him now? You wouldn't marry him."

Tayler whispered a prayer and moved forward. "He's been a friend of mine for a long time." She looked at Emerson, whose pale face was frozen in fear.

The big man shook his head. "I'm not stupid. You just want to have me arrested."

"No, I don't. You're here to collect a debt," Tayler reasoned. "Isn't that so?"

The big man nodded. "I am."

"There's nothing illegal about that. So far, you haven't committed a crime, so why would anyone arrest you?"

This seemed to momentarily stump the man. When he didn't answer, Tayler hurried on. "I can get you the money. All I have to do is have it wired wherever you like. You can go with me and oversee the telegram yourself."

"You don't even know how much it is." The man pointed the blade in her direction.

"I don't have to. I have plenty left of my inheritance. And if it's not enough, then I know Joshua will make up the difference." She stepped a bit closer. "Then you wouldn't have murder on your hands, and Emerson's slate would be clean with your boss."

Emerson looked at her strangely. It seemed the fear was passing and now confusion reigned. "Why would you pay my debt?" He barely spoke the words aloud.

Tayler smiled. "Because Someone once paid my debt to keep me from death."

Both men's brows furrowed as if they were trying to figure out what language she was speaking. Tayler shook her head. "Come on. We're missing the celebration, and Thomas and the others will be worried about where I've gotten off to."

She started back the way they'd come, then glanced back over her shoulder. "If your friend Charlie wants his money, then leave Emerson be and come with me."

The sound of movement behind her left Tayler little doubt that at least the big man was following behind. She thought of Emerson's push to see them married and finally understood his desperation. It saddened her to think he would lie before God and a congregation by making vows with her that he didn't mean. Worse still, that her mother had betrayed Joshua in the way she had. And for what? Money? Power? She shook her head. What had happened to this world?

Sin. And humans gave in to the temptation far too often.

They made their way back down the hill and into the clearing. By now the big man was at her side, the knife no longer in sight, and Emerson followed a few paces behind. Tayler saw Thomas and gave him a wave. He crossed the tracks with a worried look on his face.

"I was searching all over for you. Where have you been?"

"We were just taking a little hike." She motioned to the big man at her side. "This is Mr. . . ." She looked at the big man. "I'm sorry, I don't seem to remember your name."

"Uh . . . DeMarco. Greg . . . DeMarco."

Thomas still looked uncertain but nodded. "Mr. DeMarco."

"And of course you know Emerson." Tayler smiled. "In fact, would you be so kind as to take Emerson on over to the buffet while I assist Mr. DeMarco?" She didn't wait for an answer but looked at the big man. "We'll just go to the hotel manager. He'll help us arrange for your needs."

She left Thomas and Emerson with a wave. "I'll join you in a minute. Save me some cake."

"If you're lying, you know I'll still kill him." Mr. DeMarco's voice brushed over her.

Swallowing the lump in her throat, Tayler prayed for peace. Was she doing the right thing?

It didn't take long to get Mr. Bradley's assistance. Since it was a bank holiday, nothing could be officially managed until the next day, but Mr. DeMarco seemed to accept this without too much concern. Once he'd stated the amount and she confirmed that she had more than enough to cover it, Tayler left him with a bank draft and received from him a signed receipt for Emerson. He hadn't been overly excited to give it, but with Mr. Bradley witnessing the entire matter and assuring him that Tayler Hale's check was good, Mr. DeMarco finally relented.

"What was that all about?" Thomas asked as she joined him.

"Emerson owed the man money. That's all any of this has been about. Money."

Thomas frowned. "I don't understand."

"That makes two of us. I'm not sure what all is happening or why Emerson was suddenly depleted of funds, but apparently, he owed someone named Charlie the Chisel a great deal of money, and Mr. DeMarco was here to collect."

"And you paid him?" Thomas's voice betrayed his disbelief.

"I did." Tayler looped her arm through his. "I can't really explain it, but I felt like if I paid the debt, Emerson would see that I could truly forgive him. Remember the verses Pastor Wilcox shared about doing good to those who hate you? I just felt that this was the thing to do, even though I don't think Emerson hates me."

"But after all he's done to you—the way he tried to force you to marry him . . ." Thomas fell silent.

Tayler squeezed his hand. "I know. But I just kept thinking of all the things they did to Jesus, and He was still willing to pay. Emerson's life was at stake. All because of money. Maybe by my paying his earthly debt, there's a chance he will turn his life around and accept Jesus' payment for his spiritual debt."

"But you had no idea how dangerous Mr. DeMarco was—you put your own life at risk." Thomas pulled her closer. "Weren't you afraid?"

"More than you can imagine. But I felt at peace. Even if I had to lay down my own life, Emerson deserved another chance because that's what God does for all of us."

Thomas looked down at her with an expression of wonder. "You're really something else, Tayler Hale. I don't think I could be as forgiving if I lived a million years."

"Well, it's a good thing it's not a contest, then." She laughed and leaned in closer. "You don't do very well in those, as I recall."

Thomas pulled away. "If you're talking about our fishing contest, then that's not fair. You know I was . . . I was . . ."

"Distracted?" She grinned. "The only way I suppose we'll ever know is to repeat the contest." She sighed as if it were a huge imposition.

28

The train pulled into Curry, and Thomas stood on the platform with his arm around Tayler. Her brother Joshua was arriving today.

Telegrams had flown back and forth over the past month. Mr. Dunham had confessed to helping Mrs. Hale forge the changed will and was facing charges for embezzlement. Mrs. Hale was awaiting the judge's ruling, but neither of her children wanted to press charges against her. She'd willingly signed everything over to her son and daughter and apologized for all of it.

Thomas wasn't sure how he felt about it, but it had been shocking to hear that Tayler's mother had been a part of the scheme from the beginning. And to think that money had been the cause of all the problems to begin with. Mrs. Hale had turned to money instead of grieving for her husband. Emerson had turned to money instead of God, and it had gotten him into a whole mess of trouble. Esmerelda had made stupid choices all because of greed. What had gotten into this world? Were they doomed?

The Bible clearly stated that the love of money was the root of all evil. That was one of the reasons why Allan and Cassidy stayed in Curry, and why Jean-Michel had left France, and why Collette chose to stay here as a cook's assistant. None of them wanted to have a love of money.

Emerson had left after Tayler preached to him good and long about his need for salvation. Whether he took it to heart or not, they didn't know. But at least he knew. And Tayler had sent a telegram to Mr. Pruitt back in Denver explaining everything so that Emerson couldn't continue in his lies. The rest was up to Emerson and God. Mr. DeMarco had left immediately. Shortly after, a lovely telegram from Charlie Lorenzo arrived thanking them all for their help and assistance. If Thomas hadn't read it himself, he wouldn't have believed it.

The train eased to a stop, and steam puffed out from the base of it. Tayler tensed next to him. But Thomas knew as soon as she spotted her brother, for she gasped and ran toward him.

Thomas slid his hands into his pockets and watched the siblings reunite. Something he'd never had before he came to Curry. But he had many whom he could call family now.

But then Tayler gasped again. "Mother!"

An elegant lady stood on the bottom step of the train.

Joshua went over and offered his arm. He gave Tayler a little nod.

Thomas observed the woman he loved. Several emotions passed over her face, and then she took a deep breath and walked forward toward her mother.

The older woman broke into tears. "I'm so sorry, Tayler. Have I lost you?"

Tayler hesitated only a moment before she rushed to the woman's arms. A lot of healing had taken place over the weeks and miles. "No, you haven't lost me. And I forgive you. Just as I've been forgiven."

Thomas moved closer to her side in case she needed his support. It was one thing to learn of everything Mrs. Hale had done from a distance, but now she stood in front of them. In person.

Mrs. Hale swiped at her face. "I don't deserve your forgiveness for everything I've done—especially how I treated you—but thank you." She looked at her son. "If Joshua hadn't confronted me in love . . . I can't imagine what would have become of me." She sat on a nearby bench, looking totally spent. "Something snapped when your father died. The doctor tried to give some kind of medical explanation, but let's be honest . . . there are no excuses. I'm a sinner and what I did was wrong. So very wrong. And to think I almost lost both of you in the process." She shook her head. "I couldn't control the fact that I'd lost my husband, and Mr. Dunham convinced me I could control my future. Little did I know that he just wanted to stay in my good graces a while longer to steal more of my husband's money." She started sobbing again. "I still can't believe all I've said and done. I'm so sorry."

Joshua Hale lifted his mother to stand again and took her arm. "We're not here to say everything is perfect, but we are working on it. As a family." He stepped toward Thomas with Tayler all smiles beside him. Joshua held out a hand. "Now . . . I believe I don't need to be introduced. Thomas, it's a pleasure to meet you finally. My sister wrote me a lengthy letter about you."

He felt his brows rise. "Really? She didn't tell me that."

"It's wonderful to meet a man she deems worthy." Joshua looked back down at his sister. "That's important to me after all she's been through."

Thomas felt the sudden urge to be blunt with the man. "Well, I'd like to make it permanent."

Tayler gasped.

"But I want to do this properly. I'd like to ask your permission, Mr. Hale."

"Permission for what?"

"Permission for your sister's hand in marriage."

Joshua's face turned sour. "I'm sorry to hear that."

Thomas's heart sank down to his stomach. He swallowed. He'd flubbed it all. Jumped too soon.

"Because . . ." Joshua's face twitched a bit. "I'm only giving permission if you take *all* of her."

Laughter was heard behind them, and Thomas turned to see Collette, Mrs. Johnson, Cassidy, Allan, and the twins.

Collette gave a little squeal and rushed in and hugged Tayler. She turned and spoke in French to Thomas. "So are you going to ask her or not?"

Tayler's face turned red, but Thomas took that moment to get down on one knee. "Tayler Grace Hale, would you do me the honor of becoming my wife?"

"Wait a second!" a voice bellowed behind them.

Everyone turned and saw the fiery, redheaded Chef Daniel coming toward them with a bunch of flowers in his hand.

"Can't let the young'uns do all the proposing today." His brogue was thick and the crowd watched as he strode straight up to Mrs. Johnson and got down on one knee. "Lassie, you know what I'm asking."

Thomas straightened up. He couldn't believe what was happening, but he had to hear Tayler's answer. "Well?"

"Yes!" She jumped into his arms.

He looked down at her, pulling her close. "I love you."

"I love you too." She pushed him aside. "But we can talk later, we have to see what *she* says."

The crowd laughed as all the attention went back to Curry's head chef. Mrs. Johnson sputtered for a moment and placed her hands on her hips. She scanned the crowd gathered around, her face looking very unhappy. Then all of a sudden, she shook

her head and shouted, "Of course I'll marry you, you big lug! Now get on your feet and kiss me."

Thomas laughed along with everyone else as they noticed that this was one order Chef Daniel wasn't going to disobey.

Dr. Reilly ran up at that moment and stood next to Collette. "What did I miss?"

Collette filled him in on the two proposals, and the doctor looked stunned. Then he glanced back at Collette and wiggled his eyebrows. "Why don't we make it three?"

Applause filled the train platform.

Cassidy came close and had tears in her eyes. "Thomas, I'm so proud of you, of the man you've become, and for choosing such a beautiful young woman to join our family." She turned to Tayler. "Tayler . . ."

"TayTay!" the twins chimed as they danced around and clapped.

"TayTay?" Joshua laughed and shook his head. "I'm loving it already. I used to call her Tiny T when she was no bigger than those two, but I prefer TayTay."

"Me too." Leaning down, Thomas kissed Tayler on the forehead. It might not have been the most romantic of days, but he wouldn't trade it for the world. His whole family was right here.

Tayler reached up and patted his cheek. "Oh no, you're not getting away that easily, Mr. Smith." She tugged his face down and kissed him.

Warmth spread through him as he wrapped his arms around his bride-to-be and kissed her fully.

So this was love.

Wow.

Epilogue

Cassidy circled the bride and checked the beautiful white satin gown. "Tayler, it's absolutely perfect." She hugged the young woman who'd become so much more than just a friend. "*You* look perfect."

"Thank you, Cassidy. For everything." A sheen of tears glistened in Tayler's eyes. "I don't know what I would have done without you."

"I've always wanted a little sister, and then God brought you here."

"I'm so glad He did." Tayler turned back to the mirror. "I can't believe I get to marry Thomas today." She put her hands to her cheeks. "It's all so exciting. Am I dreaming?"

"No. It's very real. Today is your special day." Laughter bubbled up. "I remember thinking the same thing when I married Allan—it seemed like a fairy tale." She wrapped an arm around the young bride's shoulders as they stared into the mirror together. "Today is just the beginning. Thomas is a wonderful man, and he loves you so much."

321

Heart in her throat, Cassidy couldn't put the rest of her feelings into words. The two who were saying their vows today were among the most precious people in her life. In her book they both deserved all the happiness in the world. What God had done in all of their lives over the past years at the Curry Hotel was truly a miracle. Allan and her. Thomas and Tayler. Daniel and Margaret. Matthew and Collette. Jean-Michel and Katherine—who were now coming to stay in Alaska for several months. Her heart felt like it could burst with joy.

Tayler stepped away from the mirror and grabbed both of Cassidy's hands. "I've always wanted a big sister too. So I'd like to make a request. Would you pray with me before we go out there?"

"I'd be honored." Cassidy squeezed Tayler's hands and bowed her head as she prayed for the Lord's blessing on the wedding today and the marriage for the years to come.

She had no idea what the future would hold for the Curry family up in their little hamlet in Alaska, but she did know one thing: it would be joyous and full of love and life.

As she spoke her "Amen," the new song Pastor Wilcox had taught the children last Sunday sprang to her mind.

Let it shine, let it shine, let it shine. . . .

In loving memory of Cassidy Faith Hale
(March 2000–September 2015)

Recipes

Curry Hotel Rolls

by Kimberley Woodhouse

Makes 52 rolls

7 cups	King Arthur Bread Flour
½ cup	plus 1 tablespoon sugar
2½ cups	whole milk (warmed to about 110 degrees)
1 stick	real salted butter (softened)
2	large eggs
3½ tsps	salt
5 tsps	instant dry yeast
1 stick	melted salted butter (for brushing—and actually the more you use, the better they will be!)

Combine the flour and salt in a bowl and set aside. Stir the yeast into the warmed milk and set aside. In a stand mixer (I use a 6-quart for this recipe) cream the butter and sugar together until fluffy and then gradually add the milk on the slowest speed. Add the eggs and mix well. Once it's all incorporated, add the dry ingredients. Place a dough hook attachment on the mixer and mix on low speed for approximately 3 minutes, then bump it up to the next speed for another 3 minutes. The dough should be elastic but firm.

Cover the dough and place in a warm environment for about an hour and a half while the dough rises until nearly doubled.

From here, prepare the dough like a Parker House–style roll. Fold the dough gently and turn out onto a bread board or smooth working surface. Roll out the dough into a large rectangle about ⅛ inch thick. Butter the entire surface and fold the dough in half (butter side in), pressing the edges a bit to seal. Using a bench knife, cut the dough into 52 squares. Place on parchment-lined baking sheets (I like the air-bake sheets the best), brush the tops with more butter, and set to rise for another hour or so. They will really puff up, so give them space. (If you'd rather have an oval roll, follow the alternate directions below.)

Bake in a preheated oven at 400 degrees (375 degrees convection) until they are golden brown, approximately 12 minutes. Brush them with melted butter immediately after removal from the oven.

Alternate oval: Divide the dough into 52 pieces. Work each individual piece into a flat oval shape (about an ⅛ inch thick). Brush the oval with the melted butter and then fold it in half (so that the butter is on the inside), pressing lightly on the edges so they stay folded. Repeat with each oval of dough. Continue with the rest of the recipe.

Enjoy.

Curry Hotel Chocolate Mousse

by Kimberley Woodhouse

Makes 8 servings

7 oz.	bittersweet chocolate (I like Ghirardelli™)
4	large egg yolks
¾ cup	powdered sugar
1 tsp	vanilla
1 stick	salted butter (very soft)
2 cups	heavy whipping cream (divided)
¼ cup	granulated sugar
	shaved chocolate (optional)

Beat the egg yolks and powdered sugar together until the mixture is thick, then place in a double boiler (where the water is simmering underneath) and continue beating the yolk mixture constantly until the mixture is foamy (approximately 3 minutes). Remove from the double boiler and continue whisking the mixture over a bowl of ice water for another 3 minutes. Set aside.

Melt the chocolate over a double boiler, remove from heat, and beat in the butter until the mixture is creamy. Pour the chocolate mixture over the egg mixture. Mix well and then add the vanilla.

Beat 1 cup of the heavy cream until stiff peaks form and then fold into the chocolate mixture until combined. Divide into serving dishes and chill at least two hours.

Beat the remaining cup of cream with the ¼ cup of sugar until stiff peaks form. Garnish the mousse with the whipped cream and shaved chocolate (optional).

Tracie Peterson is the award-winning author of over one hundred novels, both historical and contemporary. Her avid research resonates in her stories, as seen in her bestselling HEIRS OF MONTANA and ALASKAN QUEST series. Tracie and her family make their home in Montana. Visit Tracie's website at www.traciepeterson.com.

Kimberley Woodhouse is an award-winning, bestselling author of fiction and nonfiction. A popular speaker and teacher, she's shared her theme of "Joy Through Trials" with more than half a million people across the country. Kim and her incredible husband of twenty-five-plus years have two adult children. Connect with Kim at www.kimberleywoodhouse.com.

Sign Up for Tracie's Newsletter!

Keep up to date with Tracie's news on book releases and events by signing up for her email list at traciepeterson.com.

Sign Up for Kimberley's Newsletter!

Keep up to date with Kimberley's news on book releases and events by signing up for her email list at kimberleywoodhouse.com.

More from Tracie Peterson and Kimberley Woodhouse

Cassidy Ivanoff and her father, John, have signed on to work at a prestigious new hotel near Mt. McKinley. John's new apprentice, Allan Brennan, finds a friend in Cassidy, but the real reason he's here—to learn the truth about his father's death—is far more dangerous than he knows.

In the Shadow of Denali
THE HEART OF ALASKA #1

Katherine and Jean-Michel once shared a deep love that was torn apart by forces beyond their control. Reunited in the 1920s at the Curry Hotel in Alaska, have the years changed them too deeply to rediscover what they had? And when Jean-Michel's nightmares of war return with terrifying consequences, will faith be enough to heal what's been broken for so long?

Out of the Ashes
THE HEART OF ALASKA #2

Dr. Jeremiah Vaughan has come to Alaska in hope of a better future. While working at a rural medical practice, he soon develops an attraction to nurse Gwyn Hillerman, who also grows fond of him. But when rumors begin to surface, will the truth about his past ruin his chance at love?

All Things Hidden

◆ BETHANYHOUSE

You May Also Like . . .

To escape an unwanted marriage, heiress Isadora Delafield runs away and disguises herself as a housekeeper. She finds a position at the home of self-made man Ian MacKenzie's parents. Ian is unexpectedly charmed by Isadora and her unconventional ways, but when Isadora's secret is revealed, will they still have a chance at happily-ever-after?

Flights of Fancy by Jen Turano
AMERICAN HEIRESSES #1
jenturano.com

With a Mohawk mother and a French father in 1759 Montreal, Catherine Duval finds it easiest to remain neutral among warring sides. But when her British ex-fiancé, Samuel, is taken prisoner by her father, he claims to have information that could end the war. At last, she must choose who to fight for. Is she willing to commit treason for the greater good?

Between Two Shores by Jocelyn Green
jocelyngreen.com

A female accountant in 1908, Eloisa Drake thought she'd put her past behind her. Then her new job lands her in the path of the man who broke her heart. Alex Duval, mayor of a doomed town, can't believe his eyes when he sees Eloisa as part of the entourage that's come to wipe his town off the map. Can he convince her to help him—and give him another chance?

A Desperate Hope by Elizabeth Camden
elizabethcamden.com

◊ BETHANYHOUSE